THE WORLD'S MOST SUCCESSFUL NOVELIST!

HAROLD ROBBINS

Since the publication of his first novel, *Never Love a Stranger*, he has consistently topped the best-seller lists with such titles as *The Pirate*, *The Carpetbaggers*, *The Adventurers*, and *A Stone for Danny Fisher*. It is estimated that more than 25,000 people around the world buy a Robbins novel every day.

Translated into 32 languages, his books have sold over 150,000,000 copies to date, and with the phenomenal success of his latest best sellers, *Dreams Die First* and *The Lonely Lady*, he is well on the way to his second hundred million.

"It has an aura of titillation, action instead of descriptions . . . and knowledgeable writing about the in-fighting between moguls and jet-set principals."　　　　　　　　　　　　—*Bestsellers*

Harold Robbins

THE DREAM MERCHANTS

A KANGAROO BOOK
PUBLISHED BY POCKET BOOKS NEW YORK

POCKET BOOKS, a Simon & Schuster division of GULF & WESTERN CORPORATION
1230 Avenue of the Americas, New York, N.Y. 10020

ISBN: 0-671-82342-6

First Pocket Books printing July, 1961

49th printing

CONTENTS

THE
DREAM
MERCHANTS

AFTERMATH

1938

MONDAY

I GOT out of the cab on Rockefeller Plaza. It was a windy day even for March, and my coat flapped around my trouser legs as I paid the hackie. I gave him a dollar and told him to keep the change.

I grinned as he thanked me profusely. The meter read only thirty cents. The gears meshed as the cab drove off. I stood there a few minutes breathing deeply before I entered the building. The air smelled fresh and clean. It was too early in the day for the usual gasoline odors to drift over from the bus stand on the corner and I felt good. Better, perhaps, than I had felt in a long time.

I entered the building and bought the *Times* at my usual stand near the Chase Bank and then walked down the steps into the arcade to the barber shop.

De Zemmler's was to barber shops what Tiffany's is to jewelers'. The door opened magically as I neared it. A small stubby-looking little Italian held the door for me as I walked through, his swarthy face flashing large white teeth. "Good morning, Mr. Edge," he said. "You're early today."

I looked over at the clock automatically before I answered him. It was only ten o'clock. "Yes, Joe," I answered as he took my coat. "Is Rocco here yet?"

"Sure, Mr. Edge," he grinned. "He's changing clothes; he'll be out in a minute."

I put the paper down on the counter while I took off my jacket and tie. Joe took them from me.

Just then Rocco came out from the back room and walked toward his chair. Joe seemed to signal him invisibly. Rocco looked at me and smiled.

"Rocco's ready now, Mr. Edge," Joe said to me; then turning to Rocco, he called: "Okay, number seven."

I picked up my paper and walked toward the chair. Rocco stood next to it grinning at me. I sat down and he whisked a cloth around me, tucked some Kleenex down my collar, and said: "Early today, Johnny."

I couldn't keep from smiling at the tone of his voice. "Yeah." I answered.

"Big day for yuh, Johnny." He smiled back at me. "I guess yuh couldn't sleep?"

"That's right," I replied, still smiling, "I couldn't sleep."

He walked over to the washstand in front of the chair and began to wash his hands. Looking back over his shoulder at me, he said: "I guess I couldn't sleep either if I just got a new job paying a grand a week."

I laughed aloud at that. "A grand and a half, Rock," I told him. "I wish you'd get things straight."

"What's five c's a week when you get that kinda dough?" he asked, walking back to me, drying his hands on a towel. "Pocket money."

"Wrong again, Rock," I said. "When you get that high, it's not money any more; it's prestige."

He took his scissors out of his pocket and began to peck at my hair. "Prestige is like a pot-belly. You look like a well-fed guy with it. A guy what's doing okay. But you're always secretly ashamed of it. You sometimes wish you could do without it and be skinny again."

"Sour grapes, Rock," I answered. "On me it looks good."

He didn't answer, just kept pecking away at my hair, so I opened the paper. The first page was nothing but news. Very uninteresting. I kept turning the pages until I found it.

It was on the amusement page. A two-column head in twenty-point type: "John Edge Elected President of Magnum Pictures." The story that followed was the usual thing. History of the picture company. History of me. I frowned a little at that. They didn't skip the fact that I had been divorced from that famous actress, Dulcie Warren.

Rocco looked over my shoulder at the paper. "Gonna start a scrapbook now that you're Mr. Big, Johnny?"

That one got a little under my skin. It was as if he had sneaked into my mind and sneaked out again with my thoughts. I tried not to be sore. I managed a weak grin.

"Don't be silly, Rock," I said. "I'm still the same guy. I only got a different job. It don't change things for me."

"No?" Rocco grunted. "Yuh shoulda seen yourself coming in here just now. Like Rockefeller cut you in on the joint."

I began to get a little sore. I held up one hand and looked at it. "Call the manicurist," I told him.

The girl heard me and came right over. She took my hand. Rocco tilted the chair back and began to cover my face with lather; I couldn't read the paper any more, so I dropped it on the floor.

I had the works—shave, shampoo, sun treatment, everything. When I got out of the chair, Joe rushed over with my tie. I stood in front of the mirror and knotted it. For a change I got the knot just right and didn't have to do it over. I turned to Rocco, stuck my hand in my pocket, and came up with a five-dollar bill, which I gave him.

He stuck it in his breast pocket carelessly as if he were doing me a favor by taking it. He looked at me a minute and I looked at him. Then he asked: "Did yuh hear from the old man yet? What's he think?"

"No," I answered, "And I don't give a damn. Frig him and what he thinks."

"That's no way to talk, Johnny." He shook his head gently. "He's an okay guy even if he did screw you up a little. He always liked yuh. Almost as much as his kid."

"He screwed me though, didn't he?" I asked almost belligerently.

Rocco's voice was gentle. "So he did. So what? He's an old man. He was sick and tired and desperate and he knew he had shot his load." He stopped talking for a second to light the cigarette I had put in my mouth. His face was very close to mine when he spoke again. "So he went a little crazy and took it out on you. So what, Johnny? You just can't wash away the thirty years before that happened. You can't say those thirty years never happened, 'cause they did."

I looked into his eyes. They were soft and brown and had a subtle sort of compassion in them. They almost looked sorry for me. I started to say something but didn't. Instead I walked away from him and went to the door, put on my jacket, and threw my coat over my arm and walked out.

The tourists were already in the building. There was a whole group of the yokels lined up waiting for one of the guides to come and show them around. The yokels never changed. They had the same look on their faces that they had at the carny over thirty years ago. Eager, expectant, their mouths a little open as if they could see more through them.

I walked past them to the escalator and rode up to the main floor, then went over to the second bank of elevators—the bank that went express to the thirtieth floor. I entered the elevator. The operator looked at me and then punched the button marked 32 without my saying a word.

"Good morning, Mr. Edge," he said.

"Good morning," I answered.

The door shut and then there was that slightly sickening feeling as the high-speed elevator gained momentum and rushed toward the roof. The door opened and I got out.

The girl at the reception desk smiled at me as I walked by. "Good morning, Mr. Edge."

"Good morning, Mona," I said, turning down the corridor and walking the rug to my new office. It used to be his. But now my name was on the door. "MR. EDGE," it read in gold letters. They looked funny there instead of his name. I looked closely at the lettering to see if any traces of his name remained. There weren't any. They had done a thorough job of it, and it didn't take too long either. Even if your name had been on the door for a thousand years, it only took a few minutes to take it off.

I put my hand on the door and began to turn the knob. Suddenly I stopped. This was only a dream up to now. It wasn't my name on the door, it was his. I looked closely at the name on the door again.

"MR. EDGE," it read in gold letters.

I shook my head. Rocco was right. You just couldn't wash away thirty years.

I opened the door and stepped into the office. This was my secretary's office; mine was through the next door.

Jane was just hanging up the phone as I came in. She got to her feet and took my coat and hung it in a small closet and said: "Good morning, Mr. Edge," all at once.

"Good morning, Miss Andersen," I returned, smiling. "My, aren't we formal this morning?"

Jane laughed. "Christ, Johnny, after all, you're the big boss now. Somebody's got to set the standard."

"Let somebody else do it, not you, Janey," I told her as I walked into my office.

I stopped at the door a minute to sort of get used to it. This was the first time I had seen the place since it had been redecorated. I had been at the studio until Friday evening, flew into New York Sunday night, and this was only Monday morning.

Janey had followed me into the office. "Like it?" she asked.

I looked around. I sure did. Who wouldn't like an office that looked as if it were made out of spun gold? The office was on the corner of the floor. It had ten windows, five on each side. The inside walls were lined with an artificial wood. On the large wall there was a large photo-mural of the studio made from a picture taken from a plane. On the small wall there was an artificial fireplace complete with andirons, grille, and fireplace chairs. There were other chairs made of a deep rich red leather scattered throughout the office, and my desk was of a highly polished mahogany covered with a matching leather. In the center of the leather were my initials in raised leather of a slightly contrasting color. The place was big enough to throw a ball or party in and there would still be enough room left over to have some privacy.

"Like it, Johnny?" Jane asked again.

I nodded my head. "I sure do." I walked over to my desk and sat down behind it.

"You haven't seen anything yet," she said. She walked over to the fireplace and touched a button on the wall.

The fireplace began to turn around and a bar came out. I whistled.

"Pretty slick, eh?" she asked proudly.

"I'm speechless," I answered.

"That isn't all," she said. She touched the button again and the fireplace came back into view. Then she walked a few steps and touched another button. Part of the wall slid back and the door revealed a shining tiled bathroom. "How do you like that?" she asked.

I got up and walked over to her, put my arms around her, and gave her a squeeze. "Janey, you just made me the happiest guy in the world. How did you ever guess that the one thing I wanted was a private john?"

She laughed, a little embarrassed now. "I'm so glad you like it, Johnny. I was a little worried."

I let go of her and stuck my head in the bathroom door. It was complete, stall shower and all. I turned back to her. "Your worries are over, kid. Papa likes."

I went back to the desk and sat down. I still had to get used to it. When Peter had the office, it was plain, old-fashioned, like himself. They said a man's office reflected what his secretary thought he was. I began to wonder. Did Janey think I was this fancy a Dan?

The phone in Jane's office began to ring and she rushed out to answer it, shutting the door behind her. The minute the door closed I felt alone. I felt so alone it was ridiculous.

In the old days when I was Peter's assistant, by now my office would be crowded with people. We'd be talking and the air would be blue with smoke and it would feel good. They used to tell me their ideas, about pictures, about sales, about advertising. We used to razz each other, criticize, argue; but out of it all came an easy camaraderie that I knew I would never have again.

What was it that Peter had once said? "When you're boss, Johnny, you're on your own. You got no friends, only enemies. If people are nice to you, you wonder why. You wonder what they want from you. You listen to what they say and try to make them comfortable, but you never can. They never forget that you're the boss and what you say or do might turn their lives inside out. Being boss is a lonely thing, Johnny, a lonely thing."

I had laughed at the time, but now I was beginning to understand what he had meant. Deliberately I thrust the thought from my mind and turned my attention to the mail stacked high on my desk. After all, I hadn't looked for the job. I picked up the first letter and suddenly my hand stopped. Or had I? The thought flashed through my mind and was gone in a second and I began to read the letter.

It was a note of congratulations. That's what all the rest of the mail and telegrams were about. Everybody in the industry was sending me notes of congratulations and good will. The big and little. That was an interesting thing about this business. No matter how much you were liked or disliked, whenever something happened everybody sent you notes. It was like being in a big family where every member of it watched everybody else for signs of success or failure. You could always tell what people thought you were heading for by the amount of inconsequential mail you got.

I was almost through with the mail when Jane came into my office again, carrying a large bouquet of flowers.

I looked up at her. "Who sent those?"

She put them into a vase on the coffee table and without saying anything tossed a small white envelope on my desk.

Almost before I saw the small initials "D. W." on the envelope I knew whom they were from because of the way Janey had acted. I opened the envelope and took out a small white card. There was some scrawling in a small familiar hand.

"Nothing succeeds like success, Johnny," it read. "Looks like I guessed wrong." It was signed: "Dulcie."

I threw it into the wastebasket and lit a cigarette. Dulcie. Dulcie was a bitch. But I had married her because I thought she was wonderful. Because she was beautiful. And because she had a way of looking at you that made you think you were the most wonderful guy in the world. It just shows how much you can get fooled. When I found out just how much you could get fooled we were divorced.

"Were there any calls, Jane?"

Her face was troubled while I had read the letter; now it brightened. "Yes," she answered. "Only one before you came in. George Pappas. He said for you to call back when you had time."

"Okay," I said. "Get him for me."

She left the office. George Pappas was all right. He was president of Borden Pictures and we had known each other a long time. He was the guy that had bought Peter's little nickelodeon when Peter had decided to go into the production of pictures.

My phone buzzed. I picked it up. Janey's voice came through: "I have Mr. Pappas for you."

"Put him on," I said. There was a click, then George's

voice. "Hallo, Johnny?" The way he said it, the "J" was soft and slurred.

"George," I said, "how the hell are yuh?"

"Good, Johnny. How are you?"

"Can't complain."

"How about lunch?" he asked.

"Thank God somebody thought of that," I told him. "I was afraid I'd have to eat alone."

"Where will we meet?" he asked.

I had an idea. "George," I said, "you come over here. I want you to see the office."

"It's nice, eh, Johnny?" he asked, laughing softly.

"Nice isn't the word for it," I said. "It's like the reception room in one of those high-class French whorehouses. Anyway, you come over and see it and let me know what you think."

"One o'clock, Johnny," he said, "I'll be there."

We said good-by and hung up.

I called Jane in and told her to get all the department heads up into my office. It was about time they heard from me anyway. Besides, what was the good of being boss if nobody showed up for you to boss?

The meeting lasted until almost one o'clock. It was the usual crap. They were full of congratulations and good will. I told them the company was in bad shape and that we'd have to quit screwing around and buckle down to some serious work or first thing we'd know we'd all be out of work. As I said it I felt funny. Saying something like that in an office that had cost about fifteen grand to refurnish seemed entirely out of place to me, but apparently none of them thought about it that way. They were impressed. Before I closed the meeting I told them I wanted on my desk before the week was out an economy chart from every department showing who and what we could dispense with. We had to eliminate waste and inefficiency if we were to survive this economic crisis. Then I told them to go to lunch, and as they filed out I knew from the looks on their faces behind their smiles that not a one of them would be able to eat.

When the door closed behind the last of them I went over to the wall where the bar was and looked for the button. I couldn't find it. I walked over to Janey's door and opened it.

"I can't find those God-damn buttons," I told her.

She looked startled for a second, then she got up. "I'll show them to you," she said.

I followed her over to the wall and watched her press the button for the bar. As it swung around, I told her to mix me a drink while I went down to the can. Automatically I started for the outer door, but she stopped me.

"Private," she said, "remember?" She touched another button and the bathroom door slid back.

Not answering, I went in. When I came out, George was in the office, a drink in his hand, and looking around the place. I went over to him and we shook. "Well, George," I asked, "what do you think of it?"

He smiled slowly, finished his drink and put the empty glass back on the bar, and said: "A few pictures of some naked ladies on the wall and I think maybe, Johnny, you're right."

I finished my drink and we went to lunch. We went down to the English Grill. I didn't want to go to Shor's because of the crowd and he didn't want to go to the Rainbow Room because of the height, so we compromised on the English Grill. It was in the arcade of the RCA Building and looked out on the fountain. It was still cool enough for them to have their skating rink out and George and I got a window seat and for a few minutes watched the skaters.

The waiter came. I ordered grilled lamb chops and George ordered a salad. Had to watch his diet, he explained. We looked out the window again for a while and watched the skaters.

At last he sighed. "Makes you wish you were young again, Johnny."

"Yeanh," I said.

He looked at me closely. "Oh, I'm sorry, Johnny, I forgot."

I smiled. "That's all right, George. I don't think much about it any more, and even if I did, what you said was still right."

He didn't answer, but I knew what he was thinking about. It was my leg. My right one. I had lost it in the war. I had the latest thing in prosthetics now and if people didn't know about it they could never guess it wasn't mine that I walked around on.

I remembered how I had felt that day Peter had come to visit me in the hospital on Staten Island. I was bitter, sore at the world. I wasn't thirty years old and had lost my leg. I was just going to lie in the hospital the rest of my life and Peter had said: "So you lost a leg, Johnny. You still got your head on your shoulders, ain't you? A man doesn't live by how he can run around, he lives by what he's got between his ears. So don't be a fool, Johnny, come back to work and you'll forget all about it in no time."

So I went back to work and Peter was right. I forgot all about it until that night that Dulcie called me a cripple. But Dulcie was a bitch and in time I even forgot about that.

The waiter brought our order. We began to eat. We were halfway through with the meal when I began to talk. "George," I said, "I'm glad you called and wanted to see me. If you hadn't, I would have called you."

"About what?" he asked.

"Business," I said. "You know what the setup is. You know why I've been made president. Because Ronsen thinks I can bail him out."

"And you want to?" George asked.

"Not particularly," I answered candidly, "but you know how it is. You spend thirty years helping build something, you don't like to let go just like that. Besides, it's a job."

"And you need a job so bad?" he asked, smiling.

I grinned at that. A job was one thing I didn't need. I was worth a quarter of a million bucks. "Not in that sense, but I'm too young to lie around doing nothing."

He made no reply to that. After a mouthful of his salad he asked: "And what do you want I should do?"

"I'd like you to play the terrible ten," I said.

Not a sign of what he was thinking flashed across his face. No surprise that I had just asked him to play what the trade had laughingly dubbed the ten worst pictures ever made. "You trying to close my theaters, Johnny?" he asked softly.

"They're not that bad, George," I said. "And I'll make a

good deal for you. You can play 'em anyway you like, short half or long half, fifty dollars a date; guarantee five hundred dates and you get them free after that."

George didn't answer.

I finished my chops, leaned back in my chair, and lit a cigarette. It was a good deal I had made. George had close to nine hundred theaters; that meant he would play them free in four hundred houses.

"They're not as bad as the papers say," I threw in. "I saw them and I can say I saw a lot worse."

"Don't try to sell me, Johnny," he said softly, "I'll buy."

"There's just one more thing, George," I said. "We need the dough right away."

He hesitated half a second before he answered: "Okay, Johnny, for you I'll do it."

"Thanks, George," I told him. "It'll be a helluva help."

The waiter came up and cleared the table. I ordered coffee and apple pie, and George ordered black coffee.

While we were on our coffee George asked me if I had spoken to Peter lately.

I shook my head. My mouth was full of pie and I swallowed it before I answered. "I haven't seen him in almost six months."

"Why don't you give him a call, Johnny?" he said. "I should think he'd like to hear from you now."

"He can call me," I answered shortly.

"You still sore, eh, Johnny?"

"Not sore," I said. "Disgusted. He thinks I'm one of the people in the plot to steal the picture business. The anti-Semiten he calls them."

"You don't think he believes that any more, do you?"

"How in hell would I know what he believes?" I asked. "He threw me out of his house that night I told him he would have to sell out or lose everything. He accused me of being a spy for Ronsen and part of the plot that was out to ruin him. He blamed everything that went wrong on me. The things he did that he said I should have stopped. Oh, no, George, I took it for a long time, but that was the finish for me."

He took out a long cigar and placed it in his mouth and lit it slowly, all the while looking at me. When he had it lit to his satisfaction, he asked: "And what about Doris?"

"She decided to string along with her old man. I haven't heard from her either." It hurt me even as I said it. I'd been a fool about many things, but just when I thought everything would turn out all right, it went wrong.

"What did you expect her to do?" George asked. "I know the girl. Do you think she would run out on the old man when everything went wrong? She's too fine for that."

At least he didn't say a word about my futsing around all those years, I was grateful to him for that. "I didn't want her to take a powder on the old guy. All I wanted to do was marry her."

"And how would that look to Peter?" he said.

I didn't answer. There wasn't any answer. We knew how it would look to Peter, but it made me sore anyway. People had their own lives to live and both of us had given him more than enough of ours.

George signaled for the check. The waiter brought it and he paid him. We walked out into the arcade and George turned to me. He held out his hand.

I took it. His grip was firm and warm.

"Call him," he said. "You'll both feel better."

I didn't answer.

"And good luck, Johnny," he continued. "You'll do all right. I'm glad you got the job instead of Farber. And I'll bet that Peter is, too."

I thanked him and went back upstairs. All the way up in the elevator I kept thinking about calling Peter. When I got off on my floor I finally decided to hell with it. If he wanted to talk to me, he could call me.

Jane's office was empty as I went through it. I guessed she was still out to lunch. There was another stack of mail on my desk that had been placed there while I was out. It was piled pretty high and there was a little paperweight stuck on top of it to hold it down.

The paperweight looked familiar. I picked it up. It was a little bust of Peter. I hefted it in my hand and, sitting down in my chair, looked at it. Some years ago Peter had thought that a bust of himself would prove to be an inspiration to every employee, so he had hired a sculptor, who had charged him a thousand bucks to make up this little statuette. Then we had found a small metalworks plant, had had a die cast, and soon the little bust was on every desk in the office.

The statue was very flattering. It gave him more hair than I had ever remembered his having, a squarer chin than he ever had, a more aquiline nose than he had been born with, and an air of quiet determination that belonged no more to him than to the man in the moon. And underneath it, on the base of the bust, were the words: "Nothing is impossible to the man who is willing to work—Peter Kessler."

I got up again and, holding the bust in my hands, walked over to the bathroom and pressed the button. While the door rolled back I kept turning it over and over in my hand. When the door was open, I stepped through it. On the right-hand wall were a few little shelves for bottles and things. Carefully I placed Peter's statue in the center of the top shelf and stepped back to look at it.

The not true face that looked so real stared back at me. I turned and went back into my office and shut the door behind me. I picked up some of the mail and looked through it, but it didn't do any good. I couldn't concentrate. I kept thinking of Peter and the way he had looked at me when I had put him on the bathroom shelf. It wasn't any use.

Angry with myself, I got up and went back into the bathroom and took the bust out. I looked around my office for a place to put it where it wouldn't disturb me. I settled for the top of the fireplace. It looked better there. It almost seemed to smile at me. I could almost hear his voice in the room saying: "That's better, boy, that's better."

"Is it, you old bastard?" I said aloud. Then I grinned and went back to my desk. Now I was able to concentrate on the mail.

At three o'clock Ronsen came into my office. His round, well-fed face grinned at me. His eyes looked deep and self-satisfied behind their square-cut frameless glasses. "All settled, Johnny?" he asked in his surprisingly strong voice. When you first heard him speak you wondered how such a strong, commanding voice could come from such a round, comfortable body. Then you remembered this was Laurence G. Ronsen. In his class of society you were born with a deep commanding voice. I bet when he was a baby he didn't cry for his mother's tit, he commanded her to give it to him. Or maybe I was wrong, maybe mothers didn't have tits in that class of society.

"Yes, Larry," I answered. That was another thing about him that I did not like. When I was around him I was subconsciously compelled to try to speak an almost perfect English, which was something I was constitutionally unable to do.

"How did you make out with Pappas?" he asked.

He must have his spies working overtime, I thought. Aloud I answered: "Pretty good. I sold him the terrible ten for a flat quarter of a million bucks."

His face lit up at the sound of that. I made my moment of triumph a little more complete. "In advance," I added; "we'll get the money tomorrow."

He rubbed his hands together and came over to the desk and slapped me on the shoulder. His hand was surprisingly heavy and I remembered he had also been an all-American fullback at college. "I knew you were the boy that could do it, Johnny. I knew it."

As quickly as his pleasure broke through his reserve it slipped back into its sheath. "We're on the right track now, boy," he said. "We can't miss. Let's play off that old product and tighten up our organization and pretty soon we'll be in the black."

Then I told him about the meeting of the morning and what I had asked them to do. He listened attentively, nodding his head from time to time as I stressed the various things we had to do.

When I had finished he said: "I can see you're going to have plenty to do around here."

"Christ, yes," I answered. "I'll probably stay in New York the next three months to keep on top of things."

"Well, it's important enough," he agreed. "If you don't control things here, we might as well close up shop."

Just then my phone rang. Jane's voice came through: "Doris Kessler calling from California."

I hesitated a second. "Put her on."

I heard the click-click, then Doris's voice: "Hello, Johnny."

"Hello, Doris," I said. I wondered why she had called; her voice sounded strange.

"Papa had a stroke, Johnny. He's calling for you."

Automatically I looked over at the statue on the fireplace. Ronsen followed my glance and saw it there. "When did it happen, Doris?"

"About two hours ago. It's awful. First we got a telegram that Junior was killed in a battle in Spain. Papa took it awful hard. He fainted. We hurried him to bed and called the doctor. He said it was a stroke and he didn't know how long Papa would last. Maybe one day, maybe two. Then Papa opened his eyes and said: 'Get me Johnny, I got to talk to him. Get me Johnny!' " She began to cry.

It only took a moment, then I heard myself saying: "Don't cry, Doris. I'll be out there tonight. Wait for me."

"I'll be waiting, Johnny," she said, and I hung up the phone.

I clicked my receiver up and down a few seconds until Jane came back on. "Get me a ticket to California on the next plane out. Call me as soon as it's confirmed, I'll leave from here." I hung up the phone without waiting for her answer.

Ronsen stood up. "What's wrong, Johnny?"

I lit a cigarette; my hands were shaking a little. "Peter just had a stroke," I said. "I'm going out there."

"What about the plans here?" he asked.

"They'll have to keep for a few days," I answered.

"Now, Johnny"—he held up a quieting hand—"I know just how you feel, but the board won't like it. Besides, what can you do out there?"

I looked at him and stood up behind my desk. I didn't pay any attention to his question, didn't bother to answer it. "Frig the board," I said.

He was the board and he knew that I knew it. His mouth tightened. He turned and angrily left the office.

I watched him go. For the first time since I had decided to take the job that night Ronsen had offered it to me, my mind was at peace.

"Frig you too," I said to the closed door. What did that son of a bitch know about the last thirty years?

THIRTY YEARS

1908

1

JOHNNY held the shirt in his hand as he listened to the church bell toll. Eleven o'clock. "Only forty minutes more to make the train," he thought as he savagely resumed packing. Angrily he threw his remaining clothing into the valise and snapped it shut. Placing one knee on its corner, he put his weight on it and cinched the strap around it. Finished, he straightened up and picked the valise from the bed and carried it out of the room through the store and placed it on the floor near the door.

He stood there a moment looking around him. In the dark the machines seemed to be mocking at him, jeering at his failure. His lips tightened as he walked back past them and into the little room. There was one thing more he had to do. The most unpleasant part of this whole nasty business. Leave a note for Peter telling him why he was running off in the middle of the night.

It would have been easier if Peter hadn't been so good to him. For that matter, if the whole family hadn't been so damned nice. Esther having him up for dinner almost every night, the kids calling him "Uncle Johnny." He could feel his throat tighten up a little as he sat down at the table. Somehow this was the kind of family he had always dreamed about in those long, lonesome years he had worked on the carnival.

He took out a sheet of paper and a pencil and wrote the words: "Dear Peter," across the top of it and then stared at the paper. How do you say good-by and thanks to people who have been so kind to you? Do you just casually write the words: "So long, it's been nice knowing you, thanks for everything," and forget them?

He put the end of the pencil in his mouth and chewed

on it reflectively. He put the pencil down on the table and lit a cigarette. After a few minutes he picked up the pencil again and began to write.

"You were right in the first place. I should never have opened this God-damn place."

He remembered the first day he had walked into the store. He had five hundred dollars in his pocket, was nineteen years old and cocky with wisdom. He had worked in a carnival all his life and-now, at last, he was going to settle down and get somewhere. A fellow he knew had tipped him off that there was a completely equipped penny arcade up in Rochester just waiting for him to take it over.

The day he met Peter Kessler. Peter owned the building and the hardware store that was the only other store in it besides the arcade. Peter had liked Johnny from the moment he saw him. Johnny was an easy person to like. He was tall, almost six feet of him; his thick black hair, blue eyes, and ready smile with white even teeth made a quick pleasant impression. Peter had begun to feel sorry for the kid even before he rented him the store. There was something so eager, so intense about him.

Peter had watched Johnny walk about the store, touching the machines, testing them. At last he spoke. "Mr. Edge."

Johnny turned to him. "Yes?"

"Mr. Edge, maybe it's none of my business, but do you think this is such a good location for a penny arcade?" Peter hesitated a little. He was thinking that he was a little foolish. After all, he was the landlord, his only interest in this boy was that he should pay the rent but—

Johnny's eyes grew hard. At nineteen it's hard to admit you might be wrong. "Why do you ask Mr. Kessler?" His voice was cold.

Peter stammered slightly. "Well, the last two fellers here, they didn't do so good."

"Maybe they didn't have the right idea for this kind of a business," Johnny answered. "Besides, you're right. I don't think it's any of your business."

Peter's face froze. He was a sensitive person though he tried hard not to show it. His voice became brusque and businesslike, just as it was when Johnny had first stepped into his store and introduced himself. "I apologize, Mr. Edge, I meant no offense."

Johnny nodded his head.

Peter continued in the same tone: "However, in view of my past experience with the former owners of this place, I find it necessary to insist on three months' rent as security." That should stop him, he thought.

Johnny calculated swiftly. One hundred and twenty dollars from five hundred left three eighty. Enough for him to do what he wanted. He took his money from his pocket, counted off the bills, and placed them in Peter's hand.

Peter leaned against one of the machines and wrote out a receipt. Turning, he gave it to Johnny and held out his hand. "I'm sorry to seem so rude," he said, "but I only meant good." He smiled hesitantly.

Johnny looked at him intently. Seeing no sign of mockery on Peter's face, he took his hand. They shook hands quickly and then Peter walked toward the door.

At the door Peter looked back. "If you need me for anything, Mr. Edge, don't hesitate to call. I'm right next door."

"I won't, Mr. Kessler. Thanks."

"Good luck," Peter called back to him as he stepped out. Johnny waved to him. Peter's face was unusually thoughtful as he walked into his own shop.

His wife, Esther, who had been staying in his store while he had shown Johnny the arcade, came up to him. "Did he take it?" she asked.

Peter nodded his head slowly. "Yes," he answered, "he took it, the poor kid. I hope he makes out."

Johnny lit another cigarette and began to write again.

"Believe me, I'm not sorry about the dough I've lost, only the dough I've cost you. My old boss, Al Santos, is giving me back my job at the carnival and as soon as I get paid I will send you some money on account of the rent I owe you."

He didn't want to go back to the carnival. It wasn't that he didn't like the work, but he would miss the Kesslers. He didn't remember much about his own parents. They had been killed in an accident at the carnival when he was about ten years old. Al Santos had taken him under his wing then, but Al was a very busy man and Johnny had to shift pretty much for himself.

He had been a lonely child, for there weren't many

children his own age around the carny, and the Kesslers seemed to fill a niche in his life that had been empty until now.

He remembered the Friday-night dinners with Peter and his family. He could almost smell the chicken cooking in its own soup and the taste of those matzoh balls or "*knedloch*," as Esther called them. He thought of last Sunday, when he had taken the children to the park. How they laughed and how proud he felt when they had called him "Uncle Johnny." They were nice kids. Doris was about nine and Mark was three years old.

He didn't want to go back to the carnival, but he couldn't sponge on Peter forever. He owed him three months' rent now, and if it weren't for the fact that Esther had him up to eat so often he would have spent many a hungry night.

Again the pencil scrawled its way across the paper.

"I'm sorry I got to go off like this but some creditors are coming tomorrow with a judgment against me so I figure this is the best way to do it."

He signed his name at the bottom of the note and looked at it. There was something empty about it. It was no way to say good-by to friends. Impulsively he began to write again just below his name.

"P.S. Tell Doris and Mark if the carny ever gets to town they get all the rides for free. Thanks again for everything. Uncle Johnny."

Now he felt better. He stood up and tilted the note against an empty tumbler on the table. He looked around the room carefully. He didn't want to forget anything; he couldn't afford to, there wasn't enough money left for him to replace what he might forget. No. Everything was all right, he hadn't forgotten anything.

He looked at the note lying on the table again, then reached up and turned off the light and walked out of the room and shut the door behind him. He didn't see the note flutter off the table and fall to the floor, sent there by the draft from the closing door. Slowly he walked through the store, his eyes wandering from side to side.

On his right he could see the one-armed bandits, the slot machines, and next to them the French-postcard moving pictures. A few steps farther on were the games of skill, the baseball machine with its batter and nine men facing him, the prize fighters with the long metal buttons on their jaws. On his left was the row of benches he had put in for the flicker projector he had ordered, which hadn't come yet, and at the door stood Grandma, the fortune-telling machine.

He stopped and looked through the glass at her. Her head was covered with a white shawl from which dangled peculiarly shaped coins and symbols. In the dark she seemed almost alive, her painted eyes staring out at him.

He fished in his pocket for a coin. Finding one, he placed it in the slot and pushed the lever. "Let's hear what you got to say about it, old girl," he said.

There was a whir of machinery, then her arm lifted and her thin iron fingers went skimming over the rows of neatly stacked white cards in front of her. The noise of the machine grew louder as she selected a card and laboriously turned her body and dropped it into the chute. The noise stopped as she turned back to face him. The card came out of the chute in front of him. He picked it up. At the same moment he heard a train whistle in the darkness.

"Golly," he said to himself, "I gotta run." Frantically he shoved the card in his jacket pocket, picked up his valise, and went out into the street.

For a second he looked up at Peter's windows. All the lights were out. The family had gone to sleep. A chill had come into the night air. He put his coat on, turned the collar up, and started walking rapidly to the station.

Upstairs in her bed Doris suddenly woke up. Her eyes opened; the room was dark. Uneasily she turned on her side toward the window. In the light of the street lamp she could see a man walking up the street. He was carrying a valise. "Uncle Johnny," she murmured vaguely as she drifted back to sleep. By morning she had forgotten all about it, but her pillow was damp as if she had wept in her sleep.

Johnny stood on the platform as the train rolled in. He reached in his pocket for a cigarette and found the card. He took it out and read it.

*You are going on a journey from which you think you
will never return, but you will come back. Sooner than
you think. The Gypsy Grandma Knows All.*

Johnny laughed aloud as he climbed up the steps of the
train. "You came pretty close to it that time, old girl. But
you're wrong about my coming back." He threw the card
into the night.

But it was Johnny who was wrong. Grandma was right.

2

PETER opened his eyes. He lay still on the great double bed,
the mists of slumber sluggishly clearing from his mind. He
stretched out his hands. His right hand hit the dent of the
pillow where Esther had lain beside him. It was still warm
from her. The sound of her voice in the kitchen telling Doris
to hurry up and eat or she'd be late to school completed
his awakening. He got out of bed, his long nightshirt trailing the floor, and made his way to the chair over which his
clothes were thrown.

He took the nightshirt off and got into his union suit, then
into his trousers. Sitting down in the chair he pulled on his
stockings and his shoes, and then proceeded to the bathroom.
He turned the water on in the tap, took down his shaving-
mug, and began to mix up a lather. He began to hum. It
was an old German song he remembered from his youth.

Mark came toddling into the bathroom. "Daddy, I gotta
make pee," he said.

His father looked down at him. "Well, go ahead, you're a
big boy now."

Mark finished his business, then looked up at his father,
who was stropping his razor. "Can I get a shave today?" he
asked.

Peter looked at him seriously. "When did you shave last?"

Mark rubbed his fingers over his face as he had seen his
father do many times. "Day before yesterday," he said, "but
my beard grows fast."

"All right," Peter said as he finished stropping the razor.

He handed Mark the shaving-cup and brush. "Put on the lather while I finish." He began to shave.

Mark covered his face with lather and then waited patiently for his father to finish. He didn't speak while his father was shaving, for he knew that shaving was a very important and delicate act and if you were interrupted you might cut yourself.

At last his father was through and he turned to Mark. "Ready?" he asked.

Mark nodded. He didn't dare open his mouth to speak because he had covered it with lather and if he did he would swallow some.

Peter knelt down near him. "Turn your head," he told Mark.

Mark turned his head and shut his eyes. "Don't cut me," he said.

"I'll be careful," his father promised. Peter turned the razor so that the back of it was against Mark's face and began to wipe off the lather.

A few seconds and he was through. He stood up. "You're all finished now," he said.

Mark opened his eyes and rubbed his face with his hand. "Smooth now," he said happily.

Peter smiled down at him while he rinsed the razor and dried it. Then he carefully laid it away in its case and rinsed out the mug and brush. He finished washing the spots of lather off his face, and after drying himself he picked Mark up and swung him to his shoulders. "Let's go in to eat now," he said.

They paraded into the kitchen and he swung Mark into his chair. He sat down in his own chair.

Doris came over and kissed him. "Good morning, Daddy," she said in her high clear voice.

He squeezed her. *"Gut' morgen, liebe kind, zeese kind."* That was the way he always spoke to her. Especially since Mark was born. Mark was his favorite and he had a guilty feeling about it, and so he made more of a fuss over Doris than he had before Mark was born.

She went back to her chair and sat down. Peter looked at her. She was a pretty little girl. Her golden hair was tied in braids up around her head, and her blue eyes were soft and warm. Her cheeks were fair and rosy in color. Peter felt good.

She had been a sick little child and because of her they had moved to Rochester from the crowded lower East Side of New York.

Esther came over to the table carrying a plate. Heaped high on it and giving off deliciously tantalizing odors were scrambled eggs, smoked salmon, and onions, all fried together in butter.

Peter sniffed. "Lox and eggs!" he exclaimed. "How did you manage it, Esther?"

She smiled proudly. Lox was something you couldn't get in Rochester, but she had had some sent from New York. "My cousin, Roochel, sent it from New York," she told him.

He looked at her as he filled his plate. She was a year younger than he, still slim, still good-looking, with the same quiet dark beauty that had first attracted him when he came to work in her father's hardware store right after he had come to America. She wore her thick black hair tied up in the back in the style of the times, her brown eyes gazed levelly and serenely from out of a round smooth face. She began to fill Mark's plate.

"I got a shave," Mark told her.

"I can see," she answered, giving the side of his face a rub with the back of her hand. "Very nice."

"When can I start shaving myself?" he asked.

Doris laughed. "You're too young yet," she said. "You don't even have to shave now."

"I do too," he protested.

"Be quiet and eat," Esther told them.

By the time she sat down Peter was almost finished. Taking out his watch, he looked at it; then, gulping down his coffee, he ran down the stairs to open his shop. He didn't say anything as he left the table. No one seemed to mind it. Papa was always late in opening the store and it was a few minutes after eight o'clock now.

The morning passed by slowly. There wasn't any business; it was too warm for the time of year, and the heat kept people from becoming ambitious enough to attempt any extra work.

About eleven o'clock a drayman came into the store. He walked over to Peter. "What time does the guy next door open up?" he asked, jerking a thumb in the direction of Johnny's place.

"About twelve," Peter answered. "Why?"

"I got a machine to deliver, but I find the place shut up and I can't come back."

"Knock on the door," Peter told him. "He sleeps in back of the place and you can get him out."

"I have," the drayman replied, "but there's no answer."

"Wait a minute," said Peter, reaching under his counter for a key; "I'll let you in."

The drayman followed him into the street. Peter knocked at the door. There was no answer. He looked through the window, but couldn't see anything. He put the key in the lock and turned it. The door opened and they stepped in. Peter went directly to the back room. The door was closed. Peter knocked at it softly. No reply. He opened the door and looked in. Johnny wasn't there. He turned to the drayman.

"I guess you might as well bring it in," he said; "Johnny's probably gone out for a while."

Peter went out into the street while the drayman unloaded the machine. Curiously he looked at it; it was something he had never seen before. "What is it?" he asked.

"A moving-picture machine," the drayman answered. "It throws pictures on a screen and they move."

Peter shook his head. "What will they think of next?" he wondered aloud. "Do you think it really works?"

The drayman grunted. "Yeah, I seen 'em in New York."

When the machine was in the shop, Peter signed the receipt for it, locked the door, and promptly forgot about it until half past three, when Doris came home from school.

"Daddy, why isn't Uncle Johnny open yet?"

He looked down at her, puzzled. He had already forgotten about the morning. "I don't know," he said slowly. Together they walked out into the street and looked at the penny arcade.

He peered in the window. There was no sign of movement inside. The crate delivered that morning still lay where the drayman had placed it. He turned to Doris. "Run upstairs and get Mamma to come down and stay in the store for a minute."

He stood there in the street waiting until Esther came

down. "Johnny hasn't opened up yet," he told her. "Stay in the store while I look in his place."

After he had opened the door he walked slowly to the back room. This time he entered the room and found the note on the floor. He picked it up and read it. Slowly he went back into his own store and handed the note to Esther.

She read it and looked at him questioningly. "He's gone?"

There was a hurt sort of look in his eyes. He didn't seem to hear her question. "I feel like it's my fault. I shouldn't have let him take the place."

She looked at him understandingly. She, too, had grown fond of Johnny. "You couldn't help it, Peter. You tried to stop him."

He took the note back from her and read it again. "The kid didn't have to run off like that," he said. "He could have told me."

"I guess he was a little ashamed," Esther said.

Peter shook his head. "I still can't understand it. We were his friends."

Suddenly Doris, who was standing near them listening solemnly to what they were saying, began to cry. Her parents turned to look at her.

"Isn't Uncle Johnny ever coming back?" she wailed.

Peter picked her up. "Sure he is," he told her. "He says in the note he's coming back to take you on all the carnival rides."

Doris stopped crying and looked at her father. Her eyes grew big and round. "Honest?"

"Honest," Peter answered, looking at his wife over the child's head.

3

THE stranger waited quietly until Peter had finished waiting on the customer before he went over to him. "Is Johnny Edge around?" he asked.

Peter looked at him curiously. He didn't look like one of the creditors Johnny had mentioned in his note; Peter knew most of them. "Not at the moment," he replied. "Maybe I can help. I'm Peter Kessler. I own the building."

The stranger held out his hand and smiled. "I'm Joe Turner of Graphic Pictures Company. I came up to show Johnny how to operate the moving-picture machine that was delivered yesterday."

Peter took his hand and shook it. "Glad to know you," he said. "But I'm afraid you're in for a disappointment. Johnny left here the day before yesterday."

Turner looked disappointed. "He couldn't hold out?"

Peter shook his head. "Things were pretty bad. He went back to his old job."

"With Santos?" Turner asked.

"Yes," Peter answered. "You knew Johnny?"

"We worked for Santos together. He's a good kid. Too bad he couldn't have held on for a few more days. Moving pictures would have pulled him out of the hole."

"In Rochester?" Peter laughed.

Turner looked at him. "Why not? Rochester isn't any different than any place else and moving pictures are the biggest thing in the entertainment field and getting bigger every day. Ever see them?"

"No," said Peter. "Never even heard about them until your man delivered the machine here yesterday."

Turner took a cigar out of his pocket, bit the end off it, and lighted it. He blew out a cloud of smoke and looked at Peter a moment before he spoke. "You look like a fair man to me, Mr. Kessler, so I'm going to make you a proposition. I guaranteed Johnny's machine to my office. If I have to pull it back, I'm hooked for the freight and installation charges even if the machine is never used. That's over a hundred dollars. You let me run a show for you tonight, and if you like it you open up and give it a try."

Peter shook his head. "Not me. I'm a hardware man. I don't know nothing about moving pictures."

Turner persisted. "It doesn't make any difference. It's a new business. Just two years ago a man by the name of Fox opened a picture show without any experience and he's doing all right. So did another man by the name of Laemmle. All you have to do is run the machine. People will pay to see the pictures. There's good money in it. It's the coming thing."

"Not for me," Peter told him. "I got a good business. I don't need any headaches."

"Look, Mr. Kessler," Turner said, "it won't cost you anything to see it. The projector's here already. I got some cans of film outside and nothing better to do with my time. Let me run a show for you, and you can see for yourself what it's like. And then if you don't like it, I'll pull the machine out."

Peter thought for a moment. He wanted to see the moving pictures. The few words the drayman had said to him the other day had excited his imagination. "All right," he said, "I'll look. But I'm not promising anything."

Turner smiled. He held his hand out to Peter again. "That's what they all say until they see it. I'm telling you, Mr. Kessler, you may not know it but you're in the picture business already."

Peter invited Mr. Turner to have supper with them. When he introduced Turner to Esther, she looked at him questioningly but didn't say anything. He hastened to explain: "Mr. Turner is going to show us some moving pictures tonight."

After they had eaten, Turner excused himself, saying he had to go downstairs to set things up. Peter went along with him.

As they walked into the penny arcade together, Turner looked around. "Too bad Johnny had to leave. This was just the thing he needed."

Then Peter told him why Johnny had left and about the note Johnny had written.

Turner listened attentively while he worked, and when Peter had finished, he said: "Anyway, Mr. Kessler, you don't have to worry about the money Johnny owes you. If he said he'd pay you, he will."

"Who's worried about the money?" Peter asked. "We liked the kid. He almost seemed like one of the family by now."

Turner smiled. "That's the way Johnny is. I remember when his folks were killed. Johnny was about ten years old then. Santos and I were discussing what to do with him. He had no other relatives, so he would have gone to an orphanage, but instead Santos decided to keep him. After a while Santos used to say Johnny seemed just like his own kid."

Turner finished his work in silence and Peter went upstairs to get Esther. When they came down, all the lights in the store were turned off. They sat down self-consciously in the dark where Turner told them. Excited as Peter was about seeing the moving pictures, at the same time he was glad there weren't many people on the street to see him.

"Ready?" Turner asked.

"Yes," Peter answered.

Suddenly a bright light flashed on the screen that Turner had set up in front of where they sat. Some printed words, which blurred, then became clearer as Turner focused the lens. Then the words were off the screen before they had a chance to read them and there was a train, small in the corner of the screen, smoke belching from it. It was moving toward them, growing larger every second.

Then it was upon them. It seemed to leap from the screen into their faces.

Esther made a small cry and buried her face on Peter's shoulder, her hand grasping for his. Peter held her hand tightly. His throat was dry, he couldn't speak, and his face was pale with sweat.

"Is it gone?" Esther asked, her voice muffled against his shoulder.

"It's gone," Peter answered, surprised that he could speak.

Almost before the words had left his mouth, they were on a beach and some girls were going swimming and they stood around and smiled; and then they were on a ferryboat coming into New York Harbor and the familiar buildings looked so real that they were tempted to reach out and touch them, but before they could they were out at the race track in Sheepshead Bay and the horses were running and the crowd was milling around and one horse, running mightily, finished ahead of the others and it was all over. A bright light flashed on the screen again, hurting their eyes.

Surprised, Peter still found Esther's hand in his. He heard Turner's voice saying: "How did you like it?"

Peter stood up, still blinking his eyes. He saw Turner smiling at him. He brushed his hands over his eyes wonderingly. "If I didn't see it myself, I still wouldn't believe it."

Turner laughed. "They all say that at first." He turned on the store lights.

Then Peter first saw the crowd. They were standing in the

street, their faces vague and anonymous, pressed up against the windows of the store, their eyes filled with the same wonder and amazement as his. He turned to Esther. "What do you think?"

"I don't know what to think," she answered. "I never saw anything like this before."

The door opened and the crowd came pouring in. Peter began to recognize people and faces. They were all talking at once.

"What is it?" one of them asked.

"Moving pictures, from New York," Peter heard Turner reply.

"You going to show them here?"

"I don't know," Turner answered. "That depends on Mr. Kessler."

The crowd looked at Peter.

Peter stood there a second without speaking, his mind still filled with what he had just seen. Suddenly he heard himself saying: "Sure, sure we're going to show them here. We'll be open by Saturday night."

Esther grabbed him by the arm. *"Bist du meshuggeh?"* she asked; "Saturday is the day after tomorrow!"

He whispered to her: "Crazy? Me? With all these people wanting to pay to see moving pictures?"

She didn't answer.

Peter began to feel big, his heart started to pound. He would open by Saturday night. After all, Esther didn't say no.

It was a little less than six weeks later that Johnny came back to Rochester. His valise in one hand, he walked up the street toward the arcade. He stopped on the sidewalk in front of the building. The hardware store was still the same but the penny arcade was no more. The old sign had been taken down and a new one put up: KESSLER'S NICKELODEON.

It was early in the morning and the street was still deserted. Johnny stood there looking at the sign for a minute; then, shifting his grip on the valise from one hand to the other, he walked into Peter's store. He stood in the doorway for a second, his eyes getting used to the darkness in the store.

Peter saw him first and came running up to him, hand outstretched. "Johnny!"

Johnny dropped the valise and took Peter's hand.

"You did come back," Peter was saying excitedly. "I told Esther you would. I told her. She said maybe you wouldn't want to, but I said we'll telegraph him anyway and find out."

Johnny grinned. "I didn't understand why you wanted me —especially after the way I powdered on you. But—"

Peter didn't let him finish. "No buts. What happened we'll forget. It's over." He looked around him for Doris; seeing her, he called: "Go upstairs and tell Mamma that Johnny's here." He drew Johnny farther into the store.

"I felt you should come back. This was your idea, you were entitled to something from it." His gaze fell on Doris. She was still standing there, looking at Johnny. "Didn't I tell you to go upstairs and tell Mamma?" he demanded.

"I only wanted to say hello to Uncle Johnny first," she answered plaintively.

"All right, then, say hello and hurry up to Mamma."

Doris came over to Johnny gravely and held out her hand. "Hello, Uncle Johnny."

Johnny laughed and picked her up and held her to him. "Hello, sweetheart, I missed yuh."

She blushed and squirmed out of his arms and ran to the stairs. "I gotta tell Mamma," she said, and ran up the steps.

Johnny turned to Peter. "Now tell me what happened."

"The day after you left, Joe Turner came in, and before I knew it I was in the picture business." Peter smiled. "I didn't expect it to be such a big thing though. It's too much for me. Esther has been working the cash, but I'm too tired at night after a day in the store to run movies too. So we decided to ask you to come back. Like I said in the telegram, you get a hundred a month and ten per cent of the profits."

"It sounded good to me," Johnny said. "I seen a lot of these nickelodeons around and they're getting to be a big thing."

Later they walked into the nickelodeon. Johnny looked around him approvingly. The machines had all been taken out and rows of benches had been placed in their stead, only the Grandma fortune-telling machine remained undisturbed in her corner near the door.

Johnny walked over to the machine and rapped on the glass. "It looks like you were right, old girl."

"What did you say?" Peter asked, looking startled.

"The old girl here told my fortune the night I left. She said I'd be back. I thought she was nuts, but she knew more than me."

Peter looked at him. "In Yiddish we have a saying: 'What is to be must be.'"

Johnny looked around the store before he answered: "I still can hardly believe it." He thought back to the time when he got Peter's telegram. He had shown it to Al Santos.

"I don't know why this guy wants me back after I skipped out on three months' rent," he had said.

"Two months," Al Santos corrected him. "You sent him one month's rent last payday."

"I know," Johnny answered, "but I still don't get it."

"Maybe the guy likes yuh," Al said. "What yuh goin' tuh do?"

Johnny looked at him in surprise. "Go back. What do you think I'm gonna do?"

Johnny took his hand off the fortune-telling machine. "How many shows a day do you give here?" he asked.

"One," Peter answered.

"From now on we're giving three," Johnny said. "One matinee and two evenings."

"Where we get the customers?" Peter asked.

Johnny looked at Peter to see if he was joking. Satisfied that Peter was entirely serious, he answered: "Peter, you got a lot to learn about show business. I'll tell yuh how we're goin' to get the business. We'll advertise. We'll plaster billboards all across the countryside, we'll advertise in the newspapers. We're the only picture show in the whole section. People will travel to see it, if we let them know about it. Besides, it doesn't cost us any more to run the film three times a day instead of once. We only pay one rental for it."

Peter looked at Johnny with a new respect. "The kid's got common sense. Right away he figures out how we could do three times more business," he thought, feeling a sense of relief flow over him. Now that Johnny was back, he began to realize that he didn't have to worry about the nickelodeon any more.

"That's a good idea, Johnny," Peter said aloud, "a very good idea."

Late that night when Peter fell asleep he was still thinking about it. Three times more business.

4

GEORGE PAPPAS stood across the street from Kessler's nickelodeon at seven thirty in the evening and watched the crowds going in to see the show. He took out his watch and checked the time. He heaved a sigh and shook his head. These moving pictures were changing the time habits of the town. Before the nickelodeon had opened, you could find only a few persons on the street after seven o'clock. And here it was nearly eight o'clock and people were going into the nickelodeon.

It wasn't only the townspeople that were there. Farmers and other people from out of town were coming to see the moving pictures, too. This fellow Edge that Kessler had with him was a live wire all right. He had covered the entire territory with signs telling about the new nickelodeon.

George Pappas sighed again. It was very strange, but he had a feeling the change was here to stay. He had been in to see the show before and he felt an important thing had come into his life. Just how it was going to affect him he did not know. He only knew that it would.

He owned a small ice-cream parlor about five blocks away. At seven o'clock he and his brother would close up the store and go home to eat. There wasn't any business in the evening, except on Saturday nights. But here it was Tuesday and there were more people coming in to see Kessler's show than George had seen on the streets of Rochester even on a Saturday night. He sighed again and wondered how it would be possible to attract some of these people to his ice-cream parlor.

He started to walk toward home pondering this problem, when suddenly he stopped short. A thought had come to him. It had flashed into his mind in Greek. It came so quickly and naturally that he didn't fully understand it until his mind had translated it into English. Then it was so right, so perfectly the answer to his question, that he turned back and walked across the street to the nickelodeon.

At the door he stopped. Esther was there taking change from the people as they entered. "Hallo, Missus Kessler," he said.

Esther was busy, so she answered briefly: "Hello, George."

"Is Mr. Kessler around?" he asked in his funny stilted manner.

"He's inside," Esther told him.

"I would like for to see him, plizz."

She looked at him curiously; his earnest intentness had caught her attention. "He'll be out in a few minutes, the show is about ready to go on. Is there anything I can do?"

George shook his head. "I will wait. I got some business to make with him."

Esther watched him walk over to the door and lean against the wall. Vaguely she wondered what business George had with Peter, but she was busy making change and in a few seconds had forgotten he was there.

George was busy too. As he stood by the door he counted about forty people going in. He looked in the door of the nickelodeon. The place was filled with people. Row after row, people sat close together chatting expectantly with one another, waiting for the show to start. Some of them had brought fruit with them and were eating it. George figured there were more than two hundred people in the place when Peter came out and shut the door. And there were still people in the street, and more were coming.

He watched Peter shut the door and hold up his hand. "There will be another show in an hour," he heard Peter say to those waiting. "We're all filled up, but if you'll wait you all will get in."

He heard a good-natured murmur of disappointment come from the crowd, but very few left; most of them settled down for a wait. And those that left were more than made up for by new arrivals. Gradually a line began to form that went down the street.

Peter stuck his head inside the door, "All right, Johnny," he shouted. "Start the show."

The audience started to applaud as the lights in the store

went off; then suddenly there was silence as the first picture began to flash on the screen.

Peter had lit a cigar as George walked up to him.

"Hallo, Mr. Kessler."

"Hello, George, how are you?" Peter replied expansively, puffing at his cigar.

"Prooty good, Mr. Kessler," George said politely. He looked around him. "Lots of poopuls you got come here."

Peter smiled. "We certainly have, George. Everybody wants to see the moving pictures. Did you see them yet?"

George nodded his head.

"It's the coming thing," Peter said.

"Mr. Kessler, I think so, too," George assured him. "You got good mind for what poopuls want."

Peter beamed at the compliment. "Thanks, George." He reached into his vest pocket. "Here, George, have a cigar."

George took it gravely. Although he didn't like cigars and couldn't stand smoking at all, he held it expertly to his nose and smelled it. "Good cigar," he said.

"I have 'em sent special from New York," Peter told him. "They're six cents apiece."

"If it's all right with you, Mr. Kessler," George said, putting the cigar carefully in his pocket, "I will smoke him after dinner to enjoy him better."

Peter nodded, his attention already wandering, his eyes on the crowd.

George sensed his inattentiveness, but he didn't know just how to broach what he wanted to say. At last he blurted it out. "Mr. Kessler, I would like for to open a ice-cream parlor here."

Peter's attention came back to George with a snap. "An ice-cream parlor here?" he queried. "What for?"

George was embarrassed. His face turned red. His inadequate English became even more unintelligible. "These poopuls," he stammered, "good for business. Ice cream, candies, fruits, nuts."

Peter stopped smiling; he suddenly understood what George meant. His voice became serious. "It's a good idea, George, but where can we put it? There isn't enough room."

Magically George found the words for what he wanted to say. He spoke quickly, easily. He explained to Peter how little room they would need for it. But what clinched the argument was his offer to pay rent plus a share of the profits.

While business at the nickelodeon was good, it was not without its problems. Under Peter's agreement with Graphic he was given a new show every three weeks. This was all right until they had begun giving three shows a day. Then it seemed that the first week of the show everybody in the section would see it and business would fall off greatly in the following two weeks. He had spoken to Johnny about it and they had agreed to ask Joe Turner on his next trip up if there was anything that could be done about it.

About two weeks after George had opened his little stand, Joe came up on his regular monthly visit. He stood in the small lobby watching George and his brother move busily behind the counter. After a while he went into the nickelodeon and spoke to Johnny.

The afternoon show had just finished and Johnny was rewinding the film for the next show.

"Whose idea was that?" Joe asked him.

"Peter's," Johnny answered. "What do you think of it?"

Joe nodded his head approvingly. "It's a good 'un," he said. "Makes me feel the idea will catch on in town when I tell 'em about it."

Johnny finished rewinding and set the reel in place so that it would be ready to run off for the next show. He clambered down from the little platform on which the projector stood. "C'mon out and have a Moxie," he invited Joe.

They walked out to the stand and ordered their drinks. Johnny introduced him to George and his brother. For a moment they sipped their drink reflectively, then Johnny spoke. "Haven't you got any other films? People are getting tired of the same show for three weeks straight."

Joe shook his head. "There isn't much to be had, but we just got a new one-reeler that we can send you."

"What the hell good is one reel when we need a whole show?" Johnny asked.

Joe looked at him for a moment before he answered. "I got something that might help you out, but it's gotta be kept quiet."

"You know me, Joe. I'm like a clam when I gotta be."

Joe smiled at Johnny's expression. "I guess yuh heard about the big companies gettin' together to form a combine and control the picture business."

"Yeah."

"Well, I guess yuh know one of the reasons for that is because a lot of small producers are makin' pictures an' cuttin' into their time. They want you exhibitors to play their kind of show, which is a short one, and they want to make sure that you get your pictures from them, so they combine. That way they control all the picture patents between 'em and nobody can make pictures but them."

"So what?" Johnny asked. "I still don't see how we're gonna get more pictures."

"I'm gettin' tuh that," Joe said. "Graphic's joinin' the combine an' I'm leaving them to go with one of the independents who plans to make enough pictures for a new show every week."

"Sounds good," Johnny said, "but where do we come in?" He sipped some Moxie up through his straw. "According to our agreement we can only show Graphic pictures."

"A lot of exhibitors figure what the combine won't know won't hurt 'em." Joe replied. "Look—you got to take their pictures for three weeks, but you don't have to play them for three weeks if you can't do business with them."

"I see," Johnny said, finishing his drink. "Let's go in and see Peter about it."

On their way into the hardware store Joe told Johnny all he had to do to get the film was to go down to New York and sign a rental agreement.

"Who's this guy you're goin' to work for?" Johnny asked.

"Bill Borden," Joe answered. "He's the biggest independent in the field."

"What you gonna do?" Johnny lit a cigarette. "Sell pictures for him?"

Joe shook his head. "Nope. I'm through with that. I'm gonna make the pictures. I tole Borden that what he needed was a man who knew what the exhibitors wanted, and since I knew what the exhibitors wanted, I was the man he needed."

Johnny laughed. "You haven't changed a bit since we

worked carny. You could still shoot the bull with the best of them."

Joe joined in Johnny's laugh. "But seriously, kid, it's gonna be a great racket some day. I'd like to see you get in it."

5

Johnny stopped with his hand on the doorknob. He could hear Esther's voice through it. She was talking to Peter.

"Nu?" she was saying. "Aren't you getting dressed yet? Doris and Mark you were going to take to the park today."

Johnny grinned to himself in the hall. He heard Peter's voice indistinctly as he replied to his wife, but he couldn't understand the words. Its tone was lazy and grumbling. Johnny grinned again. It was Sunday and he knew that Peter liked to spend the morning with his feet on a hassock reading the papers. He turned the knob and walked into the kitchen.

Esther looked at him in surprise and then at the clock. "You're up early, Johnny," she said. There was a big pot bubbling on the stove behind her.

He smiled at her. "I'll only be a minute, I just wanted to ask Peter if he wanted me to pick up anything for him in New York."

"You're going to New York today?" she asked.

He nodded. She seemed a little peeved. He wondered what it was.

Peter came to the door of the kitchen and looked in on them. "You're going to New York?" he echoed Esther's words.

"Yeah," Johnny answered laconically. He looked at Peter. Peter was in his shirtsleeves, the belt on his trousers loosened comfortably. Peter had put on a little weight lately, he thought. Well, why shouldn't he? Things were going pretty good.

"What for?" Peter asked.

"I promised Joe I'd be down to see him and look over some of the new pictures," he replied. "I'll be back tomorrow in time for the evening show."

Peter shrugged his shoulders. "If you want to travel eight

hours just to look at a couple of pictures, it's all right with me, but I wouldn't do it."

Johnny smiled. "If you did," he thought silently, "maybe you'd understand what I've been trying to tell you the past few months—that this is growing into a big business." Aloud he said: "I like to do it. You get an idea of what's goin' on that way."

Peter looked at him. A peculiarly fanatical light had come into Johnny's eyes as he spoke. Moving pictures had captured Johnny's mind. He ate, slept, and dreamed moving pictures. Since he had started to go into New York to buy them for the nickelodeon, he couldn't stop talking about them. He remembered what Johnny had said one day when he had come back from the city:

"This guy Borden's got the right idea. He's making two-reel films with a story in them. And there's those other guys, Fox and Laemmle, them too. They say it's gonna be a big business. They say some day there will be theaters that will show nothing but moving pictures, like they have now for plays."

Peter had sniffed at the idea, but secretly he had been impressed. All these men, maybe they had something. He had seen their pictures. They were certainly better than the combine's; maybe they knew what they were talking about.

He had wondered what it would be like to own a theater that showed nothing but moving pictures, but resolutely he pushed the thought from his mind. No, it was foolish to waste time even thinking about it. It would never pay off. He was better off the way he was.

Doris came running into the kitchen followed by Mark. She looked up at Johnny, her face radiant. She had heard his voice in the other room. "Going to the park, Uncle Johnny?" she asked excitedly.

He looked down at her, smiling. "Not today, sweetheart," he said, "Uncle Johnny's gotta go to New York on business."

Her face fell and a look of disappointment came over it. "Oh," she said in a very small voice.

Esther turned and looked meaningly at her husband. Peter caught the glance. He stepped forward and took Doris's hand. "Papa'll take you, *liebchen*," he said. He turned to

Johnny. "Wait for us, we'll walk you down to the station."
He left the room to get his jacket.

"Some coffee, Johnny?" Esther asked.

"No, thanks," he replied, smiling, "I had breakfast already."

Peter came back into the kitchen, buttoning his jacket.
"All right, *kinder*," he said, "let's go."

In the street Mark tugged at Johnny's hand.

Johnny looked down at him.

"Piggy-back!" Mark said in his little treble.

Johnny grinned and swung the child onto his shoulders.

"Whee!" shouted Mark as they walked along.

It wasn't until they had walked halfway down the block
that Peter realized Doris had gone over to the other side
of Johnny and was holding Johnny's free hand. He smiled to
himself. It was a good sign if children liked you.

"How is Joe getting along?" he asked Johnny. He hadn't
seen Joe since he had quit the combine and gone to work
for Borden.

"Good," Johnny answered. "He's turning out some swell
pictures. Borden says he's the best man he's got."

"That's fine," Peter said. "Is Joe satisfied?"

"Joe likes it, but there's one thing more he wants to do."
Johnny was trying to untangle Mark's grip on his hair. Mark
was laughing.

Peter looked up at him. "Let go Uncle Johnny's hair," he
said sternly, "or I'll tell him to put you down."

Mark loosened his grip and Peter spoke to Johnny. "What
is it he wants?"

Johnny's voice was elaborately casual. "He wants to go
into business himself. He says there is a lot of money in it."

"What do you think?" Peter was interested, though he
pretended not to be.

Johnny stole a quick glance at him out of the corner of
his eyes. Peter's face was calm but his eyes gave him away.
"I think he's got something," Johnny said slowly. "We figured it out.

"A one-reeler costs about three hundred dollars, plus the
prints. You make a hundred prints from each negative. You
lease each print at least twice for ten dollars each time. That
gives you two thousand for each picture. I don't see how
you can miss."

"Then what's stopping him?"

"Money," Johnny answered. "He needs at least six thousand for cameras and equipment and he hasn't got it."

They were at the station now and Johnny lifted Mark down from his shoulders. "You know, Peter," he said, looking at him speculatively, "it wouldn't be a bad business for us to go into."

Peter laughed. "Not me. I'm no *schlemiel*. I know when I'm well off. What happens if you can't get rid of the film?" He answered his own question. "You go broke."

"I don't think so," Johnny said quickly. "Look at us. We buy film from every place we can get it and never have enough. I don't see how it can miss." He fished out a cigarette and put it in his mouth. "And all the other exhibitors I met in New York are in the same boat we are. Their tongues are hanging out for more pictures."

Peter laughed again. This time his laugh wasn't as assured as before. Johnny could tell that he was intrigued by the idea. "I'm not greedy," Peter said. "Let the other guy have the headaches. We're doing all right."

A few minutes later the train pulled in and Johnny climbed aboard. He stood on the platform and waved to them as the train pulled out. They waved back to him and he smiled.

He knew Peter well enough by now to realize he had planted the germ of an idea in his mind. Leave it alone for a while and every now and then say a few words more about it. In time the idea would catch on and begin to grow. The station was lost to his sight as the train turned round a bend and he went inside and found a seat. He took a newspaper from his pocket and opened it, still smiling. Maybe by the time Joe was ready, Peter would be too.

Back at the station, Doris began to cry as the train pulled out. Peter looked down at her in surprise. "Why are you crying, *liebchen?*" he asked.

She sniffled. "I don't like to see anybody go away on a train."

Peter was puzzled; he scratched at his ear. As far as he knew, she had never seen anyone off on a train before. "Why?" he asked.

She looked up at him, her soft blue eyes swimming in tears. "I—I don't know, Papa," she said in a small voice. "I just feel like crying. Maybe Uncle Johnny isn't coming back."

Peter looked down at her. For a moment he stood there silently, then he took her hand. "Such nonsense!" he said gruffly. "Come on. Let's go to the park."

6

It was dark when Johnny awoke. He was in a strange room. His head felt logy, heavy. He groaned and stretched his arms.

There was a stir in the bed beside him. He started in sudden surprise as his outstretched hand encountered warm, soft flesh. He turned his head.

In the darkness he could barely see the face of the girl sleeping beside him. She was lying on her side, one arm under the pillow. He sat up slowly, trying to remember what had happened last night. He remembered Joe ordering more wine. They were all getting drunk. Painfully it began to come back to him.

It had started when he came into the studio about five o'clock. Joe had told him they would be working because it was the only day some of the girls they had hired would be free. These girls worked in a burlesque show during the week and this was a chance for them to pick up a few bucks extra.

When he got there, Joe was in the midst of a hot argument with one of the girls. She was screaming at him. At first Johnny couldn't make out what it was all about, but then he gathered it had something to do with the clothes she was wearing.

Bill Borden was standing near by, wearing a worried look that Johnny had come to recognize as customary for all picture men. Joe stood there calmly waiting for the girl to stop screaming. Johnny stopped near the door. No one even noticed his entering.

At last the girl stopped yelling. Joe looked at her for a moment, then turned to Borden. "Give her her time, Bill," he said calmly, ignoring the girl. "We can't afford temperament in this business."

Borden didn't answer. The worried look on his face grew deeper.

The girl started to shout again. "You can't do it!" she

screamed at Joe. "I'm supposed to have the lead in this picture. My agent'll sue you!" Her voice grew shrill.

Joe looked at her calmly for a moment; then he suddenly exploded. "Who the hell do you think you're gonna sue and for what?" he shouted back at her. "Why, for Christ's sake, we pay you more here for one day's work than you make all week hustling your ass on a burley line! Sue us an' you get no work from any of the picture people!" He stepped close to her and shook an angry finger in her face. "Now, if you want to play the lead in this picture, take off your God-damn dress and show your chemise! And don't give me any bull about being modest. I seen you on the stage of the Bijou without nothin' on! Thass the reason I hired you!"

The girl fell silent in the face of this sudden tirade. After a few seconds of looking at him thoughtfully, she said: "All right, I'll do it. But there's one thing!" With a sudden motion she stepped back from him, drew her dress off over her head, and threw it at Joe's feet.

A gasp rose in Johnny's throat. The girl didn't have a stitch of clothing on under the dress.

Quickly Joe picked up the dress and rushed to cover her. Borden threw his hands over his face and groaned.

The girl smiled as Joe reached her. "You'll have to lend me a chemise," she said sweetly. "It was too damn hot to wear one."

Joe began to laugh. "Yuh shoulda said so in the first place, baby," he managed to say. "We would've saved ourselves a pack uh trouble."

A few minutes later the girl was dressed in a chemise, and the camera began to roll. Joe looked up and saw Johnny. He went toward him, a smile on his face. "See what I gotta go through?" he asked.

Johnny grinned back at him. "Yeah. Pretty tough, isn't it?"

Joe laughed at Johnny's answer. "No foolin', though," he said seriously. "These kids are crazy, you never know what to expect from them."

Johnny grinned again. "I didn't see nuthin' to complain about."

Joe shoved him gently by the shoulder. "Go on into the projection room an' look at those pictures, you unsympathetic bastard," he said in a friendly voice. "I should be through by the time you are. Then we'll go to eat."

"Okay," Johnny said, starting to turn away.

Joe called him back. "I was just thinkin'," he said with a smile on his face, "it might be a good idea if we took a couple of the babes along with us. The kinda life you been leadin' up in Rochester ain't too good for yuh."

"Decent of you to worry about me," Johnny told him with a derisive smile on his face. "I suppose you can get along without dames."

Joe smiled comfortably. "I kin take 'em or leave 'em. But I remember the time when you were about sixteen an' yuh got so randy over that contortionist, Santos had to take yuh over an' get yuh fixed up."

Johnny's face grew red; he started to reply to Joe's statement, but just then Borden came up and hurried him off to the projection room. When he came out, Joe was waiting with two girls.

Joe introduced them. One of them was the girl who had been arguing with Joe; her name was May Daniels and from the way she took Joe's arm Johnny knew they were old friends. The other girl was a cute little blonde named Flo Daley.

She smiled at Johnny. "Yuh better be nice to him, Flo," Joe said laughing. "He's one of our biggest customers."

They had dinner at Churchill's. Joe was in a good mood. He had completed a whole picture that afternoon. After they had finished eating, he lit up a cigar and leaned back in his chair. "Did you talk to Peter yet?" he asked Johnny.

"Un-hunh," Johnny grunted. "Just this morning. I think he'll bite."

"I hope so." Joe leaned forward earnestly. "Borden's workin' on that new studio out in Brooklyn an' it'll be good if Peter comes in in time to take this one off his hands. It'll save us a lot of trouble."

"He will," Johnny said confidently. "I'm sure he will."

"Good." Joe leaned back in his chair again and blew a cloud of smoke toward the ceiling.

May leaned toward him. "Do you men always have to talk business?" she asked. "Can't you forget it just once and have a good time?"

Joe squeezed her knee under the table. He had drunk just enough to make him feel good. "That's right, baby," he said. "Let's have a real good time." He hailed the waiter. "More wine!"

It was late and they were arguing over how many theaters Johnny owned by the time they reached Joe's apartment. Joe had insisted it was twenty-one while Johnny insisted it was only twenty.

Flo had wondered how a man so young could be so successful. Joe drunkenly assured her that Johnny was an organizing genius and was so busy he didn't have time to remember how many theaters he had himself.

They staggered into the apartment. Johnny looked at Joe. "You're loaded," he said to him. "You better go to shleep."

Against Joe's protests they hustled him into the bedroom. He fell across the bed and passed out. They were trying to undress him when suddenly May had said she was too tired to bother and stretched out on the bed beside Joe and went to sleep.

He and Flo had looked at each other and giggled. "Can't hold their likker," he had assured her solemnly. Together they stumbled out of the room into the other bedroom.

She turned to him as the door closed behind them. There was a smile on her face; she held her arms toward him. "Like me, Johnny?" she asked.

He looked down at her. Strange, she didn't sound as drunk as she had a moment before. He pulled her toward him. "Of coursh I like you," he said.

Her eyes were on his face, the smile still on her lips. "Then what are you waiting for?" she asked in a low, excited voice.

For a second he stood very still, then he kissed her. He could feel her body clinging closely to him. His hand found the open bodice of her dress and slipped inside it. Her breast was warm and exciting in his fingers. He moved her toward the bed.

He heard her laugh. "Wait a minute, Johnny," she told him. "You don't have to tear the clothes off me."

He let her twist out of his grasp and watched her as she undressed. "Joe was right," he thought wildly, "the life I been leading ain't normal." But another part of his mind insisted stubbornly that he didn't have enough time for this and everything else he wanted to do.

Her clothes lay on the floor around her as she stepped

toward him. "See," she smiled, "it's much better this way, isn't it?"

He didn't answer as his hands pulled her to him and their lips met. Her body was as fire to his touch as he thrust all thoughts from his mind and gave himself up to the moment.

His head was pounding fiercely now. He got out of bed and, picking up his union suit from a chair, laboriously got into it. After a few unsteady steps toward the bathroom, he turned back toward the bed. He looked down at the girl for a few seconds, then he leaned forward and picked up the end of the blanket.

The girl stirred and turned toward him. "Johnny," she murmured softly, still asleep. She had nothing on.

Memories of her body, warm against him, flooded through his mind. He let the blanket fall and staggered to the bathroom.

He shut the door and turned on the light. It hurt his eyes. He went over to the washbowl and turned on the cold water. The basin filled rapidly. He leaned over it, hesitated a second, then plunged his head into the cold water.

At last he began to feel better. He picked up a towel and dried himself. He looked in the mirror over the washbowl and ran his hand over his face. He needed a shave, but there wasn't time for it.

He went back to the bedroom and dressed, then silently left the house without waking anyone. The morning air was clean and invigorating. He took out his watch and looked at it. It was six thirty. He'd have to hurry if he wanted to make the early train to Rochester.

7

JOHNNY came into the kitchen. It was warm and cozy in there, the big stove throwing off waves of heat. "Where's Peter?" he asked.

Esther put the cover back on the pot of soup and turned to look at him. "He went out for a walk," she told him.

He looked at her in surprise. "In this weather?" he asked,

going to the window and looking out. The snow was still coming down heavily; the street was already covered with drifts. He turned back to her. "There must be almost three feet of snow out there."

She made a helpless gesture with her hands. "I told him," she said quietly, "but he went anyway. He's been so restless the last few days."

Johnny nodded his head understandingly. He had noticed Peter's restlessness himself ever since they had to close down the nickelodeon three days ago because of the heavy snowfall. The summer had been profitable, but now the first snow of winter had closed them up.

Esther looked at him. Her mind was still on Peter. "I don't know what got into him lately," she said half to herself. "He was never like this before."

Johnny dropped into a chair in front of her. His brows knitted together puzzledly. "What do you mean?" he asked.

Her eyes looked directly into his as if the answer to her problem lay there. "Since the nickelodeon opened, he's changed," she said slowly. "A little business more or less never bothered him before; now every morning he stands at the window and curses the snow. 'It's costing us money,' he says."

Johnny smiled. "It ain't that bad," he said. "In the carny we knew that the sun can't shine every day. It's all in the business."

"I told him we shouldn't complain, we were lucky so far; but he only ignored what I said and went out." She sat down in the chair opposite Johnny and looked down at her hands folded in her lap. When she looked up at him again, her eyes had filled with tears. "It seems almost like I don't know him any more. Like he's a different person, a stranger. I remember back in New York when Doris was a baby and the doctor told us the only way she would get back her health was if we took her out of the city. Peter sold the business there and came out here without a second's hesitation. Now I'm beginning to wonder if he would do a thing like that again."

Johnny shifted uncomfortably in his seat. He was embarrassed by the sudden flood of her confidence. "He's been working pretty hard lately," he said, trying to comfort her.

"It isn't the easiest thing in the world trying to run two businesses at once."

A sudden smile at his poor attempt to console her broke through her tears. "Don't tell me that, Johnny," she said softly. "I know better. Since you come back he hasn't had to do a thing in the nickelodeon."

Johnny's face grew red. "But the responsibility is his," he replied lamely.

She took his hand, still smiling. "You're a good boy to say so, Johnny, but you're not fooling anybody."

The soup on the stove behind her began to boil; she dropped his hand and got up to look at it. She took a spoon and began to stir it, speaking over her shoulder to him. "No, it's not that. There's something on his mind and I don't know what it is." A discouraged tone seemed to permeate her voice. Peter seemed farther away from her now than he had ever been.

She remembered when Peter had first come into her father's store. She had been fourteen then and he was about a year older.

He had just got off the boat and had a letter from her father's brother, who had settled in Munich. He had looked like a real greenie too, his wrists shooting out from the cuffs of his too short jacket. Her father had given him a job in the small hardware store on Rivington Street and Peter had started in to go to night school. She used to help him with his English lessons.

It was the most natural thing in the world for them to fall in love. She remembered when he went to ask her father for permission for them to get married. She had watched them from behind the door that led into the back room of the store. Peter had stood there awkwardly watching her father, who was sitting on a high stool behind the counter, his little black yamalke perched on his head, reading the Jewish newspaper through his small spectacles.

At last, after a long, uneasy pause, Peter had spoken. "Mr. Greenberg."

Her father had looked up at him over the rims of his glasses. He didn't speak, he wasn't a very talkative man.

Peter was nervous. "I—uh, that is, we—Esther and I, would like to get married."

Her father had looked up at him over the rims of his

glasses, then, without speaking, dropped his eyes back to his newspaper again. She remembered how her heart was pounding so loudly that she had been afraid they would hear it out in the store. She held her breath.

Peter spoke again; his voice was strained and cracked slightly. "Mr. Greenberg, did you hear me?"

Her father looked at him again and spoke in Yiddish. "Nu and why shouldn't I hear you? Am I deaf?"

"But—but you didn't answer me," Peter stammered.

"I didn't say no, did I?" Mr. Greenberg answered, still in Yiddish. "Neither am I so blind that I could not see what you were going to ask." He turned back to his newspaper.

Peter stood there a moment as if he did not believe his ears; then he turned and started back to tell Esther. She had just time to get out of the way of the door before he burst into the room with his news.

When her father had died, Peter took over the store. Their little Doris was born in the room behind it. When she was three years old she had been a very sick little child and the big doctor they had gone to had told them the only thing they could do for her was to take her out of the city. That was how they came to Rochester, where, after a few years, Mark was born.

Now there was an urgency in Peter, a restlessness she had never seen before, something she didn't quite understand. She felt strangely excluded from his mind, somehow apart from him, and felt a vague hurt within her.

She heard the door open. Peter came into the kitchen, brushing the snow from him.

Johnny cleared his throat in relief. Esther's protracted silence had added to his embarrassment, he was glad that Peter had come in. "Bad weather," he said.

Peter nodded his head morosely. "It looks like we'll be closed tomorrow too," he said irritably. "It doesn't seem to be letting up." He took off his overcoat and dropped it on a chair, where it began to shed small drops of water as the snow on it melted in the heat of the room.

"That's what I thought," Johnny said. "I've been thinking of running down to New York and seeing Joe at the studio. Why don't you come with me?"

"What's the use?" Peter snapped, "I told you before I wasn't interested."

Esther looked up at him suddenly. Intuitively she knew from his voice that this was what had been troubling him. She turned to Johnny. "What is it you want him to do?"

Johnny turned to her, sensing an ally. "Bill Borden is opening a new studio in Brooklyn shortly and he's putting his old one on the block. I want Peter to come down to New York and look at it. If he thinks enough of it, maybe he and Joe and me will go into it."

"You mean make pictures?" she asked, watching Peter out of the corner of her eyes.

"Yeah. Make pictures," Johnny answered. "There's a lot of money in it an' it's getting bigger every day." Excitedly he began to tell her about the possibilities he saw in it.

Esther listened attentively. It was all new to her, but Peter sank into his chair with an apparent air of boredom. It was only Esther who could see that beneath the mask of indifference on Peter's face the idea had intrigued him.

Johnny talked about it all through supper. He could speak endlessly about it, and when he went downstairs to sleep, his words still lingered in Esther's mind. Peter had not commented one way or the other; he seemed wrapped up in other thoughts.

About nine o'clock they went to bed. It was still snowing and the room was cold. Esther waited for him to come to bed; when he did he was sleepy, but Esther wanted to talk.

"Why don't you want to go and see what Johnny says for yourself?" she asked him.

He grunted and turned over on his side. "What for?" he mumbled into his pillow. "The kid is all excited over nothing."

"He was right about the nickelodeon," she pointed out. "Could be he's right about this."

He sat up. "That's different," he said. "The nickelodeon we know is a novelty. When it wears off, we close up the thing; we're not out no money because we went in cheap. But this is a big business. It takes a big investment to go into it. Yet it's based on the same novelty, and when the nickelodeons close, where is it? Gone. With this when we close up, we made our money, so we don't lose no sleep."

She persisted. "But Johnny thinks it will get bigger. He

says nickelodeons are opening up at the rate of over twenty a week."

"So it'll die so much quicker." He lay back on the pillow again. A thought came to him. "Why are you so interested in what Johnny says all of a sudden?"

"Because you are," she answered simply, "only I don't go around looking for excuses why I shouldn't do something because I'm afraid of it."

Peter didn't answer. "She is right," he was thinking. "I'm afraid to take a chance. That's why I won't go down with Johnny. Because I'm afraid he's right and I'll pass it up anyway."

They were quiet for a while. Peter was just drifting off to sleep when she spoke again. "Are you up?"

"I'm up," he answered testily.

"Peter, maybe it's a good idea that Johnny's got. I got a feeling."

"I got a feeling too," he grumbled. "I got a feeling I should like to sleep."

"No, Peter." She sat up in bed and looked at him. "I mean it. Remember when the doctor told us to take Doris out of New York and how I felt about Rochester?"

He looked at her through the darkness. He wouldn't admit it, but he had a healthy respect for her hunches. Time had proved her right many times. That time he had wanted to go somewhere else. Instead they came here and prospered, while the man who had taken the other place had failed. "So?" he asked.

"Well, now I got a feeling this was one of the things we came here for and now the time is right for us to go back to New York. I never said nothing because we came here for the baby's health, but now, thank God, the baby's all right and I'm lonely. I miss my people, my family. I want Mark to go to cheder where my papa used to pray. I want to go where I can hear people speaking Yiddish and I want to stand with my children in front of the matzoh bakery on Rivington Street and smell the matzos warm from the oven like my father and I used to do. And suddenly the feeling is strong in me that the time has come to go back home. Please, Peter, go down and look. If it's not good, don't do nothing about it, but go and look."

It was a long speech for her; in that way she was a great

deal like her father, and Peter was impressed. He pulled her head down on his shoulder. There were soft wet spots on her cheek where it lay against his neck. With his free hand he stroked her hair. When at last he spoke, his voice was very soft and he spoke in Yiddish. "All right, so I'll go and look."

She turned her face toward him. "Tomorrow?"

"Tomorrow," he answered, and then suddenly turned to English. "But I'm not making no promises!"

Esther lay awake for a long time listening to Peter's slow breathing as he slept. It was funny sometimes how hard you had to work to convince a man that it was right for him to do the thing he really wanted to do.

8

THEY reached Borden's studio at three o'clock the next afternoon. Expertly Johnny led him through the studio to where Joe was working. Joe waved his hand when he saw them. "Grab yourself a seat and watch," he shouted to them above the noise of the studio. "I'll be with you in a little while."

It was almost an hour before Joe came over. Meanwhile Peter had looked around the studio. Even his inexperienced eye could recognize the aura of intense activity going on around him. There were three crews working on different platforms. Johnny explained to him they were called stages. The people themselves had an air about them that indicated a pride, a sureness, an awareness that their work was the most important thing in the world.

Peter watched Joe. Joe was rehearsing a group of actors in a scene he was about to photograph. Again and again he made them go through the motions of the scene until they did just what he wanted them to do. It reminded Peter of when he was a boy and used to bring his father lunch in the music hall in Munich. His father played second violin in the orchestra there. The orchestra had been rehearsing as Peter had come into the hall, the maestro would be shouting, and then suddenly all would be silence as they would play the number for the last time before the evening concert. When the number was finished, the maestro would nod his head if he was satisfied and say to them: "Now, my children, you are ready to play for the King if he should come."

That was what Joe was doing. He was making them play a scene over and over, and when he had it just right, he would capture it on film. For here the camera was king. A vague tightness came into Peter's chest as he watched. This was something he could understand. His father had made him practice violin day in and day out, for his father wanted him some day to play beside him in the orchestra. Peter knew how much it had cost his father to send his son to America when the Kaiser began to conscript all young men and boys into his army. Time flew by quickly for him. The hour that Joe had taken with the scene seemed but a few minutes to Peter, so completely had he been absorbed.

"So you finally came down?" Joe smiled.

Peter was cautious. "Things were quiet. I had nothing better to do," he explained.

"Well, what do you think of it?" Joe asked, waving his hand at the studio around him.

Peter was still cautious. "It's all right. Very interesting."

Joe turned to Johnny. "I think I saw the boss come in while I was working. Why don't you take Peter over to meet him? I got another scene to shoot before I can call it a day."

"All right," Johnny answered.

Peter followed him back to the office. The office was a large room with a few men and girls sitting at desks and working. At the back of the office there was a little railing. Just inside the railing was the desk of William Borden. It was a big roll-top desk that completely hid the little man who sat behind it. Only the top of his bald head could be seen over it as he occasionally moved or spoke into the telephone perched on the side of it.

Johnny led Peter through the railing up to the desk. The little man looked up.

"Mr. Borden," Johnny said, "I'd like you to meet my boss, Peter Kessler."

The little man sprang to his feet. Peter and he looked at each other for a few startled moments. Then Borden smiled and thrust out his hand. "Peter Kessler," he said in a thin high-pitched voice. "Of course. Don't you remember me?"

Peter took his hand and shook it. He looked puzzled. Suddenly a light of recognition came into his eyes. "Willie—Willie Bordanov." He nodded his head excitedly, his face smiling. "Sure, your father had—"

"That's right"—Borden was grinning—"the pushcart on Rivington Street in front of Greenberg's hardware store. You married his daughter, Esther, I remember. How is she?"

The two men were talking excitedly when Johnny left them and went back to see Joe. He had a hunch that something would come of it. Something had to come of it. Bill Borden was the best salesman the picture business had ever had. He felt more sure of it than ever when Peter told him they were going to have dinner with Borden at his home that night.

It was after dinner, while they were sitting in the kitchen of the Borden apartment, that the talk got around to the picture business. The evening had gone by and, much to Johnny's disgust, the two men had done nothing but talk of their friends and their youth. It was Johnny who brought the talk around to the subject. He had started Borden talking about the combine, which was Borden's pet anathema. Then gradually he led him around to making the statement that if there were more independent producers in the field, the combine would have to fold.

Johnny nodded his head in agreement. "I been telling Peter that, but Peter thinks the hardware business is safer."

Borden looked at Peter, then at Johnny. "Maybe Peter is right, the hardware business is safer. But the picture business has more opportunity. It offers greater rewards for those who are willing to pioneer. Look at me. I started in three years ago with fifteen hundred dollars capital. In another few weeks I will have finished building a studio in Brooklyn that cost me fifteen thousand dollars, with equipment extra. My pictures are selling all over the country and I'm doing eight-thousand-a-week business. Next year this time, with my new plant, I'll be doing twice that."

The figures impressed Peter. "How much would it cost to start in the business today?" he asked.

Borden looked closely at him. "Are you serious?"

Peter nodded his head and pointed to Johnny. "My young friend here has been plaguing me for the last six months I should be going in with him to the picture business. So I'm serious. If there's money in it, why should I make jokes?"

Borden looked at Johnny with a new respect. "So that's why you didn't take the job I wanted to give you," he said to him. "You had plans of your own." He turned back to Peter. "A dozen times I wanted Johnny to come to work for me and each time he said no. Now I know why."

For some reason Peter was touched. To think that Johnny had turned down jobs offered him and never even mentioned it. "Johnny's a good boy," he said. "He's like one of the family."

Johnny was embarrassed. "How much would it take, Mr. Borden?"

The two older men smiled understandingly at each other. Borden leaned back in his chair. "You should be able to go into business with ten thousand dollars."

"Then it's out of the question for me," Peter said. He lit a cigar. "I ain't got that much."

"But—" Borden leaned forward, his voice grew a little excited. "I got an idea." He got out of his chair and walked over to Peter. "If you really would like it, I got a proposition to make you."

"Nu?" asked Peter.

"Like I said," Borden answered, his voice once more calm, "I'm opening up in Brooklyn, a studio, in a few weeks. I had planned to sell my equipment at this studio because I got for my new place all new equipment." He leaned over Peter's chair and dropped his voice to a confidential whisper. "For six thousand dollars I can let you have my equipment at the old studio and it's a bargain."

"Willie," Peter said, getting to his feet and looking down at Borden, "you haven't changed a bit since the days you tried to sell me two-cent shoelaces for a nickel off your father's pushcart. I might be green in the picture business, but I'm not so dumb as you think. You think I don't know the condition of your old equipment? It's not for nothing I spent all these years in the hardware business not to know merchandise. If you had said to me three thousand dollars, I might have listened, but six, I laugh."

Johnny caught his breath. Was Peter crazy? Didn't he know that you couldn't get equipment in this business—that the combine controlled everything and that there were men who would jump at the opportunity of getting that equipment for six thousand dollars?

Borden's reply was even more amazing to Johnny. "Peter," he said, "the only reason I made you an offer so sensational like that is because I want you in this business. I got anyway a feeling that you're going into the picture business, so I'll make you another proposition. From you and only you I'll take three thousand dollars in cash down and three thousand dollars I'll take in chattel mortgage. Such confidence I got in you as a person, you can pay me when you make the money."

The spirit of bargaining had caught Peter. "Make it five thousand, two down and the rest mortgage, and I'll consider it. I'll even talk to Esther about it."

Again Johnny was surprised. He didn't understand why Peter said he would talk to Esther about it. He didn't see why it was necessary. After all, what did she know about the picture business?

But Borden didn't seem surprised. He looked up shrewdly into Peter's face. What he saw there must have pleased him, for suddenly he gave Peter a playful punch in the arm. "Good enough, Landsman!" he said. "If Esther approves it, we got a deal!"

9

PETER was very quiet on the train going home. Johnny didn't talk much to him when he saw that Peter wanted to be left alone. Peter stared out of the window most of the time.

The snow was still packed tightly on the ground when at last they got off the train and trudged toward home. As they drew near the house, Peter began to talk.

"It's not so easy like you think, Johnny," he said. "There's lots of things I got to do before I can even take a chance like that."

Johnny got the impression that Peter was talking more for his own benefit than Johnny's, so he didn't reply.

"I got responsibilities here," Peter went on. Johnny was right, Peter didn't expect an answer. "I got the two businesses and the house, which I have to sell so we can have some cash to operate. The hardware business is not so good right now and I got a big inventory, which I expected to clear out in the spring."

"But we can't wait," Johnny protested. "You can't ask Borden to wait until then. He will have to sell his equipment."

"I know," Peter agreed, "but what can I do? You heard he wants at least two thousand in cash and right now I ain't got it. I don't know either whether it's such a good thing to jump into anyhow. It's a risky business. What if the pictures don't sell? I don't know nothing about making 'em."

"Joe'll come in with us," Johnny said, "and he knows how to make 'em. His pictures are the best that Borden's got. We can't lose."

"Maybe," Peter said doubtfully as they came to the door. "But there's no guarantees."

Peter went upstairs to his apartment and Johnny went into the nickelodeon.

"Hallo, Johnny," George called from behind his counter.

"Hello, George." Johnny walked over to the counter and sat down on a stool.

George put a cup of coffee in front of him. "Have a good trip?"

Johnny sipped at the coffee gratefully and started to unbutton his coat. "Yeanh"—he nodded—"pretty good." "At least it would be if Peter wasn't so damn cautious," he thought.

"I didn't think you'd be down today," he said aloud. "It's so cold nobody'll be out."

"Poopuls come out," George said. "You should been here last night. Poopuls come minute she stops snowing and wait in entrance for you to open op."

Johnny was surprised. "You mean people were actually here last night in all that snow?"

"Sure," George said.

"Did you tell 'em we'll be open tonight?" Johnny asked.

"Nope," George said proudly, "did better. I go upstairs to Missus Kessler and tell her. She sticks head outside windows and sees poopuls. She comes downstairs and we put on show. Did good business too."

"Well, I'll be damned," Johnny muttered under his breath. "But who ran the projector?"

"Me," George said beaming. "Missus Kessler took the tickets and my brother Nick, he work the store. I run him putty good too. Only broke film twice."

Twice in one show was nothing. "How did you learn to work the machine?" Johnny asked incredulously.

"Watched you," George answered. "Not so hard to do." He looked at Johnny and smiled. "Sure is one good business. Make money easy. Put in film one end machine, money comes out other end."

Johnny never heard it put better. He finished his coffee and started for his room at the back of the store.

"Johnny," George called him back.

"What?"

"Missus Kessler, she say Peter go to New York. Maybe go into picture business there."

"Maybe."

"Then what he do with this?" George asked. "Sell it?"

"Maybe."

George walked over to him excitedly. He put his hand on Johnny's arm. "If he does sell, you think maybe he'll sell it to me?"

Johnny looked at him a moment before he answered. "If he decides to sell and if you got money to buy, I don't see why he won't."

George looked at the floor. His face, as always when he was excited, turned a little red. "You know when I come to this country fifteen yirrs, I'm Grik, and poor boy, but my brother Nick and me, we live cheap and save few bucks maybe for to go back to old country with some day. I think now maybe we don't go back to old country so quick. We use money to open up picture show."

"What made you think of that?" Johnny asked curiously.

"I read in papers all over the country they open. In New York they got theaters now show only moving pictures." George spoke slowly, he didn't want to get mixed up in his choice of words. "If Peter sell me the building, I take out hardware store and make regular theater like New York."

"The whole building?" Johnny didn't believe his ears.

"The whole building," George said, then added cautiously: "That is, if Peter don't ask too much money!"

Peter had just finished explaining to Esther why he thought they would not be able to take Borden's proposition when

Johnny came running up the stairs. He burst into the room.

"Peter, we got it! We got it!"

Peter looked at him as if he were crazy. "Got what?"

Johnny couldn't stand still. He picked up Esther and swung her around. Peter's mouth hung open as he watched them. "Our worries are over," Johnny sang out, "George will buy it. The whole building!"

His excitement was contagious. Peter went over to him and shouted: "Stand still a minute, you crazy fool! What do you mean George will buy it? Where'll he get the money?"

Johnny looked at him grinning. "He's got the money. He says so and he wants to buy the place."

"You're crazy," Peter said with finality. "It's impossible."

"Impossible?" Johnny yelled. He walked over to the door and opened it. "Hey, George," he shouted down the hall, "come on up!" He stood there holding the door open.

They could hear the footsteps on the stairs. They were slow and hesitating at first and then grew firmer as they came closer. At last George came into the room. His face was red and he looked at the floor as he stumbled across the room toward them.

"What's this Johnny tells us?" Peter asked him.

George tried to speak but couldn't. The English words just wouldn't come to his tongue. He gulped twice and then looked at Peter helplessly.

It was Esther who came to his rescue. Sensing the poor man's distress and divining the reasons that lay behind it, she went up to him and took his hand. "Come and sit down, George," she said quietly, "and while you men talk it over, I'll make some coffee."

And so it was settled. A week later George had bought the building and the nickelodeon for twelve thousand dollars, half cash and half notes secured by mortgage. Peter arranged for the sale of the merchandise in the hardware store to the only other hardware merchant in the neighborhood, who was only too glad to buy it because it left him with a clear field.

The very next day Peter signed his agreement with Borden and an hour later rented the building in which the equipment stood, thus taking care of his studio space.

When the papers were all signed, Borden turned to Peter

and grinned. "Now you need some help to make pictures. I got a few relatives who know the business and they could be of real use to you. Maybe I should send them over to talk to you?"

Peter smiled and shook his head. "I don't think I'll need them."

"But you got to have help to make pictures," Borden protested. "I'm thinking only of your good. You don't know nothing about how to make them."

"That's true," Peter admitted, "but I got some ideas I'd like to try out first."

"It's all right with me," Borden said, "it's your funeral."

They were seated around a big table at Luchow's on Fourteenth Street. Borden and his wife, Peter, Esther, Johnny, and Joe made up the party. Borden got up to make a toast. "To Peter Kessler and his good wife, Esther," he said, holding a glass of champagne in his hand. "All the luck in the world in producing—" He stopped in the middle of the toast.

"I just thought of something," he said. "You ain't got no name for your pictures. What are you going to call them, Peter?"

Peter looked puzzled. "I never thought of that. I didn't know I had to have a name for them."

"It's very important," Borden assured him solemnly. "How else are the customers going to know they're your pictures?"

"I have an idea," Esther said.

They looked at her.

Her face flushed a little. "Peter," she said, turning to her husband, "what did the waiter call that big bottle of champagne you ordered?"

"A magnum," Peter answered.

"That's it." She smiled. "Why not call it Magnum Pictures?"

A chorus of approval rose from the table.

"Then it's settled," Borden said, holding up his glass again. "To Magnum Pictures! They should be seen on every screen in the country just like Borden Pictures!"

They all drank and then Peter got up. He looked around the table and picked up his glass. "To Willie Borden, who I will never forget his kindness."

Again they drank. When they put their glasses down, Peter still stood there. He cleared his throat. "This is a big day in my life. Today I went into the business of producing pictures. Tonight my dear wife gave them a name. Now I would like to make an announcement." He looked around dramatically. "I announce the appointment of Mr. Joe Turner as studio and production manager of Magnum Pictures."

Borden didn't act surprised. He smiled and reached over the table and shook hands with Joe. "No wonder Peter didn't want any of my relatives," he said ruefully. "You must have tipped him off."

There was a relieved burst of laughter at that. Peter had been worried about how Borden would take it. He didn't know that Johnny and Joe had spoken to Borden some time ago about it.

"Wait a minute," he said, "I got another announcement." They looked at him.

He held up his glass. "To my partners, Johnny Edge and Joe Turner."

Joe just sat there with his mouth open; he gulped but couldn't speak.

It was Johnny who jumped to his feet and faced Peter. His heart was beating wildly and his eyes glistened moistly. "Peter," he said, "Peter—"

Peter grinned at him. "Don't get so excited, Johnny. After all, you only got ten per cent apiece!"

AFTERMATH

1938

TUESDAY

You sit back in your seat and try to look relaxed. The pressure in your ears grows heavier and heavier and you get a tight knotty feeling in the pit of your stomach. The lights in the cabin are low and you strain your eyes to see how the other people in the plane are acting when suddenly the wheels touch the ground. Without realizing it you have been chewing the gum faster and faster and now suddenly it tastes bad in your mouth.

I took a Kleenex from the container and wrapped the gum in it and put it away. The wheels bumped along the ground and slowly the plane came to a stop. The hostess came down the aisle and unfastened the safety belt.

I stood up and stretched. My muscles were tight from the tension. I couldn't help it. I was afraid of flying. No matter how many times I did it, I was always afraid.

The motors cut and died away, leaving a hollow, empty ringing in my ears. Unconsciously I listened for it to stop, for when it stopped I knew I was back to normal.

There were a man and a woman in the seat in front of me and they had been talking as the plane came down. While the engines were roaring I could hardly hear them, and now they seemed to be shouting.

"I still think we should have let them know we were coming," the woman was saying, when she realized she was talking loudly. She stopped in the middle of her sentence and looked back at me as if I had been eavesdropping.

I looked away and she resumed her conversation in a lower voice. The hostess came down the aisle again.

"What time is it?" I asked.

"Nine thirty-five, Mr. Edge," she answered.

I took off my wristwatch and set it and walked toward

the rear of the plane. The door had been opened and I walked out of it and down the ramp. The floodlights hurt my eyes and I stopped for a minute.

I began to feel chilly and was glad I had worn my topcoat. I pulled the collar up around my neck and walked toward the gate. Other people were rushing past me, hurrying toward the exit, but I walked slowly. I lit a cigarette as I walked and dragged deeply on it, my eyes wandering over the crowd.

And there she was. I stopped for a second and looked at her. She didn't see me. She was puffing nervously at a cigarette; her face was pale and luminous in the glaring light. Her eyes were deep blue and weary, with circles under them; her mouth was tense. Under the loose camelhair short coat flung over her shoulders her body was taut, and her free hand clenched and unclenched.

She saw me. Her hand lifted as if to wave and then hung there still in the air in front of her as if caught on an invisible rung. She watched me as I walked through the gate to her.

I stopped a foot in front of her. She was all wound up like a tight spring. "Hullo, sweetheart," I said.

Then she was in my arms, her head on my chest, crying: "Johnny, Johnny!"

I could feel her body shaking against me. I dropped my cigarette and stroked her hair. I didn't talk. There was no use talking, it wouldn't help. I just kept thinking the same thing over and over.

"I'll marry you when I grow up, Uncle Johnny."

She was almost twelve when she said that. I was just going back to New York with the first picture Magnum had completed in Hollywood and we were having dinner at Peter's house the night before I got on the train. We were all very happy and nervous. We didn't know just what was coming. The picture that was in the can would either make us or break us and so we all tried to joke and act lighthearted and not let the others see how apprehensive we were.

Esther had laughed and said: "Don't let some pretty girl on the train talk you into marrying her and go away and forget the picture."

I had reddened a little. "You don't have to worry. There isn't a girl that would marry me."

It was then that Doris spoke. Her face was serious and the blue of her eyes was deep and her voice was much older than her years. She came toward me and took my hand and looked up into my face.

"I'll marry you when I grow up, Uncle Johnny."

I don't remember what I had said, but everybody laughed. Doris still held on to my hand and looked up at me with a let-them-laugh look in her eyes.

Now I held her head tight against my shoulder and the words kept going over and over in my mind. I should have believed her. I should have remembered. There would have been less pain in our lives if I had.

Slowly her body stopped its trembling. For a few seconds she stood still against me, then she stepped back.

I took out my handkerchief and wiped the tears from her cheeks and the corners of her eyes. "Better now, sweetheart?" I asked.

She nodded her head.

I fished cigarettes out of my pocket and gave her one. As I lit her cigarette the glow from the match illuminated the cigarettes we had dropped on the ground. They lay there close together, the lipsticked end of her cigarette not quite touching mine. I put a fresh one in my mouth and lit it.

"We were held up in Chicago," I said. "Bad weather."

"I know," she answered, "I got your wire."

She took my arm and we started walking.

"How is he doing?" I asked.

"He's asleep. The doctor gave him a sedative and he'll be sleeping till morning."

"Any better?"

She made a small gesture of helplessness with her hands. "The doctor doesn't know, he says it's too soon to tell." She stopped and turned to me; the tears came welling to her eyes again. "Johnny, it's terrible. He doesn't want to live. He doesn't care any more."

I pressed her hand. "Hold it, sugar, he'll make out."

She looked at me for a moment; then she smiled, her first smile since I saw her. It looked good even if it took effort to make it. "I'm glad you're here, Johnny."

She drove me to my apartment and waited while I bathed, shaved, and changed my clothes. I had given the servants a few weeks off because I hadn't expected to be back for a while, and the place had an empty look about it.

When I came back into the living-room she was listening to some Sibelius records on the phonograph-radio. I looked at her. Only the light from the table lamp near her chair was on. It threw a soft glow over her face and she looked relaxed. Her eyes were half-closed and her breathing came soft and even. She opened her eyes when she felt me standing there.

"Hungry?"

"A little," she answered. "I haven't really eaten since this happened."

"Okay, then," I said, "let's go to Murphy's and wrap ourselves around a steak." I started back to the bedroom to get my coat when the phone began to ring. "Get it, will ya sweetheart?" I called back through the open door.

I heard her move and pick up the phone. A second later she called me. "It's Gordon. He wants to speak to you."

Gordon was production manager at the studio.

"Ask him if it'll keep till morning; I'll drop in at the studio," I told her.

I heard the murmur of her voice, then she called to me: "He says it can't keep, he's got to talk to you."

I picked up the phone in the bedroom. "I'm on," I said. I heard the click as she put down her phone.

"Johnny?"

"Yeanh, what's up?"

"I can't talk over the phone. I got to see you."

That was Hollywood. The federal government and the state government pass laws against wiretapping and people worry about talking over the phone. It's a fetish you don't fight; whenever something really important goes on, you can't talk over the phone.

"All right," I said wearily. "Where are you? Home?"

"Yes," he answered.

"I'll drop in on you after I eat some dinner," I said, and hung up.

I picked my coat off the bed and went back into the living-room. Doris was putting on some lipstick in front of a mirror.

"I gotta make a stop after dinner, honey. Do yuh mind?"

"No," she said. She knew Hollywood too.

It was nearly eleven o'clock when we got to the restaurant. It was nearly deserted. Hollywood is an early town during the week. Everyone who is working is in bed by ten o'clock because he has to be on the job at seven in the morning. We were given a quiet table in a corner.

We ordered old-fashioneds, steak, french fries, and coffee. She was more hungry than she had realized. I smiled to myself as I watched her eat. Say what you like about a woman's diet; hungry or not hungry, put a steak in front of her and watch it disappear. Maybe it was because some smart press agent planted the rumor that steak was not fattening. Anyway, she did it justice. I did too, but then, I always did.

Her plate was empty and she pushed it away from her with a sigh. She saw me smiling at her. She smiled back. A little of the tension had gone from her face. "I'm full," she said. "What are you smiling at?"

I took her hands across the table. "Hullo, sweetheart," I said.

She held my hands and looked at them, I don't know why. They were funny hands no amount of manicuring could make look presentable. They were square and the fingers were short and covered with thick black hair on the back of them. She looked back at me. "Hello, Johnny." Her voice was soft.

"How's muh baby?" I asked.

"Better since you're here."

We just sat there smiling at each other until the waiter came and took the empty dishes away and brought us a fresh pot of coffee. It was half past twelve when we left the restaurant.

We drove over to Gordon's house. He lived over in Westwood; it was about a half-hour drive. The lights in his living-room were on as we drove up the driveway.

He had the door open almost before we were up the steps. His hair was rumpled and he held a drink in one hand; he looked nervous. He was surprised to see Doris with me.

We said hello and followed him into the living-room. Joan, his wife, was in there. She got up when she saw us. "Hello, Johnny," she said to me, and then went over to Doris and kissed her. "How is Peter?" she asked.

"A little better," Doris answered. "He's sleeping."

"That's good," Joan said. "If you can get him to rest, he'll be all right."

I spoke to Gordon. "What's all the shootin' fer?"

He finished his drink and looked at Doris. Joan picked up the hint. "Let's make some coffee. These men want to talk business," she said.

Doris smiled understandingly at me and followed Joan out of the room.

I turned back to Gordon. "Well?"

"The rumor's all over town that Ronsen's tying a can to you," he said.

The two greatest products of Hollywood were pictures and rumors. From morning to night they manufactured pictures, from night to morning they manufactured rumors. There were several arguments as to which was the more important, but I don't believe it was ever settled to anyone's satisfaction.

"Tell me more," I said.

"You had a fight with him in New York. He didn't want you to come back here to see Peter. You did. He got in touch with Stanley Farber the minute you left and he's flying out here tomorrow to meet him."

"Is that all?" I asked.

"Isn't that enough?" he asked.

I grinned at him. "I thought it was important."

He was pouring himself another drink when I told him that. He almost dropped it. "Look; I'm not joking, Johnny. This is damned serious. He hasn't kept Dave Roth on the lot for love."

Gordon wasn't wrong about that. Dave was Farber's right-hand man, and Ronsen placed him on the lot as Gordon's assistant to act as a psychological threat to me. It added up too. Farber wouldn't let Roth stay there if he wasn't sure that something would come of it.

"What's Dave been doing?" I asked.

"You know Dave," he answered, shrugging his shoulders. "Tight as a clam when he wants to be. But he seems pretty damn sure of himself." He held out a drink to me.

I took it and sipped it reflectively. Maybe Ronsen was coming out to see Farber, but I was the guy that knew the whole organization. I knew the weak spots and the strong spots. I knew what had to be done, and until I finished the repair job, my position was good.

"Look, Gordon," I said, "stop worrying. I'll be at the studio in the morning and we'll go over the situation."

He looked at me doubtfully. "All right, but I hope you know what you're doing."

Joan came into the room with a pot of coffee. Doris followed her with a tray of tiny sandwiches. Hollywood wives and diplomats' wives have to develop a sense of timing. They have to know just when to excuse themselves and just when to re-enter a room. I often wonder how they know just when to come back.

Doris and I were too full to eat, but we had some coffee and left. It was almost two thirty when we got to her house.

The house was quiet; only a small light was lit in the living-room. Doris threw off her coat and went upstairs. She came down a moment later.

"He's still sleeping," she said. "Mother is too. The nurse told me that the doctor gave her a sedative. Poor thing, she just can't comprehend everything that's been happening. It's been one shock after another."

I followed her into the library. There was a big fire going in there. It felt good; the night had turned cold, with a sudden frost that would have the smudge pots going in the fruit groves. We sat down on a couch.

I put my hand around her shoulder and drew her head toward me. I kissed her. She put both hands on my cheeks and held my face close to hers.

"I knew you'd come, Johnny," she whispered.

I looked at her. "I couldn't stay away even if I wanted to."

She turned around and rested her head against my shoulder and we looked into the fire. After a little while I spoke. "Feel like talking about it, sweetheart?"

"You know a lot, for a man," she said, her voice low. "You knew I didn't want to talk about it before."

I didn't answer.

After a few minutes she spoke again. "It started yesterday. A telegram was delivered and the butler took it. I was near the door when it came, so I took it from him.

"It was from the State Department, addressed to Father. I read it first. It's a good thing now that I did, for it read: 'We are informed by our Embassy in Madrid that your son, Mark Kessler, was killed in the fighting near Madrid.' It was as plain as that. I stood there for a moment, my blood running cold. We knew that Mark was in Europe even though we hadn't heard from him for almost a year, but we never thought he'd be in Spain. We thought he might be in Paris with some of his old cronies, but we weren't worried. Not really. We knew Mark. When he was up against it, we figured we'd hear from him. Meanwhile Papa figured it was a good thing for him to be away for a while after what had happened."

She took a cigarette from the end table near her and leaned forward for me to light it. Then she settled back again, letting the smoke drift slowly from her mouth. Her eyes were dark and troubled.

"You know," she said, "it is something I'll never understand. Mark was one of the most self-centered, egotistical men that ever lived, he never gave a damn what happened to the other guy. And yet he went to Spain and joined the Abraham Lincoln Brigade and died fighting for a cause he never truly believed in and against a way of life that he might have admired if he hadn't been a Jew. My first thought was for Mother—how she would take it. She hadn't been well since Mark went away. He was her baby still and she was never quite the same after Papa threw him out of the house. She was always after Papa to get Mark to come back home. I think Papa wanted him to come home too, but you know him—he got his Dutch stubbornness up and kept putting it off."

She fell silent, looking into the leaping flames of the fire. I wondered what she was thinking. Peter had always favored Mark and she knew it. But she never complained. She never talked much either. I remembered the way we found out she could write. It was the year she graduated from college. She hadn't said anything at all about her writing until her book had been accepted by a publisher. Even then she had used a nom de plume, not wanting to trade on her father's name.

She had called the book *Freshman Year*. It was the story

of a girl's first year in college and away from home, and it was very successful. It was a story of warmth and homesickness and a girl's growing up. The critics made a great deal of fuss over the book. They were all amazed at the depth of understanding and perception of the girl who had written it. She was just twenty-two at the time it came out.

I hadn't paid much attention to it. Matter of fact, I hadn't even read it at the time. The first time I saw her after the book came out was when I brought Dulcie to Peter's home the day after we were married.

They were all seated at breakfast when Dulcie and I came in the room. Mark was about eighteen at the time; he was a tall, thin boy with the acne of adolescence still clinging to his face. He took one look at Dulcie and whistled.

Peter had cuffed him and told him to mind his manners, but I just laughed proudly and Dulcie blushed a little and I could tell she didn't mind. Dulcie liked people to look at her, she was a born actress. Even then, as she stood there blushing, I knew she was acting and I loved it.

That was part of Dulcie's charm for me. Wherever we went, heads turned to look at her. She was the kind of a woman men wanted to be seen with. Tall, slim, and fullbreasted, with a tawny look, she gave an impression of latent sexual savagery that carried every man back about five thousand years.

Esther got to her feet and had chairs brought out for us. Up to that moment I hadn't told them we were married. I began to feel awkward, wondering how I could tell them. I looked around the table and saw Doris looking at us curiously. There was a question in her eyes.

I had a bright idea. I spoke to Doris. "Well, sweetheart, you won't have to worry about your old Uncle Johnny any more. He finally found a girl that would marry him."

Doris's face turned a little pale, but I was too excited to pay any attention to it. "You—you mean you're getting married?" she asked, her voice shaking a little.

I laughed. "What do you mean, 'getting married'? We were married last night!"

Peter jumped up and came around the table and shook

my hand. Esther had gone over to Dulcie and put her arms around her. Only Doris sat there in her chair looking at me, her face still pale, her blue eyes dark and wide, her head tilted to one side as if to hear better.

"Ain't you comin' over and kiss your Uncle Johnny?" I asked her.

She got up from her chair and came over to me. I kissed her, and her lips were cold. Then she went over to Dulcie and took her hand. "I hope you'll be very happy," she said, kissing Dulcie's cheek.

I looked at them as they stood there. They were about the same age, but there were other things about them that suddenly struck me.

Doris's skin was pale and her hair was cut short. Standing next to Dulcie, she looked like a schoolgirl. Dulcie was studying her, too. I knew the look on her face already. To most people it seemed a fleeting glance, but I knew Dulcie well enough by then. She could tell more in a few seconds than most people in hours.

Esther turned to me. "She's lovely, Johnny. Where did you meet her?"

"She's an actress," I had answered. "I met her backstage at a theater in New York."

Peter had turned to me. "Actress, did you say? Maybe we can find a part for her."

Dulcie smiled at him.

"There's time enough for that," I had said. "We've got to settle down first."

Dulcie didn't speak.

When we had left, Dulcie said to me: "Johnny."

I was busy driving. "Yes, dear."

"You know she's in love with you."

I took a quick look at her. She was watching me with an amused look in her tawny eyes. "You mean Doris?"

"You know who I mean, Johnny," she said.

I laughed. "You're wrong that time, honey," I said uncomfortably, "I'm only Uncle Johnny to her."

She laughed too, a knowing laugh, full of amusement at male ignorance. "Uncle Johnny," she said, and laughed again. "Did you ever read her book?"

"No," I answered, "I haven't had time."

"You ought to read it, Uncle Johnny," she said with a faint mockery in her voice. "You're in it."

Doris began to speak again. Her voice was low. "I thought of calling the doctor for Mother before I showed her the telegram, and then I thought I'd tell Papa first. He was in the library. I went to the door and knocked. There was no answer, so I went in. He was seated at his desk there, the phone in front of him. He was looking at it. I often wondered why he didn't have it taken out. You know the one I mean—the direct wire to the studio."

I knew the one she meant. Involuntarily I looked at it. It stood there on the desk with a lonely unused look about it. In the old days, when the receiver was picked up, a blue light would flash on the studio switchboard. It meant that the president was calling. The call took precedence over anything else on the board at the time.

"He was looking at it, a vague longing in his eyes.

" 'Papa,' I said. My voice began to shake a little.

"With an effort he brought his mind back to me. 'What, *liebchen?*' he said.

"Suddenly I didn't know what to say. Wordlessly I handed him the telegram. He read it slowly, his face turning white under his tan. He looked up at me unbelieving for a moment, his lips moving, then he read the telegram again. He got to his feet, his hand trembling.

" 'I got to tell Mamma,' he said, his voice dull. He took a few steps, and then he seemed to stumble a little. I caught his arm.

" 'Papa,' I said, 'Papa!' Suddenly I was crying.

"He held on to me for a minute, his eyes searching mine. There were tears in his eyes too. Then he crumpled. It happened so quickly that he fell from my grasp. I tried to lift him, but I couldn't. Then I ran to the door and called the butler. Together we placed him on the couch. I ran to the desk and picked up the telephone. By mistake I picked up the wrong one. I picked up the studio phone. The operator's voice came on immediately. There was a question in her voice. 'Magnum Pictures,' she said. I hung up the phone with a feeling of shocked surprise. 'Magnum Pictures,' I was thinking. I began to hate the sound of those words. I had been hearing them all my life, it had turned all our lives inside out. Why did we ever have to go into the picture business?"

She looked at me. Her eyes were wide and strange, filled with flickering lights. "Why couldn't we have stayed in Rochester and missed all this? Mark dead and Papa lying on the floor with a broken heart. It's your fault, Johnny, your fault. I heard Papa say many times he wouldn't have done it if it hadn't been for you. He would never have come to Hollywood if it hadn't been for you. If you hadn't kept talking we could have spent our lives quietly and missed all this."

Suddenly she was crying again; then she came against me, her hands striking against my chest. "I hate you, Johnny, I hate you. Papa could have lived out his whole life and never missed the picture business. But you couldn't. You were born for it. And you couldn't do it alone, so you had to use Papa."

I tried to grab her hands but I couldn't. They were moving too fast.

"You're Magnum Pictures, Johnny, you always were. But why couldn't you stop when you got to New York? Why did you have to bring him out here and make him think he was so big that when the bubble burst, it took his heart with it?"

I finally caught her hands and held her close to me. She was crying now. Hard, bitter tears came from her eyes. She had been hitting me for many more things than she realized. For all the years I had been so blind.

At last she was quiet, her body still trembling slightly against mine, and when she spoke I could tell the effort she made to control her voice. It was low and husky, but it still shivered a little through the sheath of restraint. "I'm sorry, Johnny," she whispered so low I could hardly hear her, "but why did we ever come to Hollywood?"

I didn't answer. I didn't know what to answer. I looked over her head toward the window. The faint gray streaks of day were already beginning to cut up the night. The clock on Peter's desk read four thirty.

She was eleven years old and Peter was thirty-five and I was twenty-one when we came here. And none of us wanted to, we had to. There was nothing we could do about it.

THIRTY YEARS
1911

1

EVERYBODY was happy but Johnny. Borden was happy because he collected the money Peter owed him; Joe because, for the first time, he could make any picture he wanted without someone telling him what to do or what not to do. Peter was happy because the business had turned out even better than he had thought. He had paid all his debts, put eight thousand dollars in the bank, moved into a new apartment on Riverside Drive, and was getting a maid in to help Esther with the children. Esther was happy because Peter was happy.

But Johnny wasn't. He was content, in many ways satisfied, but still something was missing. The excitement, the feeling he had at first that big things were going to happen, were still deep within him, but covered by the commonplace layer of day-to-day activities.

If it were not for the Motion Picture Combine, Johnny might have been happy. But he had a carnival man's instinctive dislike and contempt for being forced into a pattern of routine not of his own choosing. And that was just what the combine was doing to the motion-picture industry.

The independent producers among whom Kessler and Borden had found themselves were dependent on the combine for the privilege of staying in business. The combine controlled the raw stock from which the film was made, the processes that made the film, the patents of the motion-picture camera, and even the patents covering subsidiary equipment without which a picture could not be filmed, such as the mercury vapor lamps and light synchronizers.

By the virtue of these basic controls it was able to bend the independent producer to its will, since each independent operated under a cross-licensing agreement issued by the combine. Thus the combine was able to tell the producer what type of pictures he could make and how much he could sell them for. The rules were strict and all covered by the agreement. No feature was to be more than two reels in length. The exhibitor, in order to retain his motion-picture projector, must use a set quota of combine-produced film, over and above which he could use independently produced film if he desired. And the quota set was sufficiently great to limit the playing time available to the films made by the independents.

Johnny chafed under these restraints; inside him were the unformed visions of what motion pictures were to become. In vain he would rail against the combine for retarding the progress of the screen. Deep inside him he knew that he was shouting at the moon, because no independent producer, no matter how great his complaint, would dare to challenge the supremacy of the combine. The combine was king. It was the patronizing overlord of an infant industry that tolerated the independent producers as an indulgent father would eye the escapades of his children. The lines were carefully drawn and the independent had to toe the mark. If he did not, his license would be immediately withdrawn; his notes and debts were quickly bought up by the combine, and his sources of business were rapidly closed to him. If he obeyed the rules, the combine magnanimously allowed him to remain in business and collected from him a royalty on every foot of film he bought or sold.

Johnny had learned a great deal about motion pictures in the past three years and the conviction grew in him that something was missing from them. What it was he did not know; he only knew that the combine-enforced pattern of short features did not allow the producer to tell his story properly.

With interest he watched the development of the serial pictures that some producer had developed to get around the combine's regulations. But these were still shown at the rate of two reels a week, or one chapter, as they were called in order to conform with the combine's rules. These pictures were followed avidly by the movie-goers from week to week, but for Johnny there was still something missing.

That was the intangible in the back of Johnny's mind, always annoying him. It was like trying to remember a tune he had once heard. He could hear the melody, envision the music, but when he tried to bring it to his lips the melody would not come forth. It would linger at the back of his mind and tantalize him with its sound. So it was with motion pictures.

In his mind he could see the kind of motion picture that should be made. He knew its size, its shape, its form. He knew how long it should run, he even knew how the audience would react to it. But when he tried to bring it forth, he could not. It would dance in front of his eyes in a slow wraithlike form and then disappear into the bright realities of the day around him. Thus, with a constantly growing sense of excitement to come, the successes of the present day were as nothing to him.

Then one day the idea began to take shape. It was late in December of 1910 and he was standing in the lobby of Pappas' new theater in Rochester, talking to George, when a man and a woman had come out.

The man had stopped near them to light a cigar, and the woman spoke. "I wish they had the other episodes of that serial to show here tonight. Just for once I would like to see a whole picture instead of part of one."

Her voice cut into Johnny's mind and involuntarily he stopped talking to George and listened to what they were saying.

The man had laughed. "That's how they get you to come back every week," he said. "They only show you a part of the picture at a time. If they showed you the whole thing like a play, you wouldn't have anything to come back for next time."

"I don't know about that," the woman replied as the two walked away. "It seems to me that I would be more willing to come back every week if I knew I was going to see a whole show and get my money's worth."

Johnny couldn't hear the man's reply as they had already gone out of earshot, but his mind was tingling with the glimmer of excitement that he came to recognize when he thought about what was going to come in motion pictures. He turned to George. "Did you hear that?"

George nodded his head.

"What do you think?" Johnny asked.

"Lots poopuls feel that way," George answered simply.

"How do you feel about it?" Johnny persisted.

George thought a few seconds before he answered. "I don't know," he replied at last. "Could be good, could be bad. Depends on picture. I got to see one, then I know."

On the train, all the way back to New York, the idea kept turning over and over in Johnny's mind. "A whole picture," the woman had said. What did it mean? He was puzzled, and his brows knit together as he thought about it. Was it a serial that could be shown all at once? Unconsciously he shook his head. That wasn't the answer. It would take half a day to run a picture that long. A serial was twenty reels long. Maybe the answer lay in cutting the serials down to smaller size, but what size? He had to know the answer.

It was late when he walked into the office, but the sense of excitement hadn't left him. He told Peter and Joe what he had heard and what he thought.

Joe seemed interested, but Peter was not. After listening to him Peter replied: "That's only one person talking. Most people are satisfied with the way things are. I wouldn't go out of my way to look for trouble."

But Johnny wasn't satisfied. He felt that the chance remark he had overheard held the key to the question in his mind. And the events of the ensuing days and weeks seemed to bear out his contention.

More now, so it seemed to Johnny, the exhibitors that he called on would ask him: "Haven't you got anything different? My customers are getting tired of the same old thing every time."

And Johnny knew that they were right. He knew that it didn't make any difference to the exhibitor whose pictures he played; all the producers made the same sort of picture.

He decided to get a complete serial, condense it into one picture, and see if that was the answer. But another problem then presented itself. Magnum did not produce serials and he would have to obtain one from another company. Yet what company would give him a print of a serial and let him tamper with it? And if they would, he would have to tell them what he wanted to do and he didn't want any of them to know it.

He solved this problem by asking George to get him a print of one of Borden's serials. George told Borden he liked it so much that he wanted to have a print of it for himself. Bill Borden felt so good about it that he insisted upon making George a gift of the print. If Borden had known what was to be done with his picture, he would have committed mayhem, but he didn't know and George turned the print over to Johnny.

Johnny took the print back to New York and he and Joe sat down to edit the ten chapters into one complete unit. They worked for five weeks on it before they felt they had a picture worth showing. They had a picture that ran six reels and took a little over an hour to show.

Until they had finished their work they had not told Peter about it. Now they called him in, told him the whole story, and asked him to view the finished product. He agreed to look at it and they set a showing for the next evening.

Johnny sent George a wire asking him to come down and see the picture. The next evening they all gathered in the little projection room at the Magnum Studios. Peter, Esther, George, Joe, and Johnny were the only people there. The regular projectionist had been sent home, and Johnny worked the projector.

They were quiet while the picture was on, but the minute it was over they all began to talk at once.

"It's too long," Peter said. "I don't like it. Nobody can sit so long and still enjoy a movie."

"Why not?" Johnny asked. "You sat through it without any trouble."

"It hurts your eyes looking at the screen so long," Peter replied. "It makes you uncomfortable."

"People sit in the movies that long now and it doesn't hurt their eyes," Johnny said heatedly. He was getting a little angry at Peter's continued stubbornness. "What's the difference if they look at one big picture or four little ones?"

Joe grinned. "Maybe you need glasses, Peter."

Peter exploded. His eyes had been bothering him, but he

refused to wear glasses. "My eyes got nothing to do with it. The picture is too long!"

Johnny turned to George; his voice was challenging. "Well?"

George looked at him sympathetically for a moment before he answered. "I like it," he answered quietly, "but I would like to see it in a theater before I would say more."

Johnny smiled at him. "I would too, but we can't do it."

It remained for Esther to put her finger on the weakness of the picture. "It was interesting," she said, "but it wasn't complete. Something was missing. In a serial it is all right to have excitement in every chapter; when it's condensed into one picture it's too much. It's all excitement, and then it's too much to seem possible. After a while it seems like a joke."

When Johnny thought it over he realized that she was right. The answer was not in cutting serials down to another size but in developing a new-size picture. He had viewed the condensed version of the serial several times and he had come to the conclusion that while the running time of the picture was not too long, the picture lacked other elements of appeal that were necessary to round it out. A story would have to be developed that would fit the size of the picture.

They left the projection room in a group, still talking about the picture. Only Johnny was silent. He slouched along, his hands in his pockets, his face glum.

Peter slapped him on the shoulder. "Snap out of it. We're doing all right as it is, so why worry?"

Johnny didn't answer.

Peter took out his watch and looked at it. "Tell you what," he said, trying to cheer Johnny up. "It's early yet. Supposin' we all have dinner and then go to a show?"

2

"No!" Peter shouted. "Positively no! I ain't gonna do it!" He strode angrily past Joe and up to Johnny. He stood in front of him and waved an excited forefinger in Johnny's face. "I should have to be crazy to do what you want! For almost two years now, we struggle and slave day and night to get on our feet and now that we're making a dollar you want to throw the whole damn thing away for another idea. I'm not crazy altogether yet. I won't do it!"

Johnny sat there quietly, looking up into Peter's face. Peter had been roaring ever since Johnny had come out with the idea of making a six-reel picture. Peter had listened quietly enough when Johnny proposed that they buy *The Bandit*, a play that was then running on Broadway, and make it into a picture. He had been quiet enough while Johnny told him he would hire the author of the play to write the screen version. He had been quiet enough while Johnny explained to him how they could capitalize on the play's already established market value. His interest in the idea was evident from the question he had asked Johnny: "How much would it cost?"

Johnny had anticipated the question. He had prepared a budget on the picture, and he figured it would cost around twenty-three thousand dollars. He gave Peter the budget.

Peter took one look at the budget and threw the whole thing back at Johnny. "Twenty-three thousand dollars for one picture!" he yelled. "A man's got to be *meshuggeh!* Buy a play and hire a man to write it for twenty-five hundred dollars? For the same money I could make a whole picture!"

"You'll have to start somewhere," Johnny insisted, "and some day you'll have to do it."

"Maybe some day," Peter replied hotly, "but not now. We just got into the clear and now you want to put me in hock again. Where am I gonna get that kind of money? I'm not the United States mint yet."

"Nothing ventured nothing gained," Johnny quoted quietly.

"Neither do you lose your shirt," Peter replied quickly. "Besides, it ain't your money you want to put up."

Johnny grew angry at that. "You know damn well I wouldn't ask you to put money into anything I wouldn't."

"Your money!" Peter sneered. "It ain't enough to buy toilet paper for the studio for a week."

"It's enough to pay for ten per cent of the picture," Johnny yelled. His face was getting flushed.

"Take it easy," Joe said, stepping between them. "All this hollering ain't going to settle anything." He turned to Peter. "I got enough for another ten per cent of the picture. That leaves only eighteen thousand for you to get."

Peter threw his hands in the air. "'Only eighteen thousand,' he says. Like I can pick it up on the sidewalk." He turned and slammed the top of his desk down and then looked up at them.

"No!" he shouted. "Positively no! I ain't gonna do it!"

Johnny's anger had evaporated. He could understand Peter's reluctance to endanger what he already had accomplished, but Johnny was convinced that what he proposed must be done. He spoke slowly and quietly.

"Back in Rochester you thought I was crazy about this," he pointed out, "but we didn't do so bad, did we?" He didn't wait for Peter to answer. "You got a nice apartment on Riverside Drive, eight thousand in the bank that's all clear, a paid-up mortgage, haven't you?"

Peter nodded his head. "And I ain't going to risk it on one of your crazy ideas. We was just lucky the last time. This time it's different. This time it's not only money we have to risk, but also we'd have to fight the combine. And you know how far we'd get doing that." He, too, had cooled off a little. He spoke more sympathetically now.

"I'm sorry, Johnny. Honest. Maybe your idea is good, for all I know, even if I don't think it is. But with things the way they are we can't take the chance. That's my final word on the subject." He walked to the door. "Good night," he said, and shut the door behind him.

Johnny looked at Joe and shrugged his shoulders expressively. Joe grinned at him. "Don't look so disappointed, kid. After all, it's his dough and he's got a right to his ideas." He got to his feet. "Come on out and have a beer and forget it."

Johnny looked thoughtful. "No, thanks. I'm gonna sit here awhile and see if I can figger some way to make him see it. This is one business you can't afford to sit still in. If you do, you're cooked."

Joe looked down at him. He shook his head slowly. "All right, kid, have it your way. You're beating your nut against a stone wall, though."

For a while after Joe left, Johnny sat where he was; then he got up and walked over to Peter's desk. He rolled up the top and picked up the budget he had given Peter and looked at it.

He stood there almost ten minutes looking at it. At last he put it back and rolled the top of the desk down. "All right, you old buzzard," he said to the desk as if it were Peter, "some day you'll do it."

Johnny opened his eyes slowly. The air in the room was warm. Spring had come early this year, with a more than ample hint of the summer to come. It was only mid-March, but already winter coats had been shed and men were going to work in their jackets and shirtsleeves.

Lazily he got out of bed and walked through the parlor of the apartment and opened the door. The Sunday papers were lying on the floor in front of it. He bent down and picked them up. Reading the headlines, he went back into the parlor and sat down in an easy chair.

He heard the snoring coming through the open door of Joe's room. With a grimace he got up and walked over to Joe's room and looked in. Joe was curled up in a corner of the bed, sawing wood. Quietly Johnny shut the door and went back to his chair.

He turned the pages until he came to the dramatic section. Motion pictures were not covered regularly on the amusement pages of the daily papers as yet, but the Sunday papers devoted an occasional item to the new medium. This Sunday there were two items that made Johnny sit up suddenly in his chair.

The first was an item from Paris. "Mme. Sarah Bernhardt to make four-reel motion picture based on the life of Queen Elizabeth."

The second was from Rome. "The famous novel *Quo Vadis?* will be made into an eight-reel film in Italy next year."

The items were brief. They were hidden in the corner of the page, but to Johnny they were banner headlines proving he had been right. He stared at the paper for a long time, wondering if Peter would agree with him now. At last he gave it up and went into the kitchen and put a pot of water on the stove for coffee.

The smell of coffee brought Joe from his bed, sleepy and rubbing his eyes. "Morning," he grunted. "What's for breakfast?"

It was Johnny's turn to make Sunday breakfast. "Eggs," he answered.

"Oh." Joe turned back and began to stagger toward the bathroom.

"Wait a minute," Johnny called after him. He picked up the paper and showed the items to Joe.

Joe read them and handed the papers back to Johnny. "So what does it prove?" he asked.

"It proves that I was right," Johnny said, a note of triumph creeping into his voice. "Don't you see? Now Peter will have to listen to me."

Joe shook his head slowly. "You never give up, once you get something in your nut, do you?"

Johnny was indignant. "Why should I? It's a good idea and I was right in saying that bigger pictures were coming."

"Maybe they are," Joe admitted, "but where are you going to make them? And how are you going to make them?

"Even if we get all the dough, you know our studio isn't big enough to do it in. It would take all the raw stock we use for six months' production to do a job like that. And you know the combine is dead set against anything over two reels, and if they get wise to us they'll take away our license and then where'll we be? Up the creek?"

"So we give up making small pictures for a time," Johnny answered. "We can save up enough film for the picture and make it before they find out what's going on."

Joe lit a cigarette and blew out the smoke. He eyed Johnny shrewdly. "Maybe you're right. Maybe we can get away with it, maybe we can't. If we can't, then Magnum's out of business. They're a little too big for us to take on. They'll squash us like you step on an ant. Let Borden or one of the others take them on. They got more dough to do it with, and even with that I don't see any of them falling over themselves to get into trouble."

"Well, I still think there is some way we can do it," Johnny insisted stubbornly.

"Still think you're right, huh?" Joe looked at him strangely.

Johnny nodded his head. "I am right."

Joe was silent for a moment, then he heaved a sigh. "Maybe you are, but look what you're riskin'. I'm not worried about my neck or yours. We're alone. We don't have to worry if things go wrong, 'cause we kin get along. But Peter's another story. If we go wrong on this, he's broke. If he goes broke, then what's the guy gonna do? He's got a wife an' two nice kids to look after. He put everything he's got into this business, an' if it misses out, he's finished." He stopped and drew a deep breath. He looked right into Johnny's eyes. "Yuh willin' to risk that?"

Johnny didn't answer him for a long while. He had thought about it before. He knew of the risk, Joe didn't have to tell him about it. But there was something inside him that kept pushing him on. It kept saying over and over: "The golden fleece lies just ahead. All you need to grab it is the nerve." The vision of the picture in his mind was like Circe calling to him. He could no more stop following it than he could stop breathing.

His face was set and determined as he answered. "I got to do it, Joe, it's the only thing that counts. It's the only chance the business has to become really big, really important. Otherwise we're in the nickelodeon business all our lives; this way we're something that really counts. We're an art. Like the theater, like music, like books, orly some day maybe we're better and bigger than all of them. We gotta do it."

"You mean you gotta do it," Joe said slowly. An odd sense of disappointment tugged at him. He ground his cigarette out in a tray. "You got dreams of what you want, an' you think that's what the business must have. If I didn't know yuh better an' like yuh so much, I would say you're selfish an' ambitious. But I know differen'. Yuh really mean what yuh say, but there's one thing yuh gotta know."

Johnny's face had gone white as Joe spoke. With difficulty he forced himself to ask: "What?"

"Peter's been awful good to us. Don't never fergit it." Joe turned and walked out of the room.

Johnny looked at his back and then turned to the water boiling on the stove. His hand was trembling as he turned down the gas.

3

"WHOSE apartment did you say, sir?" the elevator operator asked as he slowly shut the door and the elevator began to move upward.

Johnny finished lighting his cigarette. He hadn't mentioned any names, just the floor he wanted. He thought to himself that these fancy houses didn't miss a trick. Their tenants weren't going to be disturbed unnecessarily. "Mr. Kessler's," he answered. It was a long way from Rochester—where all you had to do was look upstairs over the store—to Riverside Drive.

His mind flashed back to his conversation with Joe that morning. What Joe had said still troubled him. They hadn't spoken very much, and soon after breakfast Joe went out. True, Joe had asked him if he wanted to come along and see May and Flo, but he had said that he was going up to Peter's that afternoon.

The elevator stopped and the door slid open silently. "Just down the hall to your right. Apartment 9 C, sir," the operator said politely.

Johnny thanked him and walked down the hall to the door and pressed the buzzer.

The maid answered the door. Johnny stepped in and handed her his hat. "Is Mr. Kessler in?" he asked.

Before the maid could answer, Doris came sweeping into the hall. "Uncle Johnny!" she cried. "I heard your voice!"

He picked her up and hugged her. "Hello, sweetheart."

She looked into his face. "I was hoping you'd come today. You don't come to see us very often."

His face reddened. "I haven't much time, sweetheart. Your father keeps me pretty busy."

He felt a tugging at his trousers. He looked down.

Mark was pulling at them. "Swing me, Uncle Johnny," he cried.

Johnny put Doris down and swung him up in the air and then onto his shoulders. Mark yelled with glee and dug his fingers into Johnny's hair as Esther came into the hall.

"Why, Johnny," she smiled, "come in, come in."

With Mark still on his shoulders, he followed her into the living-room. Peter was there, reading his papers. His shirt was off and with some surprise Johnny noticed he had developed a little paunch. He looked at Johnny and smiled.

"Look at him," Esther said to Johnny, a smile deep in her eyes. "With a maid in the house, he sits around all day in his underwear. Mr. Fancy of Riverside Drive."

Peter grunted. He spoke in Yiddish. "So what? I know the village she comes from in Germany. There, if they got shirts, it's a miracle."

Johnny looked blank and they both laughed at him.

"Go put on a shirt," Esther said.

"All right, all right," Peter grumbled as he moved toward the bedroom.

Peter came back into the doorway as Johnny put Mark down. He stood there buttoning his shirt. "What brings you up here?"

Johnny looked at him quickly and smiled to himself. Peter didn't miss much. This was the first time in weeks that Johnny had come to visit them. "I wanted to see how the other half lives," he laughed.

"You been here before," Peter pointed out with a complete lack of humor.

Johnny laughed aloud. "Not since you had a maid."

"And that should make such a big difference?" Peter asked.

"Sometimes," Johnny said, still smiling.

"Never by me," Peter spoke seriously. "I should have a houseful of servants and still I would act the same."

"Sure," Esther added. "He would still sit around the house in his underwear."

"That proves what I say," Peter came back triumphantly. "Servants or no servants, Peter Kessler is always the same."

Johnny had to admit to himself that Peter was right. Peter hadn't changed in the past few years, but he had. Peter was content with things the way they were, but Johnny wasn't satisfied. There was something more he wanted, something more he had to have, and what it was he didn't really know. Only the sense of dissatisfaction was real. He remembered again what Joe had said that morning. Peter had come a long way from the little hardware store in Rochester; he had gained a measure of security and was content with it. What right did he have to ask Peter to risk all this for an idea? But on the other hand, he reasoned, Peter would not have had even this if it hadn't been for the fact that he had pushed him. Whether this gave him the right to push Peter further, Johnny did not know. He only knew that he could not stop now. The future, no matter how nebulous it seemed, was too much a part of him to give up.

He looked at Peter quizzically. "You mean you're not too big to listen to a good idea?"

"That's what I mean," Peter said. "Always I'm willing to take good advice."

Johnny heaved a mock sigh of relief. "I'm glad to hear that. Some people say you're getting very high-hat since you lived on Riverside Drive."

"Who could say such a thing?" Peter cried indignantly. He turned to Esther and held out his hands. "The minute a man does a little all right, people start knocking him."

Esther smiled sympathetically. Johnny was leading up to something, she was sure of it. She was curious about what he wanted and she felt that it wouldn't be long in forthcoming. "People can't help misunderstandings," she said. "Maybe somebody you gave a reason?"

"Never," Peter protested indignantly. "I'm friendly to everybody like always."

"So then don't worry," she told him reassuringly. She turned to Johnny. "You would like, maybe, some coffee and cake?"

They followed her into the kitchen. When Johnny had finished his second piece of cake he asked Peter casually: "Did you read the *World* today?"

A sixth sense made Esther turn around and look at him. The question was casual, almost too casual, she thought. There was something in the way he asked it that made her feel this was only the beginning. "Now it comes out," she thought.

"Yeanh," Peter answered.

"Did you read about Bernhardt making a four-reeler? And about *Quo Vadis?*"

"Sure," Peter replied. "Why do you ask?"

"Remember what I said about bigger pictures?"

"Sure, I remember," Peter answered. "I also remember the serial you cut down."

"That was something else," Johnny said. "I was trying to work something out. But this is different, this proves what I said about making a picture out of *The Bandit* was right."

"How does it?" Peter asked. "Things are still the same."

"Are they?" Johnny said. "When you get the greatest actress of the time to make a motion picture, when you make a motion picture out of a great novel, are things still the same? Can't you see that moving pictures are growing up? That the two-reel short pants the combine is making them wear is beginning to chafe?"

Peter stood up. "This is nonsense you're talking. Once in a blue moon somebody will make a long picture. You happen to read in the paper about two being made at once and right away you're right.

"Maybe if Sarah Bernhardt would make a picture for Peter Kessler, I would make a long picture, but otherwise who would go to see an hour-long movie without any famous actors in it?"

Johnny looked at him. Peter was right. Without names that were known, it would be difficult to attract people to a picture. When he had been with the carnival, certain acts had been featured by name because it was known that they would attract customers. The stage, too, featured certain actors and actresses for the same reason, but the movies never credited any players. The combine objected to it because it feared that if the players knew of their value they would demand more money.

Yet people were recognizing certain players, and whenever they heard one of their pictures was playing, they would flock to the theater and plunk down their nickels and dimes and pay to see their favorites. Like that little funny-looking tramp who had just made some comedies. What was his name again? Johnny had heard it once, but he had to think twice before he could call it to mind—Chaplin. And that girl who was known as the Biograph girl. Johnny couldn't even remember her name. Still, the customers remembered and would turn out to see the pictures they appeared in even if they didn't particularly want to go to the movies.

He made a mental note to have Joe feature the name of the players on the title card of the picture. It would make it easier for the patron to identify the player he liked and would prove of help to the exhibitor in publicizing his attractions.

Peter looked at Johnny strangely. Johnny had been silent for so long that Peter thought he had stumped him. "Stopped you, hah?" he asked triumphantly.

Johnny shook himself out of his reverie. He reached for a cigarette and lit it and looked at Peter through the smoke. "No," he answered, "you didn't. But you just supplied the one thing I needed to guarantee the success of a big picture. A big name. A name that everybody knows. If you get the right actor, you can't object to making a big picture."

"With a big name I could see it," Peter admitted. "But who are you going to get?"

"The actor that plays *The Bandit* on the stage, now," Johnny answered, "Warren Craig."

"Warren Craig?" Peter cried incredulously. "And why not John Drew while you're at it?" He looked at Johnny sarcastically.

"Warren Craig is good enough," Johnny answered seriously.

Peter lapsed into Yiddish: "*Zehr nicht a nahr!*" he said. He noted the blank look on Johnny's face and he repeated: "Don't be a fool! You know they all look down on the movies. You can't get them."

"Maybe now that Bernhardt is making a picture, they won't be so hard to get," Johnny said.

"Maybe you could get me John Jacob Astor's money to pay them while you're at it," Peter said sarcastically.

Johnny paid no attention to Peter's last remark. He got to his feet excitedly, his cigarette forgotten in his hand. "I can see it now as it comes on the screen. 'Peter Kessler presents . . . Warren Craig . . . in the famous Broadway stage success . . . *The Bandit* . . . a Magnum Picture.'" He stopped, his hand pointing dramatically toward Peter.

Peter looked at him. Unconsciously he had been leaning

forward in his chair as Johnny spoke, trying to visualize what Johnny was saying. Now the spell was broken and he leaned back. "And I can see it now," he said, trying to cover his previous display of interest, " 'Peter Kessler files petition in bankruptcy!' "

Esther watched the two of them. First one, then the other, a vague surprise running through her mind. "Peter really wants to do it," she thought.

Peter got to his feet and faced Johnny. He spoke with finality. "Nothing doing, Johnny, we can't take a chance like that. There are too many risks involved. The combine won't like it, and if they take away our license, we're out of business. We haven't enough money to take a chance like that."

Johnny eyed him speculatively, a tiny pulse hammering in his temple. He looked at Esther, she was watching Peter. He looked through the door into the living-room. Mark was playing on the floor with some blocks. As he watched, Mark scattered them over the floor with one hand, and Doris put down the book she was reading and went to help him pick them up.

Slowly Johnny turned back to Peter. The words came out evenly; no trace of inner struggle showed in his voice. His mind was made up.

"You producers are all alike! You're all afraid of the combine! You bellyache all the time, you cry they're not letting you live, they're starving you out. But what are you doing about it? Nothing! You're all willing to hang around the edges of their table and feed on the crumbs and scraps they throw you. And crumbs is what you get. Nothing more. Do you know how much money they made last year? Twenty million dollars! Do you know how much all you independents made last year? Four hundred thousand dollars between forty of you. That's about ten thousand apiece on an average. Yet during that time you independents paid the combine more than eight million dollars to stay in business. Eight million dollars! Money you made and couldn't keep! Twenty times as much as you kept for yourselves. And there's only one reason for it! You're all afraid to buck the combine!"

His cigarette burned his fingers. He put it out in the tray on the table and went on without paying any attention to it. His voice had grown hard and intense. It was dramatic; the emotion he called on came into his voice as it was needed, and quickly was supplanted by another when its time had gone.

"Why don't you guys get wise to yourselves? This is your business as well as theirs. You made the money. Why don't you keep it? Sooner or later you'll have to fight 'em; why don't you fight 'em now? Fight 'em with better pictures. They know you can make 'em, that's why they limit what you can do. They run the business that way because they're afraid of what you will do if you ever move out on your own. Get together. Maybe you can fight them in the courts. Maybe what they're doing is against the new anti-trust laws. I don't know. But the stakes are worth the fight.

"Back in Rochester I wanted you to get into this business, remember? I had a reason then, a good one. I could have gone to work for Borden or maybe one of the others, but I wanted you. Because I felt you were the man, the only man with courage enough to fight when the time came. There were times since that I've been offered jobs elsewhere, but I stuck with you. For the same reason. And now I got to know whether I was right or wrong. Because now is the time. You either fight now, or soon the combine will put you all out of business!"

He stood there looking at Peter, trying to gauge the effect of his words. Peter's face told him nothing, but there were other things Johnny saw that made him feel the fight was won. Peter's hands were clenched like a man's about to go into battle.

Peter was silent for a long while. He didn't argue with Johnny. He couldn't. He had long felt that what Johnny had said was right. In the last year he had paid the combine one hundred and forty thousand dollars while keeping about eight for himself. But Johnny was young and too ready to tilt at the windmill. Maybe when he was a little older he would realize that sometimes a man had to have patience.

He turned away from Johnny, walked over to the sink, and drew a glass of water. He sipped it slowly. Still, there was something in what Johnny had said. If all the independents got together, they could fight the combine and maybe they would win the fight. Sometimes fighting was better than waiting; maybe Johnny was right. Maybe this was the time. He put the tumbler back on the sink and turned to Johnny.

"How much did you say it would cost to make a picture like that?" he asked.

"About twenty-five thousand dollars," Johnny replied. "That is, if you wanted Warren Craig to play the lead."

Peter nodded his head. Twenty-five thousand dollars—a lot of money for one moving picture. Still, if it went over, there was a fortune to be made. "If we made a picture like that," he said, "we must have Warren Craig to play the lead. We can't afford to take any extra chances."

Johnny pounced on his opportunity. "You won't actually need twenty-five thousand of your own," he said eagerly. "Joe and I can put up five thousand between us, you put up eight, and we can borrow the rest. I was thinking some of the exhibitors would take a chance on a thing like that. They're always crying for something different. If we can give it to them, maybe we can get the dough from them."

"But we got to get Warren Craig," Peter said.

"Leave that to me," Johnny answered confidently. "I'll get him."

"Then I can put up ten thousand," Peter said.

"You mean you're going to do it?" Johnny asked, the pulse now hammering wildly in his forehead.

Peter hesitated a moment. He turned to Esther and looked at her. The words came out very slowly. "I'm not saying I'm going to do it and I'm not saying I ain't. What I'm saying is that I'll think about it."

4

PETER waited for Borden to come out of the synagogue. The synagogue on lower Broadway was the morning meeting-place for many of the important independent picture men. He fell into step with him as he walked down the street.

"Morning, Willie," he said.

Borden looked over at him, "Peter," he said, smiling, "how's *geschäft?*"

"No complaints," Peter answered. "I want to talk to you. Got time for a cup of coffee?"

Borden took out his watch and looked at it importantly. "Sure," he said. "What's on your mind?"

"You read yesterday's papers?" Peter asked as they sat down at a table in a near-by restaurant.

"Sure," Borden answered. "To what are you referring?"

"Specifically," Peter said, "the Bernhardt picture and *Quo Vadis?*"

"Yeah, I saw it." Borden was wondering what Peter wanted.

"You think bigger pictures are coming?" Peter asked.

"Could be," Borden answered cautiously.

Peter was silent while the waitress put down the coffee and left. "Johnny wants me to make a six-reeler."

Borden was interested. "A six-reeler, huh? About what?"

"He wants me to buy a play and make a picture out of it and hire the leading man to play in it."

"Buy a play?" Borden laughed. "That's silly. Who ever heard of such a thing? You can get all the stories you want for nothing."

"I know," Peter said, sipping at his coffee, "but Johnny says the play's name means customers at the boxoffice."

Borden could see the sense in that. His interest quickened. "How will you get around the combine's regulations?"

"Johnny says we should save enough film to make the picture and then do it secretly. They won't know about it until the picture comes out."

"If they find out they can put you out of business."

"Maybe," Peter said. "Maybe they will and maybe they won't. But somewhere we got to draw the line and fight them. Otherwise we'll still be making two-reelers when the rest of the world is making bigger pictures. Then the foreign producers will come in and take over our market. When that happens we'll suffer more than the combine. We've been feeding on the crumbs from their table long enough. It's time we independents got together to fight them."

Borden thought that over. What Peter had said was the common sentiment of all the independent producers, but none of them had the desire to buck the combine. Even he would not want to take a chance on a venture as risky as this promised to be. But if Peter was willing to do it, he could see the benefits that would accrue to him if Peter should succeed. "How much would a picture like that cost?" he asked.

"About twenty-five thousand."

Borden finished his coffee. He was trying to figure out just how much money Peter had. After a few moments of silent calculation he arrived at the conclusion that Peter had about ten thousand dollars. That meant he would have to borrow the rest. He put a quarter on the table and stood up. "You going to make the picture?" he asked when they reached the street.

"I'm thinking about it," Peter replied, "but I ain't got enough money. Maybe if I could see my way clear on that, I might take a chance."

"How much you got?"

"About fifteen thousand," Peter answered.

Borden was surprised. Peter must have been doing better than he had figured. He looked at him with a new respect. "I can let you have about twenty-five hundred," he said impulsively. It was a small amount for him to risk on a venture that might lead to as much opportunity for him as this promised. He felt very smug about it. It would be better for him if Peter took the chance.

Peter looked at him appraisingly. This was what Peter wanted to know—whether Borden liked the idea enough to risk his money on it. The small amount that Borden had offered made no impression on Peter; the fact that Borden could advance him the balance of the money needed if he wanted to was lost to him. "I haven't made up my mind yet," he said. "I'll let you know if I decide to do it."

Now Borden wanted Peter to do it. "That's right," he said slyly. "If you don't do it, let me know. Maybe I'll do it. The more I think about it, the more I like it."

"I don't know yet," Peter answered quickly. "Like I said, I got to make up my mind. But I'll let you know."

Johnny looked at the door. The lettering on the glass read: "Samuel Sharpe," and underneath it in smaller letters: "Theatrical Representative." He turned the knob and went in.

The room he entered was a small one. Its walls were covered with pictures, all of them inscribed to "Dear Sam." Johnny looked closely at them. They all seemed to be in the same handwriting. He smiled to himself.

A girl came into the room from another door and sat down at a desk near the wall. "What can we do for you, sir?" she asked.

Johnny walked over to her. She was pretty. This Sharpe could pick them. He threw a card down on the desk in front of her. "Mr. Edge to see Mr. Sharpe," he said.

The girl picked up the card and looked at it. It was a simple card, carefully engraved. "John Edge, Vice-President —Magnum Pictures." She looked up at Johnny with a quick respect. "Won't you take a seat, sir?" she said. "I'll see if Mr. Sharpe is free."

Johnny smiled at her as he sat down. "You ought to be in pictures."

Her face was flushed as she left the room. She was back in a moment. "Mr. Sharpe will see you in a few minutes," she said. She sat down at the desk and tried to look busy.

Johnny picked up a copy of *Billboard* and glanced through it. Out of the corner of his eye he could see her watching him. He put the paper down. "Nice day, isn't it?" he asked pleasantly.

"Yes, sir," she answered. She put a sheet of paper in the typewriter and began to type.

Johnny got out of his seat and walked over to her. "Do you believe that your handwriting will reveal your character?" he asked.

She looked puzzled. "I never thought of it." Her voice was pleasant. "But I guess it could."

"Write something on a sheet of paper," he told her.

She took a pencil in her hand. "What shall I write?"

He thought for a moment. "Write: 'To Sam from'—whatever your name is." He smiled at her disarmingly.

She scribbled on a sheet of paper and handed it to him. "There it is, Mr. Edge, but I don't know what you can make of it."

Johnny looked at the sheet of paper in his hand. He looked up at her in sudden surprise. She was laughing. He grinned back at her and read the writing on the paper again.

"You could have asked me," it read. "Jane Andersen. Further details upon request."

He joined her laugh. "Jane," he said, "I might have known you were wise to me."

She started to answer, but a buzzer sounded next to her

desk. "You may go in now," she said, smiling. "Mr. Sharpe is free."

He started toward the inner door. At the door he stopped and looked back at her. "Tell me something," he said in a stage whisper. "Was Mr. Sharpe really busy?"

She tossed her head indignantly, then a bright smile crossed her face. "Of course he was," she replied in the same kind of whisper. "He was shaving."

Johnny laughed and went into the other room. The second room was a duplicate of the first, only a little larger. The same pictures were on the wall, but the desk was a bigger one. A small man in a bright gray suit sat behind it.

As Johnny came into the room, he got up and held out his hand to him. "Mr. Edge," he said in a thin, not unpleasant voice, "I'm glad to meet you."

They exchanged greetings and Johnny came right to the point. "Magnum Pictures is purchasing the motion-picture rights to *The Bandit* and we would like Warren Craig to play the lead in the motion picture."

Sharpe shook his head sadly and didn't answer.

"Why do you shake your head, Mr. Sharpe?" Johnny asked.

"I'm sorry, Mr. Edge," Sharpe replied. "If it had been any one of my clients other than Warren Craig, I would say you might have a chance of getting him. But Warren Craig—" He didn't finish his sentence, but spread his hands expressively on the desk.

"What do you mean, 'But Warren Craig'?"

Sharpe smiled at him soothingly. "Mr. Craig comes from one of the first families of the theater, Mr. Edge, and you know how they feel about the flickers. They look down upon them.

"And besides, from a more practical point of view, they don't pay enough money."

Johnny looked at him speculatively. "How much money does Warren Craig rate, Mr. Sharpe?"

Sharpe returned the look. "Craig gets one hundred and fifty dollars per week and you flicker people won't pay more than seventy-five."

Johnny leaned forward in his seat; his voice dropped to a confidential tone. "Mr. Sharpe," he said, "what I am about to tell you is in the strictest confidence."

Sharpe looked interested. "Sam Sharpe will respect that confidence, sir," he said quickly.

"Good." Johnny nodded, and pulled his chair closer to Sharpe's desk. "Magnum does not intend to make an ordinary flicker out of *The Bandit*. Magnum is going to make a brand-new high-type production, something that is so new it will be fit to take its place among the finest works of the theater. That is why we want Warren Craig to play the role he created on the stage." He paused impressively.

"For playing that role we are prepared to pay him four hundred dollars a week, with a minimum guarantee of two thousand dollars." Johnny leaned back in his chair and watched the effect of his words on Sharpe.

From the look on his face Johnny could tell that he was interested, that it was the kind of deal Sharpe would like to make. Sharpe sighed heavily. "I must be honest with you, Mr. Edge," he said regretfully. "Your offer seems to me a most generous one, but I don't believe I can persuade Craig to accept it. I repeat again, he does not approve of the flickers. He even goes so far as to despise them. He believes them beneath the dignity of his art."

Johnny stood up. "Madame Sarah Bernhardt does not believe them beneath the dignity of her art, and if she is making a picture in France, maybe Mr. Craig will consent to make one here."

"I had heard about that, Mr. Edge, but I didn't believe it," Sharpe said. "Is it really true?"

Johnny nodded his head. "You can believe it," he lied. "Our representative in France was very close to the deal and he assured us it is signed, sealed, and delivered." He hesitated for a moment, then added as if it were an afterthought: "Of course we would pay you the same sort of bonus that Madame Bernhardt's agent received. Ten per cent over the guarantee for yourself."

Sharpe stood up and faced Johnny. "Mr. Edge, you have been most convincing. You have sold me on the idea, but you will have to sell Mr. Craig. On a matter of this type he would never listen to me. Will you talk to him?"

"Any time you say," Johnny answered.

Johnny walked out of the office with an understanding that Sharpe would call him as soon as an appointment with Craig could be arranged.

He stopped at the girl's desk as he left. He smiled down at her. "About those further details, Jane," he said.

She handed him a typewritten sheet of paper. He looked at it. Her name, address, and telephone number were neatly typed on it.

"Don't call later than eight o'clock, Mr. Edge," she smiled. "It's a boarding house and the landlady doesn't approve of telephone calls later than that."

Johnny grinned. "I'll call you here, sugar. Then we won't have to worry about the landlady."

He left the office whistling jauntily.

Johnny didn't get to the studio until late in the afternoon. Peter looked up from his desk as he came in.

"Where were you?" he asked. "I been looking for you all day."

Johnny perched himself on the edge of Peter's desk. "I had a busy day," he said, smiling. "First thing this morning I saw Warren Craig's agent. Then I thought I'd have lunch with George since he was in town today."

"What did you go to lunch with George for?" Peter asked.

"Money," Johnny replied blithely. "It looked like we're going to get Craig this morning, so I thought it wouldn't hurt to start getting some dough for the picture. He's going to let us have a thousand."

"But I didn't say we were going to make the picture," Peter said.

"I know," Johnny replied. "But if you don't somebody else will." He looked down at Peter challengingly. "And I don't aim to be on the outside looking in when it's all over."

Peter looked up at him for a few minutes. Johnny looked back at him steadily. At last Peter spoke. "Your mind's made up?"

Johnny nodded. "My mind's made up. I'm through horsin' around."

The phone rang. Peter picked it up and answered it. He turned to Johnny and held the phone toward him. "It's for you."

Johnny took the phone. "Hello."

The voice crackled over the phone a few minutes while Johnny listened. He put his hand over the mouthpiece of the phone and spoke to Peter while the voice crackled on.

"It's Borden. Did you speak to him about the picture this morning?"

"Yes," Peter said. "What does he want?"

Johnny didn't answer him, for the voice over the phone stopped talking. Johnny spoke into the phone. "I don't know, Bill." He looked at Peter questioningly. "He hasn't made up his mind yet."

The voice spoke rapidly for a few minutes.

"Sure, Bill, sure," Johnny said. "I'll let you know." He hung up the receiver.

"What did he want?" Peter repeated suspiciously.

"He wanted to know if you had made up your mind. He said if you decided against it, for me to see him."

"The *gonif!*" Peter exploded indignantly. He put a cigar in his mouth and chewed on it furiously. "Only this morning I spoke to him and already he's trying to steal my ideas. What did you tell him?"

"You heard me," Johnny answered. "I told him you hadn't decided."

"Well, call him right back and tell him I decided," Peter said excitedly. "We're going to make the picture!"

"You'll do it?" Johnny was grinning.

"I'll do it," Peter said. He was still angry. "I'll show that Willie Bordanov he can't steal a man's ideas."

Johnny picked up the phone.

"Wait a minute," Peter stopped him. "I'll call him. There's a little matter of twenty-five hundred dollars he promised to lend me if I make this picture and I want him to send it right over."

5

PETER was silent all through dinner. He scarcely spoke two words throughout the entire meal. Esther wondered what was worrying him but kept tactfully quiet until he had finished eating. She knew him well enough to know that he would talk to her when he was ready.

"Doris brought home her report card today," she said. "She got an A in everything."

"That's nice," Peter answered absent-mindedly.

She looked at him. Ordinarily he was much interested in Doris's report card; he would want to see it and would make a great fuss over signing it. She didn't speak again.

He got up from the table, picked up the paper, and went into the living-room. She watched him go and then helped the maid clean up. When she went into the other room, the paper was lying neglected on the floor while he stared into space.

She grew a little exasperated at his protracted silence. "What's the matter with you?" she queried. "Don't you feel good?"

He looked at her. "I feel all right," he replied. "Why do you ask?"

"You look like you're dying," she said. "All night long not one word do you say."

"I got things on my mind," he answered shortly. He wished she would leave him alone.

"So it's a big secret?" she asked.

"No." He was startled. Suddenly he remembered he hadn't told her about his decision. "I decided to make that picture that Johnny wanted. Now I'm worried."

"If you made up your mind, what are you worrying about?"

"There's a big risk involved," he answered. "I could lose the business."

"You knew that when you made up your mind, didn't you?"

He nodded his head.

"So don't sit there like the world came to an end. The time for worrying was before you made up your mind. Now you got to do what you want, not worry over what might happen."

"But supposing I lose the business, then what will happen?" He puffed at his cigar. His mind clung to that one thought like a tongue to an aching tooth; the more he played with it, the more pain he felt.

She smiled slowly. "Nothing. My father lost three businesses and he always made out. We'll get along."

His face brightened a little. "You wouldn't care?"

She went over to him and sat down on his lap. She pressed his head against her bosom. "Business is not that important I should care about it. What I'm interested in is you. You do what you feel you must. That's important. Even if it's no good, you should do it. I'm happy if I got just you and the children. I don't care if we ain't got an apartment on Riverside Drive and a maid."

He put his arms around her and turned his head until it rested in the cleft between her breasts. He spoke in a low voice. "Everything I do is for you and the *kinder*. I want you should have everything."

Her voice was warm. This was what she wanted. She understood that success in business was very important to a man, but to her the way her man felt about her was important. "I know, Peter, I know. That's why you shouldn't worry. A man can do a better job without foolish worries on his mind. You'll do all right. It's a good idea and it's needed."

"You think so?" He looked up at her.

She looked into his eyes and smiled. "Of course it is. If it wasn't, you wouldn't have decided to do it."

Raising the money for the picture proved to be the easiest part of the whole project. The exhibitors whom Johnny spoke to were eager to put up money to have the picture made. They were tired of being gouged for poor combine-quality, routine pictures. Johnny received sums ranging from the thousand dollars he had obtained from Pappas down to one hundred dollars from a small exhibitor on Long Island.

It was the biggest open secret in the industry. Everybody but the combine knew about it. The other independents watched Magnum carefully to see what would happen next.

Meanwhile Peter was quietly buying up all the raw stock he could lay his hands on and Joe was busy working with the playwright whipping the script into shape for a picture.

Warren Craig's dressing-room was crowded with people while he removed his make-up. In his mirror he could see the people talking excitedly, but that pretty little girl in the corner wasn't saying a word; she just watched him remove his make-up with an awed expression on her face.

He felt good. He had turned in a good performance to-night and he knew it. There were some nights when everything just seemed to go right and nothing you could do would spoil it, just as there were the other kind of nights. He crossed his fingers as he thought about it.

The girl in the mirror saw him do it and smiled tentatively at him. He smiled back at her. Her smile brightened.

With a flourish he wiped the last of the cold cream from his face and wheeled around. "And now if you good people will excuse me," he said in his rich baritone voice, "I'll get out of this provincial costume."

The people laughed. They always did when he said that; it had become part of the performance. He was dressed in a cowboy costume and it flattered him. The bright colors of his shirt, contrasting with the dull color of the chaps, lent gentle emphasis to his broad shoulders and very flat hips.

He went behind a screen and appeared in a few minutes in regular clothes. It was the truth that he looked as well in evening clothes as he did in costume. He was an actor and he knew it. Everything he wore, everything he did and said, never let you forget that Warren Craig was the third generation of his family on the American stage.

He was ready now to receive their homage. He stood there easily in the center of the room, his head lightly inclined forward; he spoke a few words to each person as they came up and congratulated him. A cigarette in a long Russian holder dangled from his lips.

That was how Johnny first saw him as he followed Sam Sharpe into the dressing-room. Only Warren Craig wasn't happy to see Sam. Sam reminded him of the appointment he had made reluctantly earlier in the day to talk to that flicker fellow, and he was trying to find an approach to make that pretty little girl in the corner have supper with him.

Craig smiled to himself philosophically. That was the trouble with being one of the foremost actors of the American stage, he thought, your time was never your own.

Gradually the room emptied. The last to leave was that pretty little girl. She stopped at the doorway and smiled back over her shoulder at him. He returned her smile with a helpless gesture that spoke as plainly as words. "I'm sorry, my dear," it said, "but being a great actor has its drawbacks. Your time isn't your own."

Her smile answered him. He knew just what it meant. "I understand. Some other time soon." The door closed behind her.

Johnny didn't miss the byplay. He had stood there quietly sizing Craig up. He had no doubt that Craig was a competent actor, but the man's vanity hung about him like a cloak. And he had reason to be vain. He was young, not more than twenty-five the way Johnny figured. He was handsome, with thin, even features and black thick curling hair that Johnny thought would photograph beautifully.

Craig turned to Johnny and really saw him for the first time. "Why, he's younger than I am!" was his first thought of shocked surprise. "And still he's a vice-president of a flicker concern." But as he continued to look at Johnny he could see other things, things that were not at first visible to the ordinary person. Being on the stage taught you to look for certain signs of character, things that were important if you wanted to project them to an audience. Johnny's mouth was wide and generous, but firm and determined. His jaw had a slightly aggressive tilt to it, but was controlled. The most unusual thing about him, however, was his eyes. They were dark blue, and deep inside them there seemed to lurk hidden flames. "An idealist," Craig thought.

"Hungry, Warren?" Sharpe asked in his thin little voice.

Craig shrugged his shoulders. "I can eat," he said quietly, as if food meant nothing to him. He turned to Johnny. "These performances take so much out of one."

Johnny smiled sympathetically. "I understand, Mr. Craig."

Craig warmed to Johnny's voice. "I say, let's not be so formal. Warren's the name."

"Johnny to you," Johnny replied.

The two men shook hands and Sam Sharpe smiled happily to himself as they left the dressing-room. That bonus and commission were beginning to look as if they had a chance.

Craig warmed the brandy in the goblet between his hands. Slowly he rolled the goblet back and forth. Despite his protestation of not being hungry he had performed a very trencherman-like job on the large steak he had ordered. Now he was ready to talk.

"I understand you're with a flicker company, Johnny," he said.

Johnny nodded.

"Sam tells me that you're planning to film *The Bandit*."

"Right," Johnny replied, "and we would like you to play the lead. There isn't anyone else in the theater who could do justice to so difficult a role." He couldn't see any harm in flattery.

Craig couldn't either. He nodded his head in agreement. "But flickers, old boy," he said in a gentle derogatory voice, "but flickers!"

Johnny looked over at him. "Motion pictures are growing up, Warren," he said. "Now an artist of your talent can express himself more fully than on the stage."

Craig sipped at his brandy slowly. "I don't agree with you, Johnny." He smiled deprecatingly. "The other day I went into a nickelodeon and saw the most horrible things. They called it a comedy but, believe me, it wasn't funny. There was a little tramp and he was being chased by fat policemen and they were falling all over the place." He shook his head. "Sorry, old boy, I just can't see it."

Johnny laughed. He saw that the goblet Warren held in his hand was empty and gestured for the waiter to refill it. "Certainly you don't think that's the kind of picture we're going to make out of *The Bandit?*" His voice expressed amazement that Craig should think of such a thing.

He leaned across the table. "Look, Warren, first of all, this picture will be the real thing. It won't run just twenty minutes, it will run more than an hour. Then there is something new that's just been developed. It's called the close-up."

Johnny saw the blank look on Craig's face. "A man by the name of Griffith just worked it out. This is the way it works. Say you're playing a big scene—that scene with the girl in the garden. Remember that moment when you look at her and your face expresses your love for her without your saying one word? On the screen that would be magnificent. The camera would focus on your face and your face alone. That's all the audience would see. And every subtle expression, every tiny nuance that you, with your superb artistry, are capable of, would be brought forth for everyone to see, not just the people in the first few rows of the theater."

Craig looked interested. "You mean the camera would be on me alone?"

Johnny nodded his head. "And that's not all. It would be on you for most of the picture, for, after all, without you what is there to *The Bandit?*"

Craig was silent. He sipped a little more of the brandy. He liked that idea. After all, he was *The Bandit*. Then he shook his head. "No, Johnny, you tempt me very much, but I just can't do it. The flickers would ruin my reputation on the stage."

"Sarah Bernhardt isn't afraid that motion pictures would ruin her reputation," Johnny pointed out. "She can see the challenge to her artistry and goes forth to meet it. She knows that the new medium of motion pictures offers her as broad an opportunity for acting as the stage. Think of it, Warren, think of it! Bernhardt in France, Warren Craig in America. The foremost artists on their respective sides of the ocean making motion pictures. Would you have me believe that you are afraid to meet the same challenge that Madame Bernhardt is facing?"

Craig tossed down his drink. The last few words had reached him. What was it Johnny had said? He liked the sound of it. Bernhardt and Craig, the foremost artists in the world. He rose to his feet a little unsteadily and looked down at Johnny. "Old boy," he said pompously, "you've convinced me. I'll do the picture! And what's more, I don't care what anyone in the profession thinks, even John Drew. I'll show them that a true artist can meet the challenge and work in any medium. Even flickers!"

Johnny looked up at him and smiled. Under the table Sam Sharpe uncrossed his fingers.

6

Joe sat in the easy chair and watched Johnny knot his tie. Twice Johnny did it over and at last he ripped the tie off and took another one from the rack. "Damn it!" he muttered. "I can never get it right the first time."

Joe smiled. Since the morning he had spoken to Johnny about the risk he ran in prompting Peter to make that picture, he hadn't said another word on the subject. He did his share of the job quietly and well and hoped that everything would work out all right. But everything was going too smoothly. Occasionally he felt a twinge of misgiving at the easy way things seemed to be working out and would reprimand himself for being a pessimist.

"Got a date?" he asked Johnny.

Johnny nodded, still concentrating on the tie.

"Anyone I know?" Joe asked.

The tie was knotted at last and Johnny turned around. "I don't think so," he replied. "Sam Sharpe's secretary."

Joe let out a whistle. "Better be careful, kid." He smiled. "I seen that pretty little blonde once. She's the marrying kind."

Johnny laughed. "Nonsense. She's a lot of fun."

Joe shook his head in pretended sadness. "I seen that happen before. You go out with a dame for laughs and wind up with a ball and chain."

"Not Jane," Johnny answered. "She knows I'm not looking to settle down."

"A dame might know it, but she'll never believe it." Joe smiled. Then his expression changed and his face grew serious. "You an' Peter goin' over to the combine offices tomorrow?"

Johnny nodded. It was late in May and everything was ready to roll on the picture. The script and the cast were ready; the only difficulty that remained was getting a studio big enough to make the picture in, since their own was pitifully small.

They had checked several of the independents, but none was available. At last they had decided to approach the combine and try to rent a studio from them. They had several large studios that could accommodate *The Bandit*, and one of them Johnny knew was not in use that summer. They had agreed that they would tell the combine they were making a serial, and it was a logical enough excuse to get by.

"What'll you do if they turn you down?" Joe asked.

"They won't turn us down," Johnny replied confidently. "Stop being a gloomy Gus."

"All right, all right," Joe said; "I was just askin'."

The horse's hoofs stopped clattering on the pavement, and the hansom drew to a stop. The driver turned around on his seat and looked down at them. "Where to now, sir?" he asked.

"Around the park again," Johnny said. He turned and looked at Jane. "All right with you?" he asked. "You're not tired?"

Her face was pale in the moonlight. The night was warm, but she had a little scarf around her shoulders. "I'm not tired," she said.

The hansom set off again and Johnny leaned back in his seat. He looked up at the sky; the stars were out and they twinkled down on him. He put his hands behind his head. "When this picture is finished, Janey," he said, "we'll really be on our way. Nothing'll stop us then."

He felt her stir beside him. "Johnny," she said.

"Yes, Jane?" His mind was still in the stars.

"Is that all you ever think about? When the picture is finished?"

He turned toward her in surprise. "What do you mean?"

She looked at him steadily. Her eyes were wide and softly luminous. Her voice was very quiet. "There are other things in life besides pictures, you know."

He stretched himself and grinned. "Not for me there ain't."

She turned her face away from him and looked out the other side of the carriage. "Other people find time for other things besides business."

He put his arm around her shoulder; with the other hand he turned her face to him. For a moment he looked at her, then he kissed her. Her lips were warm and her arms went around him hungrily and then as suddenly dropped from his shoulders.

"You mean things like this, Janey?" he asked softly.

She was silent for a few seconds. When she answered, her voice was very small. "I wish you hadn't done that, Johnny."

Johnny's face expressed his astonishment. "Why, honey?" he asked. "Isn't that what you meant?"

She looked at him steadily. "It is and it isn't. Kisses themselves aren't important, but the things that are behind them are. I'm sorry that you kissed me because now I know there's nothing behind it. You've got moving pictures inside you, Johnny, not feelings."

The combine offices were located in a big building on Twenty-third Street. It was a twelve-story building and the combine occupied every floor. The executive offices were on the seventh floor, and when Peter and Johnny got off the

elevator on that floor, they were met by a young girl re-
ceptionist.

"Who do you wish to see?" the girl asked.

"Mr. Segale," Peter answered. "Mr. Edge and Mr. Kessler
to see him. We have an appointment."

"Won't you take a seat?" the girl asked, gesturing toward
a comfortable couch placed along the wall. "I'll check with
Mr. Segale's office."

Johnny and Peter sat down. At the end of the hall was a
large office with an open door. Through it they could see
row upon row of desks with men and women sitting at
them.

"They really are big business," Johnny whispered.

"I'm nervous," Peter answered.

"Take it easy," Johnny counseled in a whisper. "They
haven't the faintest idea of what we're going to do. There's
nothing to worry about."

Peter started to reply, but his answer was cut short by the
girl. "Mr. Segale will see you," she said. "Right down the
hall. You'll see his name on the door."

They thanked her and walked down the hall. The place
was big and oppressive. Occasionally someone would scurry
by them with an air of doing something very important. Even
Johnny was impressed.

The name on the door read: "Mr. Segale—Production
Supervisor." They opened the door and walked in. They
were in a secretary's office. A girl looked up at them and
gestured to another door against the inner wall. "Right in
there," she smiled. "Mr. Segale is expecting you."

They went into the other office. The office was quietly
but lavishly furnished. A rich wine-colored rug covered the
floor, several paintings hung on the gray painted wall, and
rich leather couches and chairs were scattered around the
room.

Behind a tremendous flat-topped walnut desk sat Mr.
Segale. He greeted them warmly and waved them to chairs.
"Make yourselves comfortable, gentlemen," he said, smiling.
He passed around a box of cigars. "Smoke?"

Peter took one and lit up. Johnny gestured no and lit a
cigarette.

Mr. Segale was a small, fat man with a cherubic face. His

blue eyes were unusually keen and his lips were thin and his mouth small and round.

It was when he looked at him that Johnny felt his first sense of misgivings. "This baby's no fool," he thought. "It's not going to be so easy to pull the wool over those baby-blue eyes." But he said nothing, he kept silent.

Mr. Segale spoke first. "What can I do for you, gentlemen?"

Peter decided to come right to the point. "Magnum would like to rent the Slocum studios for three weeks to make a serial."

Mr. Segale clasped his hands across his stomach and leaned back in his chair. He looked up at the ceiling. "I see," he said, blowing the smoke from his cigar upwards. "I believe you hold a sublicense from us for the production of short features not to exceed two reels in length."

"That's right, Mr. Segale," Peter answered quickly.

"You're doing all right with them?" Segale continued.

Johnny looked at Peter. Things were not going the way he had thought they would. But Peter was intent upon Mr. Segale.

"What a question to ask!" Peter's voice was gently amazed. "You know how we're doing."

Mr. Segale straightened in his chair. He looked forward on his desk, his chubby hands searching for a paper. He found it and looked at it. "Hmm, you produced seventy-two reels of film last year."

Peter didn't answer. He, too, was beginning to feel something was wrong. He stole a quick look at Johnny. Johnny's face was cold, his blue eyes hard behind narrowed lids. With a sinking feeling he realized Johnny felt the same thing he did. He turned back to Segale. "Why all these questions, Mr. Segale? All we're asking for is space to make a serial."

Mr. Segale stood up and walked around his desk to Peter. He stood there in front of Peter's chair and looked down at him. "Are you sure that's all you want to do, Mr. Kessler?" he asked.

Johnny watched them. He was starting to see the inside. The man was playing with Peter as a cat would with a mouse. He knew what they wanted; he had known what they wanted before they came in. Why didn't he say so immediately instead of horsing around?

Peter's voice was bland and smooth as he replied: "Sure, Mr. Segale, what else would we need all that space for?"

Segale looked down at him for a minute. "I've heard some talk that you want to make a six-reel feature out of the Broadway play *The Bandit.*"

Peter laughed. "Ridiculous. Maybe I did talk about making a serial out of it, but a six-reeler, never."

Segale walked back to his chair and sat down. "I'm sorry, Mr. Kessler, the Slocum studio is all booked up for the summer and we can't let you have it."

Johnny sprang to his feet. "What do you mean, all booked up?" he said excitedly. "That's a lot of crap. I know there isn't a thing shooting there all summer."

"I don't know where you get your information, Mr. Edge," Segale replied smoothly. "But I ought to know."

"I take it, Mr. Segale," Peter injected, "the combine doesn't want Magnum to make a serial."

Segale looked at Peter steadily, leaning back in his chair as he spoke. "Mr. Kessler," he said urbanely, "as of June 1, the combine doesn't want Magnum to make pictures at all. Under paragraph six, section A, of our cross-licensing agreement, we hereby revoke our license to you to engage in the manufacture and production of motion pictures."

Johnny saw Peter's face grow gray as Segale spoke. For a second he seemed to slump in his chair; then he straightened up and color began to flood back into his face. Slowly he got to his feet. "I take it, then, the combine is exercising its monopolistic right in restraint of trade and competition."

Segale looked at him closely. "You call it what you want, Mr. Kessler. The combine is only doing what is provided for in its contract."

Peter's voice was heavy and dull, but underneath it was a steely timbre. "You can't stop Magnum from making pictures simply by revoking its contract, Segale. Neither can you stop the free progress of the screen. Magnum will continue to make motion pictures. With or without a combine license!"

Segale looked over at Peter coolly. "The combine is not at all anxious to put you out of business, Mr. Kessler, if you will reiterate your agreement to make and produce only two-reel features."

Johnny looked at Peter. This Segale was a hard customer.

First he hit you over the head with a sledge hammer, then he offered you a Seidlitz powder. He wondered what Peter would do. Segale had offered him a way out.

Peter stood there quietly. Many things were turning over in his mind. This was a chance for him to save his business, but if he took it, he would never again have the nerve to try to buck the combine.

It was only a motion picture that he wanted to make. Strips of celluloid, thousands of feet long, with little pictures frozen on them. But when you flashed them on the screen, they came to life. They were real people and real places and they meant something. People laughed at them and wept with them. They were as capable of stirring the emotions as the stage, as literature, as music or any form of art. And an art in order to be important had to be free, even as a man had to be free and unhampered in order to live the way he wanted.

What was it Esther had said when he first went into this? "You do what you want. It's not important that we have a house on Riverside Drive. . . ."

The words flooded over his tongue. He knew just what he wanted to say to Segale, but what came out was something entirely different.

"Magnum will not enter into any agreement that will dictate to it as to what type of pictures it will make, Mr. Segale. It is not important that we have a house on Riverside Drive."

He turned his back and walked out of the room. Johnny followed him.

Behind them Mr. Segale scratched his head and wondered what a house on Riverside Drive had to do with making motion pictures.

7

THE sunlight was white and glaring and hurt their eyes as they stood in the street in front of the combine offices. Johnny looked at Peter. Peter's face seemed white and drawn to him. "Come on, let's get a drink," he suggested.

Peter shook his head slowly. His voice trembled a little

as he answered: "No, I think I'll go home and lie down awhile. I—I don't feel so good."

Johnny's voice was sympathetic. It was his fault that Peter had been brought to this. "I'm sorry, Peter. I didn't mean—"

Peter interrupted him: "Don't be sorry, Johnny. It's not your fault any more than mine. I wanted to do it." He put his cigar in his mouth and puffed at it. It had gone out. He struck a match with trembling fingers and tried to light it, but his hand was shaking so much that he couldn't get it to light. At last, in disgust, he threw his cigar away.

They stood there looking at each other morosely, each occupied with his own thoughts. For Peter it seemed the end of all his plans. Now he would have to figure out something else to do. Already his conscience was troubling him. He had been too hasty in there with Segale. He should have taken up Segale's offer, let somebody else buck the combine. Someone with more money and in a better position. He didn't know. He felt sick and confused. Maybe when he got home and talked to Esther, things would straighten out.

Johnny was already figuring on how to make the picture elsewhere. There must be another studio or place they could rent to make the picture. The combine couldn't be the only organization in New York that had a studio big enough for *The Bandit*. He would have to look around. Maybe Borden could let them have some space at his studio. He made serials and with a little squeezing there certainly was enough room to make *The Bandit*. After all, Borden had twenty-five hundred bucks in the picture and he wouldn't like to see it go down the drain.

"I'll get you a cab," Johnny said, stepping to the curb.

A cab drew up and Johnny helped Peter into it. Peter looked at him and tried to smile.

Johnny smiled back at him. The guy had guts. "Try not to worry," he said. "We'll find a way to lick the bastards yet."

Peter nodded his head; he didn't trust himself to speak. He was afraid he would burst into tears. The cab drew off and Johnny stood on the curb looking after it until it had turned the corner.

Joe was sitting at his desk reading the paper when Johnny

came in. He jumped to his feet excitedly when he saw him. "How did—?" he started to ask, but the question was never finished. He saw Johnny's face. He sank back in his chair. "No dice?" he asked.

Johnny shook his head. "No dice."

"How come?"

Johnny looked at him angrily. "They knew all about it. Some bastards just can't keep their mouth shut."

Joe nodded philosophically. "It was bound to happen."

Johnny's voice rose almost to a shout. "It didn't have to happen. We coulda got away with it."

Joe held up his hand. "Take it easy, kid. Yelling at me won't help. I didn't tell 'em."

Johnny was instantly contrite. "I'm sorry, Joe, I know you didn't. But you were right, I shouldn't have pushed Peter into it. If I'd kept my big mouth shut, we'd still be in business."

Joe let out a whistle. "It's as bad as that, eh?"

"Yeah," Johnny answered glumly. "They revoked our license."

"Now I need a drink," Joe said.

Johnny looked at him. "Where's the bottle?"

Joe opened a lower drawer of his desk and took out a bottle and two small glasses. Silently he filled them and held one out to Johnny. "Luck," he said.

They drained their glasses.

Johnny held his glass out to Joe. Again they were filled and again they drank. They sat there silently for a long while.

At last Joe spoke. "What do we do next?" he asked.

Johnny looked at him. Joe was a decent guy. He didn't rub it into him when he could have. "I don't know," he answered slowly. "Laemmle is down in Cuba making that Pickford picture, but we ain't got the dough to do that. We got to figure out a place to make the picture around here. We ain't going to take this laying down. We'll give them a run for their money."

Joe looked at him, a grudging admiration on his face. "Now I know what Santos meant when he once told me you were a scrapper. You never give up, do you?"

Johnny's mouth was set in determined lines. "We're goin'

to make that picture." He turned and picked up the phone on his desk and gave the operator Borden's number.

Borden answered the phone.

"Bill," Johnny said into the mouthpiece, "this is Johnny." There was a slight hesitation in Borden's voice before he answered. "Oh—uh, hello, Johnny."

"We were over at the combine's," Johnny said, "and we didn't have any luck there. How about us getting some space at your shop?"

Borden's voice sounded slightly embarrassed. "We're pretty jammed up out here, Johnny."

"I know you are," Johnny replied. "But maybe we could squeeze it in here and there. We're in this thing pretty deep, you know."

"I'd like to help you, Johnny"—Bordon spoke very slowly —"but I can't."

"What do you mean you can't? Johnny said angrily. "It was all right with you when Peter agreed to make the picture. You guys could see he was fighting your fight for yuh."

Borden's voice was very meek. "I'm sorry, Johnny. Honest."

A light suddenly dawned in Johnny's mind. "Did you hear from the combine?"

The phone was silent for a second before Borden replied. When he did, his voice was apologetic. "Yes."

"What did they say?"

"You're on the blacklist. And you know what that means."

Johnny felt a sinking feeling in his stomach. He knew what it meant. From now on no independent in the business could have anything to do with Magnum or they would lose their own licenses. "And you're going to pay attention to that?" he demanded.

"What can we do?" Borden queried. "We can't all afford to go out of business."

"And Peter can?" Johnny asked nastily.

"We can't help him if we all lose our licenses," Borden protested.

"Then how are you gonna help him?" Johnny asked.

"I—I don't know," Borden stammered. "Let me think about it. I'll call you tomorrow."

"All right," Johnny said, and hung up the phone. He turned to Joe. "The combine put the word out already. We're on the blacklist."

Joe got to his feet.

Johnny looked at him in surprise. "Where you goin'?"

Joe smiled at him. "Out to git a paper. Want to see what the want ads have got in 'em."

"Sit down and quit horsin' around," Johnny said. "We got enough troubles."

Joe sat down. "What we gonna do next?" he asked.

"I don't know yet," Johnny answered, "but there must be a way out of this mess. I got him into it an' I gotta get him out."

"All right kid," Joe said seriously. "Count me in. I'm with yuh, all the way."

Johnny smiled at him. "Thanks Joe."

Joe grinned back at him. "Don't thank me. I got twenty-five hundred fish in this, remember."

It was late in the evening when he called Peter's home. Esther answered.

"Esther, this is Johnny. How is Peter?"

Her voice was quiet and even. "He's got a headache. He's lying down in the bedroom."

"Good," Johnny said. "Keep his mind off the business. Make him get some rest."

"Looks bad, Johnny?" Her voice was still quiet and controlled.

"Doesn't look bright," he admitted. "But don't worry, things'll look better in the morning."

"I'm not worried." Her voice was clear. "My father, God rest his soul, used to say: 'What will be will be.' A living we can always make."

"Good," Johnny said. "Make Peter feel like that and we can't lose."

"Leave Peter to me," she answered confidently. "But Johnny—"

"What?"

"Don't you start worrying. It's not your fault and we like you too much to want you to get sick over this."

Johnny felt the tears come perilously close to his eyes. "I won't, Esther," he promised.

He hung up the phone and turned to Joe, his eyes shining brightly. "What are you gonna do with people like that?" he asked wonderingly.

8

THE summer dragged on and nowhere could they find a place that was willing to take a chance and let them shoot their picture. Johnny had been to every independent in the business, but could get no help.

They were all sympathetic. They agreed with Johnny that the only way the combine would ever be beaten was by what Magnum was doing, but that was where they drew the line. More than sympathy Johnny could not get. In vain he would argue and point out that Magnum was fighting their fight. That if Magnum won out they would all benefit. They agreed, but none of them would risk losing his license.

By the end of August they had pretty nearly reached the breaking point. Their money was almost gone. Peter had lost his paunch. Esther had let her maid go in July and now Peter found himself looking enviously and speculatively at hardware stores when he passed them.

Joe spent most of his day at the studio engaged in an endless game of solitaire. Neither he nor Johnny had drawn a cent of pay since Magnum's license had been revoked, but they all hung together. To save money they would all eat at Peter's house. The meals were simple but satisfying, and Esther did not complain at the extra work.

Several times Joe had got an odd job at one of the independents and he threw the money he earned into the pot. But it was Johnny who had changed most of all.

He seldom smiled now. Slim he had been when all their troubles had begun. Now he was thin, taut, and intense. His eyes were sunken hollows in his face. Only the flames in them had not dimmed. At night he would lie in his bed and stare sleeplessly at the ceiling. It was his fault, he would think; if he hadn't been so insistent, this would never have happened.

Making this picture became the one thought in his mind. He knew that once this picture was made, their battle would be won. Each morning he would wake up with the conviction that this would be the day he would be able to talk one of the independents into letting them use his studio. But as time went by, the producers began to get tired of his persistent cajoling. They left orders with their help to shunt him off and if they saw him coming they would try to avoid him.

When Johnny realized what they were doing and that he was being avoided, he grew bitter. "The dirty bastards," he would think, "they're all heroes when you're doing the fighting for them, but ask them to help a little bit and they won't even talk to you."

Their lawyer had been in court all summer trying without success to get an injunction against the combine to prevent it from applying its blacklist against Magnum. At last he came to Peter one day and told him there was no use in continuing the fight. The license was too cleverly drawn, the combine's position too cleverly planned for an attack to be made on it in such a manner. Besides he wanted some money instead of promises.

Quietly Peter paid him and they continued their struggle. But now it was the end of August and the day of reckoning was fast approaching.

Peter and Johnny and Joe were sitting in the office when Warren Craig came in with Sam Sharpe.

Johnny got to his feet and held out his hand. "Hello, Warren."

Craig ignored it and walked past him to Peter. "Mr. Kessler," he said.

Peter looked up at him tiredly. He hadn't slept too well last night, he had been trying to figure how much longer their money would carry them. It wasn't far. "Yes, Mr. Craig," he answered.

"Mr. Kessler, we must have a definite starting date for the picture or I must give you notice now." Craig's voice was pompous.

Peter spread his hands wearily on the desk. "I'd like to give you a starting date for the picture, Mr. Craig, but how can I? I don't know when we can start the picture myself."

"Then I must give you my notice," Craig said.

Sam Sharpe's thin voice cut in. "Don't be too hasty, Warren. After all, it's not really their fault. Maybe if—"

Craig turned on Sharpe quickly. His voice was cutting and sharp. "Maybe nothing, Sam. I let you talk me into this in the first place. When we signed the agreement, the picture was supposed to be completed by mid-July. Now here it is almost September. A new Broadway season is about to start. If you were the proper kind of agent you would see to it that I was set in one of the new plays instead of keeping me waiting for this fool's dream to materialize."

Sharpe seemed to shrink within his clothes. "But, Warren—" he began to say, when a look from Craig shut him up.

"Wait a minute, wait a minute." Johnny planted himself in front of Craig belligerently. "You've been paid for the time you stood by, haven't you?"

"That's right," Craig admitted.

"Two thousand smackers a month, every month, June, July, and August, isn't that right?"

"Yes," Craig answered, "but—"

"But, hell," Johnny shouted. "We agreed to pay you two thousand for the picture. When we found out the picture wouldn't start on time, you agreed to take two thousand a month until the picture was finished. Now that the summer is over and your dead season is gone, you want to run out on us!"

"I'm not running out," Craig answered uncomfortably. "But I have my career to think of. They forget about you quickly on Broadway if you don't come up with a new play."

"You have a contract with us to make this picture, and, by God, you're going to live up to it!" Johnny shouted, his fists clenched.

"Johnny!" Peter's voice was sharp.

Johnny turned to him in surprise.

"What's the use, Johnny?" Peter said; his voice was low. "Let him go if he wants. The whole thing is no good anyway."

"But we paid him six thousand dollars already," Johnny said.

"We could pay him a hundred thousand more if we had it," Peter answered, "and we wouldn't be any closer to making the picture than we are now." He turned to Craig.

"All right Mr. Craig, I'll accept your notice."

Craig started to say something, then changed his mind. He turned on his heel and started out. "Come on, Sam," he called to Sharpe over his shoulder.

Sharpe hung back for a moment. "I'm sorry, Johnny," he said softly. "It wasn't my idea. I tried to talk him out of it."

Johnny nodded his head.

"I'll send back my commissions and bonus in the morning," Sharpe said.

Johnny looked at Sharpe suddenly. The man's eyes were warm with understanding. "You don't have to do that," he said quickly; "you earned your money. It's not your fault."

"Our agreement was contingent upon Craig making the picture," Sharpe said simply. "He didn't make it. I don't take pay for not keeping my share of a bargain."

Johnny looked at him. The little man had his pride. "All right Sam," he said. They touched hands and the little man scurried after his client.

Silently they watched him leave. "A square little guy," Johnny said as the door closed behind him.

Peter turned back to his desk and looked at it for a while. He picked up a pencil and toyed with it. He put it down. He picked up a butt of a cigar from his ashtray and put it in his mouth and chewed on it reflectively. Then he turned to Johnny and Joe.

"Well," he said slowly, "I guess that's the finish."

"The hell you say," Johnny came back at him. "There are other actors just as good as he is."

Peter looked at him. "Do you think they'll take a chance with us after the experience he had? Even if we had the money, which we haven't?" He spoke with irrefutable logic.

Johnny had no answer. Joe turned up a red queen and put it on a black jack.

"We might as well face it," Peter said heavily. "We're licked." He held up a hand to still Johnny's protest. "Don't tell me any different. You know it too. We tried everything and it didn't work, so we might as well close up shop."

Joe took a vicious swipe at the cards. They scattered into

the air and fluttered to the floor. His lips were moving with silent curses.

Johnny said nothing. He couldn't speak even if he wanted to, his throat was all knotted up.

Peter stood up wearily. "I don't know how I'm going to pay you boys back your money."

Johnny found his voice. "You don't owe me nothing."

Joe followed right along. "Me neither," he growled.

Peter looked at them steadily for a few seconds. There was a suspicious moisture in his eyes. He stepped toward Joe and held out his hand. He gripped Joe's hand silently, then he turned to Johnny.

Johnny held out his hand. For some strange reason he couldn't keep it steady. It kept shaking.

Peter took it and held it tightly. They looked into each other's eyes for a moment. Then Peter clasped Johnny to him. Tears were running freely from his eyes now.

"You Americans!" Peter said. "What can you say with a handshake?"

Johnny couldn't speak.

"Johnny, Johnny, my boy, don't blame yourself. It's not your fault. You tried harder than any of us."

"I'm sorry, Peter, I'm sorry."

Peter held him at arm's length and looked at him. "Don't give up, Johnny. This is your business. You were meant for it. It's not for old men like me. You'll do great things with it."

"We'll do great things, Peter."

Peter shook his head. "Not me. I'm through." His hands fell to his sides. "Well, I guess I'll be going home." He walked slowly to the door. At the door he turned back and looked at them. He took a half look around the office and tried to smile. He couldn't. He made a helpless little gesture with his hand and shut the door behind him.

For a few seconds there was silence in the room. Joe was the first to speak. His voice was strained and cracked. "I think I'll go out and get drunk."

Johnny looked at him strangely. "That's the first good idea we had all summer!"

9

THE bartender looked at them threateningly. He held the two drinks in his hand close to him on the bar. "That will be seventy cents, gentlemen." His pleasant voice belied his appearance, but his grasp on the glasses indicated the firmness with which he was prepared to deal with the situation.

Johnny looked over at Joe. He didn't know whether he was weaving or Joe. He wished that Joe would weave in the same way he did. Maybe he wouldn't be so dizzy that way.

"The man inshists on cash," he said.

Joe nodded his head solemnly. "I heard him. Pay him."

"Shure." Johnny stuck his hand in his pockets and came up with some coins. Laboriously he laid them on the bar and counted them. "Shixty five, sheventy," he crowed happily. "Give ush our drinksh."

The bartender looked at the change and pushed the drinks toward them. He picked up the change and rung it up on the register.

Before the sound of the bell had faded away, Joe was pounding on the bar. "Shet up two more," he said.

The bartender looked at him. "Cash in advance."

Joe drew himself up indignantly. "Shee here, my good man," he said solemnly, "I was polite enough when you spoke to my frien' like that. But when you talk to me, thash something differn'. I am a shteady cushtomer. He ish not ash mush a drinker ash me, therefore when I order drinksh, I egshpect drinksh."

The bartender nodded to a man standing down at the end of the bar. The man came up to them and took them each by the arm. "Come along now, boys," he said quietly.

Joe shook himself loose. "Take your hands off me."

The man ignored him. Instead he put both hands on Johnny's back and pushed him out the door, then he turned back to Joe and rolled up a sleeve. "Are yuh leavin'?"

Joe looked at him disdainfully. "Of coursh I'm leavin'. Did you think I would care to shtay after sush a dishplay of inhoshpitably?" He weaved his way to the door.

At the door he turned and held his fingers up to his mouth and made a vulgar sound at the man. The man made a gesture toward him. Joe ducked quickly out of the door, missed the step down, and fell sprawling.

Johnny helped him to his feet. "Did they throw you out, Joe?"

Joe leaned on him. "Of coursh not. They know better than to try and throw Joe Turner out. I jusht mished the shtep, thash all."

They leaned against the corner of the building. "Where'll we go now?" Johnny asked.

Joe looked at him, trying to clear his head. "What time ish it?"

Johnny took his watch out of his pocket and tried to focus his eyes upon it. "Twelve o'clock," he said. He turned and tried to put his arm around Joe. "Joe, it'sh midnight!"

Joe pushed him away. "Don't kish me. You shtink from whishky."

Johnny drew back, hurt. "All ri', Joe, but I like you anyway."

"Yuh got any money?" Joe asked.

Johnny went through his pockets one by one. At last he came up with a crumpled dollar bill.

Joe took it. "Letsh get a cab," he said. "I know a saloon where we can get shome credit."

Johnny's head lay on the table. The cool marble top felt good against his face. Someone was trying to pull him up, but he didn't want to get up. He pushed the hands away. "Ish my fault, Peter, ish my fault."

Joe looked down at him, then turned to the man standing with him. "He'sh drunk, Al."

Al Santos spoke tersely. "You'ra the fin-a one to talk."

"He'sh drunker than I am," Joe insisted.

"That'sa only because he hasn't the experience with drinking that you have," Al replied. "He'sa not as old as you are. He's still a kid."

"He'sh twenty-two."

"I wouldn't care if he was fifty," Al shot back. "He'd still be a kid to me." He turned back to Johnny and shook him. "Come on, Johnny boy, get up. It's Al, I been looking for you all night."

Johnny just turned his head and mumbled: "I'm sorry, Peter. 'Sall my fault."

Al turned to Joe. "What's this he always keeps saying he's sorry for?"

Joe was beginning to sober up, his eyes were beginning to clear. "Poor kid," he said. "He wanted to make a picture that busted up the works. We all lost our dough and Johnny keeps saying it's his fault."

"Is it?" Al asked.

Joe looked at him. "No, it isn't. True enough, it was his idea, but it was a good one and nobody made us go into it. We were old enough to know what we were doing."

"Come over here and tell me about it," Al said, leading the way to another table. The waiter came up and he ordered a bottle of wine.

He listened silently to Joe's story. Every now and then he would look over at the table where Johnny was sleeping and smile to himself fondly.

Johnny Edge. He remembered the first time he had heard the name. A wagon had pulled into the carnival he had been running, late one night in 1898. That was thirteen years ago. A long time, but now it didn't seem so long ago. The years had flown by.

That was the year he and his brother, Luigi, had bought that farm in California. Luigi wanted to see things grow, raise grapes for wine, and see oranges hanging from the trees like in the old country, and he wanted to have some place to go when he retired. And here he was, fifty-four years old and retired, and going out to the farm in California.

It had been early morning and he had come out of his wagon. The purple gray mists of the dawn still hung closely to the ground as he walked around to the back of his wagon and relieved himself. He had felt someone watching him and he turned around.

It was a small boy, about nine years old. Al looked at him

closely; there weren't any boys that age around the carnival. "Who are you?" he had asked.

"Johnny Edge," the boy had answered, looking at him levelly out of candid blue eyes.

Al's face looked blank and the boy hastened to explain. "I'm with my mother and father. They just joined your show last night."

"Oh," Al said as he understood suddenly. "You're with Doc Psalter?"

"That's my father," Johnny had answered gravely, "but that's not his real name. He's really Walter Edge and my mother is Jane Edge." He turned and pointed. "That's their wagon over there."

"Well then," Al had said, "let's go over and say hello."

The boy turned and looked up at him gravely. "You're Al Santos, aren't you?"

Al nodded his head and started for the Edge wagon. Suddenly he stopped and looked down. The small boy had taken his hand as they walked toward the wagon together.

He remembered the night Johnny's parents had been killed in the fire that burned down the big tent. Jane had been caught by the tent just as the center pole came down, and Johnny's father had gone in after her. When they got to him, he was burned badly. The hair was gone from his head and face, pieces of raw flesh shone redly through the cracked skin.

They took him out and stretched him on the ground. Al knelt on one side of him, Johnny on the other.

Johnny's father looked up at them. "Jane?" he asked. His voice was so faint they could hardly hear him.

Al shook his head and looked pityingly over at Johnny. Johnny was only ten years old then and his face was dull with shock. He could not understand what had happened so quickly.

Walter Edge reached up and took his son's hand. With his other hand he brought Al's hand over to the boy's. "Look after him for me, Al," he whispered. "He's just a tyke an' he's got a long way to go." He gasped for breath and then turned an agonized face to Al. "If the time comes that he ever wants to get out of this business, Al, help him. Don't let what happened to me ever happen to him."

That was why Al didn't try to stop Johnny when he left

the carny. He remembered the way Johnny had followed him around the carny until he learned to do everything that Al could do.

Al never had time to get married and raise a family like his brother, Luigi, and after a while it seemed to him just as if Johnny had become his own son. When Johnny decided to go back to Peter, Al said nothing. If that was what the kid wanted, that was what Al wanted for him.

Now that he had retired, he wanted to see Johnny before he went out west. He had gone up to the studio, but found no one there. He called Peter on the phone, but Peter didn't know where Johnny had gone. He then called Johnny's home, but there was no answer.

And now, only through accident, he had found him. It was in the saloon on Fourteenth Street where all the carny men hung out that he had come looking for Joe. He hadn't expected to find Johnny there, but he figured that Joe would know where he was.

Joe finished his story. Al was silent for a second, then he took out a thin black stogie and lit it.

"What's this-a combine you're talking about?" he asked.

"They control all the picture patents among them. Without their say-so you can't make motion pictures." Joe looked at him curiously. He wondered what Al was getting at.

"You gotta the stuff to make-a this pitch' with?"

"It's all layin' there, up in the studio," Joe nodded.

Al turned the stogie reflectively in his hand for a moment. "Wake Johnny up," he said, "I wanna talk to him."

Joe got up and walked over to the bar. Tiny prickles were jumping around in his skin as they always did when he was excited. "Gimme a pitcher of ice water," he said to the bartender.

Silently the bartender filled a pitcher under the counter and handed it to him.

Joe walked back to Johnny and held the pitcher over his head and emptied it.

The water splashed over the back of Johnny's head and dripped down on his clothes. Johnny only stirred.

Joe went back to the bar. "Fill it up again."

The bartender refilled the pitcher and Joe went back to Johnny and repeated the treatment.

This time Johnny came up with a start. He sat up and

shook his head and stared at Joe through blurred eyes. "It's raining," he said.

Joe looked at him and then turned back to the bartender. "One more ought to do the trick," he said.

Johnny tried to focus his eyes on Joe as he came back to him, but his eyes kept blurring. What was that thing Joe was carrying in his hand?

The water hit him like a flood. It was icy cold and bit through to his marrow. Suddenly his head cleared. He stood up. He was still a bit wobbly on his feet. "What the hell are you doing?" he managed to ask Joe through chattering teeth.

Joe grinned at him. "I'm trying to sober you up. We got company," he said, pointing to Al.

10

PETER couldn't sleep. He tossed and turned on his bed all night, and the sheets were damp with sweat. Quietly Esther lay beside him. She lay awake watching him, a curious hurt within her for his suffering.

"If there were only something I could do for him," she thought, "something I could say to make him really feel that it doesn't matter what happens—that the only important thing is that he tried. But there's nothing."

Peter looked up through the dark at the ceiling. He knew Esther was awake and he wanted her to sleep. The kids kept her running around all day. It was too much that she should have to spend the night up with him. He lay quiet and tried to simulate the slow breathing of sleep.

"If I had only taken Segale's offer things would be all right now," he thought, his mind going over the same ground for the thousandth time. "Johnny wouldn't have said anything then. He knew there wasn't anything else I could have done." He reproached himself silently. "Johnny didn't have anything to do with it. I wanted to make the picture, he didn't force me. It was my own fault, I was too stubborn in Segale's office." He stirred restlessly. He wanted a cigar, then he remembered he wanted Esther to think he was sleeping, so he lay quiet.

The night wore on and neither of them slept. Each lay as quietly as possible, wanting the other to get some rest, but neither of them succeeded in fooling the other.

At last Peter couldn't lie still any more. Slowly, carefully, he sat up in bed, listening for a change in Esther's breathing. She was quiet. He slipped his feet softly into the slippers at the foot of the bed and stood up. He stood there for a second and then silently tiptoed into the kitchen. He shut the door softly behind him so that the light would not shine into the bedroom and waken her.

The bright light hurt his eyes for a moment. As soon as his eyes cleared, he went to the table and picked up a cigar and lit it. He heard the door open behind him. He turned around.

Esther stood there. "Maybe you'd like a cup of coffee?"

He nodded his head silently and watched her as she went over to the stove and lit the flame under the coffee pot. She came over to the table and sat down opposite him.

Her hair was loose and hung over her shoulders in thick, luxuriant waves. He wanted to reach out and touch it, it looked so alive and warm, but he didn't. He just puffed silently at his cigar.

"When my father used to have troubles," she said, "he always came into the kitchen and smoked a cigar and drank a cup of coffee. 'It clears the head,' he used to say, 'it helps a man to think.' It's funny you should do the same thing."

He looked down at his cigar. "I'm not as wise a man as your father was. I make too many mistakes."

She reached across the table and put her hand on his. "My father used to tell me a story that went something like this. There was once a very wise old man known in his village as Yacov the Wise. And people used to come from all the countryside to sit at his feet and thus gain in wisdom from the pearls the Wise One would drop from his lips. One day there came a young, impetuous man who wanted to learn all he could from the master in one sitting. He did not have time to sit, as the others did, for weeks at the feet of the Wise One. He had to learn everything at once so he could be about his business. 'O Wise One,' he said, 'I am overcome with the wonders of your knowledge and would like to know how I could gain the wisdom so necessary in order to avoid the foolish mistakes of youth.' The

Wise One turned and looked at the brash young man. He looked at him for a long, long time. At last he spoke. 'Impetuous young seeker after knowledge,' he said gently, 'you can learn to avoid the mistakes of youth by living to a ripe old age.' The young man thought this over and at last he got to his feet and thanked the Wise One for answering his question. For it was the truth the Wise One had spoken. A mistake is not recognized until it has been made and passed. For a mistake recognized before it was made would not be made and therefore would not be a mistake."

Peter turned his hand over and held her hand in his. He looked at her seriously and spoke softly in Yiddish. "Thy name was not given thee for nought. Thy wisdom is that of the good Queen whose name thou bearest."

The coffee bubbled over on the stove. Startled, she jumped to her feet and turned off the flame. She looked back at him over her shoulder. "Of what good is the wisdom of Queen Esther in a wife if she can't make her husband a good cup of coffee?"

They laughed and suddenly began to feel better.

Peter stood up and put out his cigar. He was smiling warmly at her. "Come," he said, "let's go to bed. The worries can keep for the morrow."

"No coffee?" she asked.

He shook his head. "No coffee. That can wait for the morrow too."

They were sleeping when the telephone began to ring. Esther sat up in bed, frightened. To her, the telephone ringing in the night meant tragedy. She sat there in the dark, her heart pounding; her hand reached out for Peter.

He picked up the phone. "Hello," he said, "hello."

Johnny's voice came excitedly through the receiver. "Peter, are you up?"

Peter answered in a testy voice: "To whom would you be talking if I was asleep?"

"It's fixed, Peter," Johnny was shouting. "We can make the picture!"

"You're drunk," Peter said flatly. "Go home and go to sleep."

"I was drunk," Johnny answered, "but honest, Peter, I'm sober as a judge now. It's all set. We can make the picture!"

Peter was wide awake. "You mean it?" His voice was incredulous, he couldn't believe his ears.

"Would I call you up at four o'clock in the morning if it weren't the truth?" Johnny asked. "Now go back to sleep and be at the studio at eight o'clock and I'll give you all the dope." Johnny hung up the phone.

Peter clicked the empty receiver in his hand. "Johnny!" he said. "Johnny!"

There was no answer, the phone was dead.

Peter hung up and turned to Esther, his eyes shining with tears. "Did you hear him? Did you hear that crazy kid?"

She was excited. "I heard him," she said.

"Isn't it wonderful?" he cried, putting his arms around her and kissing her.

"Now, Peter," she laughed happily, "remember. You want the neighbors should think we're newlyweds?"

11

JOHNNY was seated at his desk talking excitedly to a short dark man as Peter entered the studio at a quarter to eight. Peter had never seen the man before. Johnny had some sheets of paper in front of him and was just showing them to the stranger when he saw Peter.

He jumped to his feet and came halfway across the office to meet Peter. The little man in the loud plaid suit followed him. Johnny looked at Peter and grinned. "This is Al Santos," he said.

The two men looked at each other over clasped hands. Peter saw a small man, swarthy from the sun, a thin black stogie held firmly between strong white teeth.

"Al's going to let us make the picture out at his place," Johnny explained.

Peter smiled. "I'm sure glad to know you, Mr. Santos."

Al took the stogie from his mouth and waved it at Peter. "Al's the name. Nobody calls me mister."

Peter's smile grew broader. This was the kind of man he felt most at home with. Plain, regular, unpretentious. "Right, Al," he said, taking a cigar from his pocket. "I can't tell you how much I appreciate your letting us make the picture at your studio."

Johnny interrupted. "Who said he's got a studio?"

Peter almost dropped the lighted match he was holding to his cigar. "He hasn't got a studio?"

"No," Johnny answered.

Peter was bewildered. "So where then are we going to make the picture?"

"On his property," Johnny answered. "He has the space. Just last winter Griffith shot a picture out his way and he says it's perfect for moving pictures."

Peter looked at Johnny in dismay. "That picture that Griffith made last year was made in California. We haven't the money to get out there."

Johnny grinned. "We have now. Al's lending us the dough."

Peter turned to Al; his face was serious. "I appreciate your kindness, Al," he said slowly, "but you must know that we haven't any security to offer."

For a moment Al studied the man in front of him. Having heard from Joe and then from Johnny just how serious the situation was for Peter, he could understand what effort was required for Peter to tell him what he did. Johnny was right. This Kessler was a square shooter. He smiled slowly. "I've got all the security I need, Peter. Many years I have known Johnny. Since he was a littla boy. Twice now he'sa leave me to work for you. For Johnny to do this, I figure that the man he's work for is a alla right. Now from the way you talk I know."

"You're the man that owned the carnival?" Peter began to understand.

"I used to own the carnival," Al answered. "Now, I'ma retired." He turned to Johnny. "Look, Johnny, you get things settled with Peter here. I'm gonna back to the hotel and get some sleep. I'm not young like you fellas any more." He had been up all night talking to Johnny and now he was tired; weariness began to show in his face.

"All right, Al," Johnny replied. "We'll get things squared away and call you."

Al shook hands with Peter. "I'ma glad to meet you, Peter. Now don't you worry about a thing. Everythinga will be alla right."

Peter looked at him gratefully. "Thanks to you it will

be," he said. "I don't know what we would have done—"

Al didn't let him finish. "Don't thanka me, Peter. I spend a longa time in show business. To tell the truth, I didn't want to retire, but my brother, Luigi, he insist. 'Al,' he say, 'you gotta enough money. Now stoppa work and come out here and enjoy your life. We make a good wine just like in Italy, we gotta oranges and people like at home. Come outta here and live.' I think it over. He's a right. I'ma getting old. No use to work like horse no more, so I decide to do what Luigi say. But alla time I think a man shoulda have something to do. Something he'sa interest in, to keep busy. This a good thing. I know show business. With the carnival I go all over the country and see the people going to the movies. Every day it'sa getting bigger. When Johnny talks to me, I say to myself; 'It's a good thing.' So I make up my mind."

Peter smiled at him. He understood all the man had said; he saw the way Al had looked at Johnny as he spoke. His words did not tell Peter half as much as that glance had; they were just the framework upon which Santos hung the real reason for doing what he did.

Al smiled back at him, he could see that Peter understood, and without saying a word to each other each man was drawn closer to the other because of a common bond they had for Johnny. Al turned and left the office.

The three of them looked at each other after he had gone. Joe went over to Peter and grabbed him by the arm. "What a break!" he exclaimed.

"California," Peter said dazedly. The import was just beginning to dawn on him. "Why, that's three thousand miles away."

"Three thousand or twenty thousand," Johnny laughed, "what's the difference? We can't make it here."

"But Esther and the kids," Peter said, "I can't leave them here."

"Who said we're leaving them here?" Johnny answered. "We'll take them with us."

"That's good," Peter said, beginning to smile. Suddenly his expression turned to dismay, his face grew long and worried.

"Now what's the matter?" Johnny asked.

"I was just thinking," Peter replied, "the danger—"

Johnny was bewildered. He looked askance at Joe. "Danger? What danger?"

Peter's voice grew serious. "The Indians."

Joe looked at Johnny and they burst into laughter. The tears began to run down Joe's cheeks, he held his hands to his sides. "The Indians, he says," he managed to gasp.

Peter looked at them as if they were crazy. "What's so funny?"

They went off into another gale of laughter.

Arrangements were made for the cameras and equipment to be packed immediately. It would take almost a week for everything to be made ready for shipment.

Later that afternoon, after the excitement had subsided, Johnny went over to Sam Sharpe's office. With him he had taken the check Sharpe had sent them in the morning mail. He was going to return it and insist that Craig fulfill his share of the bargain.

Jane saw him come into the office. "If it ain't the vice-president himself!" she wisecracked. "How's the picture business?"

He stood in front of her desk. There was a hurt look in his eyes. He didn't speak.

She looked up at him. The light from the ceiling lamp shone brightly on him and for the first time she saw how he looked. She hadn't seen him since that night he had taken her for a ride in the park and she had felt hurt. But now when she saw him, saw how thin he had become, the newly formed lines etched into his face around his eyes and mouth, she was suddenly contrite. Now all the things that Sam had told her suddenly became real.

Impulsively she reached out and took his hand. Her voice was low. "I'm sorry, Johnny, I didn't want to be mean."

He held her hand. "It was my fault, Jane. I should have known better."

"It was mine as much as yours, Johnny. We just want different things. Now that we know, we can forget it."

He smiled at her. "It's amazing," she thought, "how bright and young he looks when he smiles."

"You're okay, Jane," he said.

She smiled back at him. "You too, Johnny." Her tone became businesslike. "You wanted to see Sam?"

He nodded.

"Go right in," she told him.

Sam was sitting at his desk when Johnny stuck his head inside the door. "Come in, Johnny," he cried. "Come in. I was just thinking about you."

They shook hands and Johnny took out the check. "I'm returning this," he said, placing the check on Sam's desk.

"Now, wait a minute, Johnny." Sam stood up. "You remember what I said yesterday. I don't take money for not doing the job."

"You'll do the job, Sam," Johnny said. "We're giving you a date for the picture. Craig will have to live up to his agreement now, whether he likes it or not."

"You mean you got a place to make it?" Sam asked. "But yesterday I thought you were through."

Johnny smiled at him. "That was yesterday, Sam. But this is the picture business, where yesterday doesn't count. Today we're set."

"Craig won't like this." Sam grinned. "But I'm tickled. Where you going to shoot the picture?"

"This is strictly confidential, Sam"—Johnny lowered his voice—"but we're going to California to do it."

"California!" Sam grinned happily. "Now I know Craig won't like it."

"We're leaving next week," Johnny said. "I'll see to it that you get his ticket in plenty of time for him to be at the station to go with us."

Sam picked up the check and tore it up. "He'll be there," he promised, "if I have to drag him by the heels."

The only people who were told where they were going were Borden and Pappas. No chance was taken of the news leaking out. The cast and crew of the picture were enjoined to keep their mouths shut about it.

Al Santos left for California promising them that he would try to have everything ready when they arrived. Esther arranged to close the apartment and put the furniture in storage until their return. She took the children out of school so they could be ready to leave.

Doris was excited. She read every book on California that she could lay her hands on and she was the first among them to become a Californian. She became a Californian the day after she was told they were going there.

It was two days before they were due to leave that the phone on Peter's desk began to ring. Johnny came in from the studio, where he had helped pack the last of the equipment, to answer it, for Peter wasn't around.

It was Borden. "Is Peter there?" he asked. His voice was shrill and excited.

"No," Johnny answered. "Why? What do you want him for?"

"I just learned that the combine bought up some of your notes and they're going into court this morning to get a judgment against you!"

"This morning?" Johnny yelled. If the combine got that judgment they wouldn't be able to move a bit of equipment. It was all combine-licensed. "But we're leaving Friday night!"

"Not if they get that judgment," Borden said. "You better get out tonight if you can."

Johnny hung up the phone, took out his watch, and looked at it. It was almost eleven o'clock. The cast had to be rounded up and notified of the change of plan, the equipment had to be shipped down to the train, Peter had to empty his apartment, and, last but not least, tickets had to be exchanged for use tonight instead of Friday.

And if they couldn't do it by tonight, they were sunk.

12

JOHNNY ran out into the studio looking for Joe. He wasn't there. The studio was empty—nothing but the cases, standing around ready for shipment.

He ran down to the saloon on the corner. Joe was there, one foot on the rail, a glass of beer in his hand.

Joe took one look at Johnny's face and put the beer down on the bar. "What's up?" he asked.

"The roof's falling in," Johnny answered tersely. "Come on back to the office."

Joe started to walk to the door with Johnny, then he stopped. "Wait a minute," he said. He went back to the bar and picked up his glass of beer and drained it. Then, wiping his lips, he joined Johnny.

On the way back to the studio Johnny explained what had happened.

"That does it." Joe's face was long as they entered the studio. "We're cooked now for sure."

"Not if we can get out tonight," Johnny said.

"Tonight?" Joe snorted. "You're crazy. We'll never make it."

"We gotta," Johnny insisted stubbornly.

"There may not be a train out tonight," Joe said dourly, "and if there is, we may not be able to get tickets." He sat down on a chair and stared at the floor. "We might as well throw in the towel. We can't lick the buggers, they're too big for us."

Johnny looked at him steadily. His voice was hard and flat. "You quittin' on me, Joe?"

Joe looked up at him. His gaze met Johnny's levelly. "You know better than to say that, kid. I was agin this fool ide in the first place, but when you got Peter to do it, I came along with yuh, didn't I? I spent the whole summer on my butt stickin' with yuh. But now you're tryin' to do the impossible. The chances are a million to one against our gettin' away with it. Even you must see it. Your luck's run out, Johnny, yuh pushed it just about as far as it could go."

Johnny let him finish speaking. His voice was cold as he repeated his question: "You quittin' on me, Joe?"

Joe sprang to his feet. "No," he shouted, "no, I ain't quittin' on yuh. But, so help me God, when this is over I'm goin' tuh kick your butt aroun' the block!"

Johnny smiled slowly. Some of the tenseness seeped out of him. He put his hand on Joe's shoulder. "If we get away with this, Joe," he said softly, "it'll be a pleasure to let yuh do it."

He went over to his desk and took out the tickets. He held them out to Joe. "Now hop down to the station an' see if you can change these for tonight. If there's no train to where we're going, you get tickets to any place out of the state. We can worry about getting to California from there!"

Joe took the tickets silently and started for the door. "And call me back as soon as you know," Johnny shouted after him.

He sat down at his desk and called Peter's home.

Esther answered the phone.

"Where's Peter?" Johnny asked.

She was surprised. "I don't know. Isn't he with you?"

"No, he isn't," Johnny answered.

"I can't understand it," she said. "He left this morning to go to the studio."

Johnny was silent for a moment.

"What's the matter?" she asked quickly. "Anything wrong?"

"Plenty," Johnny said. "We gotta get out of town tonight. Can you make it?"

"I'll try," she answered. "But what about Peter?"

"I'll try to find him," Johnny answered. "But if he calls you before I can locate him, have him call me."

"All right," she answered, and hung up. She didn't waste time in asking questions. If Johnny said they had to get out, there must be a reason for it.

Johnny called the express company and they agreed to send out two wagons right away. An hour later Joe called back and said there was a train going out, but there weren't any sleeper accommodations on it.

"Are there any coach tickets?" Johnny asked.

"Sure," Joe answered.

"Then what the hell are you waiting for?" Johnny yelled. "Get them. If we have to sit all the way to California we're going on that train tonight!"

"All right," Joe said. "I'll come right back to the office with them."

"No!" Johnny yelled. "Start callin' your people and make sure they're at the train. Then go home and pack our stuff. I'll see you at the train tonight."

As the last wagon pulled away from in front of the door, the phone began to ring. Johnny picked it up.

"This is Borden. Is Peter there yet?"

"No," Johnny answered.

"Then keep him away from the studio. The combine just got that judgment and they're planning to serve it on Peter this afternoon."

"How can I keep him away from here if I don't know where he is?" Johnny was frantic.

"I don't know where he is," Borden answered. "When I saw him this morning I thought he was going to the studio."

"You saw him?" Johnny shouted. "Where?"

"At *shool*," Borden replied, "the synagogue where we go every morning."

"Oh." Johnny was disappointed. He knew the place, Peter wouldn't be there all day.

"And, Johnny, I found something out," Borden said.

"What?"

"Somebody tipped off the combine that you were going out on Friday, but I couldn't find out who it was."

"The bastard," Johnny said bitterly. A phone on the other desk began to ring. "Bill, the other phone's ringing," Johnny said. "It might be Peter. I'll try to call you later."

He hung up the phone and went over to the other desk. It was Joe.

"What do yuh want?" he asked.

"I couldn't get hold of Craig," Joe said.

"Forget him," Johnny replied. "I'll call Sharpe. You go home and pack."

He called Sharpe. "Somebody tipped off the combine and we got to get out of town tonight," he told him. "Can you get Craig?"

"Don't worry, Johnny," Sam said. "I'll bring him to the train myself."

The day wore on. He couldn't sit still. Cigarette after cigarette was ground under his heel as he lit one from the butt of the other. Where the hell was Peter? He took out his watch. Four o'clock. Only three hours to train time. He prayed silently. "Peter, Peter, wherever you are, call in. Call Esther. But for God's sake call somebody and let us know where you are."

In seeming answer to his prayer the phone began to ring. He snached it up. "Peter?" he shouted into the mouthpiece.

"Isn't he there yet?" came the reply. It was Esther.

He slumped in his chair. "No," he answered.

"Everything's ready, Johnny. The storage men were here and we're ready to leave," she said.

Slowly he straightened up. "All right, then, go down to

the station. Joe will be there and I'll meet you there later."

"But, Johnny," her voice sounded perilously close to tears, "what are we going to do? We can't find him. Maybe something happened to him."

"Now stop worrying," he said calmly, trying to soothe her. "He was all right when Borden saw him in synagogue this morning."

There was a silence at her end of the phone. Her voice came through incredulously. "Willie saw him in *shool* this morning?"

"Yeanh," Johnny said. "Now, don't worry about—"

She interrupted him. "I'm not worried any more, Johnny. That's where he is. What a dumbbell I am not to think about it before. It's the tenth anniversary of his father's death and he must be saying *Kaddish* for him!"

"You sure?" Johnny shouted.

"Sure, I'm sure," she laughed happily. "That's where he is. In my excitement and nervousness I forgot all about it."

"Esther, I love you," Johnny shouted. "Now you go right down to the train and I'll get him to meet you there!"

Peter was sitting in the front row, his eyes on a prayer book, his lips moving with every word as he read it.

Johnny stopped opposite him. "Pssst," he hissed to Peter.

Peter looked up. He showed no surprise at seeing Johnny there. His eyes were clouded and they seemed far away. Suddenly they seemed to clear. "Johnny!" he said, motioning to the top of his head.

Johnny didn't understand him. "I've got to talk to you," he whispered back at Peter.

Several of the other men in the synagogue looked at Johnny; they seemed annoyed at the disturbance he was creating.

Peter picked something up from the seat next to him and held it out toward Johnny. It was a little black skull cap. He motioned to Johnny to put it on his head. "Your head is uncovered," he whispered.

Johnny took the skull cap and put it on. "Come on out," he said, "I got to talk to you."

Peter followed him to the rear of the synagogue. "What is it?" he asked.

"I've been trying to find you all day," Johnny said. "Why didn't you leave word where you were going to be?"

"Since when does a man have to make an announcement when he goes to *shool?* I don't ask when you go to church." Peter was aggrieved.

Johnny was exasperated. "I didn't ask you why you went, I only asked you why you didn't tell us. We're in a jam. We got to get out of town tonight."

"Tonight?" Peter shouted. The sound of his voice startled him; he looked around guiltily. "Tonight?" he repeated, this time whispering.

"Yes," Johnny answered. "The combine's got a judgment against you, and if they serve it, we're finished."

"My God!" Peter said, his voice rising again. "I got to tell Esther!"

"No you don't," Johnny told him, "I spoke to her before. She'll be at the train with the kids."

Peter looked at him. "And the equipment?"

"Shipped already. It left at two o'clock this afternoon."

"Then let's go back to the office," Peter said; "I got a few things to pick up." He started out into the street.

Johnny caught up with him. "You can't go up there. They probably are waiting for you with a summons!"

Peter was stubborn. "I got to go back. The shooting script is in my desk."

"To hell with it!" Johnny said. "We're going to the train!"

Esther was the first to see them coming as they walked to the gate. "Peter!" she cried. She ran forward and threw her arms around him. She was crying.

He spoke in Yiddish. His voice was brusque, but tender all at once. "What are you crying about?"

Johnny turned to Joe, who was grinning at him. "Is everybody here?" he asked.

"Everybody except Craig," Joe answered, still grinning.

Johnny looked around him. "I wonder what's holding him up."

"Johnny," a voice called.

Johnny looked up. Sam Sharpe was running toward him. Jane hurried behind him. He stopped in front of Johnny, gasping for breath; his usually ruddy face was pale.

"Where's Craig?" Johnny asked.

"He's not coming," Sharpe gasped. "Johnny, he told the combine about your plans, that's why they jumped on you."

"The son of a bitch!" Johnny burst out bitterly. A thought struck him. There was still time for the combine to get them here. "Where is he now?" he asked.

"In my office," Sharpe answered.

Johnny stared at him wildly. "He can still let them know of the change in plans. We got to get him!" He started off the platform.

Sharpe grabbed his arm. "Wait a minute, Johnny. He can't tell them."

"What do you mean?"

"When he told me what he did, I got so mad I knocked him down."

Johnny looked at the little man unbelievingly. Craig was almost twice Sharpe's size.

"I did, Johnny," Sharpe insisted. "That is—uh, I pushed him and Jane held her foot behind him and he tripped. And then we tied him up."

"With a clothesline," Jane added.

Johnny began to laugh. It must have been funny to watch. The little man and a girl tying up that overblown matinee idol.

Sharpe looked at him seriously. "Johnny, do you think we can go along with you? When he gets loose, it will be very embarrassing."

"Sure," Johnny gasped between bursts of laughter, "come along, we might need a couple of bodyguards out there."

The countryside was dark as the train sped through the night. Johnny, looking out of the window, could only see his reflection in the glass. Doris leaned against him sleepily. It was after nine o'clock.

Doris shifted against him. He turned to her and put his arm around her shoulders. "Tired, sweetheart?"

"No," she answered, her voice full of sleep.

He smiled at her. "Maybe you'll be more comfortable with your head in my lap."

She turned on the seat and stretched out. Her eyes closed almost as soon as her head touched his lap. Her lips moved.

Johnny leaned over her. "What did you say, sweetheart?"

"You'll like California, Uncle Johnny," she whispered. "It's very beautiful."

Johnny smiled because she had fallen asleep with the last word. He looked up as a shadow fell across him.

It was Peter. He looked down at them gently. "She's asleep?"

Johnny nodded.

"I didn't answer your question," Peter said.

"What question?" Johnny asked.

"Why I didn't let you know where I was going to be today," Peter replied. "I didn't remember it was the anniversary of my father's death until after I left the house this morning."

"Oh," Johnny said. "I'm sorry I asked. I was just excited at the time, I didn't mean to be rude."

"And you're calm now?" Peter smiled gently.

"Of course," Johnny answered.

"Then maybe you'll take off your *yamalke?*" His hand brushed over Johnny's head and came off with a little black skull cap.

Johnny's mouth fell open. "You mean I've worn that since we left the synagogue?"

Peter nodded.

"Why didn't you tell me?" Johnny asked.

Peter smiled again. "I liked to see it there," he said gently. "You looked like you were born to it."

A week later they were in a car going out to the Santos farm. Johnny and Peter sat up in front with the driver. The road on both sides was lined with orange trees as far as they could see. They came to a crossroads. A small sign stood there.

"What does it say?" Peter asked Johnny. He still refused to wear glasses.

"Hollywood," Johnny answered. "I guess this is where the Santos place is."

"It's just down the road a piece," the driver ventured.

Peter looked around him. "California," he said in a disgusted tone of voice.

Johnny looked at him.

Peter was muttering to himself. "No shooting script. Cost

twenty-five hundred dollars. No leading man. Cost six thousand dollars." He sniffed the air. It was filled with the scent of orange blossoms. "Phooey!" he said aloud.

Johnny began to smile.

Peter became aware that he had been overheard. He smiled in spite of himself.

"What am I supposed to make a picture with?" he asked, holding out a hand and pointing. "Oranges?"

AFTERMATH

1938

WEDNESDAY

I LOOKED at my wristwatch. It was almost five o'clock. The gray of the morning was slowly turning to gold. I turned to Doris, "Isn't it about time you tried to get some sleep, sweetheart?"

Her eyes were dark blue and shadowed. "I'm not sleepy," she answered, but the lines in her face belied her words.

"Yuh gotta get some rest, baby," I said. "You can't keep this up forever."

She looked at me. A faint shadow of a smile flickered across her face for a moment and was gone. Her voice was lightly mocking as she answered: "You tired, Johnny?"

It was an old joke of the family's. It had started a long time ago when Peter used to come into the studio at almost any hour of the day or night and used to find me there.

"Johnny never sleeps," he used to say, laughing. "He's got money in the bank."

I smiled at her. "A little," I admitted, "but you're the one that needs the rest. Things are tough enough around here without you falling flat on your face."

The smile on her face bloomed; its warmth spilled over into her eyes. "All right, Uncle Johnny," she said in a small girl's voice, "but you'll promise to come and see me tomorrow?"

I caught her to me and held her close. "Tomorrow and every day the rest of my life when this is over, if you want it."

Her voice was rich in my ear and full of promise as she answered: "I never wanted anything else, Johnny."

I kissed her. I liked the way she held my face close to hers, her hands cupping the back of my ears and extending round the back of my head. Her touch was light, yet firm with the

155

knowledge of an old passion. I liked the soft touch of her face against mine, the light smell of perfume that rose from her neck and shoulders, the crinkling soft sound that her hair made when I stroked it.

She stepped back and looked at me for a moment, then she took my hand and we walked into the hall. Silently she helped me into my topcoat and watched me put on my hat; then we walked to the door.

At the door I turned and faced her. "Now you go right upstairs and get some sleep," I said sternly.

She gave a small laugh and kissed me. "Johnny, you're sweet."

"I can be mean too," I said, still trying to keep my voice stern, but not quite succeeding, "and if you—"

"If I don't go up to bed, you'll spank me like you did once," she said with a mischievous smile.

"I never did," I protested.

"Oh yes you did," she insisted with the same smile still on her lips. She cocked her head to one side and looked at me speculatively. "I wonder if you would if you were angry enough. It might be fun, at that."

I put my hands on her shoulders and turned her away from me. I pushed her toward the stairs and gave her a light pat on the rump as I did so. "I'll beat you with a stick if you don't go right to bed," I told her.

She went halfway toward the stairs and then she turned around and looked at me.

I looked back at her silently.

At last she spoke; her voice was serious. "Never leave me, Johnny," she said.

For some reason I couldn't speak for a few seconds. My throat was all knotted up and I couldn't find my voice. Something in her voice, in its small, quiet sound, in its loneliness and patience, seemed to go deep inside me. Then the words seemed to come from me by themselves. I didn't form them in my mind, I didn't make them in my throat, I didn't even seem to say them with my lips; they just seemed to come from within me by themselves and build a bridge between us that no distance could ever break.

"Never no more, sweetheart."

Not an expression on her face seemed to change, but a glow came from within her, and its warmth reached out and held me close across the room. For a moment she stood there; then she turned and started up the stairs.

I watched her go. Her step was light and easy and she moved with the quiet grace of a dancer. At the top of the stairs she looked down and blew a kiss to me.

I waved to her and she went down the hall and out of sight. I turned and let myself out the front door.

The sky was bright and the air was cool. The dew on the flowers sparkled in the slanting rays of the early morning sun. Suddenly I wasn't tired. My weariness had left me with the first deep breath of the morning air. I looked at my watch. It was a few minutes after five, too late to go home to sleep.

I picked up a cab two blocks from the house. "To Magnum Studios," I told the driver as I settled back against the cushions and lit up a cigarette.

The studio was only fifteen minutes from Peter's home. I paid the driver and walked toward the gate. It was locked. I pressed the bell button on the right wall and waited for the watchman to come.

I could see the light flicker as a shadow moved in front of it in the gateman's cabin a few feet beyond the gate. The door opened and he came out toward me.

He saw me through the gate and recognized me. Almost imperceptibly his step quickened until he was almost running. He opened the gate. "Mr. Edge," he said, "I didn't expect to see you back so soon."

"It's a surprise visit," I said. "I didn't expect to be back myself."

He closed the gate behind me. "Anything I can do, Mr. Edge?"

"No, thanks," I said, "I'm going up to my office."

I walked down the long street to the administration building. The studio was quiet and I could hear the sound of my footsteps echoing hollowly behind me as I walked. The chippies woke up as I walked past them and began to chirp in the trees. They resented anyone coming in early. I smiled to myself, remembering the sound from the long years behind me. They always chirped when I would get to the studio early.

The watchman at the administration building was waiting for me as I reached it. He stood there in the doorway, sleep still showing in his eyes. The gateman must have called and told him I was on the way up. "Good morning, Mr. Edge," he said.

"Good morning," I replied, walking through the door.

He hurried down the hall in front of me and opened the door of my office with his key. "Is there anything I can get you, Mr. Edge?" he asked—"some coffee or something?"

"No, thanks," I replied. I sniffed the air. It was dull and dead in the office.

He saw my gesture and rushed past me to the windows and opened them. "Some fresh air in here won't hurt, sir," he said.

I smiled and thanked him and he left. He seemed almost to back out the door as he shut it carefully behind him. I took off my topcoat and hat and put them in the little closet. I felt like a drink, it had been a long night.

I walked through the side door in my office. Between my office and Gordon's was a little kitchen. A refrigerator, pantry, and small electric stove were in there. A coffee pot stood on the stove. I touched it; it was still warm. The watchman must have made himself some coffee, I thought. I opened the refrigerator and took out a small bottle of ginger ale and carried it back to my office.

I took a bottle of bourbon out of my desk and a glass from the small table behind it. I put two fingers of liquor in the glass and then poured ginger ale over it until the glass was almost half full. I tasted it. It was just right. I drank almost half of it and then walked over to the window and looked out.

The sky was brighter now and I could see almost to the back lot. The writers' building was almost directly behind ours, and the other executive buildings fanned out to the right and left of it, making a sort of crescent around the administration building. Behind the writers' building was Sound stage number one.

Sound stage number one. I smiled to myself as I thought of it. It was a new building, all white and modern and fire-proof. The first stage that Peter and I had opened was more of a barn than a building. It was a rambling structure with four walls and no ceiling so the sun could shine through. There was a big tarpaulin top that we used to stretch over it at the first sign of rain. I remembered how we used to have a man always sitting on a little platform near the top of the building, scanning the skies.

The rain-watcher we used to call him. In case rain threatened he would yell down and the tarpaulin would be rigged in a hurry. We used to leave it off almost until the last possible minute because the mercury vapor lamps we used for indoor lighting used to cost so much money.

Joe Turner had thought of it. When we had figured out how expensive the lamps were to use, he suggested: "Why don't we put a circus top on the building? Then when it rains we can just cover it up."

Joe had been dead almost twenty years now, but there were some things about him that were as fresh and vivid in my mind as if I had seen him each day of those two decades. I could still remember his booming laugh as he told the story of how we got the land for the studio for nothing. It was his favorite story. I smiled to myself as I looked across the forty acres that made up the studio today. It hadn't cost us a cent of our own money.

It was after I had come back to New York with the first print of *The Bandit*. Peter couldn't come to New York as the judgment against him that was held by the combine was still unsettled. The first showing was held at the screening rooms of Bill Borden's studios. The independents were growing a little braver as Fox's suit against the combine seemed more certain of success each day.

The screening room was crowded. All the important states' rights distributors were there in addition to an already large list of our creditors. I don't know who was more enthusiastic about the picture, the distributors who were clamoring to buy it or our creditors, who were beginning to entertain visions of getting their money back and maybe a little profit too.

I don't think any of us really expected in our wildest dreams the events that followed. Within two hours after I had screened the picture I had collected almost forty thousand dollars in deposits from the distributors against the showing of the picture. Borden, standing at my side as each distributor pressed me to accept his check for his territory, kept saying over and over to himself: "I don't believe it, I don't believe it."

By midnight I was talking to Peter on the phone. I was so

excited I stuttered. "We got forty thousand dollars, Peter," I shouted into the mouthpiece.

His voice was thin and crackly as it came through the receiver. "What did you say, Johnny?" he asked. "It sounded like forty thousand dollars."

"That's right," I shouted, "forty thousand dollars! They loved the picture!"

There was a silence at the other end of the phone, then his voice came through doubtfully: "Where are you, Johnny?"

"At Borden's studio," I answered.

"Is Willie there?" he asked.

"He's standing right next to me," I said.

"Let me talk to him," Peter said.

I handed the phone over to Borden.

"Hello, Peter," Borden said into the mouthpiece, "*mazeltov!*"

I could hear Peter's voice crackling at the other end of the phone, but I couldn't make out what he was saying. Borden turned and looked at me, a half smile on his lips.

He waited until Peter had finished talking. His smile grew broader as he turned back to the phone. "No," he said, "Johnny hasn't had a drink all night. He's as sober as I am." There was a few seconds' silence while Peter spoke, then Borden spoke again: "Yeah, forty thousand dollars. I seen the checks with my own eyes!"

Peter's voice crackled again and Borden handed the phone back to me. "Didn't you believe me?" I asked.

"Believe you?" Peter's voice was full and happy. "My boy, my own ears I didn't believe. Forty thousand dollars!"

"I'll transfer the money to you in the morning," I said.

"No," he replied. "Transfer half of it to me so I could pay off Al the twenty thousand dollars I owe him. The other half you use to pay off our notes in New York."

"But, Peter, that will leave us broke again. We owe almost twenty here and we'll need money to make the next picture."

"If I pay off the money I owe for this picture," he said, "I can sleep easy for one night. Tomorrow I will worry about getting money for the next one."

"But what about money for a studio? We can't keep working on a farm all the time. Pay off half now; they'll be glad to wait for the rest of it. This picture looks like it will gross a quarter of a million dollars and they know it."

"If it grosses that much we can afford to pay them now," Peter said.

"But we'll have to wait almost a year for the money," I protested. Under the states' rights method of distribution we were entitled to get our money six months after the release of the picture by the distributor. "What will we do until then? Sit around on our behinds and wait? We can't afford to wait now!"

Peter's voice was firm. "Pay the money like I said. One good night's sleep I'm getting out of this!"

I knew I was licked. When that stubborn tone crept into Peter's voice, standing on my head wouldn't change his mind. "All right, Peter."

His voice lightened. "They liked the picture, hah?"

"They were crazy about it," I told him, "especially that gun fight where the sheriff and the bandit shoot it out in the parlor of the girl's house." I knew that would please him, it was his idea. In the play the shooting took place in a big saloon, but we didn't have the money to build a set like that, so Peter switched to the girl's parlor.

He laughed. "I told you it was more dramatic that way, didn't I?"

"You were right, Peter," I said, smiling at the proud manner in which he spoke.

He chuckled again. "They didn't mind sitting through the whole picture?"

"They didn't want it to finish, they liked it so much. They applauded when it was over. You should have seen them, Peter, they stood up and applauded."

I heard him turn from the phone and say something to someone. I couldn't make out what he said. His voice came over the phone again: "I was just telling Esther that I was right about seven reels not being too long."

I laughed, remembering what he had said once before— that six reels were too much for a person to sit through.

He interrupted my laugh. "Esther just asked me who's paying for this phone call."

I looked at Borden and smiled. "We are, of course. You don't think I would make a call like this on somebody else's phone and not pay for it, do you?"

There was a second of stunned silence at the other end of the wire. When his voice came through, it sounded weak.

"Almost twenty minutes already we been talking. A hundred-dollar phone call." His voice grew stronger. "Good-by, Johnny."

"But, Peter—" I started to say, when I heard the click of the phone being hung up in the receiver. I stared at it a moment in a sort of surprise and hung up my phone.

I looked over at Borden and smiled. He shrugged his shoulders and together we walked out of his office into the general office. There was still a crowd of men gathered in there talking. The air was blue with smoke and conversation. Among them were the leading independents of the day.

One of them was saying: "I guess that proves it once and for all. The day of the two-reeler is over; from now on we have to think in terms of big pictures."

"What you say, Sam?" another of them replied. "Might be true, but where are we going to make them? In New York here the outdoor season is only three months at the most. The best we could make is five pictures in that time. What'll we do the rest of the year? Lay off?"

The first man thought for a minute before he answered: "We'll have to go some place where there is a longer season, then."

The second man spoke glumly; his manner didn't express much hope. "But where? We all ain't got friends like Kessler has. We can't all make pictures in California."

Suddenly everything clicked for me. I knew all the answers. "Why not, gentlemen?" I said, stepping into the middle of the group. "Why can't you all make pictures in California?"

I looked around at them. The expressions on their faces ranged from open amazement to restrained curiosity.

"What do you mean?" one of them asked.

I looked at them a moment before I answered. I wanted them to be properly impressed with what I was about to tell them. I lowered my voice to a confidential tone.

"Magnum has not been without foresight enough, gentlemen, to realize the effect *The Bandit* would have on the future of the picture business. And Peter Kessler has not been without gratitude to his many friends among you for standing by him when the outlook was darkest. And so, gentlemen"—I lowered my voice still more and they pressed closer to hear me—"after just speaking to Kessler over the phone to California, he has informed me that he has decided to offer you the same opportunity that he himself now enjoys. To make pictures in California! Think of it, gentlemen, think of it!" I smiled to myself; this was the old carny pitch. "An opportunity to make pictures not only thirteen weeks a year, but fifty-two! An opportunity to make pictures where the sun always shines, where there's room to make any kind of a picture you want!

"Magnum has under option almost a thousand acres of land in Hollywood. Enough land to build a hundred studios. When Lasky, Goldwyn, and Laemmle came out there, Peter got the brilliant idea that all you independents would come out too and make Hollywood the motion-picture capital of the world! And so he has authorized me to offer you the following deal. In return for your many past kindnesses and favors to him, he will transfer to you his option on as many acres and as much land as you may require for the same price that he has paid for those options! One hundred dollars an acre!

"Of course he does not expect you gentlemen to buy a pig in a poke. He will give you the option for as many acres as you wish now, subject to your approval of the site when you see it. The opportunity to select the site will be given in the same order as the option is made. That is, the first person to take an option will have the first choice of the site. If any man is not satisfied, his option money will be refunded without protest."

Borden was as amazed as any of them. "You didn't say anything about this to me before," he said.

"I'm sorry, Bill," I said, turning to him. "I was under orders from Peter not to say anything until he gave the okay. He just gave me the okay inside."

"But what about our studios here?" Bill said. "We've got a lot of money tied up in them."

"You can still use them for shorts and other subjects," I answered, "but for big pictures and big money you will have to come to Hollywood. How big is your studio here? About three blocks square. Can you drive a hundred head of cattle through here as we did in *The Bandit*? Can you run a group of men on horses and photograph them here as we did in *The Bandit*? The answer is obvious. If you stay here, you're limited. Limited by space, limited by time, and limited by opportunity."

I stopped and looked around me. Their faces showed that they were impressed. I knew I had them. There was only one hitch. If any of them asked me where Peter had got the money necessary to take all these options, I was sunk. But I didn't have to worry, because Borden was the first to sucker for it.

He took out his fountain pen and began writing a check. "I want fifty acres," he said.

In an hour I had sold options on land we didn't have amounting to sixty thousand dollars. The others, seeing Borden leap to the bait, fell all over themselves trying to get on the hook. It was easier than getting the yokels to buy a ticket to see Salome and her Dance of the Seven Veils.

At three o'clock in the morning I had Peter on the phone again, this time from my hotel, where no one could hear me.

He answered the phone. I could hear the sound of other voices talking excitedly in the room behind him. "Hello," he said.

"Peter, this is Johnny."

His voice grew excited. "I thought I told you you shouldn't call me. It's too expensive."

"Damn the expense," I said, "I had to call you. I just sold sixty thousand dollars' worth of land out there and you have to buy some right away!"

"My God," he shouted, his voice rising to a shrill scream, "have you gone crazy? You want us all to go to jail?"

"Calm down," I said as quietly as I could. "I had to do it. The suckers were falling all over themselves to get out to California. It's better that we make some dough out of it than the land sharks. What can we get an acre of land out there for?"

"How should I know?" he asked, his voice still shaking.

"Is Al there?" I asked. "If he is, ask him."

I heard Peter turn away from the phone. A few seconds later his voice came on again. "Al says about twenty-five dollars an acre."

I could feel the blood running into my face. I let out a sigh. I had guessed right. "Buy a thousand acres," I told him. "That'll cost us about twenty-five thousand dollars. I just sold six hundred acres at a hundred bucks apiece and we'll net thirty-five thousand on the works and have enough dough left over to build a studio with."

There was a moment of silence at the other end of the wire, then Peter's voice came on again. There was a peculiar tone in it that I didn't quite recognize; if I hadn't known him better, I would have called it awe.

"Johnny," he said slowly, "you're a *gonif*. But a smart one."

I turned back from the window, sat down behind my desk, and finished my drink. That was a long time ago, but somehow it seemed like only yesterday. Hollywood was built on a swindle and it never changed. It lived on a swindle today, only the swindlers of yesterday were beginning to meet their masters. The swindlers of today were taking them—not as we had in the old days, out of necessity, but because of greed. Today's swindlers not only practiced on one another, but the whole world was their feeding-place.

My eyes were tired. The lids felt hot and heavy. I thought I would shut them for a little while to rest them.

The dull sound of voices kept tugging at my ears. I turned my head to shut them out, but they persisted. I sat back in my chair and opened my eyes and rubbed them. My body ached, my back was stiff from the uncomfortable position in which I had fallen asleep. I stretched and looked around the office. My gaze fell on the clock on the desk and I snapped up with a start. It was three thirty in the afternoon. I had been sleeping almost all day.

I got out of my chair and went into the little room next to my office. I turned on the cold water and splashed it over my face. Its chill woke me up thoroughly. I took a towel from the rack and dried my face in it. I looked in the mirror. I needed a shave.

I turned and started out of the little room to go to the barber shop when Gordon's voice came through the wall.

"I'm sorry, Larry," it was saying, "but I don't see how I can agree to that. After all, my agreement with Johnny was that I was in charge of all production. Dividing it up in the manner you suggest will only lead to duplication of work and further unnecessary confusion."

That put an end to my shave. Something was going on in Gordon's office that I should know about. I put my hand on the door and opened it. Gordon was seated behind his desk, his face flushed and angry. Opposite him Ronsen and Dave Roth were seated. Ronsen's face was as calm and imperturbable as usual, but Dave looked like the cat that had just got away with the canary.

I stepped into the room. Their faces turned toward me with varying expressions written on them. Gordon's showed relief, Rosen's annoyance, Roth's fear. I smiled. "What's the matter with you guys?" I asked. "Can't you let a feller sleep?"

They didn't answer. I walked over to Gordon and held out my hand. "Hi ya, boy, good to see you."

He played along with me. No sign of our having met last night appeared in his voice. He took my hand. "What are you doing out here?" he asked. "I thought you were still in New York."

"I got here last night," I answered. "I came out to see Peter." I turned to Ronsen. "I didn't expect you out here, Larry."

He looked at me searchingly a minute. If he was trying to find out what I knew, he didn't succeed. My face was as bland as his. "Something turned up after you left, and as you weren't there, I thought I'd fly out here and handle it for you."

I let interest show on my face. "Yeah? What was it?"

"We got a call from Stanley Farber," he replied. I could see that even his calm had been shaken by my unexpected appearance; he seemed to fumble a little for words. "He made us the proposition that we put Dave here in charge of our top pictures. In return for that he would see to it that we played off in all the Westco theaters and in addition loan us a million dollars."

For the first time since I walked into the office I looked at Dave Roth. But I spoke to Ronsen. "I know Stanley," I said. "He must want something else from us for a million bucks besides putting his protégé in charge of production."

I didn't take my eyes off Dave's face while Ronsen answered: "Well, naturally we'd have to give him stock as security. You don't expect anybody to advance us that much money without some sort of security."

I nodded my head slowly. Dave's face had grown paler under my gaze. Ronsen's voice cut in eagerly; he couldn't keep the tension from showing in it. "You mean you think it's a good idea?" he asked.

Slowly I turned my head back to look at him. His eyes were burning brightly and fiercely behind his bifocals. More than ever he reminded me of a big, moon-faced tiger waiting to pounce on its prey. "I didn't say I thought it was a good idea," I said, my eyes meeting his. "But I'll think about it. A million bucks is a lot of cabbage."

Ronsen was pressing now; I could see he wanted me to agree with him. "That's it, Johnny," he said eagerly, "Farber wants an immediate answer. His offer isn't good forever."

"But once we accept it, we're hooked," I said dryly. "I know Stanley, as I said, and it won't be anything we can get out of easily if it doesn't work out. Dave here is a bright boy. I know he can run theaters. But he never made a picture in his life and, with all my respect for him, what do we do if he turns out bad? I've seen it happen to others; it could happen to him."

I turned to Roth. His face had gone white. I smiled at him reassuringly. "No offense meant, kid," I said easily, "but this is a practical business and it takes a little experience to find out just how a thing is going to work out before you do it. I know Larry means well, but I'll have to think about it first. Supposing we talk some more about it tomorrow."

With those words I succeeded in impressing Ronsen with my disregard for his judgment, Dave with my opinion of his inexperience, and closed the discussion.

Out of the corner of my eyes I could see the white anger on Larry's face, but by the time I turned to him he had it under control. I smiled at him. "If you have a few minutes, Larry," I said, "I'd like to talk to you after I get a shave."

His strangely deep voice was back to normal. "Sure thing, Johnny," he said. "Give me a buzz when you get back."

I walked to the door. At the door I turned and looked back at them. They were all facing me now. Gordon, who sat behind the others, gave me the wink. I smiled at them. "See you later," I said, shutting the door behind me.

Gordon was waiting for me when I got back from the barber. I felt good. It's wonderful what a shave and a hot towel can do for you. I grinned at him.

"What'sa matter, boy?" I said. "You don't look so good."

He let out a string of curses.

I smiled at him easily. "I gather you don't think much of our eminent chairman of the board."

Gordon's face turned red. "Why in hell can't he confine himself to presiding over the lousy board meetings and keep his Goddam long nose out of the studio?" he roared. "He's only screwing up the works."

I walked over to my chair and sat down behind the desk. I looked at him. "Now, take it easy, boy." I reached for a cigarette and lit it slowly. "You gotta remember that he don't know nothin' about the picture business. You know what he is. A guy with dough who got greedy when he saw there was a fast buck to be made in pictures. When he found out that the racket wasn't all peaches and cream like he thought, he got a little nervous and now he's scratchin' around looking for something that will either guarantee his dough back or give him an out."

When he saw how calmly I was sitting there, he simmered down a little. He watched me closely for a moment. "You got an angle?"

"Sure." I smiled reassuringly. "I got an angle. I'm gonna sit tight and let him beat his brains out. When he gets tired of that he'll come back to papa."

He looked skeptical. "He's a stubborn bastard," he said. "What if he insists on giving Farber an in?"

I didn't answer him for a second. If Ronsen insisted on that, I couldn't stop him and then I was through. Maybe it would be a good thing. I'd spent thirty years here and I had enough dough not to worry no matter what happened. Maybe it would be nice just to sit back and forget about everything. But it wasn't as easy as that. A good piece of my life had gone into this and I couldn't let it go so easy.

"He won't," I finally answered, more confidently than I felt. "When I get through with him, he'll be afraid to take Farber in if he was offered the United States mint."

He walked to the door. "I hope you know what you're doing," he said as he went out.

I looked after him. "That makes two of us," I thought.

The phone rang and I picked it up. It was Doris.

"Where were you?" she asked. "I called all over and couldn't get you."

"I fell asleep in the office," I answered ruefully. "I came

here after I left you and nobody knew I was in." I changed the subject. "How's Peter doing?"

"The doctor just left. He's sleeping normally now. The doctor thinks he's improving."

"Good," I said. "And Esther?"

"She's right next to me," Doris replied. "She wants to talk to you."

"Put her on."

I heard the receiver change hands, then Esther's voice came on. For a moment I was shocked, it had changed so much. The last time I had heard it, it was young and firm, but now it sounded old and shaken. As if suddenly she had found herself in a room filled with strange people and wasn't at all sure of her reception.

"Johnny?" It was more a question than anything else.

My voice softened. "Yes," I answered.

For a moment she was still, I could hear her breathing; then in the same strangely hesitant voice: "I'm glad you came. It means a lot to me, it will mean more to him when he learns it."

Something was wrong inside me. I wanted to cry out: "This is me, Johnny! We've got thirty years together behind us. I'm not a stranger, you don't have to be afraid to talk to me!" But I couldn't say that, I could hardly manage to say what I did. "I had to come," I answered simply. "You two mean an awful lot to me." I hesitated a little. "I'm terribly sorry about Mark."

It was her old voice that answered me now as if suddenly across the wire she recognized the someone she knew. And yet, deep within her, a feeling of pain and resignation and acceptance came and somehow spilled into her voice. It had the sound of a people that had long known the sorrows of living. "It's God's will, Johnny, there's nothing we can do now. We can only hope that Peter—" She didn't finish her sentence, her voice broke. Across the wire came the silent sound of her crying for her son.

"Esther," I said sharply, trying to bring her back.

I could almost see her fighting for control of herself— fighting to hold back the tears that were so ready to flow, the tears to which she was entitled. At last she answered: "Yes, Johnny."

"You have no time for tears," I said, feeling like a fool.

Who was I to tell her when to cry? It was her son. "You've got to get Peter well first."

"Yes," she said heavily, "I must get him well again so he can say the *Kaddish* for his son. So we can sit *shiveh* together."

Shiveh was the Hebrew ritual of mourning. You covered all the mirrors and pictures in the house and sat on the floor or on boxes for a week after the death of a loved one.

"No, Esther, no," I said gently. "Not so that you can sit *shiveh*, but that you may live together."

Her voice was docile and meek when she answered. "Yes, Johnny." It was almost as if she were talking to herself. "We must continue to live."

"That's better," I said. "That's more like the girl I used to know."

"Is it, Johnny?" she asked quietly. "Until this happened, I might have been the girl you knew, but I'm an old woman now. Nothing ever really changed me before, but this did and I'm afraid."

"It will pass," I said, "and then things will seem the same in time."

"Things will never be the same," she said with a quiet sort of finality.

We spoke a few more words and then hung up. I sat back in my chair and lit another cigarette. My first cigarette had burned itself out, forgotten, in the ashtray.

I don't know how long I sat there, staring at the phone. I remembered Mark when he was a kid. It's funny how the things you don't like about a person are forgotten when they're gone. I had never liked Mark the man, so I thought about him when he was a kid. He used to like me to swing him in the air and give him rides on my shoulders. I could still hear his little voice yelling in glee as I tossed him up. I could almost feel his fingers digging into my hair and pulling it as he rode upon my shoulders.

My leg began to ache. My leg. I always thought of it as my leg, but it was only a stump. The rest of it had been in France somewhere for the last twenty years. I could feel the pain shooting down my thigh. The stump was sore. I hadn't had the prosthetic off except for a few minutes in the past three days.

I loosened my trousers. Then I leaned back, drew in my

belly and reached in and unfastened the strap around my waist that held the artificial leg in place. Through the trouser leg I loosened the other strap that tied around my thigh, and the leg came loose. It thumped on the floor.

I began to massage the stump with the even circular motion I had learned so many years ago. I could feel the blood begin to circulate in it and the ache ease away. I continued the massage.

The door opened and Ronsen came in. He saw me sitting at the desk and walked over to me. His step was springy, his frame big and strong. His eyes were bright and piercing behind his glasses. He stopped in front of my desk and looked down at me.

"Johnny," he said in that strangely sure voice, "about that Farber matter. Couldn't we . . ."

I stared up at him. For some reason I couldn't focus my mind on what he was saying. My hands, still massaging my stump automatically, began to tremble.

Damn him! Why couldn't he wait until I called him?

I began to agree with him almost before the words were out of his mouth, before I knew what he was saying. Anything, anything to get him out of the office. Not to have to look at him standing there, so calm, so strong, so easy. Not to feel that insatiable, ruthless surge of power that flowed out of him.

His eyes first narrowed with surprise at my quick agreement. He turned and left the office as if he were in a hurry before I could change my mind.

I stared after his straight back as the door shut behind it. With trembling fingers I tried clumsily to tighten the strap around my thigh. I couldn't get it to set right. I began to curse silently as I wrestled with it.

I felt so damn helpless without my leg on.

THIRTY YEARS

1917

1

JOHNNY came out of the projection room, his eyes blinking at the strong light in the corridor. He stopped and lighted a cigarette.

A man came up to him. "Okay to print it, Johnny?"

Johnny threw his match into a sandbox. "Sure, Irving. Go ahead."

The man smiled. He was pleased. "We got some good shots of Wilson as he took the oath, didn't we?"

Johnny smiled back at him. "Damn good shots, Irving." He started to walk down the hall, the man walking with him. "Now get it into the theaters and we'll beat every newsreel in the business."

Wilson had taken the oath of office for the second term of his Presidency just that morning, less than three hours ago, and Johnny had hired an airplane to bring the negative to New York instead of waiting for a train. The way he figured it, he was at least six hours ahead of any of the other companies. Those six hours meant he would be in the Broadway theaters tonight instead of tomorrow. It was a scoop in the full sense of the word.

Irving Bannon was the editor of the newsreel. He was a short, stocky man with thick black hair who had been a cameraman before Johnny recommended him for this job. What Johnny had liked about him was that he got the picture, he did not ask for elaborate setups and preparation. All he needed was enough light to see by; that was enough for him to get the picture. He was a bustling little man, full of drive, and just the type needed for the job. Johnny was pleased with him.

He scurried along with Johnny, his short little legs taking almost two steps for every one of Johnny's. "I got those war clips from England, Johnny," he said, panting a little from the effort of keeping step with Johnny's long strides. "D'ya want to look at 'em today?"

Johnny stopped in front of his office. "Not today, Irving, I'm jammed up. Make it tomorrow morning."

"Okay, Johnny." The little man scurried off down the hall.

Johnny looked after him and smiled. The little man had it. No sooner was one reel out of the way than he was already working on the next. You had to hand it to him. It was to his credit that Magnum Newsreel was considered the best in the business. He went into the office.

Jane greeted him with a smile. "How was the reel, Johnny?"

He grinned at her. "Good," he said. "Very good. Irving did a hell of a job." He walked over to his desk and sat down. "Have you got that call in for Peter?"

She nodded and got up from her desk. She took several papers from it and put them in front of Johnny. "You'll have to look over these," she said, separating them into two neat stacks in front of him. "And these you'll have to sign."

He looked up at her, his eyes smiling. "Anything else, boss?"

She went back to her desk and looked at her memorandum pad. "Yes," she answered seriously, "George Pappas is coming in at twelve and you're taking Doris to lunch at one o'clock."

He looked at his watch. "Golly," he exclaimed, "it's almost twelve now. I better get this stuff out of the way before George comes." He looked over at her. "You're a slave-driver, Janey."

She made a *moue* at him. "Someone around here has to be," she said with a shake of her head. "Otherwise you'd never get anything done."

Johnny looked down at the papers on his desk. They were the usual contracts with the states' rights distributors, a part of the work that he detested. They were routine and annoying. Janey was right. If it were left to him, he would never look at them. With a sigh he took his pen and began to sign them.

The last five years had filled out his frame. He was still thin, but the lean, hungry look had gone from his face. Magnum had done well. They had a studio in California.

Peter stayed out there and took charge of production. Joe was with Peter. Peter determined the policy and Joe executed it. They worked well together. Magnum's pictures showed the results of that teamwork; they were among the best in the industry.

Johnny was in charge of the New York office. He had been right in predicting that the major portion of production would shift to the coast. He had been right too in his surmise that the distribution center would remain in New York and that the production of shorts would for the most part be carried on there. The unexpected victory of William Fox's suit against the combine, forcing them to give film to the independents back in 1912, had given impetus to the change. Since that time several other victories had been won. Now the fate of the combine was in the hands of the United States federal courts, and all indications were that the court would order the dissolution of the combine.

When they had learned of the initial Fox victory, Johnny persuaded Peter to let him go back to New York and reopen the studios there. Jane had been working as a script girl with Joe and he asked her if she would like to come back to New York with him. She had accepted. Sam Sharpe had joined them as casting director. He had remained in that job until the fall of last year, then he went back into business as an agent.

"There's a lot of talent out here," he said, explaining his motives to Peter, "and nobody to represent 'em. Besides, I liked the business and I haven't been happy since I left it."

Peter could understand his viewpoint. "All right Sam," he said. "What you want to do is okay with me. And for a start I'll speak to all my people here and see that you represent them."

Sam Sharpe smiled. "I already do," he said. "I got 'em all signed up already."

"That's wonderful," Peter said, congratulating him.

When they had finished shaking hands, Sam sat down in the easy chair in Peter's office.

"When do you plan to go to work?" Peter asked him.

"Right now," Sam answered. "About that Cooper contract. I think the gal ought to get more money. After all, her last picture grossed a young fortune."

Peter's mouth hung open. "Thieves have been feasting at my table," he said, beginning to smile.

Early in 1912 *The Bandit* opened on Broadway. It was the first of the big premieres in the business. Admissions were set at one dollar a ticket. They expected to do good business, but even Johnny couldn't foresee what would happen.

By noon of that day, two hours before the theater was to open, a line of people had formed in front of the boxoffice that went clear down the block. Traffic on the sidewalk was blocked and people in order to pass had to walk in the gutters. Gradually the street became more crowded and confused. Someone looking out of an office window had called the police and told them there was a riot taking place. Out came the police in full force, ready to let fly with nightsticks.

The manager of the theater tore his hair and ran out to talk to the police. He spoke to a grizzled captain and explained to him that the people were waiting to see a moving picture.

The captain, a red-faced, gray-haired man, took off his cap and scratched his head. "Well, I'll be damned," he said in a fine Irish brogue. "To think that Bill Casey would see the day people started a riot to get into a movie." He turned and looked at the crowd of people and then back to the manager. "Well, they can't stay on the street and block traffic like that. You'll have to get them off."

The theater manager turned to Johnny in despair. "What'll I do? The picture isn't starting until two o'clock."

Johnny looked at him and smiled. "Open up now and let them in," he said.

The manager was bewildered. "If I let them in now, what will I do about the two-o'clock show?"

"If you don't get 'em off the street," the captain told him, "there won't be a two-o'clock show. I got orders to break 'em up."

The manager wrung his hands in despair.

"Tell you what," Johnny said, coming to a quick decision. "Let them in now and at two o'clock start the show over again." He began to smile. "Keep running the picture until they stop coming."

"But they'll get mixed up if I let them in in the middle of the picture!" the manager protested.

"They can always stay until they come around to the part they came in on," Johnny told him. "We do it with shorts, don't we?"

The manager turned to the police captain and looked appealingly at him. The captain shook his head. Slowly the manager turned and went to the boxoffice. He tapped his hand on the closed window. The girl inside opened the glass.

He turned once more in mute appeal to the captain. There was no reply. He turned back to the girl. "Start selling your tickets," he said unhappily.

The people at the head of the line heard him. They surged against the two policemen who stood there and pushed them out of the way. They poured up to the boxoffice.

The manager struggled through the mob and over to Johnny. Johnny took one look at him and began to laugh. Buttons were torn from his jacket, the flower hung askew from his lapel, one side of his wing collar had been torn away, and his tie hung over his shoulder.

The manager stared at Johnny. "Who ever heard of such a thing?" he asked in a shocked, proper voice. "Continuous performances? You'd think this was a merry-go-round."

And it was. Magnum had grabbed the brass ring.

It was only the beginning. Other companies and other pictures followed. Later that year Adolph Zukor, a New York theater operator, brought the long-heralded *Queen Elizabeth* to New York and then formed his Famous Players Film Company to make longer features.

In 1913 it was *Quo Vadis?* followed in rapid succession by Carl Laemmle's Universal Company's *Traffic in Souls* and then by Jesse Lasky and Cecil B. DeMille with *The Squaw Man*, which starred Dustin Farnum. And every year after that there were more. The first big theater devoted exclusively to motion pictures, the New York Strand, was opened in 1914. That same year saw Mack Sennett's production of *Tillie's Punctured Romance*, starring Charlie Chaplin and Marie Dressler. The next year brought Griffith's *Birth of a Nation* and Theda Bara in William Fox's *A Fool There Was*.

Names like Paramount Pictures, Metro Pictures, Famous Players, Vitagraph, were beginning to be bruited around the trade. The public was beginning to recognize players such as Mary Pickford, Charlie Chaplin, Clara Kimball Young, Douglas Fairbanks, and Theda Bara. The newspapers woke up quickly to the news value in those names. These actors and actresses made news. Reporters were assigned to chronicle daily every action, every statement they made.

The public had taken motion pictures to its heart, and the industry was growing up. It was not without its faults, however. There were long wars within it. One producer would fight with another. Competition for star names was fierce. Stars were signed by one company at a fabulous sum, only to find that the next day they could go to another company for an even more fantastic figure. Contracts were made and broken every day. But the industry continued to grow.

As Johnny said smilingly to Peter one day, half in jest, half in earnest: "For the first time there is truly a theater for the people. They can call moving pictures their very own. They made it."

And the public backed him up, with long lines that stretched in front of the movie theaters' boxoffices across the United States.

2

JOHNNY pushed the papers away from him and looked at his watch. It was almost noon. He looked over at Jane. "Check on that call to Peter," he said. "I gotta talk to him before George comes in."

Jane picked up the phone on her desk and Johnny got up and stretched. He walked over to the window and looked out. It was raining slowly. He stood there at the window thinking.

George Pappas had done well in the last few years. There were nine theaters that carried his name and he was planning to add more. He had come to Johnny with a proposition that they form a partnership to buy up ten theaters in New York City. He would do it himself, he explained in his gentle, halting manner, only he didn't have enough money to swing it. There was this man who was sick and was almost ready to sell out. They were ten good houses spread around the city. None on Broadway, but in good locations throughout the various boroughs, and it would take a quarter of a million dollars to swing it. George would put up half if Magnum would put up the other half. They would be equal partners and George would run them.

Johnny had thought it over carefully and decided to recommend it to Peter. Borden, Fox, and Zukor owned theaters, and Johnny could see how profitably they played their own product in them. They would give their own pictures the preferred playing times, the long week-end dates; and of course they paid themselves the top prices. It worked very profitably for them, and Johnny thought it would work as well for Magnum.

Jane's voice interrupted his thoughts. "Peter will be on in a few minutes."

He turned back to his desk and sat down to wait. He hoped Peter would not run true to form this time and give him an argument on it. He smiled to himself, remembering how Peter had fought with him six years ago when he had wanted him to go into bigger pictures. But he had been right then and he felt he was right now. Peter, however, liked to argue.

Peter didn't call it arguing, though; he said he was talking a thing out. Johnny remembered some of the things Peter had talked out with Joe. Some of the ideas for ;ictures that Joe wanted to make and Peter didn't. To an outsider their discussion sounded as if the two men were almost ready to come to blows. Then suddenly there would come a silence. They would look at each other sheepishly, a little embarrassed by the unexpected heat of their argument, and then one or the other would give in. It didn't matter which one, for when the picture was made they would be loud in their praise of each other. Each would protest that the other played the most important part in the making of the picture. But the results were good and Magnum's pictures were considered among the best in the industry.

He shrugged his shoulders philosophically. Well, if Peter balked, he thought, he was ready for him. He had accumulated quite a few statistics on the profits there were to be made from the marriage of production and exhibition.

"He's on the phone now, Johnny." Jane's voice was a little

excited. The wonder of these daily and sometimes twice daily coast-to-coast calls had never ceased for her.

Johnny reached for the phone. "Let him argue—I'm ready for him," he thought. He placed the receiver against his ear and leaned back in the chair. "Hello, Peter," he said.

"Hello, Johnny," came the reply. Peter's voice was thin across the wire. "How are you?"

"Fine," he answered. "And you?"

"Good," Peter said. His voice seemed to carry a little better over the phone now. It was funny how the telephone seemed to emphasize Peter's slightly German accent. "Did you see Doris?" he continued. "She get there all right?"

Johnny had almost forgotten about her. "I was in the projection room when she came in," he explained almost apologetically. "But Jane met her and she's in the hotel now changing her clothes. I'm taking her to lunch."

Peter laughed. His voice was proud. "You won't recognize her, Johnny. She's a young lady now. She's grown a lot in the last few years."

The last few times Johnny had been out at the studio he hadn't seen her. She was away at a young ladies' finishing school. He added up the years in his mind. She was eighteen now.

He laughed with Peter. "I bet I won't!" he said. "I didn't realize how time flew by."

Peter's voice grew even more proud. "You wouldn't know Mark either if you saw him. He's almost as tall as I am."

Johnny was properly astonished. "No!"

"I mean it," Peter assured him. "He grows out of his clothes faster than Esther can get them for him."

"You don't say."

"Yep," Peter said. "I wouldn't believe it if I didn't see for myself." He was silent for a moment. Then his voice became more businesslike.

"Did you get the figures for last month yet?"

Johnny picked up a sheet of paper from his desk. "Yes," he answered. He read some figures rapidly from the sheet and concluded with the statement that they would net sixty thousand in profit for that month.

Peter's voice sounded contented. "If we keep up this way," he said, "we'll make over a million dollars this year."

"Easy," Johnny told him. "Last week's business was close to seventy thousand gross."

"Good," Peter said. "You're doing all right. Keep it up."

"We'll keep it up," Johnny answered. "I got that Wilson reel today." Now there was a note of pride in *his* voice.

"Terrific!" Already the idiom of the picture business had impressed itself on Peter's tongue.

"It will be in the Broadway theaters tonight," Johnny continued. "And at feature charges, too. When I told them it was rushed up by plane, they didn't give me any argument on its cost."

"I'd like to see it," Peter said.

"Your print will be on the train tonight," Johnny told him. "What's new out there?" He had to give Peter a chance to brag.

Peter spoke for several minutes and Johnny listened attentively. Magnum had completed several pictures and now they were editing the final picture of that season's series. As Peter came to the end of his discourse an idea struck him.

"I think I'll come to New York when we're all cleaned up here next month. I haven't been there for almost a year and Esther would like to spend Pesach with her relatives. The vacation would do her good."

Johnny smiled to himself. Peter said nothing about his own desire to visit the home office and see for himself just what was going on. "Do that," he urged. "You'll both enjoy it."

"I think I will," Peter said.

"Let me know when you've decided on the date and I'll make arrangements for you," Johnny told him.

"I'll do that," Peter said. He was silent for a second; when he spoke again, his voice was hesitant. "How do they feel about the war in New York?"

Johnny was reserved. He remembered Peter came from Germany. "What do you mean?" he asked.

"Joe wants to make a picture showing how the Germans are overrunning and oppressing the people in Belgium and France and I was wondering whether it would be a good thing to do." Peter's voice was slightly embarrassed. "I didn't know if a picture like that would do business."

"The sentiment here favors the Allies," Johnny answered carefully. He knew about the picture. Joe had called him to talk about it. Joe had also told him that Peter had objected to the idea. While Peter had no illusions about the land of his birth, he could not bring himself to the point of making a picture that would actually point a finger of scorn at it. But, on the other hand, word had leaked out to the trade and the newspapers that Magnum was planning to make a film about the German atrocities, and if Peter announced that the picture would not be made, he would be labeled pro-German. He pointed this out to Peter.

He could almost see Peter nodding his head as he made his points. Peter's voice was doubtful as he replied: "I guess we'll have to go ahead with it, then."

"That's about the situation," Johnny said. "It's a case of being damned if you do and damned if you don't."

Peter heaved a sigh. He knew when he was licked. "I'll tell Joe to put the script in work," he said heavily.

Johnny felt a twinge of sympathy for him. He could understand how Peter felt. He had heard him talk many times about his family and relatives in Germany. Some day he planned to go back there and visit them. "Tell Joe to take his time with it," he said quietly. "Maybe things will be settled before you're ready to start shooting."

Peter understood Johnny's consideration of his feelings. "No," he said, "there's no use stalling. We might as well get it over with." He was silent for a second, then he laughed half-ashamedly. "After all, why should I worry so much about it? I'm not a German any more. I've been an American citizen for over twenty years. I haven't seen the country since I left there more than twenty-six years ago. The people could have changed a lot since then."

"That's right," Johnny said kindly. "They must have changed since you were there."

"Sure," Peter agreed with him. But he knew better. He could still remember the Prussian officers riding disdainfully down the streets of Munich and their big black horses. The way everybody bowed to them and was afraid of them. He could still remember the conscription forays that dragged his cousins from their families when they were only seventeen years old. That was why his father had sent him to America. He was sure they hadn't changed.

"All right Johnny," he said with a funny sort of finality. "We'll make the picture." With that statement his doubts seemed to ebb away and he felt better. "Tell Doris to call us at home tonight."

"I will," Johnny answered.

"I'll be talking to you tomorrow, then," Peter said.

"Yes," Johnny said half-absentmindedly. He was still thinking of how Peter must feel about that picture. Suddenly he remembered. George—he had to have his answer today. "Peter!"

"Yes?"

"About those theaters of George's. He has to have an answer today."

"Oh, those." Peter's voice didn't sound interested and Johnny's heart went down into his boots. He couldn't argue with Peter after what they had just spoken about. "I talked to Joe and Esther about it and they all agree with me that it's a good idea. Tell him to go ahead with the deal."

Johnny picked up the statistics on his desk after he had hung up the phone and gave them to Jane. "File these," he said to her, "I won't need them after all." He leaned back in his chair, shaking his head slowly. You just couldn't figure the guy out. He never did what you expected.

3

DORIS stood in front of the mirror, an odd sense of excitement running through her. She nodded her head, pleased with what she saw. This dress was much better for her than the other she had put on first. It made her appear older, somehow more mature, than the other. She was glad it had stopped raining so she could wear it. All her other dresses made her look like a kid.

She looked at the clock on the dresser. He should be here any minute now, she thought as she put on her hat. She had been disappointed when she hadn't seen him at the train, but Jane had explained that he was tied up with getting out the Wilson newsreel and she had accepted it. She had long since become used to the continuous pressures and self-induced deadlines that motion-picture people lived by. She felt better when she was told that he would take her to lunch and would pick her up at the hotel.

There was a knock on the door. "He's here," she thought, and started to run across the large room to the door. Halfway across the room she stopped suddenly. She turned and took a last look into the mirror and then finished her walk to the door slowly. "You're acting like a child," she told herself reprovingly as she put her hand on the knob and turned it slowly. But her heart was pounding away inside her.

It was almost as if someone else were opening the door, not her. She could see herself standing there, waiting. She could see him, the look on his face. The smile that was there when he first saw her. She could see the smile fade away as he looked at her, the look of wonder as it crossed his face, and then the smile reappearing again. Warm and admiring.

He held a bouquet of flowers in his hand. He had been prepared to see her as she had been; he had told himself that she had grown up, but inside him he hadn't believed it. He had been prepared to pick her up and swing her to him and say: "Hello, sweetheart," as he had so many times before, but now he couldn't. He saw her standing in the doorway, then stepping back a little into the room, a tinge of color in her cheeks, her eyes warm and lively with an inner excitement, her lips trembling slightly.

He stepped into the room and gave her the flowers.

She took them silently and their hands touched. It was as if a current had flowed between them, and his fingers tingled with a sense of shock. Their hands clasped and held.

"Hello, sweetheart," he said, his voice quiet and filled with the wonder he felt.

"Hello, Johnny," she answered. It was the first time she had ever called him by his name without the word "Uncle" before it. She suddenly was aware that their hands were still clasped. She drew her hand back self-consciously, more color flooding into her cheeks. "I better put these in water." Her voice was low.

He watched her intently as she arranged the flowers in a vase. She was partly turned away from him, so that her profile was visible to his gaze. The burnished coppery brunette of her hair shimmering against her fair, faintly flushed face, the eyes deep set and blue, set over high cheekbones, the mouth curved with corners soft, and the thin line of her cheek falling away to a firmly rounded chin.

She turned and saw him watching her. She gave a finishing pat to the flowers. "There, isn't that better?" she asked.

He nodded his head affirmatively. He was confused. He didn't know just how to talk to this suddenly assured young woman he had just met. His voice was puzzled. "I can't believe it. You've—"

She interrupted him with a laugh. "Don't tell me you were going to say how much I've grown. If I hear that once more, I'll scream."

He laughed with her, a little embarrassed at himself. "That's just what I was going to say," he confessed.

"I knew it," she said, walking over to him and standing in front of him looking up at his face. "But I can't understand why people always say it. Time won't stand still for me any more than it will for them. Of course I've grown up. You wouldn't want me to remain a child forever, would you?"

He began to feel better, more comfortable, more at ease. He looked down at her teasingly. "I don't know," he said. "When you were a kid I used to be able to pick you up and swing you in the air and kiss you and call you sweetheart, and you would laugh and we'd both think it a lot of fun. I couldn't do that now."

Her eyes were quickly grave. It was strange how quickly they could change color and grow dark. Her voice was even, though very quiet. "You could still kiss an old friend when you haven't seen her for almost four years."

He looked down at her for a moment, then bent his head toward her. She turned her face toward him. His lips met hers.

For a split second a sense of shock ran through him. Involuntarily his arms went around her waist and drew her to him. Her arms went around his neck, holding his face close to her. He could taste the wine of her warmth flowing through her body to her lips and coming to him. He could smell the faint exciting young perfume of her hair in his nostrils. He looked at her face; her eyes had closed.

The thoughts ran through his mind like lightning: "This is crazy. Wait a minute, Johnny, she may look like a woman, but she's only a kid going to school away from home for the first time. A romantic kid. Don't be a fool, Johnny!"

He drew back suddenly. She buried her face against his shoulder. For a moment he let his hand run along the side of her face and then across her hair. They stood there silently for a moment; then he spoke. His voice was as grave as hers had been. "You have grown up, sweetheart. You're too big to play games with."

She looked up at him, her eyes suddenly dancing, her voice so young. A smile curved her lips. "Have I, Johnny?"

He nodded, his face still grave. He didn't speak; his mind was still trying to answer his own shocked question: "What's happened to me?"

She walked across the room to pick up her coat. When she turned back to him, there was something inside her that was singing. "He loves me, he loves me, even if he doesn't know it yet!" Aloud she said: "Where are we going for lunch, Johnny? I'm starved."

He sat there idling over his coffee, strangely reluctant to finish it and bring this luncheon to an end. They had been there almost two hours and yet it seemed to him only a few minutes. For the first time he had been able to talk about pictures to a girl who had felt the same about them as he did. He finished telling her about how the Wilson reel had worked out.

She had listened quietly and attentively as he spoke. She could feel the urgency and intensity in him as he spoke about motion pictures. What they had done up to now, what they were capable of doing in the future. This would have been shop talk to many, but it was home talk to her. It was everyday language and living because she had heard so much of it in her own home.

But she had thought her own thoughts too. Of how he looked, the color of his hair and eyes, the shape of his face, the wide generous mouth and determined chin. The length of his body and the power of his stride. The strength in his arms as they had held her.

She was glad she had not been wrong. She had always loved him, and now she knew he loved her. It would take time for him to become aware of it. He had to accept her as grown up first, but she was willing to wait. An unknown warm contentment seeped through her as she listened to his voice. It would even be fun to watch him become aware of it. A shadow of a smile crossed her lips as she thought about it. He was so good to love.

He finished his coffee and put down the cup. A rueful smile crossed his face as he took out his watch and looked at it. "I've got to be getting back to the office," he said. "I haven't spent so much time at lunch since we opened it."

She smiled back at him. "You should do it more often. It isn't good to always work so hard."

He began to get up. "It isn't often I find I can stay away from it so long. But today I didn't even feel like going back." He lit a cigarette. "I don't know why," he added reflectively.

She smiled at him. "I know why," she thought happily. She rose from her chair. "There are days like that. Days that you don't feel like doing anything," she said.

He put her coat across her shoulders. "I'll walk you back to the hotel," he said.

They passed the news-stand on the corner. The papers bore headlines: "Wilson Inaugurated! Pledges Peace!"

She turned to him, her voice serious. "Do you think he will keep his word, Johnny?"

He looked at her, surprised at the gravity in her tone. "I think he'll try his darnedest, sweetheart. Why?"

"Papa is very unhappy about it. He still has relatives in Germany, you know. And there is that picture that Joe wants him to make."

"I know about it," he answered. "We spoke this morning. He's going to do it."

They walked a few more steps before she answered. He could see she was thinking. At last she sighed. "Then he's made up his mind."

Johnny nodded.

"I'm glad," she said simply. "At least he won't be tortured by all these doubts any more."

"That's right," Johnny said.

They had walked another few steps before another thought struck her. She stopped and faced him. "But if there is a war, Johnny, will you have to go?"

He looked at her, startled. He hadn't thought about it. "I suppose so," he said as first reaction; then: "That is, I don't know." He laughed quickly. "But there's no use in thinking about it now. When the time comes we'll know soon enough."

She didn't answer. She took his arm and silently they walked the rest of the way back to the hotel.

4

JOHNNY looked up from his desk. "You sure that Doris said she'd be here before we went to the train?" he asked Jane for the fourth time.

She nodded her head wearily. "I'm sure," she replied. She wondered why he was so anxious about it. If the girl didn't come here, she knew what time the train was due in and she could get there herself to meet her mother and father. It wasn't like Johnny to be so nervous.

He busied himself signing a few more memos, then he looked up at her again. "What's the name of the man that George wants to manage those three theaters uptown?"

"Stanley Farber," she answered.

He looked down at the letter on his desk again. It was a note thanking him for confirming his appointment to the position. He was surprised by it. He hadn't confirmed that job yet; he generally didn't confirm anyone's appointment to a job until after he had talked with the person involved. And he hadn't even spoken to Farber. He tossed the letter to Jane. "Check this with George," he told her, "and let me know what he says."

He pulled his watch out of his pocket and looked at it impatiently. It was only two hours before the train pulled in. He wondered what was keeping her.

The door opened before he could put the watch away. It was Doris. She came into the office.

He got up from his seat and walked around the desk to her. "I was beginning to wonder where you were," he said, taking her hand.

She smiled at him. "I missed the fast train down from school and had to take the local," she explained.

Jane looked over at them in surprise. For a moment she sat very still, a sort of numbness in her. It wasn't that she was in love with Johnny, but that she felt she could be if he wanted her. She had long felt that he was capable of great emotional depths and some day they would rise within him. But nothing he had ever said or done had led her to think that he would turn to her. Now she knew he never would, and with it came an inexplicable feeling of relief.

Doris turned to her and said hello.

Automatically Jane asked how she was.

Doris replied and Johnny led her to a seat.

"Now if you'll be patient and wait just a minute for me to clean a few things up," he said, smiling down at her, "we can grab a bite before we meet them."

"I don't mind waiting," she answered softly.

Jane looked at Johnny as he went behind his desk and sat down. It was the first time she had ever seen him excited in just that manner. He was like a boy with his first love, she thought, he didn't even know what he felt yet.

She looked at Doris sitting demurely in the chair Johnny had placed for her. She was taking off her hat, and her hair shimmered in the office lights. She looked happy and pleased and her heart was in her eyes as she looked at Johnny. She didn't notice that Jane was watching her.

Impulsively Jane got up and walked over to her. She bent over Doris and took her hand and smiled. Her voice was low, so low that Johnny couldn't hear what she was saying. "It's like a dream, Doris, isn't it?"

Startled, Doris looked up at her. She saw the warm kindliness in Jane's eyes. She nodded her head without speaking.

Jane took her coat and hung it up on the rack. She smiled again at Doris and went back to her chair and sat down.

The door opened again and Irving Bannon came in. His face was ruddy and excited. "Something big is coming over the ticker, Johnny. You better take a look at it!"

"What is it?" Johnny asked.

"I don't know," Irving answered. "The tape just said: 'Important announcement to follow.' AP says it's a big story, I checked with them before I came in here."

Johnny got up and walked round his desk to Doris. "Do you want to look at it?"

"Yes," she answered.

They followed Irving to the newsreel office. On the way there, Johnny introduced them. The newsreel office was a small room at the end of the hall. Inside it was a desk at which Irving sat when writing up his title cards and a workbench where he edited the reel. In a corner next to the desk was a news ticker-tape machine. Bannon had persuaded Johnny to install it so that if there were any special items of news the reel could give it coverage.

There were a few people gathered around the machine as they walked toward it. They made room for Johnny to walk through when they saw him. Doris stood next to him, Irving and Jane opposite him. The machine had been silent as they came into the room, but now it began to tick.

Johnny picked up the tape and began to read aloud from it.

WASHINGTON, D.C., MARCH 12 (AP).—BY EXECUTIVE ORDER PRESIDENT WILSON TODAY ORDERED THAT MERCHANT VESSELS BE ARMED TO PROTECT THEMSELVES AGAINST THE FURTHER WANTON DEPREDATIONS OF GERMAN SUBMARINES. THIS ORDER WAS ISSUED JUST EIGHT DAYS AFTER CONGRESS HAD FAILED TO PASS A BILL GIVING MERCHANT SHIPS THIS PRIVILEGE. THE COMPLETE TRANSCRIPT OF THE PRESIDENT'S ORDER WILL FOLLOW AS SOON AS AVAILABLE.—MORE WILL FOLLOW.

For almost a minute there was a complete silence in the room while the import of the news sank in. Bannon was the first to find his tongue. "This means war," he said flatly. "Nobody can stop it now. Looks like the President finally made up his mind."

Johnny looked at him. War. The United States would have to go to war. Suddenly he galvanized into action. He turned to Jane. "Get Joe Turner on the wire at the studio, quick!"

She ran back to his office.

He turned to Bannon. "Get a special reel out on this as fast as you can, then get down to Washington with a full crew. I want pictures of everything important that might happen and I want you on the train within two hours!"

He turned and went back to his office, Doris following him. He had forgotten about her for a few seconds; now he felt her hand on his arm. He stopped and looked at her.

Her face was pale and her eyes wide in the yellow light of the corridor. Her voice was small and still. "If war comes, Johnny, what are you going to do?"

He smiled reassuringly at her and avoided the question. "I don't know, sweetheart," he said. "We'll see what happens first."

They went into his office. Jane looked up at them. "Your call will be through in about fifteen minutes, Johnny."

"Good girl," he said, and walked over to his desk, sat down, and lit a cigarette. If war came he wondered what he would do. He didn't know and yet he did. There was only one answer when your country was at war.

He couldn't sit still. He fidgeted in his chair restlessly. At last he got up. "I'm going down to Irving's office," he told them. "Call me there when you get Joe on the wire." He walked out.

Doris followed him with her eyes. She said nothing; she could see his restlessness, and something inside her seemed to shrivel and tighten until she could hardly breathe. Her face grew paler.

Jane looked at her sympathetically from a new-born freedom. She got up from her chair and walked over to Doris and took her hand. "Worried?" she asked.

Doris nodded her head. She fought hard to keep tears from coming to her eyes, but she could feel them trembling just beneath her lids.

"You love him," Jane said.

Doris's voice was husky. "I've always loved him," she whispered, "from the time I was a kid. I used to dream about him and not know what it meant. Then one day I knew."

"He loves you too," Jane said softly. "But he doesn't know it yet."

The tears stood clearly in Doris's eyes now. "I know. But if war comes—and he goes away—he may never find out."

Jane squeezed her hand. "Don't you worry, he'll find out."

Doris smiled through her tears. "Do you really think so?" she asked.

"Of course he will," Jane reassured her. And all the time she was thinking to herself: "The poor kid, it's as bad as that."

The phone rang, startling them. Jane picked up the receiver on Johnny's desk.

"I've got that Los Angeles call for you," the operator's voice told her.

"Just a minute," Jane replied. She held her hand over the mouthpiece and spoke to Doris. "Would you mind going down the hall for him, honey?"

Doris was glad to be doing something. She had felt so completely out of things before. She smiled at Jane and nodded. She left the room.

A minute later she was back, following Johnny into the office. He took the phone from Jane's hand.

"Hello, Joe?" he said.

He could hear Joe's voice booming on the other end of the wire. "Yes, Johnny. What do yuh want?"

"The President's putting guns on merchant ships," Johnny said tersely. "It looks like war for sure."

Joe whistled. "It's sooner than I expected." He was silent for a moment. "What do yuh want me to do?" he asked.

"You got that war picture finished yet?" Johnny asked.

"The last scene got into the can this morning," Joe answered proudly.

"Then ship it to New York right away. If we get it out now, we'll clean up," Johnny said.

"I can't do that," Joe replied. "It's got to be edited an' the title cards have to be made up. That's a couple of weeks' work at the least."

Johnny thought for a moment. "We can't wait that long," he said definitely. "I'll tell you what we'll do. Get your best editor and two writers to get on the train with you tonight. Take along some reel-winders and reserve two adjoining compartments. You edit the film on the way in and have them write up the cards. Have everything ready when you get to New York. We'll make up the cards here and insert them. Then we can start duping prints and rush 'em out into the theaters."

"I don't know whether we can make it," Joe said. "It's short notice."

"You'll make it," Johnny answered confidently. "I'm notifying all the distributors and salesmen that the picture will be ready next week."

"Jesus!" Joe exploded, "you haven't changed a bit. You can't wait for anything!"

"We can't wait," Johnny retorted.

"What does Peter say?" Joe asked.

"I don't know," Johnny replied. "He isn't here yet."

"All right, all right," Joe said, "I'll try to do it."

"Good," Johnny said, "I know you'll do it. Have you got a name for the picture yet?"

"Not yet," Joe answered. "We've been working it under the title 'War Story.'"

"Okay," Johnny said. "It'll have a name when you get here." He hung up the phone and looked at them. "Some good may come out of this yet," he said.

"Johnny," Doris cried out in a voice filled with anguish, "Johnny, how could you talk like that? Saying some good will come out of the Germans making war against all those innocent people? How could you?"

He stared at her. He never even noticed the reproach in her voice. He grabbed both her hands and pumped them excitedly. "That's it, Doris, that's it!" he shouted.

"What?" she asked, more bewildered than ever at his actions.

He didn't answer her question; instead he turned to Jane and spoke rapidly. "I want you to get this notice out to all distributors and salesmen. Have the advertising department start working up material and getting out stories on it. Put this down." He paused for a moment while Jane got a pencil and paper ready.

"Magnum Pictures announces the immediate release of its latest and greatest production, *The War against the Innocents*. It will be ready for immediate showing next week. This picture will expose all the terrors and bestialities of the Hun that we know so well from our daily papers."

He stopped for a minute and looked down at Jane. "Tell you what," he said, "send it down to the advertising department. Have them rewrite it and get it out."

He turned back to Doris. There was a big smile on his face. "Grab your coat, sweetheart," he said. "We don't want to be late in getting to the train!"

5

THE projection room was crowded as the first completed print of *The War against the Innocents* was run off. When the picture came to an end, the audience filed out silently and broke up into small groups in the corridor.

A selected audience had been invited to the preview of the picture. The country had been at war almost a week and interest in the picture was widespread. Representatives of the larger newspapers and press associations, government officials, and prominent distributors and theater men had been among those present.

Now they were crowding around Peter and Joe offering their congratulations. They felt that the picture would do a great deal in telling the American public why the war had become necessary.

"An excellently made and brilliant piece of propaganda for our side," one of the guests told Peter. "You're to be congratulated for striking the Hun where it hurts."

Peter nodded his head. Something inside him had turned sick as he had watched the picture. Now as he heard the man's voice, he thought bitterly: "Congratulations I'm getting for making war against my own people and family." He couldn't speak, his heart was too heavy. He was glad when the last guest had gone and they could go up to Johnny's office, where it was comparatively quiet and he could sit down. Esther, Doris, Joe, and Johnny were there with him.

They didn't talk much—just looked at each other guiltily. There was a tension in the air that all seemed to feel, and each thought it was there for a different reason.

At last Peter spoke. "Have you got a little schnapps or something, Johnny?" he asked. "I feel a little tired."

Silently Johnny reached into his desk and took out a bottle and some paper cups. He poured some whisky into each cup and passed them around to Joe and Peter. He held his cup toward them. "To victory!" he said.

They swallowed their drinks.

The liquor loosened Joe's tongue. "I made the damn picture and yet, after seeing it, I feel like goin' out and enlisting myself."

Peter didn't answer. He picked up some papers from Johnny's desk and looked at them absently. They were exhibition contracts for the picture. He dropped them as if they burned his fingers. "Money I got to make from this yet," he thought.

Esther sensed how he was feeling. She walked over to him and stood there silently. He looked up at her gratefully; they understood each other.

Johnny's voice fell into the room like a shellburst. "What are you going to do about replacing me while I'm away?" he asked quietly. They looked at him startled. There was a smile on his lips, but none in his eyes.

Peter's accent was more pronounced. "Vat do you mean?"

Johnny looked at him. "Just what I said," he answered, "I'm going to enlist tomorrow."

"No!" an anguished cry came from Doris's lips.

Esther looked at her daughter. A feeling of chilled surprise ran through her. Doris's face had drained of color. It was white, almost ashen in hue. "I should have known," she reproached herself silently. Now the many things that Doris had said and done suddenly made sense. It had always been like that. She went to her daughter and took her hand. Doris's hand was trembling.

The men didn't even notice them. "By Jesus!" Joe swore, "I'm goin' with yuh!"

Peter looked from one to the other. "This day I had to live to believe," he thought. "To see these men whom I love go out to war against my brothers." He got to his feet. "Do you have to go?" he asked aloud.

Johnny looked at him strangely. "There isn't anything else I can do," he answered. "It's my country."

Peter saw the look on Johnny's face. A feeling of hurt flooded through him. "Does he doubt my loyalty?" he thought. He forced a smile to his face. "Go if you must," he said heavily, "and don't worry about us. Just be careful, we want you both back." He reached out his hand to Johnny.

Johnny took his hand across the desk. "I knew you'd understand."

The tears began to flood into Doris's eyes. A whisper from her mother stopped them. She could hear the whisper in her mind for a long time afterward.

"You should never cry in front of your man, *liebe kind*," her mother said understandingly.

Johnny looked down at his desk. The last paper had been signed, all his work had been cleaned up. He placed the pen back in its holder and looked over at Peter. "I guess that does it," he said. "Any more questions?"

Peter shook his head. "No, everything's straightened out."

Johnny stood up. "Sure," he said. "Besides if anything turns up that you're not familiar with, ask Jane. She runs the place anyway." He turned to Jane and smiled at her.

She smiled back at him. "We'll try to get along while you're gone, boss," she said teasingly.

He grinned. "Don't kid me, Janey. I know better. I'm one of the boys." He took out his watch and looked at it. "Gosh," he said, "I'd better hurry. I promised to meet Joe at the recruiting station at three o'clock."

He walked over to the clothes tree and took his hat. He put it on and came back to Peter. He held out his hand. "So long, Peter," he said, "I'll see you after the party is over."

Peter gripped his hand silently. They held firmly for a few seconds, then parted.

Johnny walked over to Jane's desk. He reached over it and mussed her hair. "So long, baby."

She got up and kissed him quickly. "So long, boss," she said in a husky voice. "Be careful."

"Sure," he said. The door shut behind him.

Peter and Jane looked at each other after he had gone. "I—I think I'm going to cry," she said in a small voice.

He took out his handkerchief and blew his nose heavily. "Nu," he said, "go ahead. Who's stopping you?"

As Johnny stopped on the sidewalk in front of the office to light a cigarette, he heard a voice calling him. He looked up.

"Johnny! Johnny!" Doris was running toward him.

He waited for her to come up to him. "Why aren't you in

school, sweetheart?" he asked sternly, but something in his heart had lightened when he saw her.

"I didn't go back yesterday," she said breathlessly. "I wanted to see you again before you went away. I'm glad I didn't miss you."

They stood there in the street looking at each other. Neither knew what to say.

Johnny broke the silence. "I'm glad you came, sweetheart."

"Are you, Johnny?" she asked, her eyes shining.

"Very glad," he said.

They fell silent again. This time it was Doris that broke the silence. "Will you write me, Johnny, if I write you?"

"Sure," he said. And again the silence. Awkward. Embarrassing. Their eyes doing much more talking than their lips.

He took out his watch and looked at it. "I'm late," he said unnecessarily, "I've got to get going."

"Yes, Johnny." She looked down at the ground, her face lowered.

He put a hand under her chin and turned her face up to him. "Be a good girl," he said, trying to joke, "and wait for me. Maybe when I come back, I'll bring you something nice."

There were tears in the corners of her eyes. "I'll wait for you, Johnny, even if it's forever."

He felt embarrassed at the intensity in her voice. Red began to creep over his neck and into his face as he flushed. "Sure, sweetheart," he said, still trying awkwardly to joke. "Do that an' I'll bring you a present."

"You don't have to bring me anything, Johnny. Just come back the way you are now. That's all I want."

"What can happen to me?" He laughed.

6

THE long khaki-clad line shuffled wearily to a halt. The hot, white sun beat heavily down on them. The dust had caked itself into thick clots on their skin where the sweat had turned it into mud.

The orders came echoing down from the head of the column: "Break ranks. Take ten."

Johnny threw himself on the grass by the side of the road. He lay on his back, hands over his eyes. His breath drew wearily in his throat.

Joe sat on the ground beside him. "Christ," he muttered, "my dogs are killing me." He took his shoes off and began to massage his feet. He groaned.

Johnny just lay there quietly. A shadow fell across him. He took his hands from his eyes and looked up at it. It was the corporal. He moved over to make room for him on the small clump of grass. "Grab yourself a piece of grass, Rock," he said.

Rocco sank to the ground beside him. He looked at Joe rubbing his feet and smiled. "That's where being a barber gives you a break," he said; "your feet get used to being stood on."

"B. S." Joe said. "You just ain't human, thass all."

Johnny grinned at him and rolled over to face Rocco. "Did yuh find out where at we goin', Rock?"

Rock nodded his head slowly. "I think so. Some place along the Meuse River. The Argonne Forest or something."

Joe held his feet up and looked at them. "Do you hear that, doggies?" he said to them. "Now we know where we goin'."

Rocco continued as if Joe hadn't interrupted him. "They say there's a big push startin' off up there."

"How far off is it from here?" Johnny asked.

"About thirty, thirty-five miles," Rocco answered.

Joe let out a groan and sank back on the grass. They lay there silently for a few minutes. The hum of an airplane motor turned their gaze skyward.

Johnny shaded his eyes and looked up. A gray-painted Spad with French colors was winging its way diagonally across the horizon. Idly their eyes followed it.

"It must be nice and cool up there," Joe said enviously. "At least your feet don't bother you."

Johnny watched it. It was as graceful as a gull in a blue sky with the sunlight shimmering on it. Suddenly it veered sharply and came racing toward them. There was an element of frantic haste about the way it fled across the sky.

"I wonder what's the matter with him?" Johnny asked.

The question was answered for him. In the sunlight behind the Spad were three red Fokkers with big black crosses painted on their wings. They were flying in tight formation over the little Spad.

Suddenly one peeled off from the formation and dove down toward the little gray Spad. The Spad veered off sharply. It flipped up one wing and banked into a sharp turn and the Fokker dove past it.

Johnny laughed aloud. "The little frog fooled the Heinie." They watched the Spad now fleeing toward the east. "I think he's going to get away from them," Johnny said.

Another Fokker came tearing down at the Spad. They could hear the chatter of its guns over the roar of the motors. It reminded Johnny of the typewriters in the office. "Why doesn't he turn and shoot back at them?" Johnny yelled.

"That's what they want him to do," Rocco said. "Then they can box him in. He's playing it smart trying to outrun 'em."

Again the Spad escaped and the Fokker shot below it. The first Fokker was climbing slowly, but it was far behind the Spad. It would never gain height in time to make another pass at it.

"Only one to go," Joe said. "If he gets away from this one he's in the clear."

As he spoke, the third Fokker went into its dive. They held their breath as they watched. The planes were too far away for any sound to reach their ears now, the whole movement seemed to be enacted in pantomime. Again the Fokker shot under the Spad.

"He made it! He made it!" Johnny was yelling. He turned to Rocco. "Did you see that?"

Rocco didn't answer. He touched Johnny's arm and pointed.

Johnny turned and looked at the Spad. A thin stream of black smoke was pouring behind it. It seemed to waver in the air like a stricken bird. Suddenly it turned on one side and began to slip toward the earth. They could see the flames licking along the wing. It began to rush toward the ground with frightening speed. A small black object detached itself from the burning plane and fell toward the ground.

Johnny jumped to his feet. "The poor bastard jumped," he said bitterly.

Rocco pulled him back on the ground. "Stay down," he said sharply. "D'yuh want the Heinies to spot us?"

Johnny sank back on the ground. He felt oddly exhausted. He threw his hands over his eyes to keep the sun from them. Against the black of his lids he could see the small black object detach itself from the burning plane. He took his hands from his eyes and looked toward the sky. The Fokkers were circling in the sky over the spot where the Spad had gone down. After a few seconds they turned and went back toward the German lines and the sky was empty, a clear, tranquil blue. He began to feel the heat again, the weariness seeping through him.

The shrill of the sergeant's whistle startled him. "On your feet, men," he heard the voices calling. He got wearily to his feet. Joe was lacing tight his shoes, Rocco was adjusting his pack. He turned and walked toward the road where the men were forming a column.

Night was beginning to fall as they marched into the little village. The sides of the streets were lined with people who were watching them with quiet imperturbable eyes. Occasionally they could see someone holding a small American flag.

They walked automatically, one foot falling in front of the other, their eyes straight ahead. They were too tired to be curious about the people, and the people were too weary to get excited over the soldiers. They were aware of each other, they felt warmth and sympathy and even understanding toward one another, but they were too tired to show it.

Only Joe felt different from the others. At the first sign of a village he perked up. When he saw the people standing there, he looked at them. He smiled at some girls. He nudged Johnny. "Dames," he chortled, "hot zig!"

Johnny plowed along silently. He didn't look up when Joe spoke to him. He was thinking about the last letter he had received from Doris. She had said that motion-picture folks were in the forefront of all the Victory Bond drives. Mary Pickford, Doug Fairbanks, and all the stars had gone out on tours to sell Victory Bonds. Others went on hospital tours. The women were rolling bandages. Peter had made shorts and pictures for the government plugging various home-front activities. Business was booming. Many new theaters had opened and now pictures were being shipped from Hollywood all over the world. In England and the rest of Europe, where the studios had been forced to close down because of the war, American pictures were being avidly demanded and enthusiastically accepted.

Mark had grown a great deal in the past year. He had finished grammar school and Papa had sent him to a military school. He was hoping the war wouldn't be over before he was old enough to go.

Two new stages had been added to their studio and now it was one of the largest in Hollywood. Edison had demonstrated a talking film—a cylinder hooked up to and synchronized with motion-picture film. Papa, along with many other leading production men in the industry, had looked at it. It wasn't practical.

Johnny cursed to himself silently. This was a hell of a time for him to be away. They were crazy. Couldn't they see that if pictures could be made to speak, they would completely achieve the level of the stage? He wished he were there so he could see this machine of Edison's.

They were in the center of the town now. It was a big, empty, cobblestoned square. The column drew up in ranks and halted. They swung their packs from their shoulders and rested their guns on the ground. Somewhere to the north they could hear a distant rumble of big guns. It sounded like thunder in the distance.

Johnny's hand on the muzzle of the rifle could feel the vibration coming up from the ground through it. He waited quietly. Idly he wondered whether they were going on through tonight or were going to stay here.

A little French official bustled up to the captain importantly. They talked rapidly for a few minutes, then the captain looked up. "We'll stay here for the night," he announced. "We're shoving off at four a.m., your noncoms will give you sleeping-quarters. Make the most of it. You'll be lucky if you see a bed in the next few weeks." He turned and walked away with the little French official.

"The hell with that," Joe said through motionless lips to Johnny, "I'm gonna get me a dame."

Rocco overheard him. "You're turnin' in," he said to him. "This ain't no picnic we're goin' on. This is business."

Joe scoffed at him. "I heard that before. All we're gonna do is march up there an' then they're gonna march us somewhere else. This isn't a war against Germany, it's all a conspiracy against my feet."

A lieutenant was coming down toward them. "Shut up," Johnny whispered, "the looey's comin'."

The lieutenant gestured to Rocco. He stepped forward and the officer spoke to him quickly. He gave Rocco a slip of paper and went on down the line to the next platoon.

A few minutes later they were dismissed.

"Where can you get a drink around here?" Joe asked. There wasn't a light visible in the town.

No one answered him. A few seconds later they followed Rocco down the street. They stopped at a small gray house. Rocco knocked at the door.

A man's voice answered in French through the closed door.

Rocco waited until the voice had finished. "We're the American soldiers."

The door opened. A tall man with a swarthy black beard opened the door. The yellow light streamed out from behind him. He held his hands wide. "*Les Américains!*" he said. "Come in, come in."

They followed him into the house. He shut the door behind them. "Marie!" he called out. Some rapid words followed in French which they did not understand.

They stood awkwardly just inside the room. Rocco took off his helmet and the other boys followed sheepishly. A girl came into the room carrying some large bottles of wine.

Joe looked around him triumphantly. "I should have known the army would fix us up before we went into battle," he crowed.

The Frenchman smiled at him. "Fix," he said, "yess, fix." He opened the bottle of wine and poured it into glasses. Ceremoniously he passed them around. He held his glass toward them. "*Vive l' Amérique!*"

They drank their wine. He refilled their glasses, then waited. Johnny was the first to guess what he was waiting for. He smiled at the man. "*Vive la France!*" he said.

Joe was already trying to talk to the girl.

Rocco was shaking his shoulder. He awoke like a cat; one minute he was lying there asleep, the next moment he was awake. Actually he had been waiting for this moment all night. Now when it came, his first reaction was to stay in bed.

"Where's Joe?" Rocco whispered.

"I dunno," Johnny answered. "Isn't he here?"

In the dark Rocco shook his head.

Johnny sat up and swung his feet over the side of the bed. He laced on his shoes. "I'll find him," he said to Rocco.

He walked quietly out of the room into the small hall. He stood for a second until his eyes became used to it and then walked to a door. He opened it and walked in. He went over to the bed in the corner of the room. As he walked toward it, a figure on the bed rolled over and gave forth with a loud familiar snore.

He grinned to himself. He bent over the sleeping figure and suddenly shot a heavy hand down and grabbed Joe by the shoulder. With one tug he pulled him out of bed and onto the floor. "Voowolla," he whispered in his best imitation of a French accent. "Zo thees iss what happen behin' my back!"

Joe struggled fiercely on the floor while Johnny held him there. "I'm sorry, mister," Joe gasped. "I didn't mean anything."

Johnny began to laugh. He let Joe get to his feet. "Come on, sleeping beauty," he said. "We got a war waitin'!"

Joe followed him out into the hall. "How did you know I was in there?" he asked.

Johnny knelt at the door and picked up his shoes and handed them to him silently.

Joe looked at him bewildered. Then he began to grin. "The French, they are a funny race, parley vous," he half sung.

Johnny motioned for him to be quiet.

"I don't care what happens now," Joe said, still smiling. "I've had everything!"

7

It was early morning. The fog of night had not yet lifted from the ground and it rolled in heavy gray mists across the earth. The men stood silently, uncomfortably, in the deep long trench that honeycombed the earth around them.

The new captain was talking. This morning as they had filed into the trenches they found out that they had all new officers. The old ones had been transferred and new officers had been assigned to them. "They're afraid we'd plug some of them in the back," Joe had said when they learned the news.

"Bunk," Rocco had answered. "These guys got experience in this business and they ain't taking any chances with amateurs."

It looked as if Rocco was right. The new captain was young—much younger than the previous one—but there was an air of quiet competence about him that was reassuring. His young face was stolid, seamed with tired lines, and his deep-set brown eyes were continually alert. He seemed to see everything while apparently looking at nothing. His voice carried down the line; he didn't raise it or speak loudly, yet every man could hear him distinctly.

"My name is Saunders," he said, "and I'm an easy guy to get along with." His eyes looked down the line. Every man felt he was talking to him alone. "All you have to do to get along with me is to stay alive." He paused again and looked at them. "From here on, you forget everything you ever heard except what you learned to stay alive. I want men, not heroes. Men, not corpses.

"To stay alive you must remember a few simple things. One, keep your head down. By that I mean don't get curious and try to look over the top of the trench to see what the

Heinies are doing. Lookouts will be posted for that job. Don't do it if it's not assigned to you. Two, keep your weapons clean and in good working order. The guy who lets his gun get fouled up is generally a corpse before he can get around to cleaning it again. Three, do what you're told and nothing else. What we tell you to do is designed with but one thought in mind: your safety or—as little risk as can be afforded."

He stopped talking and looked down the line again. "Do you understand me?" He waited for a reply. There was no answer. He smiled. "Follow those rules and we'll all be on the same boat together going home. Don't follow those rules and you might make the same trip home, but you won't know it. Any questions?" he asked. There were none. He stood there for a few seconds looking at them; then he turned and walked to the edge of the trench.

Silently he placed his hands on a block of wood and raised himself cautiously toward the top of it. Slowly his head appeared over the top of the trench. There was a slight ping and a mound of dirt jumped into the air near his head as he quickly dropped back into the trench. He sprawled on his hands and knees for a moment before he rose and faced them. There was a strangely mocking light in his eyes as he spoke.

"See what I mean?" he asked.

The three of them formed a little triangle as they squatted on the ground at the bottom of the trench. Their hands held little metal cups of coffee, and the steam from it rose in clouds up to their faces.

Rocco lifted his cup to his lips and took a long sip of the inky black fluid. He put it down with a sigh. "I hear talk we're goin' over in the mornin'," he said.

"Crap," Joe replied comfortably. "I been hearin' that ever since we got here, and that's more'n five weeks ago."

Johnny just grunted and drank his coffee.

"This ain't the crap," Rocco insisted. "If it was, why would they be pilin' all these guys in here every night? I think we might be about ready now."

Johnny thought it over. Rocco's statement added up. Every night since they arrived more men had been coming up. Last night was the first night no new arrivals had come. Maybe they had their quota and were ready to kick off.

"To hell with it," Joe said, finishing his coffee and putting the metal cup down. He loosened his belt and leaned comfortably back against the wall of the trench and lit a cigarette. "I wish I was back in that little village where we were the night we came up. Those French babes know how to please a man. I could stand a little of that right now."

A soldier came up to them. Rocco, looking up, saw it was the lieutenant and started to get up.

The officer stopped him with a gesture. He looked down at them. "Savold," he said talking to Rocco, "get your platoon inspected. See that everything's in shape and let me know what you need by tonight."

"Yes sir," Rocco answered.

The officer walked away. Rocco got to his feet. "It's beginning to look like I was right," he said.

Johnny looked up at him. "Yeanh."

The officer came back. He seemed to be hurried. "Savold!" he called.

Rocco turned to him. "Yes, sir."

"Take over as acting sergeant," the officer said. "Johnson just got hurt. Got someone for corporal?"

"How about Edge here?" Rocco gestured with his hand.

The officer turned and looked at Johnny. After a moment he spoke. "All right. Edge, you're acting corporal." He turned back to Rocco. "Tell Edge what he has to do, then come down to meet me at the captain's dugout." He turned on his heel and walked away rapidly.

Johnny turned to Rocco. "What did you go and do that for?" he asked.

"You can use the extra ten bucks a month, can't you?" Rocco grinned.

There was a puddle of water at the bottom of the shell hole and they clung to its side to keep from getting wet. Not that it would make a great difference now. It had been raining all night and their clothes were soaked through and caked with mud. It was just instinctive—an inner desire to retain some degree of comfort.

"Where in hell are those guys Rocco said would meet us here?" Joe grumbled.

Johnny puffed at his cigarette in his closed palm. "I don't know and I don't care," he answered. "I'm willing to stay here an' wait for them for the rest of the war if I have to. I don't like it out there, it ain't healthy."

Joe grubbed a cigarette from him. He lit it carefully from Johnny's cigarette, shielding them so the glow would not reveal their sanctuary. The chatter of a machine gun rose in a crescendo over their heads. They could hear the whine of the bullets as they passed over them.

"They're gonna have to knock out that gun before we kin go any further," Joe said, listening to its noise.

Johnny looked at him. "Whatta yuh worryin' about? In a hurry?"

Joe shook his head. "Nope, but I was thinkin' maybe they expect us to do it."

"What if they do?" Johnny asked. "We're not mind-readers. Nobody told us to do it. Remember what the captain said? Just do what you're told, no more. We did what we were told. From here on out, I stay until I'm told different."

Joe didn't answer. He began to scratch his head reflectively under his helmet. Suddenly he swore. He pulled something from his hair and threw it into the water. "Those God-damn cooties are drivin' me nuts," he said.

Johnny leaned back against the wall of the crater and shut his eyes. He was tired. For three days they had been pushing forward. No rest. Now he felt he could go to sleep right in the middle of no man's land.

Joe shook him. He opened his eyes. It was night again. When he had shut them it had been late evening and the last traces of daylight still hung around in corners of the sky. "I must have been sleeping," he said sheepishly.

Joe grinned at him. "I'll say you were. You were snoring so loud I was afraid they could hear you in Berlin. I gotta hand it to yuh though, if you can sleep out here."

The chatter of the machine gun drowned out Johnny's reply. They were silent for a while. Joe fumbled in his knapsack and took out a bar of chocolate. He broke it in two and gave half to Johnny. They chewed on it, letting the rich chocolaty sweetness fill their mouths.

"I been thinkin'," Joe said.

"Yeah?"

"They must expect us to get that gun," he said. "Otherwise they wouldn't be waitin'."

"That ain't our worry," Johnny said. "Nobody told us."

Joe looked at him, his eyes narrowed a little. "This is a case where nobody can tell us and you know it. We have to make up our own minds."

"My mind's made up," Johnny answered. "I'm following orders. I'm staying here."

Joe watched him for a minute, then he shifted over onto his knees. He took two hand grenades from his belt and examined them. Then he looked over at Johnny. "I'm gonna take a whack at 'em."

"You're stayin' here," Johnny said flatly.

Joe leaned his head to one side and eyed Johnny speculatively. "You gonna make me?" he asked. His voice just as flat as Johnny's had been.

They stared at each other a moment, then Johnny smiled. He shoved Joe with the flat of his hand. "Okay," he said. "If yuh wanna be a hero I better go along and look out for yuh."

Joe took his hand gruffly and squeezed it. He smiled. "I knew you'd see it, kid."

Johnny smiled back at him. He took two hand grenades from his own belt and looked at them. Satisfied that they were in working order, he turned back to Joe and said: "I'm ready if you are."

"I'm ready." Joe began to crawl to the top of the shell hole. He looked behind him at Johnny, who was crawling up to him. "I couldn't stand those cooties any more nohow."

They were on the edge of the crater. Cautiously they peered over it. The chatter of the machine gun revealed flashes of light coming from ahead of them.

"See it?" Johnny whispered.

Joe nodded.

"You take it from the right, I'll hit from the left," Johnny whispered.

Joe nodded again.

"What's the matter?" Johnny asked nervously. He was beginning to sweat a little. "Cat got your tongue?"

Joe grinned at him. "I'm too scared to talk," he said. H

raised himself to his hands and knees. "Come on kid," he said. "Let's break their asses!" And then he was running zigzag across the field.

Johnny huddled there for a second, then he followed him.

8

HE LAY quietly on the bed listening to the music that came in the open window. His eyes were wide and staring, yet they saw nothing. He didn't turn them toward the window. He didn't want to see the kind of day it was, the sky so soft and blue, the sunlight so golden on the fresh spring green of the trees. With one hand he clutched the sheet that covered him to his chest as if he were afraid it would be torn from him.

The music stilled, leaving a quiet that echoed in his mind. Unconsciously he listened for the next tune. He knew what it would be, they always played it just when the bus was pulling out.

He reached for a cigarette on the little table next to the bed. He put it in his mouth and lit it. He drew deeply on it, waiting for the music to begin again.

The sound of voices came to him. They floated lightly and softly on the breeze. Men's voices. Women's voices. Nice words. Soft words. Tender and somehow gruff words.

"So long nursey, if yuh wasn't a looey I'd kiss yuh!"

A soft warm laugh and then the answer: "Go ahead, soldier, but watch that arm. Don't forget what the doctor said!"

Other voices. Men's voices. Man talk. "I coulda got in, bud. Honest. But then she had to go an' pull her rank on me!"

Disgusted agreement. "Yeanh. They only put out for officers."

The first two. His voice: "I'll miss you."

Her voice: "I'll miss you too."

"Kin Ah come back an' see yuh sometimes?"

A second's hesitation, and then the reply: "What do you want to do that for, soldier? You're going home!"

One at a time the voices faded away. For a moment there was a silence, then the roar of a motor being started.

His free hand tightened on the sheet. Now. Now it was coming. The music hit him like a wave in the ocean. It rolled over him until he felt he was drowning in it. It was loud. It was brassy. It was written to torment him.

"When Johnny comes marching home again, tra la, tra la."

He put his hands to his ears to shut out the sound. But the music was loud and it pushed its way past his hands. He heard the gears being meshed, the cries of farewell, and over it all beat the loud, pulsing, dissonant sound of the music.

At last the music died away. He took his hands down from his ears. They were damp with the sweat that had run down his face. He took the cigarette from his mouth and put it in the ashtray on the little table. He dried his hands on the bedsheet.

Slowly the tension seeped from him. His eyelids drooped and almost closed. He was tired. His breathing slowed. And after a while he slept.

The sound of dishes rattling in a tray awakened him. With the same motion with which he opened his eyes, he reached for a cigarette. Before he could light it, a steady hand held a match under it.

Without looking up, he dragged deeply on the cigarette. "Thanks, Rock," he said.

"I got your lunch, Johnny. D'yuh want tuh get outta bed to eat it?" Rocco's voice was as steady as his hand had been.

Instinctively Johnny's eyes turned to the crutches at the foot of the bed. They leaned against the bed, a constant reminder of what he had become. He shook his head. "No."

He lifted himself with his hands as Rocco straightened the pillow behind him and bolstered it so that it would support his back. Rocco put the little stand on the bed across his thighs. He looked down at the plate and then away.

"I'm not hungry."

Rocco pulled a chair next to the bed and sat down and looked at him. He took out a cigarette and lit it. He let the smoke out his nostrils slowly. "I can't figure you out, Johnny," he said quietly.

Johnny didn't answer.

"You're supposed to be a buggin' hero, an' yet you're

afraid to get out of bed," he continued in the same quiet voice. "You're the same guy that charged a German machine-gun nest single-handed. They pinned a medal on yuh. In fact, two medals. Ours an' the Frenchies'." His voice filled with quiet wonder. "An' yet yuh won't get outta bed."

Johnny uttered one violent ugly word. He turned and looked at Rocco's impassive face. "Let them go walk on their friggin' medals. They gave 'em to Joe too, but it don't do him any good now. I tole yuh enough times that I didn't go alone. If I'da known Joe got it, I woulda quit right there. I didn' wanna be a hero."

Rocco didn't answer and they sat there silently smoking their cigarettes. Johnny was the first to break the silence.

He gestured toward the seven empty beds in the room with him. "When is the new batch comin' in?" he asked.

Rocco turned and looked at the beds and then turned back to him. "Tomorrow morning," he answered. "Till then yuh got a private room." He looked at Johnny speculatively. "What'sa matter, Johnny, getting lonely?"

Again Johnny didn't answer.

Rocco stood up and pushed his chair back. He looked down at Johnny. The sympathy that showed on his face was not apparent in his voice; it was studiedly casual. "Yuh could've gone with 'em if yuh wanted, Johnny."

Johnny's face froze into a mask. His voice was as casual as Rocco's had been. "I like the service here, Rock. I think I'll stay awhile."

Rocco smiled slowly. "This is a transient hotel, Johnny. It ain't my idea of a place to settle down."

Johnny squashed his cigarette in the tray. He looked up at Rocco. His voice was bitter. "You can afford to have your ideas, Rock. Nobody's makin' you stay here, but if you do, keep 'em to yourself."

Rocco didn't answer; he picked up the tray silently and put it back on the little wagon. He pushed it toward the door of the room, walked back to the bed, and picked up the crutches. He looked at them and then turned to Johnny.

"We got guys here who'd think they was lucky if they kin use these. Get wise to yourself, Johnny. You can't lay in bed all your life."

Johnny turned his face to the wall, away from him.

Rocco stood there a moment. Something inside him wanted

to cry. It had been that way ever since he came across Johnny lying in the little ditch where the machine gun had been.

A few yards away was Joe's body and in the trench near the gun were three dead German soldiers. Johnny was almost unconscious, but he kept saying over and over in a mad sort of delirium: "My leg, the bastards stuck it with a lot of needles!"

He knelt swiftly at Johnny's side and rolled him over. Johnny's right trouser leg was soaked with blood. He swore quietly to himself as he quickly cut the trouser from it and saw the line of perforations made by the bullets just above the knee. The blood seemed to pulse its way through the opening.

He cut a strip from his blouse and made a rough tourniquet, which stopped the bleeding. It was after that he first tried to move the leg.

He could still hear Johnny's scream ringing in his ears. It was a sound of pain and horror. It hung high in the air over the now almost quiet battlefield.

"Rocco!" Johnny had screamed in a sudden burst of recognition. "Don't take my leg off!" Then Johnny's body had gone limp. He had fainted.

Rocco had carried him back to the medical officer. He stood there while the medic shook his head. He watched while the medic cut the flesh away above Johnny's knee and exposed the splintered bone. He watched the doctor almost casually take the amputated leg and throw it on a pile made up of others and then draw the skin of the stump down as tight as he could over the raw flesh and stitch it together, leaving only a small opening for suppuration.

It was while Rocco trudged along beside the stretcher as they took Johnny back to the small hospital after the operation that he felt Johnny's hand grabbing at his sleeve. He looked down.

Johnny's eyes were wide and staring at him. "Rocco, don't let them take my leg off. Stay with me. Don't let them!"

Rocco's eyes had filled with tears. "Go to sleep, Johnny," he said, "I won't let them hurt you."

The war was over and Rocco did not go home with the others. He transferred to the medics and followed Johnny from the hospital in France to the hospital on Long Island.

He had made a promise to himself that he would stay with Johnny as long as Johnny needed him. Maybe it was because he felt that it was his fault to begin with. Because he had issued the order that had sent Johnny on the mission. But it wasn't his fault that it got mixed up. Everything was wrong that day. He still couldn't figure out how, with everything going wrong, the attack could work out right. But it did.

And now he stood beside the bed looking down at Johnny. Pity surged within him and moved his hand. He placed it on Johnny's shoulder.

"Johnny," he said softly, "Johnny, look at me."

Slowly Johnny turned around, drawn by some inexorable warmth flowing from the hand on his shoulder. He looked into Rocco's face.

Rocco's eyes were deep with understanding. "I know how you feel, Johnny. But you're gonna have to face it. Yuh got things to do an' friends tuh meet on the outside. An' I'm not gonna let yuh hide from 'em in here." He drew a deep breath. "You're gonna walk because I'm gonna find the thing that will make you want to."

Johnny looked into his eyes and found himself slipping into their depths. Instinctively he pulled himself back. "If you want to find the thing that will make me walk," he said bitterly, "go find me my leg." He turned back to the wall.

Rocco's hand fell to his side. There was a pain inside him, a deep quiet hurt that was born of Johnny's repulse. Quietly he left the room.

At night Johnny had a dream. He was running down a long familiar street. It was a long street and its end was nowhere in sight. Yet Johnny knew what lay at the end of that street and he wanted to go there. He had been running for hours and hours and now the end of the street was coming into view. A girl was standing there. She was only a slim figure, but he knew who it was even though he could not distinguish her features.

Just then the street filled with people. They stood and looked at him running and they laughed and pointed. "Look at that one-legged cripple trying to run," they laughed.

At first Johnny didn't pay any attention to them. His mind

was on that girl who was standing there waiting for him. But as he drew nearer and nearer to her, the people began to laugh louder and louder. At last he stopped. "What's so funny?" he asked.

"You," one of them answered derisively. "Everybody knows a one-legged man can't run!"

"I can too!" Johnny said.

"You cannot!" a chorus of voices answered him mockingly.

"I can, I can!" he screamed at them. "I'll show you!"

He turned and started to run, but suddenly he realized he wasn't running at all, he was hopping. He tried desperately to run, his heart pounding, suddenly frightened. And then he fell.

The crowds of people gathered around him. "See," they said, "we were right. You can't run." They laughed at him.

"I can run, I can run, I can run," he sobbed, struggling to get to his feet. He looked down the street toward the girl. She had turned and was walking away from him. "Wait for me!" he cried desperately. "I can run!" But she was gone.

He opened his eyes in the night; they were wet with his tears. He took a cigarette from the table with trembling fingers and put it between his lips. He was looking for a match when suddenly one glowed in front of him.

He dragged on his cigarette and then looked up. Rocco's face was limned in the dim glow from the match. Johnny took another deep drag from the cigarette. "Don't you ever sleep, Rock?" he asked.

Rocco blew out the match. In the dark his teeth shone as he smiled. "How can I," he replied, "if I have to keep chasing you up and down the halls all night?"

Johnny looked at him in sudden surprise. "What do you mean?"

Rocco smiled again. "I heard yuh yelling an' decided to look in. You were poised there on the end of the bed, ready to take off. I pushed you back an' you started to holler: 'I can run.'"

"I must've been dreaming," Johnny said.

"Not for my money you weren't," Rocco said quietly. "It wouldn't s'prise me atall to find yuh doin' it. Some day maybe." He picked up the crutches and tapped them together. "After yuh learn to walk!"

9

THE recreation hall was crowded as Rocco pushed the wheel-chair toward a small space on the floor where Johnny could see the screen. Johnny looked around him. The faces he saw were eager, expectant, bright with anticipation.

Ever since the news had got around a week ago that they were going to see a moving picture in the recreation hall, the talk around the hospital had been about nothing else. Men who had not displayed interest in anything heretofore were suddenly interested, alive.

Johnny had been one of these, much to Rocco's surprise. When he had heard about it, he had straightened up in bed. "I want to see the picture," he said to Rocco.

Rocco looked at him. There was a look on Johnny's face he hadn't seen for a long time. A look of anticipation, of excitement. "Sure," he said, "sure. Walk or ride?"

Johnny looked at the crutches and then back at Rocco. "I think I'll ride," he said, trying to smile. "It's got more class and besides it guarantees a seat."

Rocco laughed. Suddenly he began to feel better. It was the first time in a long while he had heard Johnny try to joke.

During the week that followed, Johnny plied Rocco with questions. Did he know what picture it was? Who was in it? What company made it? Who directed it?

Rocco didn't know any of the answers. It seemed no one did. All they knew was that they were going to see a picture. He thought it was strange that Johnny should ask all these questions. "How come you're so curious about the picture?" he asked.

But Johnny didn't answer and Rocco thought he had fallen asleep. But he hadn't. He lay there, his head on the

pillow, his eyes shut, but his mind was awake—vividly awake
with an excitement he never thought he would know again.
He had not written to Peter or anyone since he had been
hurt. Their letters had been unanswered. He didn't want
any sympathy, any acts born of charity. If he had been un-
hurt, he would have gone back gladly, but this way, crip-
pled, he could not envision himself as being anything less
than a burden to them. So he had not written and had
closed his heart and mind to the past.

He looked around the hall. The projection machine was
not too far behind him. Lovingly he let his eyes dwell upon
it with all the fondness a man might look at his home. And
it was true. Suddenly he was homesick. Homesick for the
smell of the celluloid strips as they ran through the projector
and came out warm. For the thin, tangy, crackling ozone-
like smell of the carbon arc lights in the machine itself.

He gestured to Rocco. "Push me over to the machine," he
said, "I want to see what it looks like."

Rocco pushed him near it and he sat there quietly watching the operator thread the film into the sprockets. He felt
good just watching him.

They began to draw the curtains over the windows and
gradually the room grew dark. Then it was pitch-black and
he couldn't see anything. He wanted desperately to light
a cigarette, but he remembered he couldn't smoke sitting
near the film as he was. He heard the faintly familiar buzz
as the carbon sparks caught, and then the strong bright light
flashed on the screen.

Words flashed on. At first they were blurred and then
they were clear and distinct as the operator set the focus
on his lens. Johnny read the words, his lips moving as he
passed over them.

To the soldiers at Long Island State Hospital:

*The motion-picture equipment and the film you are
about to see has been donated to us by Mr. Peter Kessler, president of Magnum Pictures, Inc. He has made
this presentation to us on behalf of the more than fifty
of his co-workers and employees who have served with
us during the past war, many of whom have not returned.*

We can do no more than say "Thanks" to Mr. Kess-

*ler for his kind and generous gift and express our
appreciation by enjoying the show that is about to
follow.*

SIGNED: *Col. James F. Arthur, U.S.A.*
COMMANDING OFFICER,
LONG ISLAND STATE HOSPITAL

The words flashed from the screen almost before Johnny
could grasp their meaning. He had been frozen to his chair
when Peter's name had flashed on the screen, but now it
was gone.

And in its place came the familiar trade-mark, the opening shot that identified every Magnum Picture: the big
champagne bottle with the champagne flowing into a glass
until the glass was filled to the brim. Then the words
covering the whole screen in Gothic lettering:

MAGNUM PICTURES
PRESENTS

Johnny's voice reached Rocco's ears in an agonized whisper. "Take me out of here, Rock!" it said with suppressed
intensity. "Take me out!"

For a moment Rocco stood still in surprise. He didn't
understand it. Johnny had been so eager to see the picture,
and now before it began he wanted to leave. He leaned
forward. "What'sa matter, Johnny?" he whispered in his
ear. "Yuh sick?"

He could see Johnny's fists clenched on the arm of the
chair as he replied: "No. Just take me out, that's all.
Take me out!"

He steered the wheelchair to the door and out. The bright
lights in the hall hurt his eyes and he blinked for a moment; then he looked at Johnny.

Johnny's eyes were squeezed tightly shut, so tight that
tears stood in the corners of them. His face was white and
strained and drops of sweat stoood out on his pallid skin.

Quickly Rocco pushed him back to his room and helped
him into bed. Johnny's body was trembling. Gently Rocco
covered him and stood near him. "Was it somebody you
knew, Johnny?" he asked gently.

Johnny's eyes opened suddenly and stared at him. Accidentally Rocco had stumbled on the truth. He must not know any more. "No," he said slowly. What was that thing he had heard the doctors talking about the other day—claustrophobia, the fear of being shut up in a small place and not being able to get out. Make Rocco think that was what had been the matter with him.

"Suddenly I couldn't stand it in there any more," he said. "I felt I would never get out." He laughed self-consciously. "I must have that claustro—er—something the doctors talk about."

Rocco looked at him but didn't answer. His mind was working. Johnny wasn't fooling him this time. He was going to find the real reason behind the way Johnny had acted. If he had really been afraid of being cooped up in there, he never would have been able to stay in this room so long a time.

The girl came out of the officer's room. She smiled at Rocco. "You may go in now, sergeant. Captain Richards will see you."

He thanked her and went into the little office. He drew himself to attention and saluted the officer.

The officer negligently returned his salute and looked up at him wearily. "Sit down, sergeant," he said in a tired voice. "We don't hold with the formalities in here."

Rocco sat down in a chair opposite the officer's desk. The officer looked down at the paper on his desk and then up at Rocco. "Your request is a most unusual one, sergeant," he remarked.

Rocco leaned forward in his chair. "It's the only way I believe we can help him, sir."

The officer grunted and looked down at the paper on his desk again. He studied it for a few minutes and then spoke. "I have Corporal Edge's service record here as you requested, but there is nothing on it that would give us any clues as to his family or friends or background. He took no life insurance from us and the only one to be notified in case of injury to him is one Joseph Turner, now deceased." He took a pipe from his desk and filled it with tobacco. He held a match to it until it was drawing comfortably. He looked over at Rocco. "You say he says he has no place to go and that he wants to remain here."

Rocco nodded.

The captain shook his head. "Well, there's no way we can force the man to leave short of bodily ejection if he doesn't want to. The only thing I can see is to transfer him to a mental hospital."

Rocco jumped to his feet. "There's no reason for that, sir," he said quickly. "Johnny's all right. There's no more the matter with him than there is with me."

"You seem to know him very well," the officer said.

"We were buddies," Rocco answered simply. "We were in the same outfit overseas. I sent him on that mission on which he got hurt and Joe got killed."

The officer nodded his head slowly. "I see," he said, "and you feel responsible for him?"

"Sort of," Rocco admitted.

"Is that why you stayed in?" the officer asked.

"Yes, sir," Rocco answered.

The officer was silent for a while and then he spoke. "I commend you for your feelings, sergeant, but if all the people in the service took their responsibilities as deeply as you, we would have more orderlies in the hospitals than patients."

Rocco made no reply.

The officer continued: "That, however, does not resolve our problem. Have you any further suggestions?"

Rocco leaned forward in his seat. He spoke anxiously. "If you could get Joe Turner's service record, maybe something on it would give us an idea of Johnny's background."

The captain thought that over. "And if we did, sergeant, we are not allowed to investigate any further." He paused for a moment and then added: "Officially."

Rocco smiled understandingly at him. "I know that, sir," he said, "but I might accidentally stumble across something that would be of great help."

The captain stood up. He returned Rocco's smile. "Accidentally, of course."

Rocco got to his feet. "Then you will try to get a copy of Joe's service record, sir?"

The captain nodded his head.

Rocco stood on the street in front of the building. The sign over the doorway read: "Magnum Pictures Company,

Inc." He hesitated a moment and then entered the building. He was in a small reception room.

A girl's face peeked through a small window at him. "No hiring done here, soldier," she said.

"I'm not looking for a job, miss," he said. "I came to see someone."

"Oh, I'm sorry, sir," she said. "Whom did you wish to see?"

Rocco took the slip of paper from his pocket and looked at it. "Mr. Peter Kessler."

"Your name, sir?" she inquired.

"Sergeant Savold, Rocco Savold," he answered.

"Won't you sit down, please?" she said. "I'll see if Mr. Kessler can see you."

Rocco sat down. He sat there for almost fifteen minutes. He wondered if the girl had forgotten about him. The window flew up suddenly and the girl's face looked out at him.

"I have Mr. Kessler's secretary on the phone. What do you wish to see Mr. Kessler about? He's very busy at the moment. If you tell her your business, she will put you down for an appointment."

Rocco hesitated for a second. He didn't want to talk with the secretary, but she would have to do if he couldn't talk directly with Mr. Kessler. He nodded.

The girl handed a phone through the open window to him. "Hello," he said into it.

The secretary's voice was briskly efficient and impersonal. "I'm Miss Andersen, Mr. Kessler's secretary. Can I help you?"

"I—uh, I don't know, miss," he said, "I wanted to speak to Mr. Kessler on a personal matter."

"You can speak with me," the pleasant impersonal voice replied, "I'm also his personal secretary."

He thought for a second. She would have to do. "I wanted to speak to him about Johnny Edge," he said. There was a sudden silence on the other end of the phone. "Did you hear me, miss?" he asked anxiously.

The voice that spoke now was a different one from that he had heard before. "I heard you," it said. It was very faint, he could hardly hear her. "You wanted to speak about Johnny Edge?"

"That's right, miss," he said, suddenly excited. "Do you know him?"

"Yes," she answered. "Is he all right?"

"Sure," he said, smiling into the phone, "sure."

"Thank God," came the fervent whisper back into his ear.

10

Rocco pushed the wheelchair into a small walk on the far end of the grounds. They were almost a quarter of a mile away from the hospital. It was quiet here. Tall hedges growing on either side of the walk, small beds of flowers spaced carefully between them. The wheelchair stopped. Johnny looked up.

Rocco's hands were going through his pockets.

"What are you lookin' for, Rock?" he asked.

"My cigarettes," Rocco answered. "I'm fresh out."

"Take mine," Johnny said, reaching into his pocket. There weren't any there. Puzzled, he looked in the other pocket of his blouse. It was empty too. Funny, he thought; he had put some there just before they left. "I'm out too," he said.

Rocco looked at him strangely. "Yuh mind if I run back to the canteen an' get some?" he asked. "I'll be back in a few minutes."

"Go ahead," Johnny said, "I'll be all right."

Rocco turned and started back. Johnny turned the wheelchair into the sun and leaned his head back. He could feel the warm rays of it on his face. It felt good. His hand hung over the sides of the chair and toyed with the long blades of grass. Idly he pulled at a few and stuck them in his mouth. They tasted a bitter green. He smiled to himself. "You can't taste a color," he thought. He sat there basking pleasantly in the sun.

He felt drowsy and lazy. It would be good to get out of the chair and lie down in the cool grass and rest. He turned his head to one side and looked at the ground. It would be good, but it was not for him. He would not walk on the grass and throw himself on the ground as he used to. It was for others to do, not him. He shut his eyes again and faced the sun.

He heard footsteps behind him. "Rocco?" he asked without turning his head or opening his eyes. "Give me a cigarette."

He felt a hand place a cigarette between his lips. He heard a match striking. He drew on the cigarette and felt the smoke going deep into his lungs. "It's nice out here," he said.

"You like it, Johnny?" It was a familiar voice, but not Rocco's.

He opened his eyes suddenly and spun the chair around. A cry burst from his lips. "Peter!"

Peter stood there, his face pale and drawn, his eyes wet with tears. He shook his head. "Yes, Peter," he said slowly. "Didn't you want to see me, Johnny?"

Johnny sat there completely still, his cigarette frozen to his lips. He couldn't speak.

Peter moved closer to him and took his hand.

He could feel the warmth of Peter's hand on his and suddenly his feelings rose in his throat and began to choke him. He leaned forward over Peter's hand and began to cry.

Peter's other hand rested on Johnny's hair. "Johnny," he said, his voice shaking, "Johnny, did you think you could always hide from those who love you?"

11

THEY stood there on the sidewalk as the cab pulled away. Johnny looked down at his crutches. They were new and shone with a yellowish brightness. The side of his trouser leg was pinned neatly to his thigh. His one leg looked strange and lonely there between the yellow crutches.

He smiled wryly at Rocco and looked over at the building. The stone letters on the building spelled out: MAGNUM PICTURES.

"Might as well get it over with," he said.

Rocco looked at him, "Yeanh."

Slowly Johnny moved to the door and hesitated when he reached it. His face was white. There were small beads of sweat on his forehead. "I don't want anybody feeling sorry for me," he said in a low voice.

Rocco smiled reassuringly at him. "Don't worry about that. Nobody will feel sorry for you. They might feel a little strange at first and want to help you a little more than would be normal, but they'll soon get over it when they see you can manage. Then things will be the same as they always were."

"They better be," Johnny said.

"They will," Rocco answered, opening the door for him. Johnny entered the small waiting-room and Rocco followed him. The girl's face looked curiously at him through the small glass. She made no move to open it.

Rocco smiled at her and motioned to Johnny. "Through that door," he said, pointing.

Johnny looked about him curiously. They had changed the place around. He didn't say anything, but went through the door indicated and they were in a long corridor. From behind the door came the sounds of people working. Typewriters, adding-machines, people talking. They moved toward the end of the corridor. Occasionally someone would pass them in the hall and look at them curiously, impersonally.

Johnny felt as if he were in a strange place. He recognized none of the people who had passed him. They came to another door marked: "Executive Offices."

They went through it and were in a small, pleasantly lighted corridor. There were several comfortable chairs placed there, and the floor was covered with a soft red carpet. There was no sound in there.

"Doesn't sound as if anyone is in here," Johnny said.

"We're early," Rocco answered. "Peter told me that no one got in much before ten o'clock."

Johnny looked at his wristwatch. It was a quarter past nine. "Good. I'll have a chance to sit down for a few minutes before I get started."

"Your office is down the end of the hall, next to Peter's," Rocco said.

Johnny followed down the corridor. Several of the doors had names on them. Johnny did not know them. He had been gone only a little more than two years and yet the business had grown so rapidly during that time that new names had appeared on doors. He felt strange, out of place.

They passed a door with Peter's name on it. "Yours is the next office," Rocco said, stopping in front of it.

Johnny looked at the door. His name had been painted on it. The paint looked new, almost as if it hadn't dried yet. Impulsively he put his fingers on it. It was dry.

Rocco smiled at his gesture.

He smiled back at him.

"Shall we go in?" Rocco asked, still smiling.

Johnny nodded.

Rocco threw open the door and stepped back as Johnny came to the threshold.

Johnny stood there in surprise as a wave of sound greeted him. His face went strangely pale and he seemed to totter a little as he leaned there on his crutches.

Rocco put a hand out to steady him.

The room was packed with people—people whom Johnny knew and people whom Johnny had never seen before. Peter and George and Jane were standing in front of the others, looking at him.

The room was all decorated with red, white, and blue bunting, and a big painted sign hung from the ceiling in the middle of the room. "Welcome Back, Johnny," it read in big red letters.

The sound died down and he stood there looking at them. He opened his mouth twice to speak, but nothing came out.

Jane stepped forward and held out her hand. Johnny took it. "Hello, boss," she said as if he had just come back from lunch.

As if it were a signal, someone turned on a phonograph and music began to blare forth and everybody began to sing:

"When Johnny comes marching home again, tra la, tra la."

He could see the tears in her eyes and felt his own eyes beginning to smart. "Janey," he managed to say.

She threw her arms around him and kissed him.

His eyes were clouded with moisture. He tried to put his arms around her, and one of his crutches fell to the floor with a clatter. He stumbled and would have fallen had Rocco not put an arm around him and held him up.

He looked at the crutch lying there on the floor. Then, strangely, as he looked at it, its bright yellow wood gleaming against the soft red carpet, he began to feel helpless. And with that feeling of helplessness came an even stranger feeling of terror—a terror of all these people watching him.

He shut his eyes for a moment. This feeling would pass, he told himself desperately. But it persisted. He began to feel his head reeling. He could feel himself stumbling, falling, but he kept his eyes tightly shut.

He could feel people helping him to a chair. He heard Rocco's voice quietly asking people to leave. He could hear Rocco explaining to them that he was still tired, still weak, and all this excitement was too much for him.

He could sense the sudden silence in the room as the people left it. Slowly he opened his eyes and looked around him. He was on a small couch. Peter and George and Jane were watching him with frightened looks on their faces. Rocco was holding a small glass to his lips.

Automatically he drank it. The liquor burned through his throat to his stomach like a livid flame. Color crept back into his cheeks. He smiled wanly at them, but the fear that had been in him still clung to the corners of his heart.

"You all right, Johnny?" Peter asked anxiously.

He nodded his head. "I'm all right," he answered. "Too much excitement I guess. I'll feel better after I get a little rest." He shut his eyes again and let his head sink back against the pillow of the couch. He wished they would go away and leave him alone.

He heard the door open and close behind them and he opened his eyes again. Only Rocco was in the room with him now.

"Rock," he whispered.

"What is it, Johnny?"

"Rock, you gotta stay with me, Rock," he said, his voice desperate and cracked with strain. "You gotta stick with me. I'm afraid to be alone with them."

Rocco tried to smile reassuringly at him. "Whatta yuh got to be afraid of, Johnny? They're all your friends."

"I know," Johnny whispered in the same tone of voice, "but I feel so helpless without a leg. When I looked down and saw it wasn't there, I thought everybody was going to laugh at me."

"Nobody would laugh," Rocco said softly.

"I don't care," Johnny said, "I'm afraid. You gotta stick

close to me all the time, Rock. I can't face them alone."
He grabbed at Rocco's hand and held it tightly. "Promise
me, Rock, promise!"

Rocco looked down at him, his face softened. "All right,
Johnny," he said slowly, "I'll stick around."

"Promise!" Johnny insisted.

Rocco hesitated a moment. "I promise," he said reluctantly.

A little while later Jane came back into the office. She
was carrying a tray. On it was a pot of coffee and two cups.
"I thought some coffee would do you good," she said, placing the tray on a small table in front of his couch.

"It will help," Rocco said, pouring out a cup and giving
it to Johnny.

"Thanks," Johnny said to her. Suddenly he noticed her
hand. Something was sparkling on her finger.

He put his cup down and caught her hand and looked
at it. She was wearing a small engagement ring and a wedding band. "Janey," he cried out in surprise, "you're married!" He looked at her. "You should have told me. When
did it happen?"

"I wrote you," she said quietly. "It was about four
months after you went away."

"I never got the letter," he said. "What's he like?"

She looked at him a moment before she answered. "He
was a very nice guy. A soldier. I met him at a dance."

The tense in which she spoke suddenly sank into his
mind. He looked into her eyes. "He didn't come back?" he
asked softly.

She shook her head almost imperceptibly. "He—he didn't
come back."

He took both her hands. "I'm sorry, Janey. I didn't know.
No one told me."

"No one could. They didn't know where you were. We
tried to locate you, but everything was all mixed up and
we couldn't get anything straight."

They were silent for a few seconds, then she spoke again.
"But things aren't so bad. I've got the cutest little son."

Johnny looked at her. She stared back into his eyes. Her
gaze was steady, even a little bit proud. He dropped his eyes

to her hands. "There are a lot of things I got to catch up with around here," he said. "Everything has changed."

"Not everything, Johnny," she said. "Only what you think has changed."

12

ALL morning Johnny sat in his office with Peter. He listened quietly as Peter patiently explained the things that had happened while he was away. The business had grown in a manner that even Johnny had not expected. Magnum's profit last year alone amounted to over three million dollars.

They were now producing thirty feature pictures a year and a complete line of short subjects, which included two-reel and one-reel comedies, travelogues, newsreels, and animated cartoons. And, as Peter said, this was not enough. The demand for film entertainment seemed to be insatiable. Already he had plans under way to enlarge the studio to a fifty-picture-per-year capacity.

In addition to producing pictures, Magnum now owned in conjunction with George over forty theaters throughout the country and was planning to acquire or build as many more.

There was under discussion at the moment the advisability of Magnum establishing its own branch offices in principal cities throughout the country and distributing its own pictures. This would do away with the states' rights distributors, who now acted as Magnum's agents, and would save the company many thousands of dollars a year that it now paid as sales commissions. Borden last year had established his chain of exchanges as he called them, and it had been a very profitable one for him.

When Johnny had gone into the army, Magnum had employed a little over two hundred people at its studio and about forty people in New York. Now it employed over eight hundred people at the studio and almost two hundred people in its New York office, and plans were under way that would call for further expansion of both.

Johnny listened as his mind quietly assorted and catalogued what he heard. Peter no longer took complete charge of the studio. A studio manager was now responsible for production and answered only to Peter for his work. Sales were broken down into two divisions, domestic and foreign, each with a sales manager and his assistants, who were responsible for the business in their respective territories.

Next year Peter planned to go abroad with his foreign sales manager and establish offices and branch companies in every foreign country in the world.

Peter's job was now one of a co-ordinator and the responsibilities were many and varied. To do this job he needed capable assistants and people he could trust. Since his time was so taken up that he could not possibly give full attention to every matter that needed him, he had it in mind that Johnny would assume the job of his number-one assistant.

Johnny would stay in New York and everything that had to do with the running of the business would flow through him. Only those problems which absolutely needed Peter's decision would be passed on to him, and those that did not need his personal attention would be settled by Johnny.

To undertake this tremendous program of expansion Peter had instituted negotiations with the Bank of Independence, Al Santos's bank, for a loan of four and a half million dollars. When he heard the amount a low whistle escaped Johnny's lips. He was surprised not only because Peter spoke so casually and matter-of-factly about borrowing so large a sum of money, but also because Al Santos's bank was capable of lending that amount.

All through the morning as they talked, people kept coming in—men Johnny had known before, who came in to wish him welcome home, and men he had not known before, who were anxious to meet this man who was to take over the position of number-one assistant to the boss. There was throughout these meetings, no matter how brief, a feeling of mutual exploration and testing, the men trying to determine just how close Johnny actually was to the boss, and Johnny trying to fit them and their importance into the present organization.

There was also something new that Johnny, ever quick to sense the relationship of people, placed immediately and began to feel. A number of cliques had begun to form and make themselves felt. Different factions and groups within the organization were trying constantly to reach the boss's ear. He leaned back in his chair and smiled at Peter. "My head is spinning," he confessed ruefully. "I had no idea that the business had so expanded. I'll have to learn it all over again."

Peter smiled back at him proudly. "You won't have any trouble," he said confidently; "it's the same old business, only there's more of it." He got to his feet and looked down at Johnny. "Ready for lunch now?" he asked. "George will be waiting at the restaurant for us."

Johnny looked across the room to where Rocco had been sitting on the couch throughout their meeting. He had sat there quietly as if he were a part of the furniture in the office and he moved only when Johnny spoke to him or when Johnny wanted something. His dark-brown eyes had been on Johnny all morning, watching intently for any sign of weakness in him. They had seen none since the early morning. On the contrary, they had seen Johnny bloom into a new kind of life, take on an expectancy, a challenge, an excitement, that he had never seen in Johnny before. Much of what he had heard did not make sense to him, but he could see that Johnny had absorbed it all like a sponge soaking up liquid.

He had watched Johnny meet people with a sort of quiet warmth and charm that he had never thought Johnny possessed. The army was not the place to bring out such qualities in a man, he thought, but now he was beginning to understand why Joe Turner had acted toward Johnny as he did.

It was only when Johnny stood up that this quality in him seemed to disappear. His face would become strained and white and he would grow self-conscious and ill at ease and stumble and stammer over his choice of words, where ordinarily his conversation was concise and direct.

It was at such moments that sympathy for Johnny would pour over him like a wave. He could almost sense the pride that Johnny had once had in his body and in his physical appearance—the pride in having a body that matched his mind. Young and strong and healthy and filled with life and excitement and a sense of accomplishment.

He saw Johnny looking at him. In that look he read Johnny's mute appeal. Quietly he left his seat and walked over to him. He put one arm under Johnny's shoulders as Johnny adjusted the crutches. He handed him his hat as they went to the door.

"It's too bad that something can't be done about it," he said to himself, thinking about Johnny's leg. But nothing could be done about it. There was nobody on God's earth who could give it back to him.

At the door Johnny stopped and turned to Peter. "We're going to have to do something about Rock," he said in an embarrassed tone of voice. "I can't get along without him."

Peter looked swiftly from one to the other. Rocco didn't speak. "There's a job for him here with you," Peter said quickly, "if he wants it." He paused for a second, then spoke again. "It'll pay seventy-five a week," he added.

Johnny looked at Rocco. Rocco was thinking. Seventy-five per was more than he could make if he went back to a barber shop. It was nice dough. Besides, he had promised Johnny that he would stick with him. Almost imperceptibly he nodded his head.

Johnny turned to Peter and smiled. "Thanks, Peter. He'll take it."

Rocco stood in the doorway and watched them walk through Jane's office and out into the hall. Jane got up from her desk and walked over to him.

"You like him, don't you?" she asked.

He turned his gaze to her and looked into her eyes steadily. His eyes were dark and unfathomable, but there was a warmth in them that she could feel. "Yes," he answered simply. "Don't you?"

It was a moment before her reply came to him. "I loved him once," she said in a soft, puzzled voice. "And I love him now. Only they're different kinds of love." She looked down at the floor trying to find the words that would express what she felt. She looked up into Rocco's eyes; they were warm and friendly.

"It must be something when you can love a guy like mad at one time and then it is gone when you find that he doesn't love you. Not that way. And you can like him for what he is and then that liking turns into another kind of a love—a kind that seems to last without any memories of the hurt that the other had left. It must be something."

His voice was quiet. "It could be respect."

"It could be," she admitted. "But it's more than that. I can't just explain it. But it's not me I'm thinking about just now. It's Doris."

"Doris," he repeated after her. "Who is she?"

"Peter's daughter," she replied. "She is in love with him. And I think he was in love with her before he went away, even if he wouldn't admit it to himself."

"Why?"

"She's ten years younger than he. And he sort of helped bring her up since she was a kid. She used to call him uncle."

"Oh, I see," Rocco said slowly.

"But now," Jane continued as if he hadn't spoken at all, "I don't think the kid's got a chance. Somehow I feel that Johnny has closed his mind to her. He hasn't said a word about her all morning. Didn't even ask how she was. Now I feel that he is going to shut her out of his heart too."

"He's got a reason," Rocco said, coming to his friend's defense. "He doesn't want to stick the kid now that he's lost a leg."

She looked at him. "It wouldn't make any difference to her. It wouldn't make any difference to anyone who is really in love."

"It does when you're the one who feels that you're the burden," Rocco said.

Jane didn't answer. She turned to her desk and picked up her pocketbook and began to make up her face.

For a moment Rocco stood watching her, a sort of half smile on his face; then he spoke. "If you haven't a date for lunch," he asked, "how about me?"

She looked at him in surprise, then she smiled suddenly, almost mischievously. "You want to hear the whole story?" she asked.

"I'd like to," he admitted frankly.

"It began like this," she said, opening a closet and taking out her hat. "I was secretary to Sam Sharpe, an agent, and Johnny came into the office." She stopped in front of a mirror and put on her hat. In the mirror she looked at him in a sort of surprise. "No, it didn't," she said in a wondering tone of voice; "it started long before that, before I ever knew him."

Her hat was on and she turned around to face him. There was a warm, friendly smile on her lips. "Come to lunch," she said, "and I'll try to tell you the story from the beginning."

He took his hat and followed her from the office.

13

LUNCHEON had been a quiet affair. Peter and George had done most of the talking and Johnny listened. There was much he felt he had to learn and they were equally anxious to bring him up to date. Both men carefully avoided references to Johnny's injury; neither did they talk about Joe, for fear of bringing back unpleasant memories to him.

It passed quickly, and when Peter left Johnny at his office, he told him he would pick him up after the screenings that had been arranged for him were over. Johnny looked at him. "You don't have to do that, Peter," he said, "I'll see you in the morning."

Peter was surprised. "What do you mean? You're not coming home with me for dinner? After Esther has been planning all day to make your favorite dish—*knedloch* and chicken soup? And Doris is coming special down from school to be with us. It's like old times again, Johnny. You're coming home for dinner and I won't take no for an answer. I don't understand how you can think of anything else on your first night home."

Johnny looked at him dumbly. Doris. He had tried not to think of her all day, but he knew he would have to face it some time. She thought she was in love with him once, but it was silly, it was only a schoolgirl infatuation. She would be over it now.

But he knew he was wrong. He knew that it was something deeper and stronger than that. Otherwise he would not have felt as he had. And now, without a leg, a returning soldier. He could imagine her sympathy going out to him and awakening the feelings he had when he had gone away.

There was no way out, however. He would have to go and face it. And if she said anything about how they had felt and acted before he had left, he would have to tell her that it was only a kid thing on her part—that he had never felt anything but affection for her as a child.

Peter was looking at him. Peter would think it strange if he did not come—if he did not want to. He would be hurt. And Esther would feel bad too.

He forced a smile to his lips. "All right, if you want me to," he said. "I just didn't want to be any trouble to you."

Peter laughed. "Since when is your own any trouble?"

Johnny entered the office thoughtfully. Peter's voice ringing in his ears. The words kept repeating themselves over and over: "your own." Did it mean that Peter had an idea about Doris and himself? Maybe she had said something to her parents?

No, that was silly. She had nothing to tell them. It was just Peter's way of talking. They had been so close that Peter thought of him as part of the family, that was all.

He and Rocco sat in the darkened projection room and watched the screen. When the first picture had been completed he realized the screen itself had improved technically too. A great deal of the flicker from the screen had been cut down. The movements of the actors now seemed more real, more lifelike. The staccato-like movements of yesterday had been slowed down to a point where the figures no longer seemed to jump from place to place on the screen.

The methods of telling a story, too, had improved. The scenario was now a play that was easy to follow. The art of close-up, fade-out, titling, all had been related to make a more harmonious whole. He began to realize that he would have to make a trip out to the studio to learn more about these new techniques. The screen had outgrown him in the short time he had been away.

He lit a cigarette in the dark room. In the glow of the match he could see Rocco's face watching the screen, enrapt in the story. He smiled to himself. Just seeing Rock there made him feel better. It was funny how the thought that Rock was near him would steady him.

He remembered that dream he had had back in the hospital. Where he was trying to run and he fell and people laughed at him. He had been afraid of that ever since. He did not want people to laugh at him, nor did he want them to feel sorry for him. And when Rocco was around he knew that none of this would happen. Rocco had a way of foreseeing embarrassing situations and avoiding them. He had a way of turning talk away from things that might upset him. He would step between Johnny and any hurt that he felt would come to him.

He was glad that Rock had promised to stick around.

"My car is downstairs," Peter said. "I just called Esther and told her we'd be home in half an hour. She was as excited as a bride the first time her family is coming to dinner."

"I'm ready," Johnny answered quietly.

They went out into the street. There was a limousine waiting in front of the building, a chauffeur stood holding the door open.

Peter stood by and let Johnny get into the car first. The inside of the car was luxuriously furnished, all velour-lined. Peter followed him into the car, then Rocco clambered in on the other side of Peter.

Johnny looked around him. "This is class," he said. "New car, Peter?"

Peter nodded proudly. "Pierce Arrow," he said, smiling, "with a special custom-built body."

"It's okay," Johnny said.

The big car began to roll silently and smoothly. Soon they were on Fifth Avenue heading downtown. It slid to a stop in front of a large apartment house opposite Central Park.

A doorman opened the door of the car. "Good evening, Mr. Kessler," he said.

"Evening, Tom," Peter replied.

They waited for Johnny to get out of the car, then they went into the building. It was a new house.

Johnny looked around him. He didn't say anything, but he was impressed. You had to have pumpkins to live in a place like this. Now he began to realize in personal terms the import of all he had seen and heard during the day.

He followed Peter into an elevator. The car took them up eleven stories and let them out into a hall that was a luxuriously furnished as the lobby had been.

Peter stopped in front of a door and rang the bell.

Johnny looked at the door and his heart began to pound strangely within him. Unconsciously he braced himself.

The door opened. Esther stood there. For a moment ther

was an awkward silence while they looked at each other; then she came to him and threw her arms around him. She began to cry.

Johnny stood there stiffly, afraid to take his hands from his crutches because he might fall. He stared over her shoulder as she kissed his face. Doris was in the doorway. Her face was pale and thin and her eyes were wide and dark in the glow of the hall light.

Rocco, standing behind Johnny, could see their eyes talking over her mother's shoulder. He looked at Doris. Her hair hung loosely over her shoulders, framing her face into an oval mask. Her hands were clenched tightly. Her lids dropped over her eyes. It was as if someone had suddenly turned the lights off in her face. She looked toward the floor. Rocco could see the hard tears swim reluctantly toward the corner of her eyes. He saw her blink twice, trying to hold them back.

Somehow she knew then what Johnny had made up his mind to tell her. How she knew, Rocco could not determine. Not a word was spoken, but she knew. Her whole body showed that she knew it—the sudden loosening of the tense frame, the slight slumping of her shoulders.

It happened in only a moment, but Rocco knew a lifetime had passed for her.

Esther stopped kissing Johnny, stepped back from him, and holding him by the shoulders, looked at him. "My Johnny," she cried softly. "What have they done to you?"

"Mamma, don't be a fool," Peter said gruffly. "He's here, isn't he? What more can we ask?"

Dinner was a silent meal. They talked, but no one would speak of what was in their hearts. The silent tears were hidden behind smiling masks.

All through the meal Rocco could see Doris looking at Johnny. They were seated across the table from each other. Whenever he looked up he would see her watching him. Johnny's face was white and he spoke little. He didn't know what to say.

She had grown, matured, since he had last seen her. Then she had been a beautiful girl, but now she was a woman—a woman grown beautiful and somehow warm and gracious in a few years.

Dinner was over and they went into the living-room.

Johnny and Doris were last to leave; and for a moment they were alone in the dining-room. She put her coffee cup down and quietly got out of her seat and went over to him. His eyes were on her as she came close to his chair.

She bent over him. Her voice was quiet, controlled. "You didn't kiss me, Johnny."

He didn't answer. His eyes were on hers.

Slowly she pressed her lips to his. For a moment a spark leaped between them. Johnny could feel himself drawing to her, and he held himself back. The corners of her mouth trembled against his lips. He leaned away from her.

She straightened up and looked down at him. Her voice was low, with an undercurrent of hurt running through it. "You've changed, Johnny."

He looked at her. Then he looked down at his leg. "Yes," he said bitterly, "I've changed."

"I don't mean that," she said. "You've changed inside."

His voice was level. "It's possible. Everything that changes a man's appearance changes him. You change if you lose a tooth. You don't smile so often."

"But you still smile sometimes, Johnny. You don't grow cold and bitter."

He didn't answer.

She looked at him for a moment and could feel the tears come to her eyes and was ashamed of them. She tried to hold them back. Her voice shook a little as she spoke. "Remember when we spoke last—how we laughed and we looked at each other and you promised to bring me back a present?"

He shut his eyes. He remembered. "Yes," he said, knowing it would hurt her, "I remember. You were a kid then and the war was just another adventure and I promised to bring you a souvenir when it was over."

She winced as his words cut into her. "Is that all it meant to you?"

He opened his eyes wide and looked at her in apparent innocence. "That's all," he said. "Why? Was it supposed to mean anything else?"

He watched her turn from him and run to the door and out of the room. He struck a match with shaking fingers and lit a cigarette. He sat there for a moment before he struggled to his feet to go into the living-room.

AFTERMATH

1938

THURSDAY

THE sound of the drapes being drawn and the windows opened wide woke me up. For a moment I lay there in bed looking up at the ceiling vacantly. The room was strange to me and then suddenly I remembered where I was. It still seemed all wrong. I was supposed to be in New York. What was I doing in Hollywood?

Then it all came flooding back to me. I suppose it had been driven from my mind by that dream again—that dream in which I was running up a street that didn't exist to a girl I couldn't see. I had had that dream ever since the war and it always ended the same way. I fell and people were laughing at me.

They probably were laughing at me this morning. I had asked Farber in. Me. After all that had happened. I let Farber get his foot in the door. Now I had to pry him loose again and shut him out. I had done it once before. Could I do it again? I wasn't sure. This time it was my own fault.

"Good morning, Mr. John," Christopher's voice came from the side of the bed.

I sat up and looked at him. His black face was gleaming and split with a white toothy smile. "Good morning, Christopher," I replied. "How did you know I was here?" I had given him several weeks off because I didn't expect to be back for a while.

He looked at me seriously. "I read the papers that Mr. Peter was took sick and I figured that you would come back to be near him."

I didn't answer as he put the breakfast tray on the bed. Did everybody know how I would react to hearing about Peter except me? Christopher knew as well as I did about my quarrel with Peter and yet he also knew that I would be back.

I couldn't get away from it. They were right because here I was.

The papers were folded neatly on the corner of the tray. I opened them up while I sipped slowly at the orange juice. The headline in the *Reporter* was simple and right to the point:

FARBER IN AT MAGNUM

WITH MILLION-DOLLAR LOAN

In was right, but not for long if I could help it. If Ronsen hadn't come into my office just at that particular moment he never would have made it. I read the story with interest:

Speculation was rife today in the industry as to the meaning of Stanley Farber's million-dollar loan to Magnum. It was well known that Farber had been trying to get an interest in Magnum ever since Peter Kessler sold his interest to Laurence G. Ronsen. It was known at the time that Ronsen was inclined to give Farber this interest, but the one thing that held it up was the opposition of Magnum's prexy, John Edge. Edge and Farber had been feuding for fifteen years, ever since Edge had crowded Farber out of Magnum in a dispute over the theaters that Farber had been running for them.

Farber's nephew, David Roth, had been installed as studio exec at Magnum two months ago, before Edge had been elected prexy of the company. The first sign of a rift between Ronsen and Edge became apparent earlier this week when Edge, contrary to Ronsen's wishes, flew out here to be at the bedside of Peter Kessler, who had suffered a stroke.

It has been rumored but not confirmed that Farber would be given a large stock interest in Magnum as security for this advance and that he and Roth would be elected to Magnum's board of directors. It is also rumored but not confirmed that Roth would take charge of turning out Magnum's top product.

Further unconfirmed rumors are that Bob Gordon, studio manager at Magnum, will ankle the lot because of the breakdown of his responsibilities. This will leave Edge without a single representative on his home lot and in turn may cause him to leave also.

> *In addition to the loan, Farber also signed an agreement with Magnum which gave Magnum an automatic play-off for all their pictures in Farber's Westco theater chain.*

I closed the paper and finished the orange juice. Rumors were as much a part of Hollywood breakfasts as coffee. No breakfast was complete without them. I had had enough for the day.

Christopher poured coffee into my cup and took the cover off the bacon and eggs. The fresh crisp odor of the bacon rose from the plate. Suddenly I was hungry. I grinned at him. "I'm sure glad you came back, Christopher," I said.

He smiled back at me. "I am too, Mr. Johnny," he said. "I worries when you're home alone."

I stood on the sidewalk and lit a cigarette while I waited for Christopher to bring the car around. It was a fresh bright day and I had already begun to feel better. The depression that had settled upon me like a cloud when I had first heard about Peter seemed to be wearing off. It was hard to explain, but I always felt better when I had something or someone definite to fight.

Until now I had been fighting merely to hold the company together. I had never considered Ronsen a genuine problem. He was outside the industry, a stranger, a necessary evil, one that you had to tolerate as long as was necessary; then, when the need no longer existed, you got rid of him. But now that Farber was in, I had a personal interest in the fight. It was no longer a fight to hold the company together; it had turned into a fight over who would hold the company together. If Farber was interested, it meant that he thought there was still a buck to be made in the business. It was up to me to figure out what he planned to do and then screw him and do something better at the same time. This was a business where competition brought out the best in you. If you couldn't stand the gaff, there was no use in staying with it.

The car came rolling to a stop and I got into it. Christopher's face turned back to me. "The studio, Mr. Johnny?" he asked.

"No," I answered, "Mr. Kessler's house first."

He turned and put the car into gear. I leaned back against

the cushions. There was time for me to get to the studio now. It would be better for me to let Ronsen and Farber set their plans and announce them before I came to work. When I got in then, I would know what they intended to do and I would upset their little applecart. I smiled to myself. There really was no reason on earth why I should feel so good; how could one explain it? The fact remained that I did.

The nurse came into the hall and softly closed the door behind her. She spoke in a low voice so that she couldn't be heard in the sickroom. "You can go in now, Mr. Edge," she said, "but don't stay too long. He's still very weak."

I looked at Doris and she started to come in with me. The nurse put a hand on her arm. "One at a time please."

Doris smiled at me and stepped back. "Go in, Johnny," she said, "I've already seen him once this morning and I know he wants to see you."

I shut the door quietly behind me. Peter was lying on the bed, his head propped up by two pillows. He was very still and at first I thought he was asleep, for he didn't move. His face was very white and thin and his eyes were sunken deep into his cheekbones. Then slowly he turned his head toward me and opened his eyes. He smiled.

"Johnny." His voice sounded pleased even if it was faint.

I walked over to the bed and stood there looking at him.

His eyes looked up at me. They were bright and alive in his face even if he was weak. He made a slight gesture with his hand. "Johnny." There was no mistaking the pleasure in his voice now. It was a little stronger.

I took his hand and sat down in a chair next to the bed. His hand felt thin and I could feel the bones of it as he moved his fingers. I still couldn't speak.

"Johnny, I've been a fool," he said, his eyes looking into mine.

Everything inside me seemed to fill up and overflow as he spoke. "No more than me, Peter." My voice sounded strangely harsh in the still room.

He smiled wanly. "We seem to spend our lives making mistakes, which we spend our lives trying to make up for."

I couldn't answer. I just sat there holding his hand. Slowly his eyes closed and I thought he was asleep. I sat there quietly, afraid to move for fear I would disturb him. His hand was still in mine. I looked down at it. I could see a small blue vein throbbing on its back, over his fingers. I watched it fascinated. It seemed to swell slowly and then go down slowly.

His voice made me look up. The question startled me. "How's business, Johnny?" he asked. His eyes were bright and interested. For a moment it was almost like old times. It was his favorite question, the one he generally asked before anything else. The first of three. The second and third were "How's collections?" and "How's the bank balance?"

Before I knew it I was telling him. About George's deal to take the terrible ten. About Ronsen's squeeze to get Farber's million bucks. I left out all reference to the reasons why Ronsen and I differed.

As I spoke, color came back into his face and he looked more like the Peter of old. He didn't interrupt me, just listened, and when I finished, he seemed to settle back against the pillows with a sigh.

I looked at him anxiously. I was afraid I had tired him. But I didn't have to be. Hearing about the business seemed to act like a tonic to him. After a few seconds he spoke. His voice was a little firmer.

"They got no guts, Johnny, no guts," he said slowly, a slight smile playing around the corner of his mouth. "It looked very good to them, all they had to do to make money was turn out some pictures and issue some stock. But now when they're up against it, like we have been so many times, they're frightened. They run around like chickens with their heads cut off looking for somebody or something to save them." He turned his face to me. There was a real smile on his lips now. His eyes were bright on mine. "They can't win, Johnny, if we don't let them. We let their money frighten us once, but we know better now. Money never made any difference in the picture business. It was the pictures that turned the trick. And that's where we got them. We can make the pictures and they can't."

The door behind me opened and the nurse came in. She bustled importantly over to the bedside. She picked up his wrist and felt for his pulse. She held it a moment and looked at me reproachfully. "You'll have to leave now, Mr. Edge. Mr. Kessler must get some rest."

I smiled at Peter and got to my feet. I turned and walked

to the door. His voice stopped me before I went out. I looked back at the bed.

"Come and see me again tomorrow, Johnny," he said.

I looked at the nurse. She nodded her head. I smiled back at him. "Sure, Peter, sure. I'll let you know how things are going."

He smiled and let his head sink back against the pillow. The nurse took a thermometer and put it in his mouth. A cigar would have looked more natural there, I thought incongruously as I left the room.

Doris was waiting in the hall. "How is he?" she asked.

I grinned at her. "You know," I replied, "I think he wants to go back to work." I lit a cigarette thoughtfully and added: "It might not be such a bad idea at that. It might do us both some good."

And all the time I kept thinking. Back there in his room I hadn't said anything that was important. Nothing about how I felt about him, how I felt about us. The things that men can feel toward one another after having spent most of their lives together. Damn it. Damn it. Damn it. Was the only thing we could talk about, the only thing we had in common, after all these years, the picture company?

I walked into the big dining-room a little after one o'clock. The place was filled with people on their lunch hour. The air was filled with smoke and talk. I could feel eyes watching me as I walked through the main dining-room to the smaller dining-room. It was called the Sun Room. The sign over the doorway read: "All tables reserved." It was a warning for the small fry to stay out. This was a room for the top echelon only.

My table was in an alcove, raised a little higher than the rest of the room. Behind it were three wide windows that looked over the studio. It was empty as I walked to it. I looked at Ronsen's table as I passed. It was empty too. I sat down and the waitress came up.

She smiled at me. "Good afternoon, Mr. Edge."

"Hello, Ginny," I answered. "What's good for lunch?"

"The sweetbreads," she answered, "sautéed. Just the way you like 'em."

"Sold," I told her.

She went away and I looked around the room. Gordon was just coming in. He saw me at the table and began to make his way toward me. I waved him to a chair. "Hello, Robert," I said.

He plumped himself into the chair heavily. "Scotch old-fashioned, dry, no sugar," he said to Ginny, who hovered next to him. He looked at me. "I need a drink."

I smiled at him. "I've heard those words before."

"You'll hear them a lot more before this picnic is over," he said. "Farber's on the lot already, making like a big shot."

I didn't answer.

He looked at me. Ginny put his drink before him. He picked it up and finished it in one draught. "I thought you weren't going to give him an in," he said flatly.

"I changed my mind."

"Why?" he asked. "I thought you didn't want him. Yesterday—"

I cut in on him. "I still don't want him. But a million bucks is a million bucks. It saves a lot of trouble."

"It can also make a lot of trouble," he said sarcastically. "Ronsen, Farber, and Roth were in to see me this morning. They say it's all set for Dave to take over on *The Snow Queen*. They said it was okay with you."

The Snow Queen was the biggest picture we had working at the time. It was a musical starring a kid that Gordon had gone to a lot of trouble to steal from Borden. She was only fourteen years old, but Bob had worked hard on her already. She had a voice like a mature woman's. Bob had planted her on a radio program featuring one of the biggest comedians and she had made a big hit. He had spent a lot of dough screwing up her tests at Borden and fixing it that they would drop her option. The minute he got her, he had gone to work. He had whipped up a story for her, and from the script we knew it had that intangible something that spelled hit before it came out. It wouldn't cost us a hell of a lot to make either, and already we sensed the dough coming in. It was his pet project, and now that everything was set to roll, all the glory would go to Dave if he took over. I didn't blame Bob for being sore.

Bob was on his second old-fashioned before I spoke. "That's interesting," I said casually.

He almost choked on his drink. "That's all you got to say?" he asked.

I nodded my head.

His face went red and he started to get up from the table. I grinned at him. "Sit down, sit down. Keep your shirt on. I'm not letting anybody screw you. We'll let Dave get associate-producer credit if we have to, but it will still be a Robert Gordon production."

"That ain't the way I heard it," he said indignantly.

"That's the way its gonna be, an' if they don't like it, they can go hump 'emselves."

He settled back in his chair. He sipped slowly at his drink now, his face was thoughtful. "Got an angle, Johnny?" he asked.

That was Hollywood too. Everything had to have an angle. You could get a guy to hang himself with pleasure if he thought he was in on an angle to screw somebody he didn't like.

"A million-dollar angle," I said smiling.

He was smiling now. "I should have known better, Johnny. I'm sorry for blowing my top."

"Forget it, Bob," I said generously. I could afford to be generous. I wasn't giving anything away.

"What's the gimmick?" he asked, lowering his voice to a conspiratorial tone.

I looked around the room and lowered my voice to match his. The best actors in this business weren't always on the screen. There was more acting in every minute of our end of the business than went on in a year before the cameras. "This is no place to talk about it, Bob," I said softly. "I'll talk to you later."

He was completely happy now. He looked around the room expansively. He even smiled and nodded to some people. His every gesture exuded confidence. It was amazing how that changed the atmosphere in the room.

Before this, people had been talking quietly, looking at us apprehensively out of the corners of their eyes. They were wondering whether we'd still be their bosses tomorrow. They were already making plans in case we weren't. New people had to be cultivated, flattered, new asses to be kissed. Maybe new jobs would have to be found by some. But now, from the way Gordon looked, most of them figured they were good for a while.

I looked over Gordon's head to the doorway. Ronsen, Farber, and Roth were standing there. Ronsen caught my eye and started toward me. He and Farber walked together, his hand most deferentially on Farber's arm. Dave brought up the rear like a puppy trailing after its masters.

Watching them, I almost smiled. Peter was right. I looked at Ronsen. His every action indicated solicitude for Farber.

Ronsen had changed a little since he had first muscled his way into the place. He was confident then. I remember what he said: "The trouble with this business is that there is too much dependence on personalities and too little faith in the good old American principles of running a business. There need be no such conditions. It's very simple, really. The studio is nothing but a factory. All they have to do is make pictures and have them marketed properly. That's my job here. To show the picture business how it should be run. Before I get finished with this place it will run like the Ford Motor Company."

I almost laughed aloud when I thought of that. The Ford Motor Company. He took a leaf right out of their books and the first thing he tried to do was break our contracts with the unions. He almost broke us instead. For nine weeks not a picture rolled on our lot. He had raged up and down the place, yelling: "Communistic labor principles." It didn't do any good. Then, in the last week of the strike, when the projectionists across the country refused to run a single Magnum picture in their theaters and we were faced with a complete loss of revenue, he finally gave in and I had to go out and straighten up the mess.

Peter was right. In the final analysis they had to come back to us. Maybe it was because we had nothing to lose and they had everything. We were broke when we started. We could afford to go out broke if we had to. We knew that the business was built upon a hypothecation, a gamble. We knew that every picture we turned out was a gamble, and like gamblers we were not satisfied to wait for the results of one bet. Before that picture was out we bet that it was good and hocked it against another picture, another gamble, and kept on going.

That was something they couldn't afford to do. They came to us with pockets loaded, with money that they had had for years, that their fathers had had before them, and if they lost that their world was at an end and there was nothing left for them.

They had to come to us.

I stood up as they neared my table. I looked at Stanley. The years had changed him but little. He was still the same guy. Maybe his hair had gone gray, his face had filled out along with his stomach, but he still had the same ready smile that lacked warmth. His eyes still gave the impression that they were constantly adding and subtracting. He hadn't changed much. I still reacted to him the same way I had when I first met him. He rubbed me the wrong way. I didn't like him.

Larry spoke first. "Hello, Johnny," he said in that deep voice of his that carried to every corner of the room. "You know Stanley, don't you?"

Every eye in the room was on us. I smiled and held out my hand. "Sure," I said, "recognize him anywhere." He took my hand. It was still the same old handshake—just like picking up a dead fish. "How are yuh, boy?" I continued. "Glad to see yuh."

His face was a little pale under its ruddy color, but his eye had an unmistakable glint of triumph in it. "Johnny," he said, "it's been years."

He let go my hand and we stood there smiling at each other. To all outward appearances we were buddies who had just seen each other after a long while. And all the time we would have gladly cut each other's throat if there was any way we could get away with it.

"Sit down, gentlemen." I waved them to the chairs.

There were only four places at my table. Since Bob and I were already seated, there were only two more places. Larry dropped into the chair on my right and Stanley seated himself heavily on my left. That left Dave standing up and looking for a place to sit.

Ginny saw him standing there and made a motion to get a chair for him; but I caught her eye. She stopped and, half smothering a smile, turned and went toward the kitchen.

Dave stood there uncomfortably for a moment looking for someone to bring him a chair. He looked at me helplessly. I smiled up at him. "Grab yourself a chair, son," I said pleasantly, "and sit down." I turned to the others, still smiling. "I don't know what's the matter with these waitresses. They're never around when you want them."

Dave had to walk over to the wall and bring back a chair. I watched him. Without turning I spoke to Stanley in a quiet voice, but one that could be heard all through the room. "Bright kid, your nephew," I confided. "Reminds me of you, the way you were years ago. He'll go far if he doesn't let his head run away with him."

From the corner of my eye I could see the color run into Stanley's face. I saw Dave stop for a second as my words reached him; then he picked up the chair and turned around. His face was pale as he walked back to the table with it. He came back and sat down.

I turned to Stanley. "Yuh look good, boy," I said. "Put on a little weight though, haven't you?"

The conversation went on, but I didn't remember much of it. I was thinking about the last time Stanley and I had sat at a table together; that time he had come to me with the proposition that we unite our forces and take over the business for ourselves. It wasn't so long ago at that. Only fifteen years. It was 1923.

The little man got slowly to his feet. His blue eyes twinkled brightly at me; the fringe of gray hair around his bald head seemed to stand out like a wire brush from the sides of his head. He smiled at me. He spoke with a thick German accent. "I think that ought to do it, Mr. Etch," he said.

I looked down at my legs. There were two of them. One was mine and gleamed with a ruddy fleshlike color. One wasn't. It was made of wood and had joints of aluminum. It fitted tightly over the stump and was held with two straps. One went around my thigh and one fastened onto another strap that went around my waist. I looked at him doubtfully.

He seemed to read my mind. "Don't vorry, Mr. Etch," he said quickly, "it vill vork all right. Put on your trousers and then ve'll try it."

Suddenly I was eager to try it. If it worked I could walk again. I could be like other people. "Why can't I try it before I put on my trousers?" I asked.

"No," he said, shaking his head, "the trousers first. Take my vord for it, I know. Vitout trousers you will look at it and it vill be no good. You must not think about it."

I put the trousers on and he helped me while I buttoned them and slipped into the suspenders. He left me sitting there while he rolled a contraption over to me. It looked like one of those walkers they make for babies, only bigger. There were two parallel steel bars held up by four upright bars. On the bottom were four coasters, round little wheels.

"Now, Mr. Etch," he said, "hold onto these bars and lift yourself up between them."

I put one hand on each bar and lifted myself up. The little man stood next to me anxiously.

"Rest each bar under your armpit," he said.

I did as he told me.

"Now," he said, going to the other side of the room, "valk toward me."

I looked at him and then down at myself. My trouser legs fell straight to the floor. Both of them. They looked strange there, two of them, instead of one going to the floor and the other pinned to my side.

His voice was sharp. "Don't look down, Mr. Etch. I said: 'Valk toward me!'"

I looked at him again and took a tentative step forward. The carriage rolled under my arm and I almost stumbled, but the bars held me up.

"Don't stop, Mr. Etch! Keep valking!"

I took another step, then another and another and another and another. I could have walked a thousand miles. The carriage moved easily with me. I reached him.

He put his hand on the bars and stopped the carriage. "So far, so good," he said. He knelt by my side for a moment and tightened the strap around my thigh. "Now," he said, straightening up, "valk after me."

He stood in front of the walker and, facing me, walked backwards. Slowly I followed him. He kept walking backwards in a wide sort of a circle. He never looked behind him; his eyes were watching the movement of my legs.

I was beginning to get tired. There were shooting pains in my thighs, and the back of my neck hurt from my shoulders pressing against the bars. The belt across my waist cut into me every time I breathed.

At last he stopped. "All right Mr. Etch," he said. "That's enough for the first time. You can sit down now and take off the leg. Vith a month of pragtice you vill be like perfect."

I sank into the chair, breathing hard. I opened my trousers and he slid them off. Then he quickly loosened the straps and the leg slipped off. He massaged my thighs with expert fingers.

"It is sore, yah?" he asked.

I nodded my head.

"It is alvays like that at the beginning," he said. "But you vill get used to it and it vill go avay."

The sense of power I had felt when I first stood up seemed to drain out of me as the leg had come off. "I'll never get used to it," I said. "I'll never be able to use it for more than a few minutes at a time."

He pulled up his trouser leg and looked at me. "If I could do it, Mr. Etch," he said, "a young man like you should not haff any trouble."

I looked at his leg. It was artificial. I looked at him. He was smiling. I began to smile back at him.

He laughed aloud. "See," he said, "it is not so bad."

I nodded my head.

"I told Mr. Kessler ven he vass in Chermany that it vould vork for you," he continued. "And it vill. He said to me: 'Herr Heink, if you can give this friend of mine to valk, I personally vill see that you go to America vit your family to live.' And I said to him: 'Herr Kessler, I am as goot already as an American citizen.' Is it not so?"

I grinned at him. I felt good. As busy as Peter had been, he had not forgotten to try to help me. It would have been easy for him not to go out of his way to this small town where he had heard of Herr Heink but continue about his business. But Peter had taken the time even though it had thrown his schedule more than a week out of place.

Then he sent this guy and his whole family to America and paid their way because that was the price the man had asked. He hadn't said anything to me about it. He knew of the disappointments I had had with the artificial legs made here. They weren't legs at all. They were clumsy stumps.

The first I knew about it was when Herr Heink had come to the office and sent in his card and a note from Peter. The note read simply: "This will introduce Herr Joseph Heink, who has come to the U.S. to start in business. He makes artificial legs. Maybe he can help you." Signed: "Peter."

No word about what it cost him. It was only after I had spoken to Heink that I learned what Peter had done.

This guy had something too. It was the way the joints worked. Naturally. Like your own legs. The movements were free and easy to make. You could not tell from looking that the man had an artificial leg himself. I had not known until now.

Peter was still in Europe. Doris and Esther were with him. They would be there for another six months and the business was all on my shoulders in the meantime.

I stood up and leaned on my crutches.

"You come back tomorrow morning, Mr. Etch," Heink said, "and ve vill give you another lesson in valking."

When I got back to the office, Rocco was waiting for me. "How was it?" he asked.

I smiled at him. "Good. I think this is gonna work."

He grinned. "That's swell."

I sat down behind my desk. He took the crutches from me and leaned them against the wall. "Anything special come up this morning?" I asked.

"The usual crap," he answered. He started to turn away and then came back. "Oh yes," he said, "Farber called and wanted to know if you were free for lunch."

"What did you tell him?"

"I told him I didn't know, you hadn't come in yet."

I thought for a minute. I didn't like Farber. I never had and I didn't know why. He knew his business all right, but there was something about him that I didn't like. Maybe it dated back to that letter I had got from him before I went into the army—the one where he thanked me for a job I hadn't given him yet.

George had okayed him and I let the thing stand. I was going into the army anyway and didn't think too much about it. But now he was in charge of all theater operations and we had over two hundred theaters. George was busy with his own theaters, which came to at least as many, and we had both agreed that Farber was logically the one to handle our jointly owned theaters.

"Do you know what he wanted?" I asked.

Rocco shook his head.

I thought for another minute. "Oh, what the hell," I said, "I suppose I might as well see him and get it over with. If I don't he'll only bother me until I do. Tell him I'll meet him at the club at one thirty."

Rocco turned and left the office. I could hear him talking to Jane through the closed door.

Stanley Farber was waiting for me in the lobby of the club

as I walked in the door. There was another man with him, a tall heavy-set man with steel-gray hair and sharp eyes.

He came forward to meet me, the tall man with him. He held out his hand. I took it. "Hello, Johnny, how are you?" His laugh was a little too loud, too forced.

I put a smile on my face and looked at him. I wondered why he was so nervous. "I'm all right, Stan," I said. "How are you?"

"Never better," he answered, still laughing.

I said nothing, just leaned there on the crutches and looked at him. Suddenly he stopped laughing in the same way he started. He looked at me. "Johnny, I'd like you to meet my brother-in-law," he said. He turned to the other man. "Sid, this is Johnny Edge, the man I told you about." He turned back to me. "My brother-in-law, Sidney Roth."

We shook hands. I liked the way the man shook hands. It was strong, firm. I liked the way the man looked at me—straight, honest.

"Glad to know you, sir," I said.

His voice was soft and quiet for so big a man. "I'm honored, Mr. Edge."

Stanley turned and started toward the table. "Shall we eat?" he asked, laughing foolishly again.

I followed him, wondering why the hell he had me to lunch with his brother-in-law. I didn't have to wait very long to find out. Stanley started in with the soup.

"You're in this business a long time, aren't you, Johnny?" he asked.

I looked at him. He knew as well as I how long I'd been in the business. I was polite, though. I answered him. "Fifteen years," I said, "since 1908." I was surprised myself when I said it. It hadn't seemed that long a time.

"Have you ever thought about going into business for yourself?" Stanley continued.

I shook my head. "I always thought that I was," I answered.

Stanley darted a quick look at his brother-in-law. It was a sort of I-told-you-so kind of look. It had a funny expression of condescension about it. He turned back to me. "I mean, start your own company or take over another?"

"No," I said to him. "Saw no reason for it. I always got along with Kessler all right."

For a moment Stanley was silent. When he spoke again, he

had taken another tack. "From what I heard," he said, his voice lower now, "you were the brains behind Kessler all the time. Everything he did was because of you. You were responsible for his success."

I didn't like the way the talk was going, but I kept my temper. I wanted to find out what was coming. "I wouldn't say that, Stan," I said easily. "We all worked at it."

He laughed confidently now. "Don't be falsely modest, Johnny. You're among friends. You did all the brainwork and Peter got all the money and glory."

"I didn't do so bad," I protested mildly.

"What did you get out of it?" Stanley waved his hand airily. "Peanuts. Do you know he's a millionaire out of this? And when you met him he was a hardware-store keeper in a small town."

I tried to look interested. I leaned forward across the table. I didn't speak.

He looked at his brother-in-law again and then turned to me. "Don't you think it's about time you got a fair deal out of the old man?" he asked.

I spread my hands out on the table in a gesture of helplessness. "How?"

"Everybody knows Kessler listens to you. It's very simple really. His note at the Bank of Independence is coming due this year and it's common knowledge he will ask for a renewal. Why don't you suggest that he sell an interest in the business and retire the note?"

I played dumb. "Who's got that much money to buy in?"

"My brother-in-law could be interested for a fifty-per-cent partnership."

I looked at Mr. Roth. He hadn't said a word throughout our discussion. "And where do I come in?" I asked gently.

"With us," Stanley said. "If we can buy our way into equal partnership in the picture company, I can buy out Pappas's half of the theaters. That will give us control of the theater company. From there it's a short step to control the whole works."

I leaned back in my chair and looked at him.

Stanley was suddenly eager. He leaned toward me excitedly. "I'm tellin' you, Johnny, we'll clean up. With what you know about the picture company and what I know about the theaters, we'll make a fortune between us. We got the whole business by the balls!" He held a match to the cigarette I had placed between my lips. "It won't be no time at all before we can crowd Kessler out!"

I drew deeply on my cigarette and looked at him, then I looked at his brother-in-law. The older man looked back at me steadily. His eyes were right on mine. "Mr. Roth, what business are you in?" I asked suddenly.

His voice was calm as he answered me. "The junk business."

My voice was as calm as his when I spoke. "Business must be pretty good if you can throw four million bucks into this."

He shrugged his shoulders. "It's not bad," he said noncommittally.

"It must be pretty good," I persisted.

"There was a lot of money in it during the war," he answered easily. "It's not quite that good now, but it's all right."

I was silent for a moment while I looked at both of them. Then I spoke again. "What do you think of a deal like this, Mr. Roth?"

He shrugged his shoulders, elaborately casual. "It sounds like a good one, Mr. Edge."

I waved my hand. "I'm not talking about the dollar-and-cents outlook, Mr. Roth. I'm talking about the moral aspect."

He smiled at me slowly. I could see a look of real warmth leap into his eyes. "The moral aspect is your concern, not mine, Mr. Edge." He put his hands on the table before him and looked at them. "What do you think about it?"

I was still leaning back in my chair, still casual in my movements, but I was surprised at the sudden savagery in my own voice. "I think it stinks to high heaven, Mr. Roth." I leaned forward and spoke to him. "And if you don't get that slimy rat away from my table I'll kill the little bastard with my bare hands!"

Stanley jumped to his feet. His face had gone white. His voice was hoarse. "You mean to say you're not interested?" he shouted. "After letting me think you were?"

I could see faces in the restaurant turn toward him. Mr. Roth kept looking at me. I turned and looked up at Stanley. My voice was cold. "When I get back to the office I expect to find your resignation on my desk."

Stanley stood there, looking at me with a furious expression on his face. I turned and looked at Mr. Roth.

There was a look of quiet understanding on his face. Stanley started to speak again, but Mr. Roth stopped him with an upraised hand. "Go into the other room, Stanley," he said quietly, "and wait for me. I want to speak to Mr. Edge alone."

Stanley looked at both of us for a moment and then turned and walked away.

We sat there quietly for a long while, not speaking. We just looked at each other. At last Mr. Roth spoke. "I apologize for my brother-in-law, Mr. Edge," he said in that soft, quiet voice of his. "I suspected for a long time he was a *schlemiel,* but now I know he is."

I didn't answer. We were quiet for a few moments, then he spoke again. "I also want to apologize for myself, Mr. Edge. I'm ashamed to feel I've been a part of this thing."

I still didn't answer.

He got to his feet and looked down at me. I looked up at him. His face was grave, stolid. "There is nothing a man would not do for his only sister, Mr. Edge. I am a good twenty years older than her, and when my mother died I promised I would look out for her. I thought I was helping my sister's husband and so helping her. I realize I've been wrong." He held out his hand.

I looked at it and then at him. Slowly I rose to my feet. I took his hand. His face was somehow sad, but his eyes met mine. He inclined his head slightly in a kind of bow and turned and left the room.

Stanley's resignation was on my desk when I got back to the office and I forgot about him for a while. I heard he went back to Chicago with his brother-in-law and that he opened some theaters back there, but I didn't pay much attention to him. I was too busy learning how to walk.

I looked around the table. Larry was talking now, but I didn't know what he was saying. Suddenly I was curious about this man I had seen but once fifteen years ago. I looked at Dave. For the first time I realized that he was the son of the man I had met.

I spoke across the table to him, cutting into Larry's talk as if he didn't exist. "How's your father, Dave?" I asked.

Dave was surprised at my question. His face grew flustered. "Who, me?" he stammered.

I smiled at him. Larry fell silent in surprise that I had interrupted his talk. He wasn't used to it. I ignored him. "Yes," I said to Dave, "your father. I met him once many years ago. A very fine gentleman."

Dave's face looked pleased at what I had said. When he relaxed he looked very much like his father. But his face didn't have the strength his father's had. "My father is dead," he answered simply. "He died two years ago."

For a moment I was genuinely sorry and I said I was. "Too bad we didn't get to know each other better," I said. "I feel he would have made a good friend."

I looked at Dave and then at Stanley. A crazy thought was running through my mind. Can relatives through marriage grow to look like one another? They both had the same selfish, sensual expression on their faces. Their mouths were round and thin and spoiled.

I began to smile slowly. I turned and looked at Stanley again. He looked uncomfortable. That business he was giving us about hard work was so much crap. He didn't make his dough. It was his wife's. She inherited it from her brother. She and Dave. That's why Stanley kept pushing him forward.

I laughed aloud. They looked at me as if I had gone off the nut. I laughed again. This wasn't going to be as tough as I thought.

THIRTY YEARS

1923

1

Johnny held his hand over the mouthpiece of the phone and spoke to Rocco. "Get the car around and I'll meet you outside as soon as I finish talking to Peter."

Rocco nodded and left the office, closing the door behind him.

Johnny took his hand from the phone and spoke into it. His voice was patient. He had been listening to Peter complaining about his man, Will Hays, whom the industry had hired to head its association. According to Peter, Hays was going to ruin the industry. "Look, Peter," he said, "stop worrying about Hays. He's only trying to do the job you and the others hired him for. The picture business isn't a peanut stand any more. It's a big business and the eye of the public is on it. That's why you formed the M.P.P.D.A. To protect yourselves—"

Peter interrupted him. "But you know what he wants to do? He wants us all to give him information on how much business we're doing in each territory. Can you imagine what Borden, Laemmle, Fox, or Mayer would do if they knew that Magnum was doing two million a year in New York and in their theaters into the bargain? They'd tighten up on us. We wouldn't get half that time in their theaters and if we got the time we wouldn't get the prices. I know those guys, I tell you, and I don't trust 'em!"

Johnny's voice was soothing. "So what? Their pictures are playing our theaters upstate and down South. One hand washes the other. Besides, Hays said all the information given would be held confidential and that only total industry figures would be used. No company would know anything about any other company, so stop worrying."

Peter grumbled. "All right, all right, but I don't like it. I still think we should have let Hays stay in Washington delivering letters or whatever he was doing before we took him."

Johnny smiled at that. He could just imagine the Postmaster General of the United States delivering letters. He changed the subject. "What about the pictures, how are they coming?" he asked. "You know we got some pretty tough competition out here with Paramount plugging *The Covered Wagon*, Universal's *Hunchback of Notre Dame*, and Pathe's *Safety Last*, with Harold Lloyd. We better get something hot soon or we won't have a good date left in New York."

Peter sounded genuinely depressed now. "I got troubles there too," he said. "I come back from Europe ready to go to work and instead nothing's ready to shoot, everything's in a mess. Pictures that should be ready ain't. I can't leave here for a minute, Johnny, and I tell you I can't be in fifteen places at once. What I need is a man like Louey Mayer got over at Metro, a guy like Thalberg, who wouldn't let the studio fall asleep when I turn my back."

"So get one," Johnny said. "We need pictures."

"So get one!" Peter mimicked his tone of voice. "Like you can pick Thalbergs from the orange trees out here." His voice grew excited. "The trouble with you, Johnny, is that you stay in New York all the time. You just don't realize what problems we got out here now. We got to make forty pictures a year."

"I know," said Johnny calmly. "But if we can sell 'em, you ought to be able to make 'em."

Peter's voice rose to a shrill screech. "If you know so much, why don't you come out here and help? It's easy to sit on your behind in New York and say we need pictures, but it's a different story when you come out here!"

Johnny grew a little angry. His voice was challenging. "I'll come out there if you want me to!"

Peter's voice was emphatic. "So come out! I want you should see for yourself what I'm up against, then maybe you'll have some appreciation for what you do get. When can you get away?"

Johnny thought quickly. He needed a few weeks to clean up his desk. He tacked a few weeks on that for good measure. "Supposing I come out for New Year's?" he asked.

"That's about four weeks," Peter said. "Good."

For a moment there was an embarrassed silence at both ends of the wire, then Peter cleared his throat and added:

"I'm glad you're coming, Johnny. It will be like old times. We always do better together when things are tough."

Johnny's voice was suddenly warm. "I hope I can help."

"You can help," Peter said sincerely. "I know you will. I'll tell Esther you're coming and she'll get your room ready."

Johnny smiled. "Tell her I'll be looking for some chicken soup and *knedloch*."

"You'll have it," Peter promised.

They spoke a few more words and Johnny hung up the phone thoughtfully. He turned in his chair and looked out of the window. A light snow had begun to fall and already the street was white. He got up and walked over to the closet and put on his hat and coat.

He walked out the door and toward the street, his mind occupied. Peter had sounded tired ever since he had come back from Europe. He had accomplished a tremendous amount of work over there. Magnum Pictures now stretched all over the globe. It had offices in England, France, Italy, Germany, Belgium, Austria, Switzerland, Spain, and in every little country that he could think of. They had set up companies and offices in Asia, in the Near East, in South America. Magnum could boast of the biggest foreign distribution setup in the industry, and one man had done almost all of it himself, Peter.

No wonder he was tired. He had worked eighteen hours a day. He hadn't spared himself for a moment, and now he came back to a studio that had fallen terribly behind. It was just too much to ask one man to do, and yet Peter had done it. And still found time to think of Johnny.

Johnny looked down at his legs. If you didn't know which was the artificial one and which the real one, you couldn't tell them apart. Peter had found time to send that funny little man to Johnny even if he had been busy. Thinking about it, Johnny shook his head. You just didn't work for a guy like that, you loved him.

The street wasn't as cold as Johnny had thought it would be. Rock had the motor of the car running while he was waiting for him. Johnny opened the front door and climbed in next to Rock. He looked in the back seat. Jane was sitting there. "Are you warm, Janey?" he asked.

She nodded her head.

Rocco had started the car by the time Johnny had turned around. "What did the old boy want?" he asked Johnny.

"He wants me to come out there and give him a lift," Johnny said.

Rocco didn't answer.

Johnny looked at him. "What's the matter?"

"Nothin'," Rocco growled.

"A trip to the coast would be nice at this time of the year," Johnny said.

Rocco kept his eyes on the road, steering carefully.

Johnny watched him for a few seconds. "What's the matter, Rock?" he asked. "Wouldn't you like to go?"

Rocco growled something that Johnny didn't understand.

Johnny took a pack of cigarettes from his pocket and took out two. He placed one between Rock's lips and one between his own. He struck a match and held it carefully while Rocco lighted up and then lit his own. He leaned back smoking for a few seconds and not saying anything. Everyone was so jumpy lately, even Rock, who was usually so calm. He wondered why. He watched Rocco driving the car for a few minutes and then decided to say nothing. A few weeks in California would make a new man out of him. He leaned back against the car cushions comfortably.

The car swung into the curb in front of the theater. Rocco turned toward him. "You and Jane get out here and I'll park the car an' meet yuh in a few minutes."

They got out of the car and watched him drive off. Johnny looked at Jane with a puzzled look on his face. "I wonder what's eatin' him?" he asked.

She looked at him strangely. "Don't you know?" she asked. He shook his head.

"He's been like this for a while now," she said. "Haven't you noticed?"

"I been noticin' some things," Johnny answered, "but I figured he was off his feed or something."

She started to speak again, but just then Rocco came up and they walked into the theater. For a moment there was an almost awkward silence, then she laughed. "It seems funny to be going to see a show with Warren Craig in it after everything that's happened."

Johnny laughed with her. "It would be funnier still if he knew we were out here." He stopped for a moment and then continued: "I wonder what he would say if we went back-stage to see him."

"From what I heard," Rocco said, "he'd probably throw you out on your ear."

2

THE applause grew louder as the curtain lifted slowly. Johnny watched Warren Craig stand there on the stage. In spite of himself he applauded with the rest of the audience. He looked over at Jane. She, too, was applauding.

She caught his look and made a face at him. "I don't like him any more than I did before," she said, "but—"

Johnny interrupted her. "I know just how you feel. The son of a bitch is an actor."

He looked back at the stage. The years had dealt well with Warren Craig. He had matured subtly without losing any of the natural charm of his youth. He was more poised, his voice richer and more expressive.

Slowly the curtain came down, hiding him from view. The applause faded away and the audience began leaving the theater. Johnny sat there lost in thought.

"Ready to go?" Janey asked.

He looked up at her, startled.

She caught the expression on his face. "What were you thinking about, Johnny?" she asked suspiciously.

His face broke into a guilty smile. He looked like a small boy caught in the cookie jar. "You guessed it," he confessed.

"Oh, Johnny!" she exclaimed. "Not again!"

He nodded his head. "Again. He's too good to pass up. We need a guy like that."

"Johnny, he won't even talk to you!" she protested.

He stood up. He had made up his mind. "I can't lose anything by asking," he said. "Want to come with me?"

She shook her head. "Uh-uh, not me," she answered. "You may have forgotten what Sam and I did to him, but I'll bet he hasn't."

He turned to Rocco. "Would you mind taking Janey home?" he asked. "I got a hunch he might listen to reason."

Rocco smiled. "I wouldn't mind a bit."

"I can get home all right," Janey put in quickly, "Rock can go with you."

Johnny knew what she was thinking. He smiled reassuringly at her. "Don't worry about me, Janey," he said, tapping his artificial leg, "I can get along all right now."

"You sure?" she asked.

"Sure, I'm sure," he told her.

When they were out in the street, she said to Rocco: "I guess it's silly of me, but I was worried about his getting along."

Rocco looked at her. "You don't have to worry about him any more. He can get along all right." He was quiet for a moment as they walked along, then he added: "He don't need nobody to look after him any more. I'm beginning to wonder what I'm doing hanging around."

She looked at him, her face thoughtful. "Why, Rock, you're doing a job," she protested. "Johnny couldn't get along without you."

His face was impassive. She couldn't tell how he felt. His voice was questioning as he answered: "I'm not so sure he can't." He looked at her. For the first time she saw a look of pain in his eyes.

Involuntarily she put her hand on his arm as they walked along. She could feel his arm tense underneath his coat. Slowly it relaxed as they walked along. After a while she asked: "What's on your mind, Rock? You're not yourself."

He looked at her swiftly. Her eyes were on his; they were warm and invited his confidence. "Nothing," he said quickly, "I guess I just feel low, that's all."

She looked at him. He could see the sudden look of hurt that flashed across her face when he refused her his confidence, and strangely something inside him warmed and glowed. Before he had felt lonely and unwanted, and now suddenly he felt differently. He didn't understand it. He stopped abruptly and faced her. "You're really interested?" he asked.

She lowered her eyes and didn't look directly at him. Her voice was low. "You know that I am, Rock," she replied.

A new and heady feeling of elation began to run through him. He took her hand as they began to walk again. Oddly enough, what was bothering him before did not seem too important now. Her hand felt good in his. He looked at her. "The car is only on the next block," he said.

She smiled at him, but didn't answer.

He liked the way she smiled at him. She had never smiled at him in just this way before. Maybe the way he felt before was not important now, but it would be good to talk to her about it on the way home.

Johnny pushed his way into the crowded dressing-room. It was a newer theater and a larger room, but the scene was the same that Johnny remembered.

Craig sat at a dressing-table removing his make-up and watching the people in the room in his mirror. Here, as on stage, he was the center of attraction.

Johnny was sure Craig had seen him enter, but as he gave no sign of recognition, he walked toward a seat on the far side of the room and sat down. He lit a cigarette and looked around him.

People were always the same, they never changed. When, at last, Craig stood up and turned around, they surged up to him. Several women gave him their programs to autograph. Others smiled and spoke a congratulatory word. For each Craig had a smile and a pleasant reply. Johnny thought he looked happy in his element.

Bored with the scene in the dressing-room, which looked as if it would last for a while, Johnny looked out into the hall. Through the open doorway he could see down the corridor to the other dressing-rooms. From one of them a girl was just emerging. She came toward Craig's room. In the dim light of the corridor there was something strangely fluid about the way she walked, something strangely and deliberately feminine. For a moment Johnny had the impression he could see through the clinging pleated dress she wore, see the flowing muscles of her thighs, the outline of her breasts.

He stared at her as she came into the room. Startled, in the full light of the room, he realized that the light in the corridor had been playing tricks on him. She was a young girl with honey-colored hair flowing down to her shoulders. She blinked her eyes a little as the light struck them; then, as they cleared, she made her way through the crowd to Craig.

Involuntarily Johnny's eyes followed her. There was something about this girl that was almost magnetic. At first Johnny didn't know what it was, then suddenly he understood it. The styles of the times called for thin figures and boyishly cut hair. This girl catered to neither of these fashions. She was slim, but feminine, and wore her hair in long blond waves.

Her voice was deep and full and Johnny could hear what she said from where he was sitting. It was a trained voice and from it Johnny knew she was in show business.

"Warren," the girl said, "Cynthia will be a little late."

Craig looked at her and nodded. "Tell her I'll wait, Dulcie," he replied.

The girl turned and silently went back out into the hall. Johnny watched her as she walked back to the dressing-room from which she had come. Again the dim light of the corridor performed its strange revealing trick. She disappeared into the room.

Johnny shook his head as he turned back to Craig. He was smiling to himself. "She'd slap my face if she knew what I was thinking," he thought.

The crowd was beginning to leave. He lit another cigarette and settled himself for a patient wait. He didn't have to wait long, for suddenly they had all gone and Craig was walking toward him. He stood up slowly.

For a moment they looked at each other, then Craig held out his hand. "Hello, Johnny," he said.

Johnny took his hand. "Hello, Warren," he replied.

Craig looked right into Johnny's eyes. He smiled slowly, hesitantly. "I never expected to see you here."

"I didn't expect to be here," Johnny replied candidly. "But I just caught the show and had to come back and tell you how much I liked it."

"I'm glad you did, Johnny," Craig said slowly. "Many is the time I wanted to apologize for making such an ass of myself, but I never seemed to get around to it. I watched your company's progress and was really glad it worked out all right."

There was no doubting the sincerity in his voice. Johnny knew instinctively that Craig wasn't acting. He smiled suddenly. "I'm glad you feel that way, because I came back here for the same reason I did the last time."

Craig threw his head back and laughed heartily. "Still the same old Johnny."

Johnny nodded his head. "One-track mind. Don't forget you still owe me a picture."

Craig's face grew serious. "I don't know whether I can, Johnny. After all, you know my position in regard to pictures."

Johnny knew his position. Since he had failed to live up to their agreement to make *The Bandit*, Craig had publicly announced that motion pictures were not important enough for him to be interested in. He looked at Craig candidly. "I've heard about it," he admitted, "but times change. You can always change your mind. The Barrymores are going into pictures; so can you." He stopped for a moment, then added as an apparent afterthought: "I know it's not important to you, but you can make as much money in one month's work in the movies as you can in one year on the stage."

Craig looked interested. This play was almost at the end of its run. It might go until the end of the year, it might not. It had been playing almost a year now, and he had no plans for the future. "Tell you what, Johnny," he said, "supposing you come to supper with me and we'll talk it over. You tell me what you've got in mind, and though I'm not promising anything, I'll listen."

Johnny nodded his head. "Fair enough," he replied. "That's all I ask. If we can do business now, we'll both forget what happened."

Craig grinned ruefully. "Go ahead, rub it in." But there was no malice in his words.

Johnny smiled at him and watched him get his hat and coat. He came back to Johnny. "We'll pick up Cynthia in her dressing-room on the way out," he said.

Johnny protested. "Wait a minute, I don't want to be breaking anything up."

Craig laughed. "Don't be silly, old man. You're not breaking anything up. Cynthia and I always eat together after the show." He snapped his finger suddenly. "Fact is, you'll be a welcome addition. My cousin, Dulcie, is coming with us. She's ambitious to become an actress, and even though my wife and I have been trying to discourage her, she'll be thrilled at meeting a big moving-picture man like you."

Johnny was surprised for a moment; then he remembered he had read in the program that during the run of the play Craig and the leading lady had been married. He smiled back at him and held out his hand. "I forgot for a moment that you're a newlywed. Congratulations."

Craig shook his hand. "Thanks," he said. "Ready to go?"

Johnny nodded. He turned and picked up his coat from the chair where he had put it. It was an awkward turn and he almost slipped as he made it.

Craig grabbed him with his hand. He grinned at Johnny. "Charley horse or one too many?"

Johnny smiled ruefully back at him and shook his head. "Neither," he replied, "I wish it were. I left a leg in France."

A look of sympathy rushed across Craig's face. "Forgive me," he said quickly, "I seem bound to make a fool of myself, but I didn't know."

"That's all right," Johnny said easily as they started to walk out of the room. He tapped his artificial leg. "The nice thing about this is that sometimes you can forget about it yourself."

3

HE CAME into the office whistling. Janey looked up at him in surprise; it had been a long time since she had seen him so carefree. "How did it go last night?" she asked with a smile. "Did he sign up?"

Johnny stopped in front of her desk and smiled happily at her. "No," he replied easily. "We went out to supper together, but he wasn't interested." Still whistling while she looked at him bewilderedly, he took off his hat and coat and hung it up. He turned back to her. "Anything special this morning?"

"George Pappas is in your office waiting for you," she replied. "You had a nine-o'clock appointment with him, remember?"

He looked at his watch. It was almost ten o'clock. He had completely forgotten about it. He hurried into his office.

George was waiting there. He got to his feet as Johnny came into the room.

"George," Johnny said smiling as he walked over to him, "I'm sorry I'm late. I didn't mean to keep you waiting, but I overslept this morning."

George smiled back at him. "That's all right, Johnny. Sometimes is good for to sleep a little later."

Johnny sat down behind his desk. "How are things going?"

George nodded his head. "Good, Johnny, too good. I'm getting nervous about it."

"What do you mean?" Johnny asked.

George sat down in the chair opposite Johnny's desk and looked at him seriously. "You see in the papers lots theaters being built and sold every day. Prices paid are climbing all the time. Two years ago we pay for twelve-hundred-seat house thirty thousand dollars. Today same house cost almost twice."

"What's so bad about that?" Johnny asked with an indulgent smile. "All I can see that it means is that our properties are worth twice as much as we paid for them."

George shook his head in disagreement. "Maybe if same number theaters are standing. But soon there will be so many theaters that price must come down."

Johnny sat forward in his chair, suddenly interested. He could see the logic in George's statement. It was all right while there was still a shortage of theaters, but what would happen if there were more theaters than there were patrons to go to them? "What are you suggesting, George?" he asked.

George was silent for a moment before he answered. "We got now more than two hundred houses," he said carefully. "For a few years yet I figure they're good; after that"—he shrugged his shoulders expressively—"who knows?"

"So?" asked Johnny.

"So I'm thinking it good thing if we examine theaters carefully, see what houses look like they will hold up, and sell the others while the price is good." He leaned back in his chair and looked at Johnny.

Johnny took a cigarette and lit it. He exhaled a cloud of smoke. "I don't know whether Peter would like that. He's very proud of the chain of theaters that carry the Magnum name."

"Peter should be told to understand some time even the gravy gets cold and tasteless and makes the stomach sick." George's face was calm.

"What if he doesn't want to sell?" Johnny pursued.

"My brother Nick and me, we talk about that. Maybe in that case he buys our share."

Johnny's face grew thoughtful as he looked at George. "You really believe there's a bust coming, then?"

George's voice was gentle. "Maybe not bust, but things certainly come down."

"Do you know what theaters you want to get rid of?"

George opened up his little briefcase, took out a sheaf of

papers, and put them on Johnny's desk. "Here is analysis of all theaters. Is marked in red, theaters we should sell and reasons for selling."

Johnny picked up the papers and leafed through them slowly. When he had finished, he looked up at George. "That's more than half of them."

George nodded his head. "One hundred fifteen."

"If we did decide to sell them," Johnny asked, "who would buy that many theaters at one time?"

Again George shrugged his shoulders. "Maybe Loew, maybe Proctor. Maybe even Borden. He is expanding his theaters rapidly."

"What do you think we can get for them?"

"Should get four million dollars if sold together, maybe more if sold one at a time."

Johnny leaned back in his chair. Half of what they would get for the theaters would be Magnum's share. He calculated what they had paid for them and realized the profit on the sales would be close to a million dollars for Magnum alone. He looked at George respectfully. His share would be as much. No wonder he wanted to get rid of them. It wasn't every day you could pick up a million bucks.

"I'll tell you what, George," he said finally, "I'm going out to the studio in a few weeks and I'll talk to Peter out there. When I get back I'll let you know what he thinks. All right?"

George stood up. "Sure," he said. "Is no hurry. Maybe got time yet for one year, maybe two. Just being careful."

Johnny stood up and smiled at him. "I understand." He walked around the desk and took George's hand. "You're being fair to us, old friend."

George smiled at him fondly. "And what is old friends for?" he asked. "You help me, is only natural I help you."

He watched George leave the office and went back to his desk and sat down. It would have been easy enough for George to sell his share on the open market without talking to them first. He knew in a case like that he would be giving someone a chance to cut in on the Magnum Theaters Company the way that Farber had wanted to do. An expression of distaste flitted across Johnny's face as he thought about Farber.

It was a good thing he had got rid of him when he did. He hadn't realized just how deeply entrenched in the organization

Farber had made himself. Most of the theater personnel had been hired by him and he had made many connections in the picture company too. It wasn't until after Farber had gone that Johnny found out just how thorough and far-reaching his activities had been.

He picked up his phone. Jane answered it. "Is Rocco in yet?" he asked. Rocco had gone to park the car.

"He just came in," Jane answered.

"Tell him I want to see him." Johnny hung up the phone.

Rocco came into the office. "What do you want, boss?" he asked with a smile.

Johnny looked up at him. "Go over to a good florist's and pick out a dozen of their best American Beauty roses. No"—he hesitated for a moment—"you better make it two dozen, and send them to Miss Dulcie Warren at the Plaza with my card."

Rocco looked at him in surprise for a moment. He recovered quickly. "Sure, boss," he said, starting out the door.

Johnny stopped him. "You got the name right?" he asked.

Rocco smiled. "Sure, Johnny. Dulcie Warren at the Plaza. Two dozen American Beauty roses with your card."

Johnny nodded. He was pleased. "That's right," he said.

Rocco closed the door behind him and swore softly to himself. He walked over to Jane's desk and looked down at her. "What happened to him last night?" he asked her.

She shook her head. "I don't know. He came in whistling and I asked him if Craig signed and he said no as if he didn't care. Then he went in to see Pappas, who was waiting for him. Why?"

Rocco scratched his head, puzzled. "Do you know what he wants me to do?"

"No. What?"

"He wants me to send some flowers to a dame at the Plaza. Two dozen American Beauty roses, no less, to Miss Dulcie Warren at the Plaza. Who is she, anyway?"

"I don't know," Jane answered, "I never heard of her."

Rocco looked down at her challengingly. "So I was wrong last night when I told you all he needs me for is an errand boy? It's 'Rock, bring the car around,' 'Rock, get my briefcase over there, will yuh?' Who's crazy, me? Now he wants me to buy him some flowers for a dame. I tell yuh, Janey, I'm nuthin' but a flunky around here and I don't like it!"

"Shh—" Janey tried to quiet him. "He might hear you!"

"What if he does?" Rocco asked savagely.

She didn't answer—just looked up at him appealingly. There was nothing she could say. Last night in the car he had told her how he felt, told her why he had hesitated about taking the job with him because he was afraid he would turn into a servant for Johnny. "I'd be better off if I went back to my old job in a barber shop," he had said. "At least there I would be doing a job and not have to be any man's flunky."

She had told him it wasn't so, he had the wrong idea. She was sure as soon as Johnny had time to think about it, he would give Rock a worth-while job to do.

He had scoffed at her. "Doing what?" he asked. "This ain't my racket. What could I do?"

Again she didn't have an answer. But something had grown between them last night. He had held her hand and she had felt alive again. She was no longer a woman alone with a child and without a man to make her complete. When he had stopped the car in front of her door, she had suddenly leaned toward him and kissed him.

His arms had gone around her and he kissed her again. His voice was suddenly soft. "Is that how it is?" he had asked huskily.

"That's how it is," she had answered, putting her arms around his neck.

She had been humming to herself as she let herself into her apartment and had gone over to her son's bed and looked in it. She had smiled and covered the child and started to undress. She remembered she had felt so foolish and young again.

She looked up at Rocco in surprise. Johnny had come into the office whistling. She had been so happy herself she didn't have time to reason why he had been whistling. But now it made sense. Suddenly her heart sank in her breast. Doris would be unhappy. Somehow she had always felt that when he snapped around to normal, he would turn to Doris and things would be right for them.

But imperceptibly it had happened. She should have seen it herself. Ever since he had started to move around on his artificial leg. Day after day he grew more like the Johnny of old. Bit by bit, as his confidence in his ability to get around grew, he snapped back. And now he was the same old Johnny as before, with the same purpose and selfish viewpoint that he had before he went away. It was pictures and himself now. That's all he had thought about then and that's all he thought about now.

Her voice was almost a whisper. "What did you say the girl's name was?" she asked Rocco.

"Warren," he answered, putting on his coat, "Dulcie Warren."

She nodded her head slowly. She didn't like the name. It was too carefully picked, too cute, too feminine. And she wouldn't like the woman either. Somehow she knew that even before she met her.

4

She liked the needle spray of the shower on her body. Some women liked bathtubs, but not her. She liked the feel of the stinging water on her body. It made her tingle and feel alive. She arched her body and let the water beat against her breasts. She could almost feel her blood circulating and, looking down, she could see her nipples slowly thrusting out against the stimulation of the water. It was almost like a lover's hands seeking her. She laughed aloud. She liked her body. She was proud of it.

Women could have these flat boyish figures if they wanted to, but not she. She had a woman's body and she wanted everybody to know it. And she knew that they knew it too. When she walked into a room, she knew that the men's eyes would automatically turn toward her. How long they would look depended upon whom they were with. If their wives or sweethearts were with them, they would turn away hurriedly and steal occasional glances at her out of the corners of their eyes. If they were alone they would continue to look and she could see the wanting in their eyes. She liked to have them look at her that way.

She had been like that in school, too. Soon enough other girls knew it and were afraid to have their boy friends and sweethearts meet her. The silly fools! What did she care for their boy friends? They were just kids, while she was destined to be a great actress.

She had been born to be one. Her family had been on the stage ever since she could remember and before that. Her father had been on the stage with his sister, Warren Craig's mother. He had told her many times about the marriage of the two greatest families on the American stage, the Warrens and the Craigs. Everyone of importance had been there. The Colts, the Drews, the Barrymores, the Costellos, everyone. And Warren Craig was the only son. He had been given the name Warren in honor of his mother's family. At his christening his father had said boastfully: "Some day he'll be the greatest name in the theater!" And it was coming true.

That was why she could never understand why they wanted to keep her from the stage. As a child she had loved to act. Her home life was a constant struggle for the center of the stage. Sometimes it would be she, sometimes her father, very rarely her mother. They were too much for the poor woman. The only big scene they allowed her was when she lay dying, and even then her father had tried to ham it up.

She remembered it well even though she was only eleven years old at the time. The room had been darkened and quiet, when suddenly her father had broken into loud sobs and laid his head on the bed. "Don't leave me, darling," he wept vainly, "don't leave me." It was very touching. The other people in the room, the doctor and the nurse and the servant, shifted awkwardly. She had put her hand on her father's shoulder. Her voice carried only to his ears, the others in the room could not hear her. "You're overacting, Papa," she said. He had nodded his head quickly and whispered back to her: "I know it, honey, but that's the way your mother likes it."

The theater was in her blood and she couldn't help it. She was born to act just as some people are born to paint or make music. She had come to New York sure that her Cousin Warren would give her a chance. But she hadn't figured on Cousin Warren's new wife.

Cynthia Craig took one look at Dulcie and silently screamed for help. This natural-born cocotte was not the ideal thing to have around in a marriage that was still in its honeymoon stages. But there was nothing she could do about it. Warren insisted stubbornly that Dulcie could stay around as long as she felt like it. And Dulcie stayed.

Cynthia even tried to get Dulcie some parts in shows that were going on the road, but Warren peremptorily rejected them for her. "It's not right for her," he would say. "What she needs is dramatic training first and I'll see to it that she gets it."

Cynthia, looking at Dulcie, would think to herself that a girl with a figure like that should not try for the dramatic stage, but should go right to Ziegfeld. He would know what to do with her. He would take ninety per cent of her clothes off and let her walk around the stage. But Cynthia forgot one important thing: Dulcie could act and all she needed was a chance.

At last Cynthia gave in and offered some advice to Dulcie. "You wouldn't have any trouble getting parts if only you'd slim down and get your hair cut in an attractive boyish bob. Then you wouldn't look like a girl out of yesterday, and maybe some producer would give you a break."

Dulcie looked at her disdainfully. She let her eyes run up and down Cynthia's slim figure until Cynthia flushed. Then she tossed her head and her hair shimmered in the light. "I'm happy the way I am," she had said.

The water felt good on her. She turned around, letting it run down her back. Suddenly she cocked her head to one side. The phone was ringing. She waited a moment for someone to answer it before she remembered that the maid had gone out and she was alone in the apartment. With a reluctant sigh she stretched out one brown arm and turned off the water.

She stepped from the tub hurriedly and threw a towel around her and went into the living-room to pick up the phone. "Hello," she said.

"Dulcie?" came the voice.

She recognized it immediately, but didn't let on that she knew who it was. "This is Dulcie," she said.

"This is Johnny," the voice came back happily. "What are you doing for dinner tonight?"

Johnny Edge was nice all right, but there was nothing particularly exciting about him. All he knew was pictures. He didn't understand how she felt about the theater. She had gone out with him several times and he had sent her flowers every time they had a date, but she wasn't in the mood to see him today. Her voice was reproachful. "Oh, Johnny, why didn't you call earlier? I just made a date with a girl friend of mine I had been promising to visit and just simply couldn't put off any longer."

Johnny's voice sounded disappointed. "How about tomorrow, then?"

"Cynthia and Warren might have arranged something," she said. "Why don't you give me a call in the morning?"

He sounded a little more cheerful. "All right, I'll call you then. So long, Dulcie."

"So long, Johnny." She hung up the phone, wondering what kind of excuse she could give him tomorrow. She started suddenly. Someone had come into the room and was watching her. She looked up.

Warren was standing there looking at her.

She pulled the towel around her. It had somehow loosened while she had been on the phone. "Warren!" she said. "You frightened me."

He grinned at her. "That I would like to see. Nothing frightens you, Dulcie. Not even Cynthia."

She looked at him in surprise. His speech was a little thick, he had probably just had a few cocktails. "What do you mean?" she asked innocently.

He laughed. "You don't have to act for me, Dulcie. I've seen how you and Cynthia get along. I think she's a little afraid of you."

Dulcie smiled and stood up. She could see him looking at her legs where they showed under the towel. She knew the look and delighted in it. It was the first time Warren had ever looked at her in that way. She shook her head. "I don't know why she should be. I've never given her any reason to worry."

She started to walk past him to the bathroom. He shot out an arm and stopped her. She turned and faced him.

"No?" he asked, smiling quizzically. "Are you sure? After all, walking around the house like this would make her worry."

Dulcie looked at him levelly. She didn't push his hand from her arm. "She shouldn't," she replied quietly. "There isn't anybody home."

For a second they stared at each other, then he pulled her toward him. She came to him willingly enough and held her lips up to him. The towel fell to the floor unheeded as he picked her up and carried her toward his room.

At the door she stopped him for a moment. "Cynthia?" she asked.

His voice was gruff. "Cynthia's having dinner with her agent. I'm to meet her at the theater."

There was quiet in the room. It was almost dark outside. She turned over on the bed and looked at him. "Give me a cigarette," she said.

He took a pack of cigarettes from the table next to the bed, gave her one, and took one himself. He lit his and then gave her his cigarette to light hers from. He watched her sit up in the bed as she drew on the cigarette. Against the shadow of the window he could see her breasts rise. He put his hand against her body. It was warm and firm. She placed his hand on her thigh.

"What are you thinking about, Warren?" she asked.

He sat up suddenly. "You know damn well what I'm thinking about. I've been afraid of this happening ever since you came here and yet I couldn't let you go."

She guided his hand over her. "So it happened," she said matter-of-factly. "There's nothing to worry about now."

He flicked on the night lamp and looked at her in amazement. Her gaze was clear and untroubled. He couldn't believe that just a few minutes ago she had clung to him whimpering and frantic in passionate frenzy.

"Nothing to worry about!" he exploded. "How long do you think you can stay here without Cynthia finding out?"

"Cynthia doesn't have to find out," she said.

He smiled ruefully. "Don't underestimate her, Dulcie. She's not stupid." He got out of bed and slipped into a robe. "I'm going to have to send you away. As far away as I can get you. This isn't going to happen again."

She dropped her eyes from his and looked down at the bed. Her voice was small. "Why, Warren? Don't you like me?"

He began to laugh suddenly. "Because I like you too much!" He walked over to the dresser and began to comb his hair. "Now let's see," he said half to himself. "Where can I send you?"

She got out of bed and walked over behind him. She pressed herself against his back and put her arms around his waist and inside his robe. "What if I don't want to leave you?" she asked wistfully.

He turned to her. "That's one thing you can count on, Dulcie," he said definitely. "You're going."

She kissed his chest. "You're mean."

He pulled her head back by her hair so that her face looked up at him. He kissed her. "Not mean," he said, "smart. This is no good for either of us." He turned back to the mirror and finished combing his hair. "Who was it on the phone when I came in?" he asked.

"Johnny Edge," she answered.

He raised an eyebrow. "He's been seeing a lot of you, hasn't he?"

"Yes," she answered, "but I'm tired of him. All he talks about is pictures." She tilted her head on one side and looked up at him. "I think he's in love with me, but I'm going to get rid of him. He's beginning to bore me."

He was suddenly interested. "Do you think he wants to marry you?"

"He probably does," she said casually.

"Why don't you marry him?" he asked. "He can do a lot for you." He puffed at his cigarette. "There's a lot of money in the movies."

"I want to act on the stage," she said. "Besides, even if he didn't bore me I couldn't marry him. He's a cripple."

"Don't be a fool," he said savagely, ignoring the latter part of her objection, his hands gripping her arms. "There's nothing the matter with acting in pictures. Don't you think I would if I could find some way of getting out of the publicity I've let build up?"

She looked at him. "Do you want me to marry Johnny so you can get rid of me?"

"No, you little fool," he replied, "but if you were married we wouldn't have to worry about Cynthia. She'd think everything is all right!"

She put her arms around him and kissed him. They stood there for a long moment. She took her arms from around his neck and walked into the other room. He followed her wondering. She went over to the phone and picked it up and gave the operator a number.

"Who are you calling?" he asked.

She looked at him, her eyes wide. "Johnny," she replied. "He asked me to have dinner with him."

He took the phone from her hand and placed the receiver back on the hook. "You can do that tomorrow," he said smiling. "I'm having some naked hussy for dinner tonight."

5

THE phone on Jane's desk began to ring. She picked it up. "Mr. Edge's office."

It was a woman's voice that answered. A strange voice, husky and deep. "Mr. Edge in?"

Something inside Jane told her who it was even before she asked. "Who is calling?"

"Dulcie Warren," the voice answered.

"Just a moment," Jane said impersonally. "I'll see if I can get him." She turned the cut-off key closing the extension and pressed the buzzer on her desk.

She could hear it ring in Johnny's office. His voice came on the wire: "Yes, Jane?"

"A Dulcie Warren is calling," she told him.

There was a sudden lightness in the tone of his voice. "She is?" he exclaimed excitedly. "Put her on!"

She threw open the cut-off key. Her voice was cold. "Mr. Edge is on the wire. Go ahead, please," she said coldly, flipping over the key that carried the call through into Johnny's office.

A few minutes later Johnny came out of his office. His face looked flushed and happy. "A Miss Dulcie Warren will come here at noon. Let me know as soon as she comes in, I promised to show her the place."

She made a note on her desk pad and looked up. "Anything else?" she asked sarcastically.

He missed the sarcasm in her voice. "No," he answered, going back into his own office.

Jane was maliciously happy when an unexpected coast call from Peter came through just as she was ushering Dulcie into Johnny's office.

He smiled apologetically at Dulcie. "I have to take this

call," he explained to her. "It's from the boss." He turned to Jane. "Hold the call for a minute and get Rock for me. He can show her around while I'm tied up."

As Jane left his office she could hear Dulcie telling him that she wouldn't mind waiting. The door closing behind her shut off Johnny's reply.

The faint odor of Dulcie's perfume still hung in the air as Jane furiously began to dial the interoffice phone, looking for Rocco. Dulcie was all that Jane thought she would be. Grudgingly Jane admitted to herself that Dulcie was beautiful. She could see why Johnny was attracted to her and she instinctively disliked her.

She finally located Rocco in the newsreel office. He came on the phone. She was so angry, the words spilled out of her mouth. "She's here, Rock," she said.

He was bewildered. "Who's here?"

"She is. The girl Johnny's been sending flowers to," she explained. "Johnny wants you to come up here right away to show her around the place!"

He whistled slowly. "From the way you're burning, she must be a knockout!"

"Don't be silly, Rock," she replied heatedly. "She doesn't mean a thing to me."

"Of course she doesn't, Janey," he said soothingly. "But I'll be right up there to see for myself what she's like!"

The phone went dead in her hand. The red light on her desk began to flicker on and off. That meant that Peter was getting tired of waiting. She pressed the buzzer. There wasn't any answer from Johnny's wire. She pressed it again.

This time Johnny answered. "Peter is still waiting," she said.

He hesitated for a moment. "Sit down over there, Dulcie; Rock will be up in a moment," she heard him say with his mouth away from the phone. Then his voice was louder: "All right, put him on."

She turned the key down as Rock came into the office. He looked at her questioningly. She pointed with her hand to Johnny's office. He went in, leaving the door open behind him.

"Rock," she heard Johnny saying through the open door, "This is Miss Warren. Would you mind showing her around while I'm talking to Peter?"

She didn't catch Rocco's reply because just then Peter came on the phone. "Hello, Johnny," he said.

"Yes, Peter," she heard Johnny say into the phone. She switched off her key and hung up the phone.

Rocco and Dulcie came into her office. He closed Johnny's door behind him. There was a strange smile on his face as he brought Dulcie over to her desk.

"I'd like you to meet Miss Andersen, Johnny's secretary," he said politely. "Miss Andersen, this is Miss Warren."

Dulcie smiled at her. Jane thought the smile was condescending and her dislike for Dulcie deepened. "I'm glad to meet you," she said politely, not meaning a word of it.

Rocco took Dulcie's arm and steered her toward the door. They stepped out. A few seconds later Rocco popped back into the office, alone. He looked at her and whistled softly. "No wonder Johnny's standing on his ear." He grinned mischievously at her. "What a babe!" He shook his head from side to side. "She sizzles when you touch her!"

Jane made a face at him. "You men are all alike."

His grin grew broader. "I just came back to tell you not to worry 'bout me, baby. I'll be true to you!" He turned to go out the door again and then stopped. His words floated back mockingly over his shoulder. "But poor Johnny—oh!"

6

DULCIE knew that he was looking at her but she kept her face turned away from him, watching the dancers on the floor. The lights were soft, the music was sweet, and the dancers were moving slowly as if caught in a dream world of their own.

She was thinking about what Warren had said to her that morning before Cynthia had come into the room. "How are you making out with our big picture man?" he had asked mockingly.

"All right," she had answered. "I think he's trying to screw up enough courage to pop the question."

He had grinned derisively at her. "You better turn on more

charm, sugar," he said, "or the fish will get off the hook. I see in the paper that he's going to the studio in the morning."

Johnny's voice interrupted her thoughts. "Dulcie."

She turned and looked at him, her eyes wide and clear. "Yes, Johnny."

He smiled apologetically at her. "I don't suppose there's much fun in it for you going to a dine-and-dance place with me."

She knew what he meant and a sudden inexplicable wave of sympathy for him ran through her. She put her hand on his. "That's not so, Johnny," she said softly. "If I didn't want to go with you, I wouldn't be here."

He turned his hand over and held hers. He looked down at her hand. It was thin and small-boned and soft in his. "It's been very kind of you to spend so much time with me the last few weeks," he said humbly, not looking up from the table.

She restrained a smile. "I wanted to, Johnny," she replied.

He didn't look up. His voice was still humble. "It's meant a lot to me that you did," he said. "It's difficult for some people to understand how a guy like me feels. We watch people living and having fun and somehow we're always on the sidelines, never in the crowd." He looked up at her. His eyes were a dark blue and there was an honest warmth in them. "By being so kind, you've made me feel for a while like I was one of the crowd."

"The fool," she thought desperately. "Why doesn't he say it and get it over with?" But she didn't genuinely understand what he had been saying—that he felt he couldn't ask her what he wanted to. She didn't speak. She sat there waiting for him.

His eyes were still on her. "I like being with you," he said. "And I'll miss you."

He didn't ask her. The surprise she felt showed in her voice. "You'll miss me?"

He looked at her. His heart leaped within him at the disappointment in her voice. "Yes," he said. "Have you forgotten? I'm going to California in the morning."

"Oh, Johnny," she said, and this time there was genuine disappointment in her voice. "Must you go?"

He nodded his head. "I have to. Business."

She tossed her head angrily. He liked the way her eyes

flashed at him. "Sometimes I think that's all you really care about! Business! The trouble with you is you don't know how to relax and have fun."

He smiled at her. "A guy like me isn't set up to have fun. All I can do is work."

She leaned forward, her face very close to his. "Stop feeling sorry for yourself, Johnny!" Her lips parted a little, showing the white ends of her teeth. "You're no different from anybody else! What happened was an accident and doesn't really make any difference to anybody and shouldn't to you." She closed her eyes and waited for him to kiss her. "That should do it!" she thought triumphantly.

She felt his hand press hers and heard his voice. She opened her eyes, feeling a little ridiculous. "It's kind of you to say that, Dulcie," he was saying. "I won't forget it."

He looked at his watch. "My God, I didn't realize it was this late!" He looked at her. "Ready to go?"

She looked back at him. For a moment anger flared through her. What the hell was he doing, she thought, playing with her? As quickly as the feeling had come, it vanished. No, he really meant what he was saying. He didn't want to impose himself upon her. She took her lipstick from her evening bag. "I'm ready," she said. "Be with you in a minute."

They were silent in the cab on the way home. He paid the driver and followed her into the lobby. They waited silently for the elevator and rode up to her apartment.

He waited while she opened the door and then followed her into the foyer. There was a small light glowing and it cast a dim shadow over their faces. She turned to him.

He held his hat awkwardly in his hand. His free hand reached for hers. "So long, Dulcie," he said.

She took his hand. "Will you be gone long, Johnny?" she asked wistfully.

"Till March," he said.

"Oh," she said disappointedly. "That's a long time."

He smiled at her. "It's not so long, Dulcie. I'll see you when I get back."

She turned her face away from his in the darkness. "Maybe you won't," she said, her voice small and plaintive. "Warren wants me to go home and give up the idea of going on the stage."

He watched her. His voice wasn't steady when he finally

spoke. "Maybe Warren has the right idea. It's a pretty tough life."

She turned her face toward his. In the dark it was glowing with an inner incandescence. True feeling rushed into her voice. "No, it isn't right, I know it!" Her shoulders drooped helplessly. "But there isn't anything I can do about it. I guess I'll have to go home."

He put his hand under her chin and turned her face up to his. His voice was sympathetic. "Don't feel blue, Dulcie. If you really want something, you'll get it."

"Do you really think so, Johnny?" Her voice was excited. "I want to be an actress, a great actress. Do you think I will be?"

He looked down at her reassuringly. "You will be if you want it bad enough."

She threw her arms around his neck and kissed him. He almost stumbled in his surprise; then his arms went around her. She let her body press against him. "I don't know what I'll do without you, Johnny." she said against his ear.

He drew away from her stiffly and looked at her. He was suddenly aware of his clumsiness. Coldly his mind told him that she couldn't be interested in him. A man with only one leg. He felt a pain stab through his breast. All she could really do was feel sorry for him.

"I've got to be going, Dulcie," he said uncomfortably.

She stared at him unbelievingly. The man was crazy. What did he want? A written invitation? In a sort of daze she held out her hand.

He took it. "Good-by," he said.

She didn't answer. Still dazed, she watched the door close behind him. Then suddenly she came to life. In a rage she took off one of her shoes and flung it at the door.

The light flashed on in the foyer and she whirled around. Warren stood there mockingly, leaning against the inner door. He silently clapped his hands together. His voice was low. "Curtain, act two," he said.

"What did you want me to do?" she snarled at him. "Hold him by his trousers?"

He walked over to her, shaking his head gently. "Temper, temper," he said. "Can't you see the man has ideals and is a gentleman?"

With an effort she controlled herself. She smiled and came

toward him, put her arms around him, and looked up into his face. "What are we going to do now, Warren? I tried."

He disengaged himself from her clasp. "I don't know what you're going to do, honey," he said quietly, "but you're going to have to leave here."

She stared at him for a moment. Rage flashed across her face, and suddenly it was gone and she smiled. She turned, walked over to the door, and picked up her shoe from the floor. She walked back to him slowly. "Darling," she said sweetly, "did you ever want something you couldn't have?"

His face was puzzled. "No," he answered. He watched her walk past him to the inner door. "Why?"

She turned and faced him. The light of the room fell across her. She let her evening wrap fall from her shoulders. "Then take a good look, darling," she said slowly, "because some day you're going to want it an awful lot and you won't get it!"

Johnny looked out the window of the train. They were rolling through the Jersey meadows. He settled back against the cushions comfortably. There was a knock on the door.

He looked up. It must be Rock with the papers. His hands were probably filled and he couldn't turn the knob. He got up and opened the door.

"Can I come in, Johnny?" the voice asked him plaintively.

He stood there for a moment in shocked surprise. "Dulcie!" he exclaimed. "What are you doing here?"

She came into the compartment and closed the door behind her. "I wanted to be with you, Johnny," she said breathlessly, looking up at him.

Happiness gradually replaced the look of surprise on his face. He reached out an arm to her. She took his hand. "But what about your plans?" he asked bewilderedly.

She put her arms around his neck and clung to him. "Last night when you kissed me I suddenly knew what I wanted. I didn't want to be an actress any more. All I want is you!"

"But—" Johnny insisted.

"No buts!" she said swiftly. "I'm free, white, and twenty-four and I know what I want!" She pressed her lips to his.

He held her close to him. Her lips told him what she said was true. He could hear the words in his ears: "I know what I want!" The only thing the matter was that he didn't know how true they were.

7

The sound of the water running in the shower woke him up. For a moment he lay listening to it, then, slowly, he rolled over on his back. He had been sleeping on his stomach. He opened his eyes. The bathroom door was open and through it came the sound of the running water.

He sat up and reached for his watch on the table next to the bed. It was almost six o'clock in the morning. He reached for the crutches that lay next to the bed and lifted himself up. The bed squeaked as his weight came off it.

Dulcie's voice came from the shower. "Darling, are you up?"

He grinned to himself. If he hadn't been awake before he heard her voice, he was now. He was suddenly alive. Alive in every part of his body in a way he hadn't been for many years. "Yeah," he called back.

"There's a note on the dresser for you," she called in to him. "I found it under the door this morning when I woke up."

He went to the dresser and picked it up. It was a white square envelope with the hotel's imprint up in the left-hand corner. On it was his name scrawled in Rocco's familiar handwriting. He opened it.

"Dear Johnny," it read, "I ordered the car to pick you up at seven fifteen downstairs as you wanted and took the five ten this morning back to New York. There's no place for an extra man on a honeymoon. Good luck." It was signed: "Rocco."

He tapped the letter thoughtfully against the dresser. He thought Rock had been acting strangely yesterday when they had been married at that whistle stop just inside the California border. They had got off the train at Pasadena at ten thirty last night and had come directly to the hotel.

290

He had told Rock to have a car ordered for seven fifteen in the morning. Rock had looked at him and laughingly said: "Do you think you'll be up that early?"

He had grinned back at Rocco foolishly. "Sure," he had said. "I told Peter I'd be out at his house for breakfast."

Awkwardly they had shaken hands and bidden each other good-night. He had gone up to their room and knocked on the door.

"Come in." Dulcie's voice was small.

He had gone into the room. She was in bed already, a small robe flung across her shoulders. The light from a small table lamp next to the bed was the only light in the room. She was watching him.

He smiled reassuringly at her. "Nervous?" he asked.

She nodded her head. "A little," she replied. "I was never married before."

He laughed at her small joke and sat down on the bed next to her and put his arms around her. She turned her face to his and he kissed her. He looked down at her; her eyes were closed. He kissed them tenderly. "Don't be afraid, darling," he whispered. "I'll be gentle with you."

He didn't know it, but the shoe was on the other foot. She was gentle with him. So gentle he hadn't suspected her experience.

She came out of the bathroom, a robe hanging loosely around her shoulders. "What is it?" she asked.

It was a moment before he realized she was referring to the note he held in his hand. The robe hung open and she was lovely beneath it. "From Rock," he said looking at her.

She tied the robe around her and walked toward him. "What does he say?"

He handed her the note and she read it swiftly. A feeling of elation ran through her. There was something about Rock and his devotion to Johnny that she was afraid of. She gave it back to him. "It's funny, he didn't say anything last night," she said.

"Yes," he said slowly, "it is funny." He laughed shortly. "I feel strange."

She had turned and was running a comb through her hair. At his words she turned back to him. "How?"

He was uncomfortable. "This is the first time since the war Rock hasn't been around."

She came to him and put her arms around him. "You don't need him any more, darling," she said. "Now you've got me."

He smiled down at her and kissed the lobe of her ear where it peeked out from under her hair. "It's not that, sugar," he said. "It's something else." There was a guilty feeling inside him. Strangely he couldn't help thinking he had let Rock down.

She snuggled closer to him. "What else?"

He laughed embarrassedly. "Like who's going to drive the car to take us out to Peter's house this morning?" and was ashamed of his words as soon as they were out of his mouth, for that wasn't the way he felt at all.

She kissed him. "I'm quite talented, darling," she said, taking him at his word. "I can drive, too."

She was curious about Peter and his family and asked him many questions about them as they drove out to his house. She asked him so many questions he didn't realize most of them were about Doris.

At last he turned to her and laughed. "Don't be such a busybody, you'll meet them for yourself in a few minutes."

She kept her eye on the road. "I'm only asking because they have known you so much longer than I," she said in a hurt tone of voice. "And I wonder if they'll like me."

He kissed her cheek. "Stop acting, darling," he said, smiling. "You know they'll love you."

She drove silently, following his directions. She was no fool. When she had made up her mind to marry Johnny she decided to learn all she could about him. Warren had told her as much as he knew. She added to that by careful questioning of some friends of hers who worked on theatrical papers. From them she had learned all about Peter and his family. She had especially been interested in Doris. An instinct told her to learn more about Doris. She had checked and found out that Doris had written a novel that had been published just a few months before. She read the book. When she finished it she knew she was right about Doris. The man in the story was enough like Johnny to be him.

Johnny's voice interrupted her thoughts. "This last turn here and we're right at the house."

She looked at him. His face was intent, watching the side of the road for the first sign of Peter's home. There was also a look of happy anticipation there. For a moment she was very fond of him. He was such a nice guy; he had acted toward her like a schoolboy with his first love. She took a hand off the wheel and placed it on his. "Happy, Johnny?" she asked.

He looked at her. "What do you think?" he asked in return, squeezing her hand.

Doris looked at them blankly. Her mind was still numb, her heart seemed to have turned into a lump of ice within her breast.

His words still hung in the air. "We were married last night!"

She watched her father jump up and go around the table and excitedly pump his hand. Hours seemed to go by. What was Johnny saying? She tilted her head a little to one side as if to hear better. He was talking to her. Desperately she tried to hear him.

"Ain't you comin' over and kiss your Uncle Johnny?" he was asking as if she were a little girl.

Stiffly she got to her feet. She wished she was a little girl again. Little girls didn't hurt inside the way she did.

8

CONRAD VON ELSTER put his elbows on his desk and his head in his hands and stared at the photographs spread out before him. He was unhappy. And he was worried too. He was looking for a woman and couldn't find one.

Not that there was a shortage of women in a personal sense for Herr von Elster. That there never was. In spite of a carefully cultivated rudeness of manner, unkempt, sandy-colored hair that never looked washed, slightly bulging, gimlety blue eyes and a pale, oily skin, he had attracted many women. This time he didn't want a woman for himself, he wanted a woman for a picture he was about to make.

Conrad von Elster was a director of motion pictures. He had come to America at the personal request of Peter Kessler, who had told him that America was waiting for his pictures. He had come to America for one thousand American dollars every week. Inflation was rampant in Germany when he spoke to Mr. Kessler. The dinner they were eating at the time Mr. Kessler extended his invitation cost two hundred thousand marks, which Mr. Kessler paid with one American ten-dollar bill with an eagle on it. It was a good dinner. Von Elster belched politely and said he would be glad to come to America. That was four months ago.

He had arrived in Hollywood with Mr. Kessler about the middle of November and was installed in an office and told to go to work. He had already approved the script of the picture he was to work on and his first job was to select an adequate cast. He had no trouble until he came to the part of the leading woman. None of the actresses under contract to Magnum would suit him. Obligingly Mr. Kessler told the casting department to extend all possible aid to Herr von Elster. Immediately von Elster was swamped with photographs of pretty girls. His phone rang every minute with a request from the casting department to interview the newest hopeful.

Von Elster had looked at all of them and found none of them satisfactory. The photographs now spread on the desk before him were the best of all those he had seen. He shook his head and sighed. He didn't like any of them.

He had to choose one of these girls to play the role in his picture or he might have to give up that thousand-dollar check he received every week. The idea of that one-thousand-dollar check made him happy until he thought of the note he had found on his desk when he arrived at the office that morning.

It was a simple note from Mr. Kessler. It was a small piece of paper. Across the top of it were printed the words: "From the desk of Peter Kessler, President Magnum Pictures." The message was typed carefully underneath it: "Be at my office at 11:30 a.m." It wasn't signed.

If this note had come before January 1, von Elster would not have been perturbed. Indeed, he would have looked forward to the meeting with anticipation. Mr. Kessler and he found many things in common to talk about; but things were different now. On January 2 a Mr. Edge had come to the studio from New York to help Mr. Kessler.

Von Elster was no fool. He could sense the almost immediate change in the atmosphere around him. Even the secretaries were at their desks early. The pleasant calls he would get from Mr. Kessler twice a week chucklingly asking him if he had found the right girl yet had stopped. It was now almost the end of January and this was the first word he had had from Mr. Kessler all month.

His fears were not entirely without other foundation. He had heard of the summary dismissal of certain directors, writers, and producers because of their inability to get their pictures into production. At first he had ignored these signals. Hadn't Mr. Kessler told him every time he spoke to him that he didn't have to start until he was perfectly satisfied with everything? But then as Mr. Kessler stopped making his bi-weekly calls, von Elster couldn't ignore what was happening. That was why he was so unhappy. He didn't want to stop receiving that one-thousand-dollar check.

He looked at his wristwatch. It was almost eleven o'clock now. At eleven o'clock the messenger would come with the check. Sometimes the messenger would be late. He hoped the messenger wouldn't be late today. He would feel better with this week's check safely in his pocket before he left for Mr. Kessler's office.

There was a knock at his door. Von Elster smiled happily. The check was on time. The messenger placed the envelope containing the check on his desk and waited patiently while von Elster signed and returned the receipt to him. The messenger left the office and von Elster placed the envelope carefully in an inside pocket of his jacket.

He looked down at the desk again in disgust. In America they called these women? Bah! In the old country they had women—real women. Here they were all alike. Made in mass production like the automobiles that covered the roads. Too skinny. Too much make-up. Too short haircuts. In Germany they had women. There the women had what he called the three B's—breasts, bellies, and behinds. Without them what good was a woman?

Worriedly he walked over to the window of his office and looked out. From his window he could see the entrance to the casting department. He took a cigar from his pocket and stuck it in his mouth and chewed on it morosely.

The door of the casting department opened and a girl came out. She stood there on the steps for a moment and opened her purse. She took a cigarette from the purse and lighted it. The sunlight falling on her hair made it seem like a ring of gold. She puffed at the cigarette, and when she was sure it was going she started down the steps. Admiringly von Elster contemplated her. That was a woman. She had the three B's all right.

She was wearing a white simple sports dress that clung to her body. Her short skirt swirled, showing long, slim legs. For a moment she stood on the walk in front of the casting building as if undecided in which direction she should go. She turned and came toward his window.

The phone on his desk began to ring. He turned and walked back to his desk and picked it up. "Hello," he said into the phone, still looking out the window. "This is Conrad von Elster." The girl was almost opposite the window now.

"Mr. Kessler would like to change the time of your appointment to four thirty this afternoon. Will that be all right?" a woman's voice asked him.

"Yes," he replied, "it vill be all right."

"Thank you," the voice said, and the phone clicked off.

He placed his phone back on the desk, his mind still on the girl outside the window. He saw her face for a moment as she walked by. "*Gott in Himmel!*" he swore to himself. "That one is a beauty. Why can't they send me one like that?" He turned and picked up a match from the tray on his desk. He snapped it against his thumbnail and held it up to his cigar. Absently his eyes looked at the photographs on his desk and suddenly his hand shook and the match fell to the floor.

"*Dummkopf!*" he almost shouted aloud at himself. He turned and ran to his door and opened it. Leaving it open behind him, he ran down the corridor to the street entrance.

In the street he looked frantically from side to side. He didn't know which way the girl had gone. At last he saw her. She was walking toward the administration building, her white skirt swinging in the sunlight.

"*Fräulein!*" he shouted, forgetting his English, "*Fräulein!*" He began to run after her. His heart pounded against his side; it had been a long time since he had demanded such effort from his body.

He was drawing closer to her. "*Fräulein!*" he shouted again. She didn't hear him and kept on walking. He tried to run faster; his side began to ache. "*Fräulein!*" This time his voice was shrill, it was almost a scream.

The girl heard him and turned around. He slowed down to a walk and held both hands in the air waving to her to wait for him. He was breathing heavily as he came up to her.

A lifted eyebrow and a studied disdainful smile was on the girl's face as she watched him approach. Her body stood quietly, perfectly poised, ready to move on if it was a case of mistaken identity.

He gasped for breath with which to speak. It was as it should be. The girl was too young to have appreciation for the difficult exercises of middle age. And those ignoramuses in the casting office had sent her away. He found his voice. "Are you an actress?"

The girl looked puzzled for a second, then nodded her head.

"That's right," he said. "In pictures you don't have to speak!" He waved his hands in the air dramatically. "I, Conrad von Elster, will make you the greatest star on the screen!"

Dulcie had a wild impulse to laugh. For a moment she thought of telling this funny little man who she was. Then she changed her mind. It would be fun to see what would happen. Johnny was tied up all day and she had nothing better to do anyway. It was like that almost every day and she was getting bored with sitting around and waiting for him.

Von Elster didn't wait for her to speak. He took her arm and was leading her back to his office. "Ve must immediately make for you a screen test."

"A screen test!" Dulcie thought. "Johnny would get a kick out of that!" But deep inside she knew he wouldn't like it and was preparing an explanation for him. If she did anything, she would do it for herself and because she wanted it and not for anyone else, even Johnny.

They were in von Elster's office now. He motioned her to a seat and picked up the phone. "Mr. Reilly in casting, please," he said into the phone. He waited for a moment, then a man's voice answered.

"Mr. Reilly, this is von Elster. I haff a girl here in my office I vant immediately to test." He paused for a moment. "No, Mr. Reilly, not this afternoon. Right avay! I haff a meeting vit Mr. Kessler to look at it at four thirty." He was silent for a moment while the man spoke, then he looked at her. He put one hand over the mouthpiece of the phone. "Qvick, vat iss your name?" he hissed at her.

Dulcie hesitated for a moment. She could still back out and end this little farce. But she didn't want to. She wanted to be an actress. She had always wanted it. Why should things be any different now because she was married to Johnny? She stared back at von Elster. "Dulcie," she said, "Dulcie Warren."

Her breath caught in her throat as von Elster repeated the name into the phone. Suddenly her tenseness was gone and she felt relaxed and at ease again. Johnny wouldn't like it, but what did it matter? What had she married him for if not this —among other things?

The test was good. No one had to tell Dulcie, she knew it. She had spent enough time around the theater to know when something was good. She could tell from how the people on the set had acted. At the beginning they were bored. It had been just another job to them, another test. They made dozens of these every week. There wasn't any reason for them to think this would be different from any of the others. But it was.

Maybe at first they had been attracted by that nervous little foreign director. He had been so excited that they could hardly understand his instructions. When they finally understood him they had opened their eyes wide in amazement. His style, his technique, was certainly different, something they had never seen before. But their professional minds had grasped it at once and wondered why no one had used it before. It was that simple and that good.

Up to the moment when Dulcie took her place before the cameras, the interest, the excitement, had all been intellectual. A style, a technique, a way of mechanics. But when Dulcie stood there, with all the lights beating down on her, everything the little man had done suddenly made sense. Emotionally as well as intellectually. It was then they realized that this funny little man had created a new technique especially for this actress, and they looked at him with a quick and deep respect. The little man gave the actress her final instructions; then he stepped back from the set and sat down in his chair.

All eyes turned to the girl when the little man dropped his hand. Quiet fell across the small set; only the clicking of the cameras could be heard; the intense heat coming from the overhead lights could be felt as the girl began to act.

The sweat was pouring from von Elster's pale face as he watched her. This had to be right. He was convinced now that fate had given him this one last chance. Suddenly there was a tension in the air. It was as if a spark of electricity had reached out from the girl and made contact with every person there.

Von Elster's breath whistled out between his lips in a long sigh of relief. Slowly he turned his head away from the girl and looked at the others. The script girl had forgotten her script, it lay on her lap as she watched the girl. He turned his gaze to the men. It was the men who would feel the full impact of this woman. He was right. The props men, the grips, the electricians were staring at her. The same look was on all their faces.

It was a look as old as time. Von Elster turned his gaze back to the girl and settled back comfortably in his chair. His eye saw with the eye of the camera. He had been right about the girl. She projected. He smiled happily to himself at the thought, visions of a long line of one-thousand-dollar checks dancing before him. She projected in more ways than one. He didn't have anything to worry about.

9

SHE put the paper down and drew the bed jacket around her shoulders. It was growing chilly. She looked over at the clock. It was almost midnight and Johnny hadn't come in yet. It had been an exciting day.

She could still hear von Elster's panicked cry through the closed doors of the projection room as she waited in the outer hall. "But, Mr. Edge, how did I know she vas your vife? She didn't tell me!" And then she fled.

Something of the panic in von Elster's voice had transferred itself to her. She could imagine the mood Johnny was in that could bring it about and she didn't want to face him. Not there. Not on his grounds.

She would face him in their apartment in the hotel, where she could meet him on her terms. Where she could talk to him not only with her lips but with her body. She had confidence in her body. She knew Johnny.

She had remained close to the phone all afternoon. She expected Johnny to call her and ask her about it. But he didn't call until it was almost seven o'clock.

Then his voice was cool and impersonal. "I'll have to miss dinner, darling," he said. "I'm stuck at the studio for a while tonight. You have dinner and go to bed. I'll be home about midnight."

"Yes, Johnny," she breathed obediently into the phone, and waited for him to say something about the test.

He hesitated for a moment, she could hear him clear his throat. "So long, Dulcie," he said.

"So long, Johnny," she said into the phone, and heard the click of the receiver being put back on the hook. A vague feeling of disappointment swept over her. He hadn't spoken about it. Then she smiled to herself. Good. The battle would be fought on even more favorable grounds for her than she had expected.

She heard footsteps in the hall and the sound of a key being inserted in the lock. Quickly she reached up and turned off the lamp near the bed, plunging the room in darkness. She threw her bed jacket onto a chair and lay back against the pillow.

The door opened and she could hear him walking through the other room to the bedroom. He stopped on the threshold and stood there.

She sat up in the dark. "Johnny?" Her voice was low and almost frightened.

She could hear him expel a deep breath. "Yes."

She reached out an arm toward the bed lamp. She felt a shoulder strap of her gown slip as she reached out. She let it slip all the way before she snapped on the light.

There was a hurt look on his face as he stood there.

"I must have dozed off while I was waiting for you," she said lamely.

He didn't answer. He walked over to the closet and took off his jacket. He moved stiffly as if he weren't sure of himself.

She watched him from the bed. "Did you have a tough day, darling?" she asked in a sympathetic tone of voice.

He turned and faced her. His face was impassive and she couldn't tell what he was thinking. He was silent for a long moment while they looked at each other. At last he spoke. "You didn't make it any easier," he said heavily.

She looked at him appealingly. "You're angry with me," she said in a very small voice.

He took off his tie and placed it on the tie rack in the closet before he answered. He unbuttoned his collar and looked down at her. "No, I'm not angry, Dulcie," he said.

slowly, "I'm hurt." She could see a muscle working in his face. He turned away, stiffly walked to the dresser, and put his cuff links on it. His voice was filled with pain. "Dulcie, why did you do it?" He didn't turn around.

She scrambled from the bed and ran to him. He half turned toward her and she slipped her arms under his and around him. She placed her head against his chest. His arms hung loosely at his side.

"Oh, Johnny." she cried in the same small voice, "I didn't mean anything! I thought it would be fun and you would get a laugh out of it!"

Involuntarily his arms went around her. He looked down at the top of her head. She was so warm against him. His voice was softer now. "It wasn't funny," he said, his voice trembling a little.

She kissed his chest where the shirt was open. She didn't look up, she knew she had him. Her voice seemed almost at the point of tears. "We're quarreling, Johnny."

He put a hand under her chin and turned her face up to his. He looked deep into her eyes, then he kissed her and placed his cheek against hers. "We're not quarreling, darling," he whispered. "But why did you do it? Aren't you happy with me? I thought you'd forgotten about being an actress."

"I had, Johnny," she said quickly. "Honest, I had. But something happened. I don't know what it was. Maybe it was being alone all day. You're always at the studio. You're so busy. When that funny little man came up to me on the street, I didn't think. It happened almost before I knew it. It was something different to do, something to do to fill up the time until I saw you." She hesitated for a second and then looked up into his face. "It's so lonely staying here in the hotel all day waiting for you. I don't know anybody here."

His voice was sympathetic now. "I'm sorry, darling," he apologized. "I should have realized how it was for you." He kissed her cheek and smiled. "Anyway, we won't be here for long. Soon we'll be back in New York." A thought struck him, and his smile grew a little broader. "Maybe soon you won't have to worry about taking up your time," he added meaningfully.

She stood very still within his arms. It was time for him to learn his first lesson. That was not the time-killer she wanted.

Ever. She looked at him silently. Slowly the tears began to well into her eyes.

He looked down at her. A puzzled expression began to creep over his face.

Suddenly she broke from his arms and flung herself face-down on the bed and began to sob.

He followed her to the bed and sat down beside her. He put his hands on her shoulders and tried to turn her around. She wouldn't turn, only sobbed harder. His voice was frightened. "Dulcie, honey, what's the matter? What did I say?"

Slowly she turned around and sat up. Her gown slipped to her waist and the tears ran down her cheeks. "Johnny," she wept, "You're going to hate me! I fooled you!"

He put his arms around her and drew her to him. He pressed his lips to her ear. "I'm not going to hate you," he whispered tenderly. "What are you crying about?"

She buried her face against his shoulder. "I should have told you before, but I was afraid you wouldn't marry me!"

His voice was genuinely frightened now. She fought an impulse to keep her triumph from showing on her face. His hands gripped tightly into her shoulders, hurting her. She welcomed the pain. It was a sign of the power she had over him.

"Dulcie, what do you have to tell me?" His eyes were staring into hers searchingly.

She looked up at him bravely. Her voice was low and full of self-reproach. "I had an accident. Years ago. When I was a kid." Her gaze fell from his. She looked down at the bed. "The doctor said I could never have a child." She looked up at him again, her eyes filled with tears.

Slowly the tenseness was disappearing from his face.

"Johnny, you're disappointed!" she cried, the tears contorting her face once more. "You wanted a child!"

A look of tenderness came to his eyes. She had never seen them so soft and warm. She didn't know they were mellowed by his disappointment. She didn't guess how close she was to the truth.

He pressed her head to his chest. "No, darling," he lied, his eyes looking somberly over her head to the picture of Peter he had on the dresser. He was going to name his first son after him. "It really doesn't matter."

She kissed his cheek, his chin, his lips. Short, quick kisses

Light as the flutter of a butterfly's wings. "Johnny, you're so good to me!"

He smiled slowly. "Why shouldn't I be?" he asked. "Ain't you my baby?"

She snuggled her head against his shoulder. "Then you're not mad at me?" she asked in a small and hesitating voice.

He kissed her neck for an answer. He held his face against her and guided it toward her breasts. She bent forward and kissed the top of his head and smiled. He was so simple. It was so easy to keep him happy.

Her voice was still low and small. "Johnny," she asked, "how was the test?"

She could feel him start with surprise. He tried to raise his head, but she wouldn't let him. Her hands kept his face between her breasts.

His voice was muffled as he replied. "It was very good."

She was silent for a while. She could feel his hands seeking her out. She let her body warm to his touch. "Was it really good, Johnny?"

He wasn't thinking of his answer. "It was one of the best we ever saw."

She reached over and turned off the lamp. She started to unbutton his shirt. He laughed happily and got out of bed. She could see him move in the dark as he undressed. A few minutes later his lips were against hers, her body warm against him.

They were quiet. The glow of their cigarettes in the darkness of the room cast their shadows on the white sheets. Slowly she placed her hand on his body and ran her fingers lightly across his chest.

"Johnny," she said.

"Yes," he answered, his voice filled with contentment.

"Johnny, I was thinking."

There was a lazy curiosity in his voice as he spoke. "What about?" he asked.

"This picture of von Elster's—" She didn't finish the sentence. Her heart began to pound excitedly inside her, lending a breathless quality to her voice. "We're going to be here until the end of March."

He turned and looked at her in the dark. He was silent for a moment. "And you want to make it?"

She didn't dare answer. She nodded her head in the dark. "Why?" he asked simply.

She hesitated. Then the answer seemed to flood from inside her. "Because I always said I could be an actress, a good one. Because Cynthia and Warren didn't believe me. I want to show them, Johnny. They used to laugh at me all the time. You said I was good yourself. Please, Johnny, just this one. That's all I ask." She was really begging now, she wasn't acting. "Let me do this one picture. It's the only chance I've got to show them. I'll never ask again. Just let me make this picture!"

He drew deeply on his cigarette. He could feel the acrid smoke deep inside his lungs. Slowly he let it out through his nostrils. Only one picture. That was all she was asking. She was good. It wasn't as if she were not. The test she had made was the best he had ever seen. That was why he had been so angry when he saw it. A cold fear had swept over him when he saw her face on the screen. He could not hope to hold so vivid a talent for his own, to keep her to himself.

His gaze had swept around the darkened projection room. The faces he saw were enraptured. They were alive to the emotions expressed by her. After a first startled word even Peter had responded to Dulcie on the screen.

Peter had been nice about it, too. He had not pressed him for any decision.

He loved her and he loved motion pictures too. Something inside ached when he thought that he would have to keep her from being where he suddenly knew she belonged. But he was afraid that if she once appeared in a picture, he would lose her.

Slowly he puffed at his cigarette. He could hear her breathing, she was sitting so still, almost as if she were afraid to move, afraid to do something that would displease him. Tenderness and love for her swept through him. She was so good to him, when he had thought no woman could ever be. He began to feel a little sorry for her, a little angry with himself. How could he be so cold, so heartless toward her when all she asked was so little of him?

He ground out his cigarette in the ashtray and turned to her. "Just this one picture?" he asked softly.

"Just this one," she repeated.

He looked at her in the dark. The light from the window

fell across her face. She was beautiful. Her eyes were on his, deep with an unexpressed hope, her lower lip trembled slightly, her cigarette was forgotten in her hand.

"All right," he said quietly.

Suddenly she was upon him, her body pressing his against the bed. She was kissing him. "Johnny, Johnny!" she was saying excitedly.

He could feel her trembling. He shivered with a strange unknown fear and pulled her face down to his with a desire to feel her warmth around him.

"Johnny," she was saying, her teeth biting excitedly against his lips. "Johnny, I love you!" And strangely enough, at the moment, she meant every word she spoke.

10

PETER put the empty coffee cup on the table and looked at Esther. "I don't like it," he said flatly. "I don't like it at all. The idea of a young girl like Doris going off to Europe by herself! It's not right."

Esther smiled at him tolerantly. "Sometimes it's necessary for a girl to get away from things and be by herself for a while," she said, coming to her daughter's defense.

Peter looked at her belligerently. "What does she have to be by herself for?" he asked. "What does she have to get away from? Everything here is fine."

Imperceptibly Esther shook her head. Men were sometimes such blind fools, and Peter could see no more than the others. Couldn't he see what was the matter with Doris? The way she had acted ever since Johnny came out here that morning with his wife? She didn't answer.

A crackling sound of gunfire came through the open windows. Peter pulled out his watch and looked at it. "Holy smokes," he exclaimed, jumping to his feet. "It's late. Already the Western on the back lot is shooting and I planned to be down there this morning."

The back lot was just down the hill from their house. He took his hat, walked to the door, and turned to look back at his wife. "I'm going," he announced, "but I still don't like what Doris is doing."

Esther came up to him and kissed his cheek. "Go, Papa," she said. "Don't worry about her. She'll be all right."

He looked at her curiously. "Nobody ever listens to me around this house," he said as he left. "I'm only the father!"

Peter stopped at the crest of the hill and looked back at his house. He shook his head. Something had been wrong for the last month. He didn't understand it. He couldn't put his finger on just what it was, but he felt certain it concerned Doris. In the past month she had lost a great deal of weight and she looked peaked. Black circles had sprung up under her eyes as if she hadn't been sleeping well. He stood there lost in thought.

The sound of horse's hoofs against the ground and men shouting made him turn around. He looked down into the valley. At the bottom of the hill on which he stood was a narrow dirt road. An open car with a camera mounted in the back was speeding along it. Behind the car about a dozen men on horses were riding desperately after it, clouds of dust coming up from the flying hoofs.

Peter smiled to himself and started down the path that led to the road. Some day he would have to build a house away from the studio, where the noise of the Westerns would not wake people up on the mornings they wanted to sleep late. But now he loved it. The sound that reached him at his breakfast table every morning would send the same thrill of pride shooting through him, the same pride he had felt when he first made *The Bandit*.

He reached the road and stood there waiting. They had gone past him, out of sight around a curve in the road, but they would be back in a few minutes. He calculated the time it would take for a setup to be made and for them to return. About seven minutes. He took out his watch and looked at it. Nothing like checking up on his units personally to gain the most efficiency from them.

Exactly five minutes later he heard them yelling as they came around the bend. He put his watch back in his pocket and stepped out into the road and held up his hand. This director was good, he had completed his setup in two minutes less time than the average.

The driver of the car saw him and slowed the car to a halt. In the back seat behind him the director waved his hand for the riders to stop. They pulled up sharply, their horses panting heavily. The cameraman snapped the shutter down on his camera to keep out any stray beams of light. They turned around.

Peter walked slowly to the car and looked up at the director. He recognized him. He wasn't the director who should be working on this road, he was a unit manager. A young fellow named Gordon, he couldn't remember his first name. "That was a quick setup, Gordon," he said, complimenting the young man.

"Thanks, Mr. Kessler," Gordon replied.

Peter looked into the car. "Where's Marran?" he asked. Marran was the director in charge of this unit.

Gordon looked uncomfortable. Marran was stinking drunk back in his office. He had come in too drunk to work and Gordon had dropped him on the couch in the office and taken the unit out to do the chase scenes. "He wasn't feeling well," he said hesitantly. "He told me to take the unit out."

Peter didn't answer. He had heard rumors of Marran's indispositions. He climbed into the car. Forgotten was his pleasure at the efficient timing of the return setup. He wasn't paying a director two hundred dollars a week so a fifty-dollar unit man could take his picture out. "Drop me at the end of the road," he said surlily. That would leave him only five minutes from the office.

The car started up again. Gordon turned and signaled for the riders to follow. "Might as well keep shooting," he said to the cameraman, looking up at the sky. "This sun doesn't look as if it will last forever."

Peter heard him and nodded approvingly to himself. Good boy, this Gordon, he didn't waste any light. Light was the most valuable thing in this business. You had to be ready to use it whenever you could. He turned in his seat and looked back.

Gordon's back was turned to him. He was leaning against the back of the car, his knees braced against its side, his body hanging over it dangerously. He waved his right hand in a circle. A rider dove from his horse and tumbled over and over on the ground.

Peter nodded his head again and turned around in his seat. He sat there silently, oblivious of the sounds and noises behind him. There were many other things on his mind. He stared ahead morosely.

There was this business of George wanting to sell out the theaters. He felt that George was worrying over nothing, and he was sure that he did not want to break up the theater chain. He felt they played an important part in establishing the Magnum name across the country. He had told Johnny that he wanted to buy George out. Johnny pointed out that it would take more cash than they had available. He had suggested they go to see Al Santos and try to borrow the capital necessary. They were to see Al today at Al's office in downtown Los Angeles. He wasn't at all sure he could get the money from him; he owed him almost four million dollars already.

The car stopped. Peter looked up, surprised the ride was over so soon. He got out of the car and turned to the unit man. "Nice work, Tom," he said to him.

Gordon corrected him. "Bob, Mr. Kessler."

Peter looked at him closely for a moment, his eyebrows pulled together. "Yes," he said absently, "Bob. Nice work." Without waiting for a reply he turned and walked down the road.

11

AL SANTOS's office was in the rear of the two-storied Bank of Independence, and through the glass he could see what was going on all over the bank. The office was very plain. Al's clothes, too, were of a sober and conservative cut. Little trace remained about him of the carnival operator of fifteen years ago. He now looked like an exemplary representative of the banking profession. Only his eyes were the same, warm, brown, and twinkling. And the tanned leathery wrinkles on his face and the black, thin, Italian stogie clenched between his teeth.

Right now he was feeling good. Thin spirals of smoke arose from the end of his cigar as he leaned back in his chair and through half-lidded eyes looked at Johnny while Peter was speaking.

Johnny looked tired, he thought. He was working too hard at the studio. He had heard how much Johnny was doing out there and he knew just how much had been accomplished.

Very little went on at any of the studios that did not reach his ears sooner or later. Somehow he felt proud of the job that Johnny had done. In a little more than a month Magnum was humming like a beehive and he knew a great deal of it was due to Johnny's effort. He was as glad that Johnny had been able to accomplish it as if he had done it himself.

But Johnny looked too tired. There were lines of fatigue across his face and around the corners of his mouth. He couldn't keep working at a pace like that forever. It was killing.

And Johnny's new wife. Al smiled to himself at the thought. A man sixty-two years old could think of things like that only in retrospect. There was a woman to wear out the buttons on a man's trousers. He looked at Johnny more closely. He supposed that didn't help much either. A man had to have some rest.

He listened to Peter with half an ear. He was used to having picture people in his office asking him to lend them money. It was a peculiar business. No matter how much they had, they always needed more to do something else they couldn't manage without. It was a funny thing, too. Generally he loaned them money and it had turned out all right.

He remembered when he had first come out here. He was retired. The last thing he expected to do was to become a banker. A former carnival man a banker. He wouldn't have believed it himself if someone had told it to him then. But one day while he was sitting on the front porch of his farm talking with his brother, Luigi, and sorting out the notes he kept in the little box in the dresser, he added them up. The picture men around here owed him almost a quarter of a million dollars. He had jokingly passed the remark to Luigi that he might as well open a bank for them since they couldn't seem to get any money through the banks already established. His bookkeeper, Vittorio Guido, a neighbor's son, who was a bookkeeper in a bank in Los Angeles during the week and helped Al on week-ends, had come out on the porch just at that moment. He had looked down at Al and had asked: "Why don't you, Mr. Santos?"

And he had, in a small store at first. Over the door they hung a small sign, made of wood, and printed on it in small raised letters were the words: "The Bank of Independence," and underneath that in smaller letters: "Loans Made to the Motion Picture Industry."

The picture business grew and so did the bank, almost hand in hand, it seemed. It was a long step from that first little store to this big building in Los Angeles of today. The gold letters on the door now read: "Capital $50,000,000."

Peter had finished talking and was waiting for him to answer. Al pulled himself away from his thoughts and looked at Peter shrewdly. He had heard enough of Peter's request to understand it. He wanted to borrow an additional two million dollars to buy out George's share of the theaters they owned jointly. "Why does George want to sell?" he asked.

"He wants more time to devote to his own theaters," Peter answered quickly.

Al leaned back and thought about it. He didn't think that was the whole reason behind George's willingness to part with his share of the Magnum theaters, but there were other factors to be considered before he made the loan. "You owe me three and a quarter million dollars now," he said pleasantly. "I persuaded the board to renew it last year when the notes came due. It will be hard to get them to approve an additional two million on top of that."

"But there was a reason for it last year," Peter said. "We were building up our foreign exchanges and it took money." He opened the briefcase on his lap and rummaged through it looking for some papers. He found them and placed them on Al's desk. "This year, however, we won't have those expenses and we'll be able to meet the notes."

Al didn't look at the papers. He never did. They were always ready to show him papers containing budgets and plans and results. He turned them over to his loan and collateral departments for study. Let them try to figure it out and make sense of it. He never could. Whether he lent a man one dollar or one million he always based his loan on his personal opinion of the borrower. "How are you going to do it?" he asked Peter.

Peter cleared his throat nervously. Sometimes he wondered why he kept pushing himself to make more money in this business. The bigger he got, the more he had to worry about. He didn't understand it, but that was the fascination the business had for him. There seemed to be no limit to how far a man could go. "This is my idea." He leaned toward Al and unconsciously lowered his voice. "We'll convert the present loan into seventy-five-thousand-dollar notes, one payable each week. That way this loan would be paid off within the year and would go through a process of reduction that your board can't object to. Against the new loan we'll give you a ten-year chattel mortgage on all the Magnum theaters. They're worth approximately twice what I want to borrow and I don't think your board would mind that." He sat back in his chair and looked at Al, satisfied with himself.

"Seventy-five thousand is a lot of money to pay off every week," Al said thoughtfully. "You sure you can do it?"

"I'm sure I can," Peter said, more confidently than he felt. "We're grossing three hundred thousand and better each week now, and by the end of the year, when the foreign offices are moving in full swing, we should be doing four."

In his mind Al checked the figures Peter quoted against the figures he knew. They were right. Magnum was grossing fifteen million a year. "Who would run the theaters if George left?" he asked.

Peter answered: "Johnny," his head nodding toward him.

Al turned to Johnny. "And you think this will be okay?"

Johnny looked at him. He had been silent while Peter presented his request. "It will take a lot of hustling," he answered honestly, "but I think it will work out all right."

Al turned back to Peter and puffed his cigar thoughtfully. He wasn't entirely satisfied about George's viewpoint, but the other bases for the loan were good. Four million collateral against a two-million mortgage was reasonably safe. He stood up, indicating the interview was at an end. "It sounds all right to me," he said to Peter, picking up the papers on his desk. "I'll turn these over to Vittorio and I'll let you know in a day or two."

Peter smiled in relief. Past experience had taught him that when Al said it would be all right, it generally was, no matter what Vittorio thought. He got to his feet and held out his hand. "Thanks, Al," he said.

Al shook his hand and they started toward the door. At the door Al put his hand on Johnny's shoulder and said reproachfully: "You've only been out to the farm once since you been here."

Johnny looked at him swiftly. It was true, but he had been busy and Dulcie didn't want to go out to the farm. She said the place depressed her because it was so quiet. "I've been working pretty late," he said apologetically.

Al smiled at him. His eyes were warm and fond as they looked at Johnny. "Well, don't be a stranger," he said. "After all, I'd like to see more of your pretty wife. I'm an old man, but I'm not that old I can't appreciate a beautiful woman, especially when she's practically in the family."

Johnny's face colored and Al smiled at it. He turned to Peter and laughed. "These newlyweds are all alike."

He walked them through the bank and watched them get into Peter's car and drive away. Then he turned and walked back to his office, shaking his head a little. Something was bothering Johnny. It wasn't only business, either. He knew Johnny too well for that. Maybe it was his wife, he guessed shrewdly. She didn't look like the kind of woman who would stay at home and raise a family. Especially after once working in a picture. He closed the door of his office behind him and walked over to his desk and sat down heavily. He picked up the papers on his desk and pressed the buzzer for Vittorio.

While he waited for Vittorio, he thumbed idly through the papers. They were covered with figures, but he wasn't looking at them. He was thinking about Johnny. Too bad he hadn't got anywhere with Peter's kid. For a while it looked like they would. She was more his style. The door opened and Vittorio came in.

"What do you want, Al?" Vittorio asked, standing in front of his desk.

He held the papers toward him. "Take a look at these and let me know if they look all right," he said heavily. "We're going to lend Kessler another two million dollars."

Vittorio didn't answer. He took the papers from his employer's hand and went out the door.

Al stared at the closed door. He let out a heavy sigh and lighted up a fresh cigar. He felt suddenly depressed. He looked at his thin cigar. It was his fourth of the day already. The doctor had told him not to smoke more than three. He looked at it thoughtfully for a moment. "I guess I'm getting old," he said aloud in the empty room.

Peter was quiet almost all the way back to the studio. When they neared the studio gates he finally spoke to Johnny. "I walked down the back lot this morning," he said, "and I found out Marran wasn't out with his crew. A kid named Gordon was running it. He was doing good, too."

"I know," Johnny answered. "Marran was cockeyed when he came in this morning."

Peter looked at him in surprise. Johnny didn't miss much. "I guess I'll have to fire him," he said heavily. He didn't like to fire anybody.

"I already did this morning," Johnny answered shortly.

Peter looked at him, relief showing on his face. "We'll put Gordon in charge, then."

"Yeanh," Johnny answered. "I've watched him. He's a worker."

They were silent again as the car rolled through the gates and stopped in front of the administration building. They got out of the car and Johnny followed Peter into his office. In the office Peter turned to him. His voice was humble. "I guess you'll have to hustle back to New York right away if we get that loan. We'll have to keep after business to make that seventy-five every week."

Johnny looked at him. He didn't answer. He walked over to a window and looked out. From the window he could see a truck rolling over to Stage Number One.

Peter walked over and stood beside him looking out. "You've done everything here that needed to be done. I'll be able to manage all right now. We need you back in New York to make sure things will be all right."

"What about Dulcie?" The words sprang bitterly from Johnny's lips.

Peter looked at him uncomfortably. It was a shame to break up their honeymoon. They had been married just a little over a month. He walked back to his desk and sat down. "I'll look after her," he said awkwardly. "I'll send her back as soon as the picture is finished."

Johnny walked over to the desk and looked down at him. He knew there wasn't anything he could do about it. The picture had been working two weeks already and too much money had gone into it to be thrown away. Besides, Peter was right. If they got this loan he had to return to New York. They couldn't take any chances, having to pay out seventy-five thousand every week.

He looked down at Peter. "Remind me not to bring any of my wives out here in the future," he said angrily. He regretted the words as soon as they were out of his mouth. It wasn't Peter's fault. It was this crazy business. You never knew what was going to happen next.

12

"Rock!" His voice seemed to echo in the lighted apartment. He stood there listening for an answer, a puzzled look on his face. There was no answer.

He turned and went back into the hall and brought in his valise. He closed the door behind him and, valise still in hand, walked to Rocco's room and opened the door. "Rock," he called softly.

There was no answer. He turned on the light. The room was empty.

He carried the valise to his room and put it on the bed. Rocco wasn't home. Strange. Maybe Jane forgot to tell him about the wire he had sent, but no, Jane wouldn't forget. He wondered where Rocco had gone.

Still puzzled, he took off his hat and coat and began to unpack. The first thing he took out was a photograph of Dulcie, which he placed on the dresser, and then he stood back smiling fondly.

It had been taken by one of the still photographers out at the studio just a few days ago. It was a good photograph, bringing out the depth of her eyes, the attractive curve of her lips over the even white teeth, and the careless line of her hair falling down to her shoulders.

Good kid, he thought as he turned back to his unpacking. She had been upset over his having to leave so suddenly. She wanted to quit the picture. He smiled to himself as he thought of how he had had to argue to persuade her to stay on while he went back. A few weeks before, she wanted to make the picture more than anything in the world and he didn't want her to. Now she wanted to quit and he had to persuade her to stay with it.

She had no idea of how much there was involved once a picture got under way. It wasn't only the money, he had told her, there were a lot of other things too. The people that worked with her would suffer if she pulled out. What really convinced her was what he said about pictures being like the theater. The-show-must-go-on business and all that kind of crap. He remembered the way her face had lighted up. She could understand that. Not for nothing had her family been in the theater for so long.

Her face smiled warmly at him from the photo on the dresser, where it leaned against the mirror. He smiled back at it. Good kid. He'd have to get a frame for it in the morning. He'd do it before he went into the office. She deserved it. She had even cried a little before he left. She had tried to hide it from him, but he had noticed it. He felt good remembering it.

His unpacking was done. He straightened up and began to take off his shirt. Unconsciously he glanced at his wristwatch. It was after two in the morning. His brows knitted together. Where the hell was Rocco?

Suddenly he laughed aloud. "You're getting to be a regular old woman," he told himself accusingly. "A guy's entitled to have some fun out of life."

He finished undressing and went into the bathroom to brush his teeth. When he came out he put on his pajamas and sat down on the edge of the bed to take off his leg. He paused for a moment. He felt uncomfortable. Alone.

He looked over at the clock on the night table. It was nearing three o'clock. Maybe Rock had left a note for him in his room. He got up and walked back to Rocco's room.

The light was still on; he had forgotten to turn it off. He walked into the center of the room and looked around. No note. Acting on impulse, he pulled open a dresser drawer. It was empty. He pulled open the other drawers. They were empty too.

He turned and walked over to the closet and looked in. Rocco's clothes were gone. He shut the door slowly and walked out of the room thoughtfully. Where had Rock gone and why hadn't he told him, he wondered.

Rocco couldn't tell him, he remembered; they hadn't spoken to each other since they had parted that night in California, and when he had called New York he had had no occasion to speak with him. He lit a cigarette and sat down on the edge of his bed.

It was strange not having Rocco around. The apartment seemed empty without him. It was almost lonely.

Suddenly he brightened up. That was the answer. Of course, Rocco had thought he would return with Dulcie, and that was why he had moved out. Silly of him not to think of it before. It was like Rock to do something like that.

He smiled to himself as he put out the cigarette. He would tell the guy off when he saw him in the morning down at the office. What was the idea of worrying him half to death?

He loosened the straps that held the leg in place and lay down on the bed. He reached over and turned off the light. For a long time he lay there in the dark staring upward in the room. He would miss having Rock around all the time. Dulcie's face intruded on his thoughts. "Hell, you can't have everything," he thought as he drifted off into slumber.

But all the same he slept restlessly. There was a feeling of being alone in the world that haunted him even in his sleep. Strange that Dulcie's face in his dreams didn't drive that feeling away.

He walked into the office briskly. "Good morning, Janey," he said, smiling.

She got up from her desk and ran over to him. She held out her hand. "So you went and done it." She laughed with mock seriousness. "You got away from me, dammit."

He laughed aloud. He looked pleased as he took her hand. "Is that the way you talk to your boss when he gets married?" he asked.

She looked at him for a moment. Her eyes were still laughing as she pretended to look behind him. "Well, the coast seems clear enough," she said. "I don't see your wife around. I guess I could kiss you."

He still held her hand. "I guess you could," he nodded.

She kissed his lips swiftly and then looked up at him. Her gaze was serious now. "Good luck, Johnny," she said sincerely. "I hope you'll be very happy."

"I will be," he said confidently, "I'm a very lucky guy." He took off his hat and coat, gave them to her, and walked to the door of his office. He looked back at her. "Tell Rock to see me when he comes in," he said, still smiling. "I got something to tell that guy."

She nodded as she hung up his coat, and he disappeared into his office.

He sat down at his desk. The mail was spread out before

him. He began to look through it. His phone rang. He picked it up.

"Irving Bannon wants to talk to you," Jane's voice said.

"Okay," he answered. "Put him on." He heard the click of the phone. "Hello, Irv."

"Johnny, you old son of a bitch, you been holding out on us." Irving's voice was effusive.

Johnny smiled into the phone. He supposed he would have to listen to this all day. He might as well get set to expect it. "I wasn't, Irving," he said. "It was as much a surprise to me as anybody."

"Don't gimme that," Irving laughed. "But I promise to forget you're keeping it a secret if you'll gimme a knockdown to the missus when she comes back to town. I seen some pitchers of her from the studio and she's a beauty."

Johnny felt pleased at the flattery. "I'll do that," he promised.

"I'll hold you to that, Johnny," Bannon laughed. "Now I can wish you luck, and may all your troubles be little ones."

Johnny winced at the old wheeze. "Thanks, Irv," he said. "I'll tell my wife you called. She'll be pleased. I told her a lot about you."

"Wait'll she hears what I got to tell her about you," Irving laughed. "Good-by, Johnny, and the very best to you both again."

"Thanks, Irv. Good-by." Johnny hung up the phone, smiling. He guessed there must be a great deal of curiosity about Dulcie around the office. When she got back and they settled down, he would have to give a party and have her meet the gang.

He picked up the phone again. "Get me George Pappas," he told Janey.

He waited. George's voice came on the phone. "Hallo, Johnny." It sounded pleased. "Congratulations."

"Thanks, George," he said.

"When I read in the papers you were married, my brother Nick and me we said: 'Just like Johnny to get married where his friends can't make excitement for him,' so instead we decide to wait till you come back. How it happen?"

Johnny laughed. "Don't ask me, George," he replied. "I still can hardly believe it myself. I'm just a lucky guy, I guess."

"You sure lucky," George agreed. "Your wife, she's one beautiful woomans."

A thrill of pleasure ran through Johnny. Everybody said that. He felt proud of the fact that he had been able to win a woman whom everybody admired. "Thanks again, George," he said, changing the subject. "I spoke to Peter and I've got news for you."

George chuckled. He was still thinking about Johnny's sudden marriage. What a pretty girl! She must be nice, too, or Johnny wouldn't have married her. "What news?" he asked absently.

"Peter doesn't want to sell the theaters," Johnny answered.

George was silent for a moment. When he spoke, his voice was businesslike. "Then what he want to do, Johnny?" he asked.

"He would like you to continue the joint operation of the theaters."

"And if not?" George asked.

"Then he wants to buy your share if the price can be arranged," Johnny said.

George thought about what Johnny meant by "if the price can be arranged." Did he mean the price they had paid? That would be foolish. It wouldn't only be foolish, it would be bad business. The theaters were worth more now than when they had bought them. Peter must know that. "The price can be arranged," he said cautiously, "based on the present market values, of course."

"You know they're inflated," Johnny said.

"Sure," George agreed readily. "But that's what they're worth today."

Johnny laughed suddenly. "Look, George, we're old friends, so we can stop kidding each other and talk honestly. We got a million and a half that we can afford to shell out for your share of stock in those theaters. We'll pay all the legal expenses in connection with the transfer, and that will leave you a half million to the good."

George hesitated. The offer was fair enough based on what he had invested, but the properties were worth much more than that right now. Besides, he needed more than that to embark on the theater-building program he contemplated. He had some ideas that would cut the present costs of building theaters almost in half. "Make it a million and three quarters and it's a deal," he said.

"Done," replied Johnny promptly. "I'll have the lawyers go to work on it immediately." He felt good. Peter would be pleased that he had been able to save that two hundred and fifty thousand. It was more than he expected.

George was satisfied too. Actually he felt he had got more than the theaters were worth and enough to provide him with a safe margin for his future plans.

They agreed to meet for lunch on the next day and discuss it further; then they hung up.

Johnny pressed the buzzer on his desk, and Jane came in. "Where's Rock?" he asked.

She looked at him puzzled. "I don't know," she answered. She started for the door. "I'll call Bannon," she said. "Maybe he stopped in there after parking the car."

Johnny was bewildered. "Parking the car?" he asked. "What car?"

Jane turned and looked at him. She had a sudden premonition that something was wrong. Maybe it was the look on Johnny's face. She didn't know. "Your car. After he dropped you off," she said, her heart pounding inside her.

"My car?" Johnny's voice was incredulous. "I came down by cab."

She could feel the color running out of her face. "Didn't he bring you down?" she asked, her voice trembling.

"No," Johnny answered. "He wasn't home when I got there last night. I haven't seen him since my wedding day, when he left for New York."

"Left for New York?" Jane's voice was suddenly weak. Suddenly she knew what had happened. Rocco had quit, just as he said he would. The tears began to come to her eyes. "He hasn't come in here." She seemed to stagger slightly.

Johnny sprang from his chair and caught her. Her body was shaking. "Wait a minute," he said, suddenly realizing that there was a strong emotion affecting her. "What's going on here?"

She hid her face on his shoulder. "Don't you know?" she asked without looking up.

He stood there dumbfounded for a moment; then he looked down at her. "You and Rocco?" His voice was filled with surprise.

She nodded her head.

"Well, I'll be—" he breathed half to himself, not finishing his sentence. What a fool he was! If he had half an eye he would have noticed. Here he was thinking of himself while it had meant a great deal more to her. He looked down again. There was a new sympathy in his voice. "Maybe he decided to take himself a vacation," he suggested hesitantly. "He hasn't seemed to—" He stopped abruptly. He had been about to say that Rock hadn't been too well lately, but that would only make matters worse. Now he didn't know what to say.

She seemed to gain control over herself. She stepped back. Automatically her hand went to her hair. "I must look a fright," she said.

In spite of himself Johnny smiled. Trust a woman to worry about her looks at a time like this. He walked over to his desk and took out a bottle and two glasses. "What you need is a drink," he said.

He filled her glass and handed it to her, then filled his own. "*L'chaim*," he said, remembering Peter's drinking toast. It meant "good luck." She would need it.

She swallowed the drink, and the color began to flow back into her face. "That's better," she said.

"All right now?" he asked anxiously.

She nodded her head. She even managed a tight little smile. "I'm okay."

He smiled back at her. "We're probably worrying over nothing," he told her more confidently than he felt. "Rock probably decided to take himself a vacation like I said, and since he didn't expect me back so soon he didn't show up."

She looked at him for a moment, not answering. She began to feel a little sorry for him. He just didn't understand what had happened. But it wasn't up to her to tell him; he would have to find out in his own way. The phone rang in her office. "The phone," she said quickly, and left, closing the door behind her.

Johnny stared thoughtfully after her. He sat down at his desk. He looked at the letters on it. He had to read them, but he didn't feel like it just now. Rocco should have said something to him about his plans. There was a strange feeling of hurt inside him, an unconscious sense of his own failure. He thought of Jane, the way she looked when she first realized what had happened. She had been frightened.

He looked at the door through which she had gone. Strange thing Rocco had done. It wasn't like him, either. An anger began to rise in him. It was a hell of a trick for Rocco to pull on him.

A little voice seemed to whisper in his ear just then: "What the hell are you complaining about? Rocco don't owe you nothing. It's the other way around."

He turned his head quickly as if someone were in the office with him. "But what about Jane?" he seemed to ask himself.

"That's none of your business," the little voice answered. "It's Rocco's and hers. You didn't worry about it before. You didn't even notice it!"

"What are you trying to say?" he asked himself.

The phone on his desk began to ring. He picked it up and spoke into it. When he hung up and tried to remember what he had been thinking, he couldn't. There was only the realization of a dimly understood failure left in him—a feeling that was to persist and grow stronger before the day was over.

13

TUESDAY night was always a late night at the office for Jane because it was make-up night for the newsreel and Johnny would go down to Bannon's office until the reel was finished. They would send out for coffee and sandwiches, and after they had finished eating, it would be around seven o'clock and time for Johnny to go. He would come back to the office about nine o'clock and they would leave. Jane used the time he was out of the office to clean up the various matters on her desk and type the letters that had accumulated during the first two work days of the week. The mail was always the heaviest then.

This Tuesday night, though Johnny had just returned from the studio that morning, was no exception. It was about eight o'clock when she finished her last letter and heaved a sigh. It had been a long day. A strangely disturbing day, and she was very tired. For a moment she thought of going home and leaving a note for Johnny, informing him, but she decided to wait until he came back. He was upset enough about Rock; she didn't want to disturb him any more than he had been.

The door rattled. She looked up. Maybe they were through early down there. It would be good if they were; she wanted to get home and climb into a hot tub and just lie there and soak out her weariness.

The door opened and Rocco stood there. There was a half-ashamed look on his face, but there was also a new look of contentment and pride mixed with it. He walked into the office silently and closed the door behind him.

Unconsciously her hand went to her breast as she looked at him. Inside her, her heart was singing: "He didn't go away! He didn't go away!" She didn't speak until he was near her desk and then, suddenly, she was in his arms. "Rocco, Rocco, Rocco"; she kept saying his name over and over as if it were a song she was singing.

"Baby," he said, his hand stroking her hair.

The name, tenderly spoken, sounded funny to her ears. She began to smile through the tears that had flooded into her eyes. She looked up at him, her eyes shining radiantly. "Say it again, Rocco," she whispered, "say it again."

He kissed her. His lips were hard against hers. He drew a deep breath and looked at her. "Baby," he said.

It was soft, tender, and reverent all at once. Some people liked to be called darling or sweetheart or lover, but she would be satisfied with "baby" all her life if he always said it like that. "Never stop saying it, Rocco," she whispered.

He smiled slowly. "I never will—baby."

Her arms went around his neck; she could feel his arms tighten around her. He was strong and she could feel her breath rushing out of her. She pressed her lips to his and closed her eyes. It was like hanging onto a rainbow; she could feel the world going round beneath her but she didn't care. Not so long as Rocco loved her.

They parted and looked at each other. Her eyes roamed over his face. He looked well; certain lines on his face had disappeared. A frown that had become almost habitual had gone from the corner of his mouth. His eyes looked back at her, clear and confident.

"You've made up your mind?" she asked.

His hand still held hers as if he were afraid to let go. "Yes," he answered slowly, "I made up my mind."

"What are you doing?" she asked.

His hand let go of hers; he looked at her with a half-defiant look as if he were afraid that she would mock him. He turned from her for a half second, and then, as if he had made up his mind, he turned back to her. He didn't speak, his fingers flew down the front of his coat, leaving the buttons open behind them. He threw the coat back over his shoulders. His eyes looked into hers searchingly.

She stared at his jacket. It was made of white linen. There was a pocket high on his breast. On the pocket in small red letters there were some words. She came closer to read them. "Hotel Savoy Barber Shop." She looked up at his face incredulously. He had said he would go back to barbering, but she hadn't believed him. She had thought he was just talking.

His eyes were still on hers, his voice was challenging as he spoke. "Anything wrong with it?"

His eyes were warm and brown and she could see right into his heart through them. He was afraid of her answer. He didn't have to be. "No, there's nothing wrong with it"—she hesitated a moment and looked levelly at him—"as long as you're happy."

She could see the hidden fear leave his eyes. Slowly they began to shine as he smiled. "I'm happy," he answered simply. "This racket was never for me."

He was right, she thought. It was not for him. This business had to be inside you the way it was inside Johnny. You were good for it then, but it left you room for little else. It did something to you, something you couldn't put into words. She could feel it in Johnny—in the way it had obsessed him even from that very first time he had walked into Sam Sharpe's office. Suddenly she was very happy that it was not for Rocco. She wanted him to stay the way he was.

"Johnny won't like it," she said.

"It really won't matter very much to Johnny," he said with rare insight. "It's only his pride will be hurt a little, but he really doesn't need me any more. I'm like the crutch he keeps near his bed now. He only uses it the times he hasn't got his leg on. And then it's mostly to go to the toilet with."

She smiled at the allegory. He was tired of doing Johnny's dirty work. He was right, too. Since Johnny had learned to walk again and now especially that he had married, Rocco would be nothing but that extra crutch.

He watched her smiling. He began to smile. "What are you thinking about?" he asked.

Her smile broadened to a mischievous grin. "I was wondering when you were going to ask me to marry you," she answered.

He laughed merrily. "And I suppose you have your answer ready."

"Yes," she answered, laughing with him.

His voice was suddenly serious. "What is it?"

She looked at him, the laughter fading from her eyes, leaving them tender and excited. "You just heard it," she said softly.

He pulled her to him. "Then what are we waiting for?" he asked happily.

They were seated on the couch when Johnny came back into his office. He stopped in the doorway and stared at them in surprise. Then he strode toward Rocco with outstretched hand, a look of genuine pleasure on his face.

Rocco got to his feet slowly and took Johnny's hand. They looked into each other's faces, smiling embarrassedly.

It was Johnny who broke the silence. "What's the idea of scaring hell out of us?" he asked. "Janey almost passed out on me this morning."

Rocco looked at Jane quickly. She hadn't said anything to him. They smiled at each other and he turned back to Johnny.

Johnny saw the look that passed between them. He laughed and walked around his desk and sat down. He leaned back in the chair comfortably. He felt better now. "Where the devil have you been?" he asked good-naturedly.

Rocco walked up to the desk and stood there looking down at him. "I been working," he said quietly.

"Working?" Johnny exploded. He leaned forward with a sudden motion that threatened to send his chair flying out from under him. He looked up at Rocco. "Where?"

"In a barber shop," Rocco answered in the same tone of voice.

"You're joking." Johnny laughed.

Rocco's face was serious. "No, I'm not," he said. "My mind was made up when I got back to New York. There's nothing for me to do around here."

"What do you mean, nothing to do?" Johnny asked. "You got a job here working for me."

"An errand boy could do the work for a lot less than you're payin' me." Rocco said scornfully.

Johnny was silent. He looked at Rocco for a minute. Rock was right but he hadn't thought of it in just that way. He took out a pack of cigarettes and offered them to Rock silently. Rock took one and put it in his mouth. Johnny struck a match and held it for him, then lighted his own. He was suddenly ashamed of himself.

"I'm sorry, Rock, I didn't think it was like that. I should've known better," he admitted. "Name the job you want. Any job. It's yours."

Rock looked down at him. Johnny was right. He hadn't known how it was, he really couldn't know. There really wasn't anything bad about Johnny. He just thought the picture business was the only thing in the world. He began to feel sorry for him. "I got the job I want," he said softly.

"In a barber shop?" Johnny asked unbelievingly.

"In a barber shop," Rocco repeated.

"Wait a minute," Johnny said, getting to his feet and walking around the desk. "You don't mean that."

Rocco smiled at him. The guy just didn't believe that anyone could like barbering better than the picture business. "I do mean it."

Johnny stared at him. He really meant it. "Well then," he said, "why don't you at least open a place of your own?"

"Maybe I will some day," Rocco answered slowly.

Johnny looked at him. He thought he saw a way to repay Rock for all he had done. "I can put up the dough," he suggested. "You can do it now if you want."

Rocco looked at Jane and smiled; then he turned back to Johnny. The guy really meant well. "It isn't the dough, Johnny," he explained. "I got enough to do it if I want. I didn't spend a cent of my own since I been with you, an' I got over fifteen thou in the sock. I just don't want to right now."

There was a look of distress on Johnny's face. "Then isn't there anything I can do?" he asked helplessly.

"No," Rocco answered slowly.

Johnny looked from one to the other. He seemed to slump somehow. Tired lines sprang suddenly into his face. "I'm sorry I loused things up, Rock," he said in a low voice.

Rocco looked at him pityingly. "It wasn't all your fault,

Johnny," he said. "I only want there should be no hard feelin's between us over this." He held out his hand.

"I haven't any," Johnny replied in the same low voice. "I only feel I owe you a great deal that I can't repay." He took Rocco's hand. "Thanks for what you've done, Rock."

Rock was embarrassed. "You don't owe me nuthin', Johnny." He tried to joke. "Just get your haircuts by me, that's all I ask."

Johnny tried to smile. "Yeah, Rock, I'll do that."

They looked at each other uncomfortably, neither knowing what to say next. This time it was Rocco who broke the silence. "Is it okay if I take Janey home? We got some things to talk about."

Johnny smiled wanly. "You don't have to ask that," he replied. "You know it's okay."

He leaned against the desk and watched them walk to the door. At the door they turned to him. "Good night, Johnny," they said almost together.

"Good night," he answered, and watched the door close behind them. He stood there in the office thinking. He felt strangely alone. Suddenly he wished Dulcie were there.

He walked around the desk to his phone. He half picked it up, then looked at his watch. It was nine thirty. That made it six thirty at the studio. She would still be working. He knew they were working late that night to make time. She wouldn't be home until eleven. He put the phone down slowly. He would call her from the apartment later. He felt drained and empty. There was a bitter taste in his mouth as he stared down at his desk. He would feel better when he spoke to Dulcie.

The cab pulled to a stop in front of the hotel. The doorman stepped forward and opened the door.

"Don't be late tomorrow, Dulcie." Von Elster smiled. "Ve got some important scenes to rehearse before ve can get down to business."

Dulcie looked at him and smiled. This funny little man had a charm all his own in spite of the way he looked. Maybe it was because he was an artist and really knew his business. She was suddenly curious about him. "It's early, Conrad," she said. "Why don't you come upstairs and have a drink? That way we can go over it tonight and we'll be that much ahead tomorrow."

Von Elster looked at her in surprise. He wondered what she meant by her invitation. He knew what such invitations usually meant, but in this case he was doubtful. After all, she was a newlywed, and her husband was young, attractive, and rich, but he was willing to explore the possibilities. If he was wrong—mentally he shrugged his shoulders—at least they would gain some time for tomorrow, as she pointed out. "A good idea," he said.

He raised his eyebrow when he followed her into the suite. A table was set with places for two. Next to the table was a small wagon with a casserole tray on it. There was a flame under the casserole.

"There's liquor in the cabinet over there," she said, pointing to the wall. "Help yourself to a drink. I must get out of these clothes and take a shower. I'm simply dying, it's been so hot under those lights all day."

He bowed politely after her as she left the room; then he turned to the liquor cabinet. He opened the door. A row of bottles looked out at him. He took one down and opened it. He sniffed at the neck of the bottle. This was real schnapps, like in the old country. The liquor they got here with this silly prohibition business was awful. He would have to find out who their bootlegger was. He poured a drink into a small glass and tasted it. Ach, goot! He swallowed it and poured himself another. The sound of water running came to him through the closed doors. It was oddly exciting. Quickly he downed his second drink and refilled his glass.

She came back into the room less than fifteen minutes later. "I wasn't too long, was I?" she asked, smiling.

He struggled to his feet from the comfortable chair he had been sitting in. His face was flushed with the five drinks resting comfortably in his stomach. He bowed to her. "No, Dulcie, not long at all."

He straightened up and suddenly he was staring. *Gott in Himmel!* She had nothing on under that negligee she was wearing! Her body seemed to be glowing underneath the diaphanous peach-colored silk. She was beautiful, positively beautiful.

She seemed unaware that he was staring at her. "Stay where you are," she said. "I'll bring something to eat over to you." She filled two plates with some food from the casserole and took two napkins from the table and carried them over to him.

She gave him one plate and pulled up a hassock in front of his chair and sat down on it, looking innocently up at him. "Now we can talk," she said prettily. She looked almost like a little girl with her long, blond hair tied behind her head with a thin blue ribbon.

He looked at her. Maybe she wasn't aware that the neck of her negligee had parted slightly when she sat down and he could see into it. He leaned forward and looked down at her. "You know, you're a very beautiful woman, Dulcie," he said, "ant a dangerous one, too."

Her laughter tinkled in the room. "Am I, Conrad?"

"Yes." He nodded solemnly. "Maybe the most dangerous woman I haff ever met." He put his plate down carefully on the floor and placed his hands on her shoulders. He leaned forward and kissed her chastely on the forehead. "You make fires to start burning inside men."

He looked down at her to see the effect of his words. He was surprised to see that the touch of his hands had caused the negligee to slip from her shoulders, revealing her body naked to the waist. He was even more surprised by her answer.

"Is that all the fire I start in you, Conrad?" she asked demurely, a look of daring on her face.

Johnny looked at the clock. It was time for the call to go through, she would be home now. The phone rang. He picked it up. "Hello."

"This is the long-distance operator," a voice answered. "I have your California call for you. Go ahead, please."

"Hello, Johnny!" It was Dulcie's voice now. She sounded pleased and excitedly breathless.

"Dulcie," he said, "how are you, darling?"

"Oh, Johnny, honey," she said, "I'm so glad you called. I miss you."

"I miss you too, darling. Everything going all right?"

"Just fine," she answered. "But I wish you were here."

He laughed happily. "That's the picture business, darling. You never know what's going to happen next. How's the picture coming along?"

"All right, I guess. But I wish I hadn't started it. I'm working so hard and I'm so tired I can hardly keep my eyes open when I get home." He could hear her yawn over the phone.

A wave of sympathy for her ran through him. Poor kid, she hadn't known what she was asking for. Picture-making was hectic and exhausting work at its best. "Look, honey, I won't keep you up, then. You got to get your rest so you can look pretty for the camera in the morning. I just wanted to hear your voice, I felt so lonely."

"Don't hang up, Johnny." She seemed to be pleading. "I want to talk to you."

He laughed. Sometimes you had to be firm with her. "Now look," he said with mock sternness, "we'll have the rest of our lives to talk. Tonight you're gonna get some sleep."

"All right, Johnny." Her voice was filled with surrender to his masculine assertiveness.

"I love you, Dulcie."

"I love you too, Johnny," she answered.

"Good night, darling," he said tenderly.

"Good night, Johnny."

He hung the receiver back on the hook and stretched out on the bed. He smiled at her picture. It was a few minutes before he realized he hadn't told her about Rocco. That was what he had wanted to talk to her about. Slowly the empty feeling seemed to creep back into him.

Von Elster watched her put down the phone. "Too bad he won't let you stay in pictures. Some day when they will have talking pictures you will be even more wonderful an actress."

She looked at him, a wise and knowing look on her face. "Who said he wouldn't let me stay in pictures?" she asked softly.

He looked at her for a moment, then he raised her hand to his lips. "Forgive me, Dulcie," he said, his voice filled with wonder. "You are a greater actress even than I thought."

She looked over his head. Her eyes grew dark and thoughtful. It was easy to fool Johnny now, he was so in love with her. She felt a twinge of conscience and shook her head. Why should it bother her?

She had never loved him and had married him for only one reason. He was getting what he wanted, she held nothing back from him. It was only fair that she should get what she wanted.

She knew deep inside her that she would never be satisfied with one man. There was a constant driving inside her, challenging her. She would only be happy when every man in the world could see her and want her. She smiled to herself.

Soon every man would. When her picture came out.

AFTERMATH

1938

FRIDAY

IT WAS the kind of day I should've stood in bed. Nothing went right. And there was nothing I could do about it. Fridays just weren't my days.

It started in the morning when I got to Peter's house. They wouldn't let me in to see him. His temperature had gone up and the doctor had forbidden visitors.

I talked awhile to Doris and Esther and tried to cheer them up a little. I don't know whether I was convincing enough for them, but I do know that the more I talked, the more depressed I grew.

It was an intangible sort of feeling. It started off small, a little foreboding deep inside you. Then it seemed to grow larger like a black cloud moving in from the distance on a rainy day. At first you shrug it off, pay no attention to it. It isn't going to bother you, it isn't even coming your way. And then suddenly it's pouring. That was the way it was with me.

I paid little attention to it when I left their house for the studio, but when I got to my office, I knew I had it. I was caught in the midst of a downpour with no shelter in sight and everything was all bollixed up from there on out.

I had spent more time at Peter's house than I had expected, so I got to the studio after lunch. It was about two o'clock when I looked down at my desk and saw Larry's note.

"Call me when you get in," it read. It was signed by Larry.

I had the strangest impulse to leave the office and go home and put off seeing him until Monday, but I didn't. Instead I pressed down the interoffice communicator and he answered.

"Stan and I would like to see you when you have a few minutes," he said, the intercom giving his voice a queer metallic ring.

I hesitated a moment. "Come on in now," I told him.

"Good," he replied. "We'll be right in."

I sat down in my chair and wondered what he wanted. I didn't have to wait long to find out. The door opened and he ushered Farber into my office.

I lit a cigarette. "Have a chair, boys," I said more cheerfully than I felt. "What's on your mind?"

Ronsen came right to the point. The words came from his lips and Farber's mind. "I've decided to call a special meeting of the board for next Wednesday in New York. I think we ought to clarify Stan's position without delay."

I was still smiling. "Sounds all right to me," I agreed readily. "What do you have in mind to clarify?"

"For one thing," Ronsen said uncomfortably, "I think we ought to do something about creating a definite post for Dave. He's been on the lot for several months now and he's neither fish nor fowl. His responsibilities should be clearly designated. The way it stands now, nobody knows just what he's supposed to do."

"I have a good idea what to do with him," I murmured gently. "But I don't suppose it will coincide with yours."

Farber flushed a little at my answer, but Ronsen grimly ignored it. "What we—uh, I mean—I have in mind," he stammered a little, "is to have him elected vice-president. He will be in charge of production."

I looked at him. "That's a very nice-sounding title." I nodded my head. "Vice-president in charge of production. A guy named Thalberg once had it over at Metro. Zanuck's got it over at Twentieth Century-Fox." I stopped for a moment to let them get my point and then continued: "But those guys knew their business. What the hell does this kid know? He doesn't know the front end of a camera from his asshole." I shook my head sadly. "Besides, gentlemen, we've got a production manager who does know his business. If you want to make a vee pee out of him, that will be all right with me, but I can't see Dave in the job. He doesn't know enough about it."

Ronsen glanced uncomfortably at Farber. Farber returned his look implacably. Ronsen turned back to me. His voice was conciliatory. "There's really nothing to get excited about, Johnny. It will only be a working title. Roth won't really be in charge of production. Gordon will still stay in that job, but we have to give him a title of some importance."

I didn't answer for a moment. I looked at him steadily. I

could see he was uncomfortable under my gaze; he shifted slightly in his seat. "Why?" I asked gently.

For the first time since he came into the office Farber spoke. "That's part of the price you have to pay for a million dollars," he said, his eyes staring into mine.

I turned my chair toward him. The chips were down and the cards were beginning to turn up on the table. This was it and I might as well get it over with as quickly as possible. "What's the rest of the price we gotta pay, Stan?" I asked softly.

He didn't answer; again it was Larry who did the talking, but I kept looking at Stan.

"Stanley will be elected to the board at that meeting along with Dave. He will be given a special authority to revamp the sales department along the lines of certain ideas he has."

My voice was sarcastic as I answered. "And what ideas has he got, may I ask, or are there some relatives of his around that I don't know about?"

"Wait a minute, Johnny," Ronsen said quickly. "You haven't heard his plans yet. You're prejudiced, but the board has already agreed with them in principle."

I turned and looked at him. "How come I haven't heard about them? I'm on the board too, remember?"

His eyes shifted behind his glasses. "This came up the day after you left and we had to act right away. We tried to get in touch with you, but couldn't."

In a pig's eye, they tried. I settled back in my chair comfortably and looked at them. "As president of this outfit I'm responsible for its operations. Those operations include sales policy and production policy. In other words, anything that pertains to the particular industry that this company is operating in. Your responsibility, Larry, is financial—to see that the company is always on a sound financial basis. When you start meddling in operations that are not your concern, you are endangering its financial standing and so imperiling your responsibility. I can well appreciate your concern and that of the board to protect the investment you have made thus far in the company. But an important factor to be considered is the qualifications of you people to pass upon any changes in how the company is to be run."

My cigarette had gone out and I lit another. I looked at them in the manner a teacher looks at his class. "Let us examine those qualifications. Yours first. Your previous experience in this business has been confined to an association with the bankers who are presently in control of the Borden Company. These bankers, upon gaining control, tried for a while to run it along their lines of thinking. In the time they did so, they lost millions of dollars and were forced to turn to the industry to find a man that could operate the company profitably for them. They found one—George Pappas. And from there on out the responsibility was clearly his. The correctness of that decision is apparent in their financial position today.

"And our other estimable members of the board—what do they know about the picture business? As little or less than you. One is a member of a banking concern. One a member of a brokerage house on Wall Street." I was ticking them off on my fingers as I spoke. "One is a member of a wholesale food-packing company, and still another a hotel man. And the last, but not least, is a sweet retired gentleman of means whose inherited fortune allows him to maintain residences in all the socially correct places, to which he shuttles back and forth as the seasons demand and serves on various boards of directors of companies in which his money is invested. He brings to all these boards the same sweetness and general lack of knowledge that he brings to ours."

They were staring at my fingers, fascinated as I held my hand on the desk in front of them. I looked at them. "Shall I continue, gentlemen?" I asked gently. "Or is that enough?"

My voice grew cold. "I will not permit the same degree of incompetence to the operating management of this company that characterizes its board. This is a motion-picture company that at present faces a difficult and uncertain future. It needs experienced personnel, not amateurs. If your desire is to protect the money you have already invested, my advice to you people is simple. Proceed cautiously before you try to apply your experience to this business. It's like nothing else you've ever come in contact with before."

I smiled gently at Larry. His face was white and strained. "The one thing that you bring to this business that is needed is capital. You people either have money or know where you can get it. I do not underestimate its importance when I tell you: you work at your end of the business and let me work at mine."

Larry's voice was trembling with fury as he answered. He

had probably never been spoken to so bluntly since he had been a baby. The veneer of politeness had been stripped from him. His words were savage. "Contrary to your stated opinion, Johnny, the board has already approved Stan's suggestions and will proceed to make it official. They are running the company, not you. This is no longer a one-man concern as it was in Kessler's day, and if you have any ideas of trying to run it on that basis, forget them." He had risen to his feet in anger as he spoke.

I looked up at him easily. This was the kind of language I could understand. Plain talk. To hell with this business of being subtle and beating around the bush. My voice was calm, matter-of-fact. I smiled slowly. "You and your boys lost three million bucks screwing around with this outfit before you called on me to pull your nuts out of the fire. Well, if I'm gonna pull 'em out, I'm gonna do it in my way. I'm not gonna try to carry an added load of incompetent people who will only throw more monkey wrenches into the works."

He stopped short as he started to sit down again. I almost laughed aloud at the way he looked, suspended in the air over his chair. A flash of fear crossed his face and quickly disappeared. He hadn't thought I would go as far as I intimated. He thought I wanted the job more than anything else in the world. It was good he didn't know how right he was. He searched for words and finally found them. His control had returned, his voice was once more bland and smooth. "What are we getting upset about?" he asked in a conciliatory voice. "It's just a difference of opinion. I'm sure we can work something out that will be satisfactory to all of us." I could see the three million dollars working around in his mind as he turned to Stanley with a placating look on his face. "Can't we, Stan?"

Farber looked at me. My face was expressionless. He looked at Ronsen again. There was a familiar whine in his voice; I had heard it a long time before. "Then what do I get out of it? After all, I'm putting up the million dollars."

Ronsen looked at me. His voice was reasonable, persuasive. When he spoke, I knew I had them temporarily. That was the trouble. I knew it would be temporary, that it wouldn't last. It would become more difficult to deal with once they entrenched themselves. I knew what would happen. Sooner or later I would be out. The only way I was sure of winning was to keep them out now, but I couldn't do that. I'd already agreed to accept the million dollars. The best I could hope for was to keep the pay-off price down as much as possible.

I leaned toward them as I spoke. "I'm not an unreasonable man," I said gently. "I mind my own business and all I ask of people is to mind their own. I'm perfectly willing to have Stan elected to the board as an ordinary member without any special authority and I'm willing to give Dave a chance here at the studio. When there is time for him to develop, I'll even be willing to give him a chance at running it, but not right now. There is too much at stake for us to take any risks."

Ronsen looked at Farber. "That sounds fair enough, Stan. What do you say?" His voice was smooth enough to wrap around a baby's behind.

Farber looked at me. I could see the desire well up into his eyes to tell me to go to hell, but his lips were pressed tightly together. His million bucks were in the pot already and there was nothing he could do about that. He got twenty-five thousand shares of common stock for it, which was all he could get —on paper. The new S.E.C. rules would not let any written agreement go further than just that. I could almost see him make up his mind to go along with my proposal and I knew that the fight had only started. I could see, too, that his mind was made up to get me out. He would wait for the right time, though. He felt certain it would come.

He got to his feet. From the look on his face I knew he had thought of something else. "I'll think about it," he said, and started out of the office.

Ronsen jumped to his feet quickly. He looked at me and then at Farber, who was walking to the door. I almost felt sorry for him. He was in the middle of it. For the moment it was a fight between Farber and me and he was out of his depth completely. The door closed behind Farber.

I smiled at Larry. For the first time I was in a position to give an order. "You better chase after your boy, Larry," I said patronizingly. "And see if you can make him see the light."

He didn't answer. The veil dropped from his eyes again for a second and his blazing resentment shone through; then he turned and hurried after Farber.

I watched the door close behind him and I knew I had made him an enemy as well as Farber. But somehow I didn't care about it any more. I would rather have them face me in the open light of day than have to look out for them in the dark. And yet inside me I knew that I was wrong. For whatever we could agree on during the day would have to be canceled when night fell. That was the kind of business this was.

The lights glowing on the clock on the dashboard of Doris's car showed it to be after ten. The radio was playing softly as we rode along. The night was warm and the tiny stars were twinkling in the dark blue-black of the sky.

I looked at her as she turned the car into the driveway and climbed the hill toward her house. She had been silent since we had left the restaurant.

She pulled the car to a stop and turned off the ignition key. We lit cigarettes and sat there silently listening to the music coming from the radio.

We both started to speak at the same time. It was funny and we laughed and the tension that had descended on us ever since we saw Dulcie in the restaurant seemed to fall away.

"What were you going to say?" I asked, still smiling.

Her eyes were serious as she looked at me. "Nothing."

"You were going to say something," I pointed out. "Now come on, what was it?"

She drew on her cigarette. It glowed and I could see the shadows in her eyes. "You loved her very much once."

I looked across the field in front of her house. Did I? I sometimes wondered now. Had I ever really loved Dulcie? Had I ever really known her? I doubted it. But she was such an actress, I had loved what I thought she was, or rather what she let me know of her. Now I was older and I knew more. If I told Doris that I hadn't loved Dulcie or that I didn't know, she wouldn't believe me, so I played it straight. "I did love her—once," I answered.

She was silent again. I watched her smoke her cigarette. I knew there was more coming. I waited. I wasn't wrong.

"Johnny," she asked, her voice very low, "what was she like? I mean really like. I heard so many stories about her, but I never really knew her."

What was she really like? I wondered. Thinking back over all that had happened, I knew now that I didn't know. I shrugged my shoulders. "You heard the stories?"

She nodded her head.

"Well—they were all true," I said.

She was silent again. Her cigarette burned down and she snapped it over the side of the car. We watched it make a glowing spiral in the air as it fell toward the ground. I felt a movement against my side. I looked down. Her hand was in mine. I looked at her and smiled.

Her voice was low. "It must have hurt terribly."

It had, but not as badly as I thought at the time. I remembered how I felt that night when I discovered Warren Craig in her bed. I shut my eyes. I didn't want to remember it. But I could still hear her screaming after me—words I had never thought I would hear from any woman's lips. Then the sudden silence when I hit her. I could remember how she looked lying there nude on the floor, looking up at me with a crazy sort of triumph in her eye, a cold smile on her lips, as she said: "That's what I always expected from—a cripple."

I looked at Doris. Her eyes were on me sympathetically. "No," I said slowly, "I don't think she ever really hurt me. What did hurt, though, came afterwards. Long afterwards. When I learned what I had been missing these many years."

She was watching my face carefully. "What was that?" she asked.

I looked into her eyes. "You," I said softly. "It really hurt then, for I knew that all the years before had been lost and I could never get them back. And I was afraid to try, I didn't know how."

She looked into my eyes searchingly for a long moment; then she turned and rested her head on my shoulder and looked up at the sky. We sat like that for a long time.

At last she spoke, her voice warm and contented. "I was afraid, too," she said.

I smiled down at her. "Afraid of what?" I asked.

She shifted her head on my shoulder and looked into my eyes. They were soft and trusting. "Afraid you would never forget her, afraid you would never come back. I was even afraid you thought of her now." I kissed her. She looked up at me. Her voice was small. "You don't know what it means to be afraid like that. Not to be sure of someone you love."

I kissed her again. Her lips were soft against mine. "You don't have to be afraid any more, sweetheart."

She smiled gently up at me. I could feel her breath against my cheek. "I know that—now," she sighed contentedly.

The night was still again and we could hear the sound of the crickets chirping in the bushes. Occasional fireflies sparkled in the night. Below us in the valley were long lines of lights. They came from homes, from street lamps, from neon signs. They matched the stars in the sky above us.

She sat up suddenly and looked at me. "What's going on at the studio, Johnny?" she asked. "Is something wrong?"

I lit a cigarette before I answered. "Nothing important," I answered.

The look on her face was skeptical. She knew too much about this town to believe me. "Don't tell me that, Johnny," she said quietly. "I can read the papers. I saw what the *Reporter* had to say yesterday. Is it true?"

I shook my head. "Part of it is," I admitted, "but I think I got it licked."

"You did get into trouble because you came out to Papa," she said. She hesitated a moment. "I should have thought of that when I called you."

I looked at her. Her eyes were questioning. She was worried about me. Strangely I felt good about it. With all that she really had to worry about that was more important, she was thinking about me. I picked up her hand and kissed its palm. "I wouldn't have it any other way, sweetheart," I said. "Even if it meant that I had to leave Magnum. Being with you again and seeing Peter is more important than anything I have to do at the picture company."

Her eyes were clouded with a sort of mist. "I hope you won't have any trouble on account of it."

I squeezed her hand reassuringly. "Don't worry about your old Uncle Johnny, sweetheart," I said more confidently than I felt. "He's got the situation under control."

I don't think it was more than ten minutes later that I found out how wrong I was. We heard the sound of a motor coming toward us in the driveway.

Doris looked at me puzzledly. "I wonder who that is," she said.

"It's Christopher," I said, glancing back at the headlights and recognizing the car. "I told him to pick me up here a little after eleven."

The car pulled alongside ours. Christopher stuck his head out the side. "That you, Mr. John?" he called.

"Yes, Christopher," I answered.

"I got a special message for you from Mr. Gordon. He says for you to call him right away. It's most important."

"Thanks, Christopher," I said, getting out of the car. I turned to Doris. "I'll use your phone."

She nodded and I hurried off to the house, wondering what he wanted now. I could hear Christopher's pleased voice behind me:

"Hello, Miss Doris. How is Mr. Peter?"

I didn't hear her reply because I was already in the hall and picking up the phone. I dialed Bob's number and waited. I could hear the buzz of the phone at the other end. It rang only once, then he picked it up. He must have been waiting for the call. "Bob," I said, "this is Johnny."

His voice sounded angry. "I thought you told me everything was going to be jake," he shouted into the phone.

What the hell was he so sore about? "Pipe down, pal," I said dryly, "or I won't need a phone to hear you. Sure I told you everything was going to be jake. Now what's wrong?"

He was still shouting. "Everything's wrong. You've been feeding me a line of bull, that's all. I just want to tell you I'm not gonna take it any more. I quit."

Now I was sore. "What the hell's going on?" I asked. "Stop the crappin' around and tell me what happened. I still don't know."

"You don't know?" There was a sound of skepticism in his voice.

"I don't know," I answered.

He was silent for a minute. When he spoke again, there was a new tone in his voice. "Then we're both getting jobbed," he said. "I just got a call from Billy at the *Reporter*. He said an announcement just came from Ronsen's office that at a special board-of-directors meeting held in New York tonight Roth and Farber were elected to the board and that Roth was also elected vice-president in charge of production!"

It was my turn to be silent. The sons of bitches had called my bluff. Farber must have done some fast talking to get Larry to pull a stunt like this. I could just imagine his arguing: "Take a chance and do it. Edge won't pull out. He's with this company too long. It's his baby." And he would be right too. He knew I wouldn't pull out even if Larry didn't. I found my voice. "Don't do anything until I see you, Bob. Sit tight, and if I don't see you over the week-end, I'll see you at the office Monday."

I hung up the phone. I waited a minute, then picked it up again and called the long-distance operator. "Get me New York," I said, and gave her Janey's number.

It was almost two o'clock in New York, but I had to find out what had happened.

Rocco answered the phone; his voice was fuzzy with sleep. "Hello," he growled.

"Rock, this is Johnny," I said quickly. "I'm sorry to disturb you so late, but I gotta talk to Janey."

He was awake in a moment. "Okay," he said. "Hold on."

Janey's voice came on. "Yes, Johnny."

"What time did that directors meeting take place tonight?" I asked.

"About nine o'clock," she answered. "The teletype calling for it came through at six, but it was nine before they could get enough of them together for a quorum. I thought you knew about it, but I didn't take any chances. I sent a notice back to you on the night wire."

"I see," I said slowly. I certainly did. There were probably two notices on my desk in the studio right now, placed there after I had left the office. I had left early because I wanted to try to see Peter that afternoon.

"Is there anything else, Johnny?" she asked anxiously.

Suddenly I was tired. "No," I said slowly. "Thanks a lot. I'm sorry I woke you up."

"That's all right, Johnny," she said.

"Good night Janey." I heard her answer and then hung up the phone and turned around.

Doris was standing there looking at me. I looked at her. My face must have told her the bad news. She took a deep breath. "Trouble, Johnny?" she asked.

I nodded my head slowly. Nothing but trouble. It was up to me now. Put up or shut up. If I took it, I was through. If I didn't, I was through anyhow. Slowly I sank into a chair. What a day! Black Friday.

I should've stood in bed.

THIRTY YEARS

1925

1

JOHNNY walked through the crowded room looking for Dulcie. She had been with him a moment ago, but suddenly she had disappeared. He wondered where she had gone.

A small, thin-faced woman called him. "Johnny dear," she said in a thin high-pitched voice that was not unpleasant to the ear, "come here a minute and talk to me. We have so little time to chat with each other, I'm beginning to forget how sweet you are."

Johnny turned and looked at her, then he smiled slowly and walked toward her. Nobody dared to ignore Marian Andrews. She was small and nervously intense and wrote a column that was syndicated in almost every newspaper in the country and throughout the world. Her subject was Hollywood, and Hollywood was her subject. Her words were known to make or break people. She knew how important she was and hesitated but little in using her power when she so willed. But the power was cleverly concealed beneath an over-friendly, gushing, inquisitive manner that carried somehow into her column and gave the reader a feeling that he or she had just heard the news over the back fence that separated his own home from his neighbor's.

"Marian," Johnny said pleasantly, taking her hand, "I didn't see you."

She looked at him a moment, an eyebrow lifted archly. "For a second," she said lightly, "I thought you didn't want to see me."

"How could you imagine such a thing?" He laughed easily. "I just had something on my mind, that's all."

She looked at him shrewdly. "Such as where is your lovely wife?"

He looked at her in surprise. "That's one of them," he admitted.

She laughed, happy at her guess. "You don't have to worry about her, dear boy, she just went outside for a bit of fresh air. Her cousin Warren is with her and you can sit down here beside me and we can have a talk." She patted the seat beside her.

He looked down at her and smiled again. "You see everything, Marian, don't you?"

A glint of pride came into her eyes. "That's my job," she replied. "Don't forget I'm a reporter. Now come on, do sit down."

He dropped into the chair beside her. Reporter was what she liked to think of herself as being; town gossip was more like it, he thought.

She turned to him. "Isn't it a lovely party that Peter is giving for her cousin? He's so pleased that Warren's first picture is to be made by him and you must be so happy that Dulcie is playing opposite Warren."

"Yes," he said slowly. "We're all very happy over it. Warren Craig is one of the biggest names in the theater and it means a great deal to us that he consented to do this picture." He looked at her directly. "It means a great deal to the whole industry too. We've been after him for years."

"I heard somewhere that's how you met Dulcie," she gushed. "When you went backstage to his dressing-room." She laughed gaily. "It must seem all too wonderful to you. You go backstage to sign one of America's greatest actors for the movies and meet his cousin, fall in love with her, and come away with a wife and not the actor you were after. And then two years later he finally agrees to make a picture, and your charming wife, now one of the most important stars in pictures, is to play opposite him. It's just like the movies." She looked up at him smiling. "It's a wonderful story. May I print it? I think everybody would love to know about it."

He returned her smile. "Go ahead," he said easily. "You would use it even if I said no," he thought. He took out a cigarette and lit it.

"You must be very proud of Dulcie," she continued. "It's not every girl that becomes a star in her first picture and then proves it wasn't just an accident by making two others in which she is even better than in the first. I hear her pictures are the biggest grossing pictures you have."

He wished she didn't have the habit of probing in two directions at once. It made it rather difficult for you to decide which one to follow first. He drew on his cigarette. "I am proud of her," he answered. "She always dreamed of being a great actress and I knew it was in her, but I don't think any of us realized just how great a success she would be. You know she only made that first picture to pass the time while I was busy at the studio."

"And then she was so good you couldn't keep her from the screen," Marian said.

He grinned wryly. "That's about it. She was too good."

She looked at him sharply. "Would you have wanted her to stay off the screen after that first picture?"

He looked at her openly. "Off the record, Marian?" he asked.

"Off the record," she assured him.

"Frankly, I would have, but after I saw that picture I knew I didn't stand a chance," he said, hoping she would keep her word.

"That's what I thought," she said, nodding her head, satisfied with herself. "It must be very unhappy being married to one of the most beautiful and admired women in the country and living three thousand miles away from her."

"It's not as bad as that," he said quickly. "We both understand that our work keeps us apart and we get together as often as we can. I come out here four times a year and she comes to New York almost as much."

She leaned forward and patted his cheek. "Johnny, you're such a dear understanding boy. Sometimes I must feel sorry for you."

He looked at her inquisitively. What did she mean by that? Sometimes during the last few visits to the studio he had got the impression that people were feeling sorry for him. Why should she come out and say it? "Don't be," he said dryly. "We're actually very happy and, in spite of the distance between us, very close to each other."

"Of course, Johnny, of course," she said quickly—almost too quickly. She glanced across the room. "Oh, there's Doug and Mary. I must talk to them, will you excuse me?"

He smiled tolerantly at her. Having exhausted him as a source of gossip, she was now looking for another. "Sure," he said getting to his feet with her. "Go right ahead."

She hesitated for a moment. Her face was serious as she looked at him. "I like you, Johnny," she said unexpectedly. "You're a very decent guy."

He was surprised by her statement and the sudden undercurrent of earnestness in her tones. "Thank you, Marian," he said simply. "But why—?"

She interrupted his question. "This is a very funny business, Johnny," she said, putting a hand on his arm. "We live in a sort of goldfish bowl out here. I know, because in some ways I helped to make it so. And I know, too, that many things are said about the people out here that aren't true and that these things sometimes make a lot of trouble and hurt other people."

He looked at her strangely. "I know Marian," he said gently.

An expression of relief crossed her face. She took her hand from his arm. "I'm glad you understand, Johnny," she said. "Because I wouldn't want to see you hurt unnecessarily. Take everything you read and hear with a grain of salt. Don't believe anything unless you see it for yourself. There are many small and vicious people who are envious of your happiness and wouldn't hesitate to destroy it." And then with typical birdlike quickness she left him.

He watched her cross the room with her small hurried steps. Strange turn the conversation had taken. He wondered what she meant. He didn't know of anyone who wanted to hurt him. He looked across the room. Dulcie and Warren were just entering the room from the veranda. A sudden light of comprehension came into his eyes.

So that's what Marian was trying to warn him about. Dulcie was laughing and her face looked young and happy and excited. She had risen so quickly that there must be people envious of her success. Marian was trying to tell him that these people wouldn't hesitate to hurt them if they could get at Dulcie that way. He smiled to himself confidently as he made his way toward them. Let them try. He knew better than to believe any of them or anybody. Even Marian Andrews.

2

PETER held the door open and let them enter the room before him. Then he followed them into the room and closed the door. The little study was quiet after the sound of the party outside. There was a small fire glowing in the fireplace and it cast a cheery reddish light across their faces.

He turned the key in the door and straightened up. "That's so we won't be disturbed," he said smiling. "These big parties make me nervous. All day my stomach is upset thinking about it."

"I know how you feel," Willie Borden said. "That's why I'm glad I'm moving back to New York. This ain't the kind of life I like. I like making pictures, but I don't like the things you got to do to keep up with the crowd out here. Sometimes I think we're slaves to our publicity men's ideas of how to run our business."

"That's how you guys might feel," Sam Sharpe injected. "But from my point of view you can't do without it. Outside in that room there you got maybe twenty people whose business it is to tell the whole world about what happens here. In Marian Andrews's column tomorrow ten million people will read that everybody in Hollywood turned out for Peter Kessler's party in honor of Warren Craig, who, incidentally, is appearing in a picture with Dulcie Warren for the Magnum studios. And that's just one column. Like I said, there are twenty of them. It's money in the bank for you guys, and you complain."

"But you ain't got to worry about nothing," Peter objected. "You're a ten-per-center. All you gotta do is collect your cut of the clients' pay. We gotta worry about making them worth the pay. We gotta worry about whether the people who count come to the party. We got all the trouble building them up.

"I still say it's worth the trouble," Sam insisted. "It brings customers to the boxoffice."

Peter shook his head and walked to a cabinet. He opened it and took out a bottle of liquor. He took down three glasses and poured a measured drink in each. He handed the glasses around. "This is the real stuff," he announced proudly, "not the junk I got out there." He held up his glass. "*L'chaim*," he said.

"*L'chaim*," Borden replied.

"Here's luck," Sam said.

They swallowed the drinks.

Peter sank into a chair in front of the fire. He leaned forward and slipped off his gleaming black shoes. With a sigh he put his feet up on a hassock. "Sit down, sit down," he said to them, waving to the comfortable chairs in front of him. "Ah, this is good, my feet were killing me. Esther made me put on my new shoes."

Borden sat down opposite him, and Sharpe sank into the chair next to him. They were silent for a while, each man thinking his own thoughts.

"Another drink?" Peter asked at last. Without waiting for a reply he refilled their glasses.

Borden looked at him. "You look tired," he said.

"I am," Peter answered.

"Maybe you're working too hard," Borden suggested.

"It's not that," Peter denied. "I feel upset like. Ever since Johnny got here the day before yesterday, I'm worrying."

They both knew what Peter meant.

"His wife?" asked Sharpe.

Peter nodded his head wearily.

"I've met women like that before," Borden said. "In this business you can't help it, but I've never met any as bad as she is. The stories I've heard about her!" He shook his head. "It's almost unbelievable."

"She's a mental case," Sam said bluntly. "If she keeps on the way she's going I don't think there will be a man left in Hollywood she hasn't shared her bed with."

Peter looked at them. "You fellas don't know the half of it. If she stayed in her own bed all the time, it wouldn't be so bad. But any place, any time, whenever she feels like it. Already I got to fire three men because they were talking about it. One day a guy comes to me with some pictures he took. She was in a corner of a set with one of the gaffers. Her dress was up around her waist and she was leaning against the wall. It cost me a thousand dollars for the negatives and prints and I still don't know whether he didn't hold out on me and keep some." He looked down at the drink in his hand for a moment, then back at them. "I called her into my office and handed her the pictures. I was too ashamed to say anything to her. I just put the pictures in her hand without a word. And what do you think she said? You wouldn't believe it. She looked at me and laughed. 'The man who took this picture must have been an amateur,' she says. 'If he'd waited another minute he could have caught me at a better angle!' "

He waited for them to speak. They were silent. He continued: " 'Dulcie,' I said to her, 'You should be ashamed acting like that. People will talk.'

" 'They'll talk anyway,' she says.

" 'But, Dulcie,' I said, 'there's no reason for it. You got a nice husband. What if he should hear about it? How would he feel?'

"She looks at me with a funny look on her face. 'Who's gonna tell him?' she asks. 'You?'

"I didn't answer. She knew as well as me that I wouldn't say nothing to Johnny. How could I tell him something like that? When I didn't answer her, a funny smile came on her face and she says to me: 'I thought you wouldn't.' She half turns as if to go out of my office and then turns back to me. She stands there almost a minute without talking. I could see she's thinking. I wait for her.

"Then I could see tears come to her eyes slowly. Her lips began to quiver. 'You don't understand, Peter,' she says, crying. 'I'm a very emotional person, and when I married Johnny I thought I would be very happy. But I wasn't. Johnny's wound is more than just his leg. He can't do anything. And I'm an actress and sometimes it's important for me to feel the emotions I project, otherwise I wouldn't be any good to you at all.'

"For a second I'm feeling almost sorry for her. Then I think that's no excuse for a woman to act like a whore. If it's that important for her she could do it discreetly and nobody would be any the wiser. I told her to behave better or I would have to put her off the lot. She promised she would and I chased her out of the office. I was so glad it was over."

"Poor Johnny," Borden said, looking into the fire. "Is he really like that?"

Peter's face seemed to grow redder. "She was lying," he said.

"How do you know?" Sam asked.

"Later in the day I was thinking about what she said and I called Johnny's doctor in New York. He said there was nothing the matter with him that way." He coughed embarrassedly.

"I wonder what would happen if Johnny should find out," Sam speculated aloud.

"I'm afraid to think," Peter said quickly. "She's got him fooled a hundred per cent, she's such a good actress."

"That's just the trouble," Borden said. "Why couldn't such talents have been given to a nice girl? It doesn't seem right that a bitch like that should have so much."

Peter nodded his head in agreement. "It doesn't seem right, but that's the way it goes. The good always have to struggle for what they get, the bad just stand there with their hands out and everything comes to them."

Sam reached over to the bottle and refilled the glasses. He turned to Borden. "When are you planning to leave for New York?"

"In a week or two," Borden replied. "As soon as I straighten up a few things. I bought a place out on Long Island and my wife is filled with excitement over furnishing it."

"You're going through with that deal?" Peter asked, looking at him curiously.

"Sure," Borden said. "Why not?"

Peter didn't answer for a moment. Borden was going to put his stock on the open market, keeping only the amount sufficient to ensure him control of his company. He had made arrangements with a group of bankers down on Wall Street to represent him and was following their advice to the letter. The entire company was being refinanced in accordance with their suggestions. There were two classes of common stock being issued, one with voting privileges, the other without. A preferred stock issue and debenture issue would be floated later. From the proceeds derived from the sale of these stocks Borden hoped to reduce his outstanding bank loans and eliminate expensive borrowings in the future.

"I don't like it," Peter answered at last.

Borden laughed. "You're too old-fashioned, Peter," he said.

"You should learn that that's how they do business today. No longer does one man try to run everything by himself. It's crazy. Today everybody is a specialist. Why should I try to be a banker, a borrower, a producer, a theater operator, a sales manager, all at the same time? My idea is to hire the best specialists in each field and watch over them and guide the whole thing. This business is still growing. Who knows how big it will get? And for big business there are specially trained men too. Men who all their lives are in big business."

"I don't trust them," Peter insisted. "They're all right now when everything looks good, but who knows how they will act when things are bad? I remember what they used to say years ago when we walked into the banks in New York. They used to look down at their noses on us. You could see them thinking: 'Jew pushcart business,' when they turned down our loans. Now that they see we're making money, they want to come in and help us. I don't trust them. Where were they when we really needed help? Looking down their noses. When we needed money we went to Santos. He trusted us, took a chance on us."

"At practically twelve-per-cent interest," Borden interrupted.

"Twelve per cent was cheap enough when that was the only place we could get money," Peter retorted. He looked at Borden shrewdly. "How much stock are they keeping for themselves?" he asked.

"Only five per cent," Borden answered.

Peter shook his head. "That five per cent is enough to make plenty trouble when things go wrong."

"What can go wrong?" Borden asked. He answered his own question. "Nothing. Look at the stock market. It's never been so high and it's climbing higher every day. The country is booming, I tell you, booming. Besides, you don't know these men. They're gentlemen. With them everything's open and aboveboard. They're not the kind of people we got in this business. They got so much money they don't have to screw anybody to get along. All they want to do is make things easy for us."

Peter looked at him cannily. "And since when are you such an expert on them? What do you know about them?"

Borden laughed easily. "I know them all right," he replied confidently. "Last year when I bought that property in Long

Island, it was right in the middle of where they lived. I was the first Jew ever to buy property out there and at first I was worried whether I'd get along with them. But I didn't have anything to worry about. They invited me to join their clubs and to their houses and made me feel right at home, they were so nice. They never once reminded me I was Jewish." There was a proud look on his face.

Peter looked glum. "Because of that you think they're all right?" He shifted uncomfortably in his seat. "It would be a good thing maybe if they reminded you you were Jewish. Maybe you're forgetting you come from a dirty cold-water flat on Rivington Street with rats running in the back yard and toilets in the hall."

Borden looked a little angry. "I'm not forgetting nothing," he retorted hotly. "But I'm not such a fool to blame them for where I come from. What counts is that they take me for what I am now."

Peter could see that Borden was growing a little angry, but he couldn't resist one more gibe. "Maybe next year," he said with a smile, "I'll be finding your name in the Blue Book."

Borden rose to his feet and looked down at Peter. "And what's wrong with that? This is America. Anything is possible. I'm no snob. If they want to put my name in the Blue Book, I say let them!"

Peter stared up at him; his mouth almost hung open. Borden was really interested in getting into the Blue Book. He half shook his head wonderingly. Little Willie Bordanov of Rivington Street with the pushcarts in the Blue Book. He raised a hand placatingly. "Don't be a fool, Willie," he said in Yiddish. "I'm only talking for your own good. Be careful, that's all I'm telling you."

Borden relaxed slowly. "Don't worry, Peter," he replied with a smile. "I'm careful. Nobody is putting anything over on Willie Borden!"

Peter put his shoes on and got to his feet heavily. "I guess we'd better be going back inside before Esther starts looking for me."

Sam Sharpe looked at them. They were a lot alike in many ways, he thought: life had not been gentle with either of them. They had to fight for everything they got. That was not the only trouble they faced, either. He could sense the basic insecurity of each, no matter what they had. In the back of their minds they would always worry whether they would be accepted because they were Jews. Maybe that was why they fought so hard for what they wanted.

He followed them slowly to the door. When the door opened he could see the mask with which they met the world settle on their faces. It was an intangible mask made up of nothing you could really say you saw. A brightness of the eyes, a tightening of the lips, a tilting of the head. For a moment he felt sorry for them. "It was tough to be a Jew," he thought; "I'm glad I'm not one of them."

3

HE STOOD there alone for a moment, with a drink in his hand as the woman approached him. He watched her absently, knowing she was going to speak to him, but he was thinking of what Dulcie had said out on the veranda.

He had tried to kiss her, but she had evaded his grasp. She laughed at him. "Why, Warren," she had said with a teasing sound in her voice as she looked up at him, "so soon?"

He had reached for her again, and again she had slipped away from him. She stood there with one eyebrow raised, a mocking look in her eye.

"Dulcie," he had said, "you don't know what it's been like without you. I couldn't eat, I couldn't sleep, I couldn't do anything. Why do you think I finally called Johnny up and told him I was ready to make a picture for him?"

She had laughed again. It was a sure laugh, filled with confidence in herself. She came close to him. He put his arms around her waist. He could feel the warmth of her body against him through her thin evening gown. He was sure she would kiss him now. He smiled down at her as he bent his head toward her.

She did not speak until their lips had almost met. Her voice was soft and carried only to his ear. "Remember what I said that night, the last time I saw you?"

He smiled again. "You were beautiful. I never saw you so beautiful before," he whispered. "And angry. I remember."

She closed her eyes, and her body seemed to cling to him. He could feel the heat rising in him. He moved his lips closer to her when suddenly her eyes opened. For a second they glared at him with a venom that frightened him. Then the words came from her lips in a cold angry rush. Her voice was still soft, still controlled, however. "I meant it then," she had said, "and I mean it now. Anybody that I want can have it for the asking—except you!"

His arms had fallen from her and the cold of the night seemed to run through him. He stared at her.

Suddenly she smiled sweetly and took his arm. "Shall we join the party, Warren?" she had asked as if nothing had happened.

In a daze he had come back into the room with her, but he was too much an actor to show how he felt. The minute he stepped across the threshold of the room and felt the eyes upon him, his face was as bright and smiling as hers had been.

"Mr. Craig," the woman was saying, "I've been simply dying all night to meet you, but I wanted to meet you without a crowd of people around so that we could really talk. I mean really have a chat."

He smiled at her politely and bowed a little. "I'm honored, ma'am," he said, managing to look both pleased and inquiring at the same time.

The woman smiled at him brightly. "I do love your voice, Mr. Craig, it is so—" she searched her mind for the right word—"so trained. Most actors out here don't know how to speak at all." She finished her sentence triumphantly.

"Thank you again, Miss—uh, Miss—" He paused pointedly.

She put a hand to her hair and patted it unconsciously. Craig's voice was known to have that kind of effect on some women. "How silly of me!" she cried, laughing gaily. "I forgot you were new out here and couldn't know who I am." She paused for an impressive moment and held out her hand. "I'm Marian Andrews."

He raised one eyebrow and looked politely amazed. "Not *the* Marian Andrews," he said, taking her hand and bowing over it. "I'm honored indeed," he said, "as well as surprised."

The woman laughed. "Surprised at what, Mr. Craig?"

"You are much younger than I thought possible for a world-famous reporter to be," he replied. He had heard somewhere that she liked to be called a reporter.

"You are charming and most tactful," she said shrewdly. "But as I am most susceptible to flattery I will accept your kindness at its face value, Warren." She looked at him. "That is, if I may call you Warren," she added. "We Westerners are not as formal as the people back East. You call me Marian."

He smiled again. "Formalities have their place, Marian," he said. "But not if people are to become really close friends."

Her voice became lighter. "I've just been talking to Johnny Edge. He's so happy that you finally agreed to do *Rendezvous at Dawn* for him. It must be exciting for you too, to be playing opposite your lovely cousin, Dulcie."

He laughed. "It is, Marian," he replied. "You don't know how exciting it can be. I've thought about doing a picture for a long time, but I never could make up my mind until one day just a few weeks ago. Then I couldn't wait until I got out here. Johnny has been after me for years."

"I know," she said, returning his smile. "I think it's so romantic too, how Johnny and Dulcie met. Is it true that they met in your dressing-room?"

He nodded his head. "That's how it happened."

There was a calculating look in her eyes. "And how does your charming wife feel about it?" she asked. "She's not making the picture with you, is she?"

He looked at her swiftly. "That's the one bad thing about it, Marian," he answered. "Cynthia has to return to New York to start rehearsals in a new play." He looked up. Cynthia was approaching. He looked back at Marian. "But wait a minute," he said. "Here's Cynthia now. You can ask her how she feels yourself."

Cynthia came up to them. "Cyn," he said, smiling, "I'd like you to meet Marian Andrews. She wants to know how you feel about the movies."

Cynthia smiled at her. "The movies, Warren?" she asked with a quizzical look on her face.

"Isn't it too exciting for words to have your husband making his first picture with his cousin playing opposite him?" Marian gushed.

Cynthia looked at Warren and smiled, then turned back to Marian. "It certainly is exciting," she answered in a sweetly sarcastic voice. "But not for some of the words I know, Marian."

Marian liked her at once. She had a deep-seated respect for honesty, and the one who did not kowtow to the power of her pen was a rare person indeed. Her smile was genuine. "Cynthia," she said, "I know just what you mean." She held out her hand. "I think we'll be friends."

Laurence G. Ronsen was leaving his first Hollywood party. He felt vaguely disappointed; he had rather expected it to be a gay bacchanalian revel, complete with houris and dancing girls. He looked at Bill Borden, talking excitedly in the foyer. He would be glad when their business was completed and he could go back home.

4

PETER sank into a chair with a sigh and looked up at Esther. "I'm glad it's over," he said.

She looked down at him and smiled. "You're glad?" she asked. "Maybe I'm not? Who does all the work when you play big-shot and give a party like this?"

A glint of humor came into his eyes. "You do, Mamma," he said pacifyingly. He leaned forward and began to unlace his shoes. "But my feet were killing me all night." He slipped his feet out of the shoes and into a pair of slippers. He stood up and began to take off his tie. "You know, I've been thinking about building a bigger house. This place is getting too small for us."

She paused in the middle of taking off her dress. "What's the matter with this house, I would like to know," she asked.

He turned to her. "Nothing's the matter with it. It's just small and old-fashioned, that's all. Don't forget we built it before the war." He waved his arm vaguely around him. "I got my eye on a nice roomy place out in Beverly Hills. We can build a swimming pool and tennis court and still have room to spare."

She turned her back to him. "Unlace my corset," she said. He bent behind her and fumbled with the laces. "We need a swimming pool?" she asked. "You can swim, maybe? Or a tennis court? In your old age you are becoming a athlete?"

His voice was muffled behind her. "It's not for me, Esther. It's for the children. How do you think they feel with everybody having a swimming pool and they haven't?"

"I ain't heard them complaining," Esther said, turning

around and facing him. "Maybe you feel we should have a bigger house, not them?"

He looked at her sheepishly and began to smile. He advanced toward her and put his arms around her. "There's no fooling you, Mamma, is there?"

She pushed him away with a smile. "Act your age, Peter," she said.

He stood there, a foolish grin on his face, watching her. "I'm not so old yet," he said.

She smiled at him. "You can't be if you want a swimming pool and don't know how to swim."

"But, Mamma," he protested, "I'm the owner of a big company and I live in a smaller house than half the people who work for me." He walked across the room unbuttoning his shirt. "It's ridiculous, that's what it is. People must think I'm a miser."

She turned away to hide her smile. Sometimes he acted more like a child than the children ever had. "Nu," she said, "so build a bigger house. Who said no?"

"It's all right, Mamma?" he asked, crossing the room quickly to her.

She looked at him and nodded her head.

The sound of an automobile in the driveway came through the open windows. He walked over and looked out. Two headlights were coming up the driveway. "I wonder who that is," he said.

"It must be Mark," she answered lightly. "Doris told me he went over to Georgie Polan's."

He pulled out his watch and looked at it. "It's after three o'clock," he announced. "I'll have to speak to him in the morning. I don't like for him to be out so late."

"Don't worry so," she said with a mother's pride, "Mark is a good boy."

"I still don't like it," he said, standing by the window and shaking his head.

She looked at him. "Come away from the open window before you catch cold," she told him.

Doris lay on her bed and looked out the window. The stars were bright outside and the moon threw a bright shadow across the window sill. The night was quiet and in the distance she could hear the sounds of field crickets calling to one another. She drew in a deep breath and held it for a moment in her lungs before she slowly expelled it. A lazy, contented feeling was slowly stealing through her. It had been a long time since she had been able to feel like that.

"Go and talk to Johnny," her mother had urged. "He won't bite you."

Hesitantly she had done as her mother had told her. At first she had felt strained and awkward. She wondered if he realized she had been deliberately avoiding him every time he came out. Then she grew gay and confident as she saw he didn't have the faintest conception of what she had been doing.

Her mother had been right. There was really nothing to be afraid of. She had been running away from shadows.

Suddenly she felt the warm tears trembling on her eyelids. She put her hands wonderingly up to her eyes. They came away wet. She blinked her eyelids quickly. It was good not to be afraid and have to run away any more. She marveled at her mother's understanding. How long would it be before she would know as much?

Maybe never, she thought. But it really didn't matter now. For the first time in a long while she fell into a deep, contented, dreamless slumber.

Mark was tired as he climbed the stairs to his room. He wondered whether his parents were still awake. Pop wouldn't like his staying out so late. But what the hell, you were young only once. He could feel the blood running through his veins as he thought of the night. Suddenly a chill of fear swept over him. What if the girl was sick? He had heard of lots of fellows who had picked up a clap from extra girls. As quickly as the fear had come to him it left him. Not this girl, she was too clean. He was the first, she had said.

He went into his room and undressed quickly in the dark. He put on his pajamas and went to his pocket and took out a little tube. Holding the tube in his hand, he groped his way to the bathroom in the dark. All the same, he wasn't taking any chances.

Johnny looked down at Dulcie's head lying on his shoulder. The perfume from her hair came up to his nostrils. He rubbed his cheek against its silky softness. "Dulcie, are you awake?" he asked in a lazy, contented voice.

She shifted within the circle of his arms like a cat. "Uh-hunh," she murmured.

He smiled in the dark. "Marian Andrews was trying to warn me about you," he said.

She sat upright, suddenly wide awake. She tried to read his face in the dark. "She did?" she asked, a sudden fright in her voice. "What did she say?"

He looked at her. "Nothing to get excited about," he replied, pulling her head back on his shoulder. "She just said that many people were jealous of you and I shouldn't believe any stories I might hear."

Her breath rushed out of her and she felt limp and drawn. "That's nice," she said in a weak voice, "but I don't know of anyone who would want to carry tales about me."

He looked over her head in the dark. A wise and knowing smile was on his lips. She was too young to know how mean people in this town could be. It was a good thing for both of them that he knew. "You know how it is," he said gently. "People like to talk."

Her voice was sleepy again. "Unh-hunh," she said. "People like to talk."

The light in Marian Andrews's room was still on when the sun began to rise over the horizon. She sat in front of her typewriter. A cigarette lay burning in a tray next to it. There was a soft smile on her face.

She was thinking about that young doctor she had met a few weeks ago when she had gone to have her finger lanced. It had become infected and she had gone to see Dr. Gannett. She was surprised that instead of Dr. Gannett this young man had lanced her finger.

She had asked where Dr. Gannett was. He was on vacation, getting a much needed rest, the young man told her. He was pinch-hitting for him until Dr. Gannett returned. He introduced himself.

"Haven't you a practice?" she had asked. He shook his head. He was looking for a place to settle down. Why not here, she had asked. Again he had shaken his head. "I don't like the people," he had said. "Too many hypochondriacs, too few real ailments." He had laughed. Maybe it was better that way.

She had seen him several times after that. For practically no reason at all, either. He had always been very polite and considerate. Never said anything to her that would let her know he knew she really didn't have to see him.

Until that day she had laughingly said that he must think she was as bad a hypochondriac as the rest. Then he had looked at her, his gray eyes suddenly laughing. No, he had said, he didn't think she was.

Then what was it, she asked, feeling more and more foolish. His gray eyes had darkened seriously. "We're in love," he had said.

"Why, that's ridiculous," she had answered.

"Is it?" he had asked, taking her hand. "You're a very powerful woman, Marian," he had said. "Maybe you think you can't fall in love?"

"That's not it," she had insisted.

He had laughed again and let go of her hand. "All right, then," he had said, "you tell me what it is. You won't admit it because I'm one person your power can't help."

She had gone away wondering at what he had said.

She picked up the cigarette and puffed at it. Maybe he was right, maybe they were in love. But he was wrong about one thing. When they were married he would find out she could help him.

She smiled and looked down at the page in her typewriter. She began to type with a sure quick-fingered touch. She didn't look down at the page as her fingers flew across the keys. Quickly the words began to appear on the sheet of paper.

MARIAN ANDREWS'S LETTER FROM THE STARS

Saturday, Aug. 22, 1925

Dear Reader,
I went to Peter Kessler's party last night in honor of the Warren Craigs and it was the most wonderful party. I'll never forget it. Everybody, but everybody, was there. . . .

5

CARROLL RAGIN's face was wrinkled with worry as he walked wearily into Johnny's office carrying a bundle of papers in his arms. He stopped in front of the desk and dropped the papers on it. His voice was tired and discouraged. "There they are, Johnny," he said. "Another hundred and twenty of them in the morning mail."

Johnny looked up at him. "More cancellations?" he asked.

Ragin nodded. "Look at them," he told Johnny. "Some of our best accounts are in there."

"Sit down, Carrie," Johnny said. "You look beat."

Ragin dropped into the chair opposite him. "I am beat," he admitted. "I've been on the phone talking to every one of those guys this morning and all I get is the same answer from each. 'Come out of the dark ages,' they say. 'When are you fellers going to make talking pictures? Sound is here to stay.'"

Johnny didn't answer. He picked up a contract and looked at it. Written across the face of it in big red pencil were the words: "Rejected, Sept. 10, 1929." Under it was the name of the exhibitor. Johnny recognized it as one of Magnum's earliest customers.

"You talked to him too?" he asked Ragin, tapping the contract.

"Yeanh," Ragin grunted. "He said the same as the others. He was very sorry but—" He paused, shaking his head unhappily.

Johnny thumbed his way through some of the other contracts. He recognized more names. He looked up at Ragin as he came to another familiar signature. "What did Morris say?" he asked.

Ragin closed his eyes wearily. "He was nicer than most of the others, but it added up to the same thing."

"He was the first exhibitor to play *The Bandit*, back in '12," Johnny said bitterly.

Ragin opened his eyes and looked at Johnny. "I know," he said, "I even reminded him of it, and he said: 'What do you want me to do? The public wants talkies and every time I book a silent the house is empty like I got a plague sign on the door.'" He laughed angrily. "Everybody wants talking pictures except Peter." He leaned forward, his voice grew vehement. "I tell you, Johnny, you gotta talk Peter into it or I won't give two cents for our chances to stay in business through next year!"

Johnny looked at him sympathetically. He had a right to grow excited and vehement. He was Magnum's domestic sales manager and until this year had an enviable record. Now, no matter how he tried or how hard he worked, he was helpless.

If only Peter had listened to him at that party two years ago. There was talk about sound then, but Peter had laughed at him. "It won't work," he had said. And then when Warner's opened *The Jazz Singer* later the same year with Jolson singing and talking but one line of dialogue in the whole picture, Peter had declared: "A novelty. It won't last." But Peter had been wrong. The *Mammy* singer had turned the movie business inside out.

One picture after another came out with singing and talking. Several all-talking pictures had been made and still Peter had clung to his attitude. It was over a month ago that Fox had come out with banner headlines in the trade and even the daily newspapers that he had discontinued the making of silent pictures and henceforth his product would be all in sound. Borden had followed with the same announcement the very next day and the others soon after. It was then that it really began to hurt.

By the end of that week they had received over forty contract cancellations, the following week over one hundred, and now they were coming in at the rate of almost one hundred a day. Johnny calculated swiftly. At that rate, Ragin was right. It wouldn't take long for the nine thousand contracts they had to evaporate.

"All right, Carrie," he said at last. "I'll talk to him again, but I don't know what good it will do. You know Peter, and when he gets an idea in his head—" He left the sentence unfinished meaningfully.

Ragin stood up and looked down at Johnny. "I know him," he said darkly, "and you can tell him if he don't change his mind I'm goin' out and look for another job, because there won't be one here."

"You really think that?" Johnny asked.

"Yeanh," Ragin replied. "I'm not kidding myself even if Peter is." He walked to the door and stopped there. "I'm goin' back to my office and see what the second mail brought in. I'll be there if you want me."

Johnny nodded at him and he left. Johnny began to leaf through the papers on his desk again. At last he put them down. A feeling of dismay began to seep through him as the implications of what was happening crystallized in his mind.

It wasn't a simple matter of getting Peter to change his mind any more; it had become more a matter of whether they could afford the change-over if Peter should change his mind. The time lag between the production of a picture and its appearance in the theater was almost six months and in some cases even longer. There were many reasons. After a picture had finished shooting, it had to be edited and titled, which took almost three months. Then advertising plans had to be drawn up and prints had to be made and shipped to the different exchanges throughout the country and the world. In addition to these problems there were the problems of the various censorship boards in the different cities and foreign countries. Each had its own regulations and ideas, which often forced the picture to be withdrawn and re-edited, and sometimes some scenes had to be retaken. It was a long and hazardous road with many strange and tortuous turnings that a picture traveled before it appeared in a local movie house.

So the industry began to keep a backlog of pictures on hand. Magnum was no exception. There were sixteen pictures in the cans, completed and awaiting release. There were five pictures in work at the studio.

Johnny's lips tightened as he thought about them. Ordinarily it was a situation that every picture-maker wished he were in: to have enough pictures to guarantee releases over the next six months. There was only one thing the matter with them. They were all silent pictures.

He picked up a pencil and scratched some figures on a piece of paper. Four pictures at about one million dollars apiece. Six pictures at an average of five hundred thousand apiece. Eleven pictures at an average of about eighty thousand apiece. He stared down at the paper. The total came to seven million eight hundred and eighty thousand dollars, not counting anything else, such as shorts, Westerns, and serials. All tied up in silent pictures, which, according to the public's opinion, were not worth paying admissions to see.

Eight million dollars' worth of junk, he thought. If they switched over to sound pictures, that was what they would become. Every one of these pictures would have to be remade.

He picked up the phone. "Get me Fred Collins," he told Jane. Idly his pencil scratched on the paper while he waited. Collins was the company treasurer and controller.

"Hello, Johnny," Collins's voice came on.

Johnny held the phone away from his ear. Collins was a big man with a big voice and in ordinary conversation you could hear him a half mile away without trying. Except when he was talking to Peter. Then in some strange way his voice became soft and meek. "Fred, what's yesterday's bank balance?" Johnny asked.

Collins's voice boomed in Johnny's ear. "Nine hundred thousand one forty-two dollars and thirty-six cents," he answered promptly.

"That's a bit low, isn't it?" Johnny queried.

"Yes," Collins answered, his voice making Johnny wince. "But we're getting that million and a half from the Bank of Independence today."

"That brings our loans to six million dollars, doesn't it?" Johnny asked.

"Yep," Collins answered. "That's the maximum we can borrow under our agreement with the bank. We can't get any more now until we reduce the borrowings to three million."

"Okay, Fred." Johnny thanked him and hung up the phone. His ears were still ringing with Collins's voice despite his precaution of holding the phone away from his ear. Why did Peter have to hire a foghorn for a treasurer, Johnny thought. Then he smiled for a moment. Collins was all right, he did a good job. The smile disappeared from his face as his mind went back to the problem.

He picked up the phone again. "Ed Kelly," he said into it.

A few seconds later Kelly's quiet voice came on the phone. "Yes, Mr. Edge."

"How many approved contracts have we got on the twenty-nine/thirty program as of yesterday, Ed?"

"Just a moment Mr. Edge," Kelly replied. "I'll check and see. Can I call back?"

"I'll hold on," Johnny told him. He heard the sound of the phone being put down. Kelly was the head of the contract department. It was his job to record and send out the billings according to the sales contracts. It was the custom of the industry to sell a whole year's program in advance before many of the pictures were made, even before some of the pictures were decided upon. This was done by listing as many of the pictures on the contract as they knew about at the time the contracts were drawn and covering the balance of the program by classifications. These classifications bore such names as "Specials," "Double A's (AA)," "Single A's (A)," "Exploitation Pictures," "Idea Pictures," "Westerns," "Serials," and "Shorts." The rental paid by the exhibitor for each picture he played was very often determined by the manner in which the picture was classified. Statistical summaries based upon these contracts would be prepared under Kelly's supervision, and they enabled Magnum to know approximately how much revenue would be forthcoming on each year's program.

"Hello," Kelly's voice came back on the phone.

"Yes, Ed."

"As of last night's closing, there were eight thousand one hundred and twelve contracts." Kelly's voice was dry and matter-of-fact. "I understand Mr. Ragin received some additional cancellations this morning. The figure I gave you is before deducting them."

"I understand, Ed," Johnny said. "Thanks."

"You're welcome, Mr. Edge," Kelly replied politely.

Johnny put down the phone and wrote some additional figures on a scratch pad and then sat back in his chair and looked at them. It didn't look so good.

They had lost almost a thousand exhibition contracts in the past month. Each contract represented an average of fifty dollars a week business. The loss in business as a result of the cancellations would amount to over two and a half million dollars for next year.

Johnny turned his chair toward the window and looked out. It was a beautiful fall day, but he didn't notice it; he was still calculating. If the cancellations kept pouring in at the present rate for another three months, they would have to close up shop. There wouldn't be enough coming in to carry the overhead, much less continue production of new pictures.

He took out his handkerchief and wiped his forehead again. No one could predict what might happen in the next few months but there was one thing he did know. Whether Peter liked it or not they would have to switch to talking pictures. But where would they get the money? They couldn't get any more from the banks. The pictures they had on the shelf would not bring in the money to make the change-over at this rate. He wondered whether Peter had enough money of his own to do it. No, he decided, Peter couldn't have. It would cost close to six million dollars to do it and Peter couldn't possibly have that kind of money of his own.

That still left the problem where it was. They would have to switch to talking pictures even if they didn't have the money to do it. He would have to find a way.

6

HE TOOK his hat and coat from the closet, walked into the outer office, and stopped at Jane's desk. "I'm going to lunch," he announced.

She looked up at him in surprise. He was going out early. He usually left about one o'clock and it was only twelve thirty now. She looked at her calendar pad. "Don't forget, you have an appointment with Rocco at two." She smiled.

He smiled for a moment. "I won't forget with you around to remind me."

She grinned back at him. "Gotta keep the guy busy," she replied. "After all, he is my husband."

For a moment he envied them. There was something about the proud way in which she spoke that betokened a closeness, an understanding, between them. Dulcie and he never felt like that. He supposed it was because they were apart so much. If they could spend more time together, maybe things would be different. He sighed almost unnoticeably. Maybe some day. "What should I get?" he asked her, still smiling slightly. "Just a haircut?"

She looked up at him mischievously. "You do and I'll quit."

She laughed. "I won't settle for nothing less than the works. Don't forget my boy works on a sixty-forty split."

He held up a hand in mock terror. "Okay, okay, the works it is. I haven't got the time to break in a new girl. But I think it's blackmail, that's what it is."

She helped him on with his coat. "That's part of the price you have to pay for my services," she said, still laughing.

"I give up." He laughed. His laughter turned into a spell of coughing. The tears came into his eyes.

A look of concern crossed her face. "Be careful," she warned. "Keep your coat buttoned. You haven't got over that cold yet."

He could feel a pain in his chest. Suddenly he was warm and he knew he was sweating. He tried to smile at her. "It's those damn cigarettes," he gasped.

"Be careful anyway, Johnny," she told him.

He nodded and left the office. The air was cool with the chill of fall, but the sun felt warm on his face. He loosened his coat and lit a cigarette. The smoke irritated his lungs and he coughed again. "God-dammit," he muttered, and began walking to the hotel.

He picked up a newspaper in the lobby of the hotel and went into the dining-room. The head waiter came up to him.

"Alone, Mr. Edge?" he asked, bowing.

Johnny nodded. "Give me a nice quiet table," he told the man. He followed him to a table in the corner of the large dining-room and sat down. He ordered lightly as he wasn't hungry, and looked around the restaurant. There was no one there to disturb him. That was why he had left early. He wanted to be alone, to have time to think quietly. It was too early for the regular crowd to be there.

He opened the paper and turned to the movie page. His glance fell upon Marian Andrews's column, "Letter from the Stars." The first paragraph caught his eye:

> *The Warren Craigs are getting a divorce. I spoke to Cynthia Craig when I heard about it and asked her if it were true. "Yes," she told me, "it's true. Warren and I have come to an amicable parting of the ways. His work keeps him in Hollywood all the time and mine in New York and we decided that it was the best thing for both of us." I felt very badly about this news for I have*

*known Warren and Cynthia ever since they came to
Hollywood several years ago and they are such a charming couple. I do hope they will reconsider their decision,
but I'm afraid they won't. Matters have gone too far and
besides I hear that Warren is interested in another young
lady, also a famous movie star, whose reputation as a
heartbreaker is already the talk of Hollywood. Too bad,
too bad.*

He read further down the column, but there was nothing
else that interested him. He turned the page, thinking that at
least Dulcie and he were not too badly off. At least they had
an understanding, and the fact that they were separated so
much had not affected their relationship. Maybe they were not
as close as Rock and Janey, but that would come in time.

The next page was filled with photographs of a Hollywood
party. A large picture in the center of the page attracted his
attention. It was a picture of Dulcie and Warren, seated at a
table, holding hands and smiling at each other. The caption
beneath it read:

Dulcie Warren *and* Warren Craig, *stars of* Magnum's *latest production,* Day of Mourning, *caught in a
moment of relaxation at the* John Gilbert *party. Miss*
Warren *is married to* Magnum's *affable executive,*
Johnny Edge, *and Mr.* Craig *has just announced his
forthcoming divorce from* Cynthia Wright, *prominent
stage actress. Miss* Warren *and Mr.* Craig *are first
cousins.*

Johnny smiled to himself as he looked at the picture.
Dulcie had written to him and told him that the publicity
department wanted them to be seen together. It was good
publicity for their pictures. He nodded to himself. They were
right. He had noticed quite a few pictures of them together in
the papers lately.

Johnny folded his paper and turned to the plate of soup
the waiter had just placed before him. The soup was hot and
flavored just the way Johnny liked it, but he didn't finish it
His mind kept working on the situation he had left behind
him in the office.

He felt sure that Peter would have no objections to making

talking pictures after hearing what he had to tell him. But where would the money come from? There was a chance they could raise the money if they turned to Wall Street, but he knew that Peter would never do that. He put down his knife and fork and called for the check. He couldn't eat.

The head waiter hurried up. "Monsieur is not satisfied with the food?" he asked, glancing at Johnny's almost untouched plate.

"No," Johnny replied, "it's not that. I'm not hungry, that's all."

He paid the check and walked out into the lobby. He looked at his watch. It was half past one. Maybe Rock wasn't busy and could take him a little early.

He walked into the barber shop. Rock was there. The porter took his coat and he walked toward Rocco's chair.

Rock smiled at him. "You're early."

Johnny nodded. "I took a chance you wouldn't be busy." He sat down in the chair. "I've only time for a shave."

Rock tilted the chair back and began to lather his face. "How've you been, Johnny?" he asked.

"All right," Johnny answered.

"Janey said you had a whopper of a cold."

"I got over it," Johnny answered shortly.

They were silent while Rocco worked. When he had finished, Johnny got out of his chair and began to knot his tie in front of the mirror.

Rocco watched him silently. "You look tired," he said.

"I've been pretty busy, Rock," he answered, turning to face him. "You look good, though."

Rock smiled. "Why shouldn't I? I got everything I want."

Johnny looked at him for a moment. "Yeanh," he said with a slight touch of envy in his voice. "I guess you have." He turned back to the mirror to finish knotting the tie. "I wish I could say the same."

A look of sympathy flashed across Rocco's face for a moment and then was gone. "Guess who came in here today?" he asked, trying to change the subject.

Johnny patted the tie. At last he had it right. "Who?" he asked casually.

Rock smiled at him. "Bill Borden. Boy, was he surprised to see me!"

Johnny grinned at him. "I'll bet he was. What did he have to say?"

"Not much," Rocco answered, "but he looked good, though. He said they were planning to enlarge their theater chain."

For a second Johnny's mouth hung open and he stared at Rock. Then suddenly he began to smile. What a fool he was to have forgotten! Last year Borden had wanted to buy their theaters, but Peter had refused to sell them. That was the way out. He threw his arms about Rocco's shoulders and hugged him. "Rock," he said happily, "you're the best damn barber in the world and I love you!"

He ran to the door and took his hat and coat and hurried out without paying his check.

The manager came over to Rock. "What's the matter with that guy?" he asked, nodding his head after Johnny. "Is he crazy?"

Rock grinned at him. "Crazy like a fox," he said affectionately.

"He certainly is," called out the cashier, who had heard Rock's reply. "He just stuck you for the check!"

Rocco shook his head as he walked toward her to pay it. Johnny hadn't changed a bit. You never knew what he would do next.

He came into the office, his face flushed and excited. "Get me Bill Borden," he told Janey, and went into his office without taking off his hat and coat.

A few seconds later the phone rang and he picked it up. "Hello, Bill?" he asked.

"Yes, Johnny," came Borden's familiar voice. "How are you?"

"Okay," said Johnny. "I just called to ask if you're still interested in our theaters?"

"Sure," replied Borden promptly. "Why? Did Peter change his mind?"

"No," Johnny answered, "Peter didn't, but I was thinking he might."

"What do you mean?" Borden asked.

"Well, I'm going out there and I was thinking I could get him to change his mind," Johnny answered.

"Do you think you could?" Borden asked curiously. He

wanted those theaters, but he knew how stubborn Peter could be.

"I think I could," Johnny said. He hesitated a moment. "Especially if I could wave your check under his nose."

Borden cleared his throat. "It's most irregular," he said. "Giving you a check for six million dollars and not knowing whether it will be accepted or not. If the stockholders heard about it, they wouldn't like it. I got them to consider too. I just can't do anything I want to."

"Nobody will have to know about it," Johnny said persuasively. "If Peter says no, I'll return it and nobody'll be any the wiser. If he says yes, which I think he might, then you'll be a hero to them." He stopped for a moment. "Don't forget those theaters are worth almost eight million bucks the way things are today," he added.

Borden's mind was made up. Johnny was right. If Peter accepted his offer, the Borden Theaters Company would be the biggest theater chain in the world. "What time are you leaving?" he asked.

"Not later than five o'clock," Johnny answered quickly.

"I'll have the check in my office," Borden told him. "Will you arrange to pick it up?"

"I'll pick it up myself," Johnny replied.

He hung up the phone and walked out into Jane's office. He still had his hat and coat on. "Get me through tickets to the coast on any train from five o'clock on," he told her, "I want to get out today." He walked back into his office and closed the door.

She was still looking at the closed door in surprise when her phone rang. She picked it up. "Mr. Edge's office."

It was Rock. "What's the matter with your boss, baby?" he asked. "He beat it outta here without payin' my check?"

"I don't know," she answered bewilderedly. "He just came out and told me to get tickets to the coast for him right away."

Just then Johnny's light flashed on. "Hold on a minute," she said to Rock, "he's buzzing for me." She pressed down the switch that disconnected Rock and brought Johnny on. "Yes, Johnny?" she asked.

"Call Chris at my apartment and tell him to pack a bag for me right away and bring it down here."

"All right," she answered. "Is there anything else?"

"No," he said, and hung up the phone. He leaned back in his chair and lighted a cigarette. It was Friday afternoon. If he could get the five o'clock train out of here today, he would be in Chicago about four in the morning. That would put him in Los Angeles about eleven o'clock Sunday night.

He reached for the phone again, about to call Peter and tell him he was coming, but he stopped before he picked it up. It would be better if he surprised him. The psychological effect would be more impressive.

"Maybe I ought to call Dulcie," he thought. Then he smiled fondly. "No, I won't. I'll surprise her too." He looked affectionately at her picture on his desk. His smile grew broader.

He could just imagine her saying reproachfully, but with a tone of tender affection in her voice: "Oh, Johnny, you frightened me. You should have told me you were coming."

He puffed at the cigarette and began to cough. With a grimace he threw it away. He hadn't entirely shaken the cold, he thought, but a few days in the warm California sunshine would straighten him out.

7

HE LOOKED out the window as the train pulled into the Los Angeles station. The rain was spattering against the train with a wind-swept violence. He shivered as a chill ran through him. He put his hand to his cheek. It felt warm to his touch and he wondered whether he had a fever.

His cold had come back with increased intensity on the train. His throat was dry and sore and he had pains in his chest; his body throbbed with a dull ache. He opened a small box of aspirin and put two tablets in his mouth and chewed on them dully. Their clayish lemon bitterness eased the soreness in his throat a little. He looked up.

The porter stood next to his seat. "Ready to go, now, Mistuh Edge?"

Johnny nodded. He got up and buttoned his coat and followed the porter, who had taken his bag down the swaying aisle. The train lurched to a stop as they reached the platform.

A redcap came up as they walked down the steps. The porter gave him Johnny's bag and turned to Johnny. "Hope you have a pleasant trip, Mistuh Edge." He smiled.

"Fine, George," Johnny answered, giving him a bill.

"Thank you, Mistuh Edge," the porter said as Johnny started off.

"Cab, mistuh?" the redcap asked.

"Yeanh," Johnny answered. He looked at his watch. It was a few minutes past ten o'clock. He would go directly to Peter's house and then go home.

The rain beat down on him as he stood in front of Peter's house and pressed the doorbell. He coughed and pressed the bell again. It was near midnight and the house was dark. He could see a light flash on in the windows near the door. He stood there waiting for the door to open.

The door opened a trifle and the butler's head peered through the small opening.

"Let me in, Max," Johnny said, "I'm drowning out here."

The door opened wide and the butler came forward and took his bag from him. "Mr. Edge!" he exclaimed in a surprised voice. "We weren't expecting you, were we?"

Johnny grinned as he stepped into the lighted room and took off his coat. "No," he answered, "I wasn't expected. Is Mr. Kessler home?"

"He's already retired, sir," the butler replied.

"Wake him up," Johnny ordered. "I have to talk to him. I'll be in the library." He left the butler in the hall and walked into the library and turned on the light.

There was a dull glow of embers in the fireplace. He stirred them and put some small blocks of wood on them. The wood caught fire and began to burn. He turned around. There was a decanter on the cocktail table. He poured himself a drink.

Peter's face was frightened as he came into the library and saw Johnny standing in front of the fire with a drink in his hand. Esther was right behind him.

He ran up to Johnny. "What are you doing here?" he asked in a surprised tone. "I didn't believe Max when he told me you were down here."

Johnny swallowed the rest of his drink. He could feel its warmth travel along his throat. He coughed. "I came out to see if I could knock some sense into your thick Dutch head," he said pleasantly.

Peter sank into a chair. "Is that all?" he said with a tone of relief. "I thought something terrible happened."

"Something terrible will happen if you don't listen to reason," Johnny replied.

Peter looked up at him. "Business?" he asked.

"Yes."

Peter got out of his chair. "It can wait till morning," he said. "First we'll get you something hot to eat while you change your clothes. They're soaking wet."

"It won't keep," Johnny said tersely. He began to cough. The cough racked through him and he put his hand on his forehead. To make matters worse, now he had a throbbing headache.

Peter looked at Esther. "Mamma," he said, "go get him something hot to drink."

She turned silently and left the room.

Johnny finished his coughing and held up a protesting hand. "You didn't have to do that," he said. "I'm going home as soon as we're through here."

Peter looked at him strangely. "Dulcie is expecting you?" he asked.

Johnny shook his head. "No, but I thought it would be fun to surprise her."

Peter looked out of the window. "On a night like this you shouldn't go out any more. Stay here tonight, you can surprise her in the morning."

"No," Johnny answered, "the worst of the storm is over."

Esther came back into the room with a pot of coffee. She put it on the cocktail table and poured a cupful and handed it to Johnny. "Here, drink it," she said, "you'll feel better."

He took the hot drink from her gratefully and held it to his lips. "Thanks," he said to her.

She smiled at him. "You don't look so good," she said worriedly.

"I got a bit of a cold," Johnny answered, "but it's nothing."

They sat down opposite him. Esther pulled her wrapper around her. It was damp and chilly in here, even with the fire going. She was glad she had made Peter put his bathrobe on. When he had heard Johnny was downstairs he had wanted to run down in his pajamas.

Peter looked at him. "Nu," he asked, "so what was the big

emergency that made you come out from New York and get here in the middle of the night?"

Johnny was quiet for a moment; then he put his coffee cup down and faced him. "We've got to make talking pictures," he said flatly.

Peter jumped to his feet. "I thought we got that all settled," he said angrily. "I said once before it won't last and that's all there is to it."

Johnny looked up at him. "We lost a thousand contracts last month through cancellations. They're coming into the office at the rate of more than a hundred a day right now. All for the same reason. No talking pictures. Ragin says he might as well quit and look for another job if he doesn't get any to sell, because in three months there won't be any job left for him. We'll be out of business."

"It will pass, it will pass," Peter said excitedly, waving his hands in the air. "What does he want me to do? Throw out all the pictures we got made? We got all our money tied up in them."

"We'll never get our money back if the exhibitors won't play them," Johnny retorted.

Peter looked down at him. For the first time doubt began to appear on his face. "You really think they won't play them?" he asked in a hesitating voice.

Johnny returned his gaze levelly. "I know they won't," he answered with conviction.

Slowly Peter collapsed into the chair. His face had suddenly gone gray and strained. "Then I'm ruined!" he whispered in a cracked voice as the implications of Johnny's statement sank into his mind. His hand reached out for Esther. It was as cold as ice.

"Not if we can get some talking pictures into work right away," Johnny said.

Peter held up his hands helplessly. "How can we?" he cried. "All our money is in this program."

"You can always go to Wall Street like Borden did," Johnny prodded. He hated to say it, but he had to make sure that Peter would agree to his plan.

Peter shook his head. "It's too late," he replied. "We owe Santos six million dollars, and our agreement says we can't borrow any more money anywhere until the loan is down to three million."

Johnny reached into his pocket and took out an envelope. He looked at it a moment, then melodramatically handed it to Peter. "Maybe this will solve our problems."

Peter looked questioningly at him as he opened the envelope. The check fell out of it and fluttered to the floor. He picked it up and looked at it, then back at Johnny. "What does Borden want to give me six million dollars for?" His face was dull and disbelieving.

"For the Magnum theaters," Johnny answered slowly, watching Peter's face.

Peter looked down at the check in his hand and then back at Johnny. For a moment he was silent. "But they're worth close to eight million," he protested weakly.

Johnny looked at the check in Peter's hand. He almost smiled at the tight grip with which Peter held it. If he wanted to refuse the offer, he would have thrown it back at him. "I know," he said softly, "but we're in no position to bargain. Beggars can't be choosers. We either take that check and give up the theaters or lose the whole thing."

Peter's eyes seemed to fill with tears. He looked at Esther helplessly.

Johnny caught the look and something inside him seemed to tighten up in sympathy. He got out of his chair, walked over to Peter, and put a hand on his shoulder consolingly. "Who knows, Peter?" he murmured. "It might all be for the best. When we get on our feet, maybe we can get them back. We may be smarter than we think. George Pappas thinks the theater market is due to break any day now. We might even be lucky to get out in time."

Peter's hand reached up and patted Johnny's. "Yes," he said, "we might be." He stood up slowly. "I guess there's nothing else we can do," he said questioningly.

"That's right," Johnny answered, looking into his eyes. "There's nothing else we can do."

Peter looked down at the floor. "I should have known better," he said quietly. "I guess I'm getting to be an old man." He looked up at Johnny. "I ought to retire and leave the business to young fellers like you."

"Baloney!" Johnny exploded brusquely. "There's nothing the matter with you. Everybody is entitled to make a mistake once in a while. And you made less than anybody else in this business that I know about!"

Peter smiled. He began to feel better. "Do you really think so, Johnny?" he asked, his eyes shining.

"Of course I do," Johnny answered promptly. "If I didn't think so, I wouldn't say it."

Esther looked at Johnny and smiled gratefully. He was such a good boy, she thought, he knew what it meant to be kind.

Johnny insisted upon going home and Peter ordered the car out. He watched Johnny climb into it and waved to him as the chauffeur put it into gear and started down the driveway. He saw Johnny begin to cough as the car moved away.

He closed the front door and walked back to the library thoughtfully. He had been a fool not to see that talking pictures were a logical development of the business. He would have lost everything if Johnny hadn't decided to come out here and surprise him. There weren't many people like Johnny in this business who would look out for someone else the way he did.

He stopped suddenly as a thought came to him. Johnny had said Dulcie didn't expect him either. A cold fear began to sweep through him. He knew Dulcie, but he didn't know what Johnny would find when he got home. He went to the telephone and gave the operator Dulcie's number. He didn't want Johnny to be hurt. He didn't care what happened to her, but he didn't want Johnny hurt.

He stood there for almost five minutes listening to the phone ring without an answer. At last he hung up and went upstairs to bed heavily. He had a strange premonition of dread. Something was going to happen. He knew it.

He stopped at the telephone in the upstairs hall again and tried the number. Again no answer. Slowly he put the phone down. Maybe he was being foolish to worry about it. She was probably sleeping and didn't even hear the phone.

He walked into the bedroom. Esther looked at him. "Who were you calling?" she asked.

"Johnny's wife," he said lamely, strangely reluctant to say her name, "I didn't want her to be frightened."

Esther's eyes were understanding as she looked at him. She spoke in Yiddish. "A shame," she said, shaking her head, "a shame."

8

THE ringing of the phone woke him up. He reached over and turned on the table lamp next to the bed.

Dulcie's eyes were open. She was watching him. "What did you do that for?" she asked lazily.

He looked at her. "The phone is ringing," he said unnecessarily, reaching out to pick it up and hand it to her.

She put out a hand to stop him. "Let it ring, Warren," she said softly. "I don't expect any calls."

He took his hand from the phone. "Maybe it's something important," he said.

"It's probably a wrong number," she replied unsmiling.

The ringing of the phone disturbed him. It had a warning sound in the stillness of the night. It seemed to be trying to tell him something. He sat up in bed and took a cigarette from the night table and lit it. His hands were trembling slightly.

She shifted her head on the pillow and looked up at him. "Why, Warren," she said with a teasing smile, "I do believe you're nervous."

He didn't answer. He got out of bed and walked to the window and looked out. The rain was pouring from the skies, he could hear the dismal howling of the wind. He turned and looked at her. "It's the weather," he said irritably. "It's enough to drive anybody nuts. Nothing but rain for three days."

She sat up in bed and looked at him. He had been upset ever since the announcement of his impending divorce had been given out. She held out her arms toward him. "Come back to bed, baby," she said in a low husky voice, "Mamma's got something that will soothe your jumpy nerves."

He looked at her. The phone stopped ringing.

"See?" she said, tilting her head to one side and smiling,

"I told you it would stop." Her blond hair cascaded over her shoulder.

Slowly he walked back to the bed. The springs creaked beneath him as he sat down beside her and put his cigarette out in the tray. "Nothing frightens you, does it, Dulcie?" he asked.

She laughed merrily. She shrugged her shoulders quickly and the nightgown slipped to her waist. "Why should it?" she asked, taking his hands and pressing them to her breasts. "I've got nothing to be afraid of."

The phone began to ring again and she could feel him start. "Take it easy," she said softly. "It will stop in a minute."

He sat there tensely, listening to it ring. She was right. It rang only a few times and then stopped.

She laughed again. "See, I was right." She reached over and took the receiver off the hook. "Now it won't bother us any more." She leaned forward and kissed him. "You're all alike," she whispered against his ear softly, "afraid of noises. Like babies."

She was warm within his arms. Slowly he could feel the tension leave him, and replacing it came a sense of growing excitement. For a little while the only sounds in the room were the sounds of their breathing.

He reached over to turn off the light. Her hand stopped him again. He looked down at her.

Her breasts were rising and falling with the rapidity of her breathing. "Leave it on," she said, her eyes glowing with strange fires, the pupils wide and dark. "I like to see where I'm going."

He bent his head toward her and their lips met. He could feel her teeth biting into his lower lip, her arms coming up and closing around his neck, holding him down to her.

He shut his eyes and minutes passed. There were senses in his body he had never known he had before and they were all alive and tingling with an uncontrollable excitement. He could feel himself sinking, drowning in a rolling sea of sensation and feeling.

Once he opened his eyes and looked at her. Her eyes were half-closed and through the narrowed lids they shone at him with strange lights of pleasure born of the knowledge of the powers and needs of her body. Her tongue was pink between the white teeth that gleamed from her parted lips. Her breath came and went against his face with the excited tempo of tom-toms.

He closed his eyes again and gave himself up to this dark rolling sea of pleasure. Suddenly he froze. A strange sound had come to his ears. He started to turn his head. The door-knob was turning and the door opened slowly.

Johnny leaned back against the seat as the car drove off. He closed his eyes. He was tired and his head was aching fiercely now. He shivered as a chill swept through him. He lit a cigarette and the first breath of smoke he drew into his lungs set him off into a spasm of coughing. He took out a handkerchief and wiped his face. He was sweating.

He turned his face and looked back at Peter's house as it disappeared behind the car. He could see the splashes of the raindrops in the swimming pool as the car drove past it. He smiled to himself. Peter was so proud of that new house, especially of the swimming pool. Despite how rotten he felt, he was glad he had decided to come out. It was worth getting that damned cold back to see the grateful look on Peter's face when he realized that everything had not been lost.

He lowered the window next to him a little and threw the cigarette out. He fished in his pocket for the tin of aspirin. He opened it, took out two tablets, and put them into his mouth. He shut his eyes wearily.

He was cold, terribly cold. His body was shaking and he couldn't stop it. He opened his eyes.

The car had stopped and the chauffeur was looking back at him. "You're home, Mr. Edge," he said.

Johnny looked outside the car. He was home. The entrance to his apartment house was empty and deserted in the rainy small hour of the morning. He was shivering.

"Do you want me to take your bag up for you, Mr. Edge?" the chauffeur asked.

Johnny looked at him. The poor devil looked tired, he had probably been awakened from a sound sleep to ferry him home on a night like this. "No, thanks," he replied, "I can manage."

He took the bag and got out of the car and ran for the door-way of the house. He could hear the car start behind him, and when he turned around, it was already halfway down the block.

He went in the door. The night man was asleep at the desk. He smiled to himself and walked into the self-service elevator and pressed the button. The car began to go up.

He slipped his key silently into the lock and turned it. The door swung open quietly. He took his bag into the room and put it down, his footsteps making no sound on the thick, heavy carpeting.

He looked toward the bedroom. The door was closed, but a thin white stream of light shone through the crack at the bottom of it. He smiled to himself. Dulcie had probably fallen asleep again with the light on. It was a habit of hers.

He walked quietly toward the bedroom door. It felt good to be home. A good night's rest was all he probably needed to feel well again. He hadn't slept very much on the train.

He put his hand on the door and turned the knob. It opened slowly before him.

Suddenly he was sick. There was a nauseous retching at his stomach and he fled from the door and ran to the kitchen. He leaned against the sink retching helplessly. His eyes were filled with tears and burning against his lids. Again and again his stomach heaved. At last the vomiting stopped and he turned from the sink and walked dully back into the living-room.

His mind was blank and empty, the lids of his eyes were almost closed as if they could shut from his mind what he had just seen. A shrill voice tore at his ears. He opened his eyes slowly; it took a terrible amount of effort, they weighed so heavily upon him.

Dulcie was standing naked in front of him, her face contorted with rage, her voice screaming at him.

He walked around her to his bag and picked up his hat and coat. His face was empty of expression, he said nothing.

She followed him, still screaming at him.

He looked at her blankly. What was she trying to say? He forced his mind to listen.

The shock of her words reacted in his mind. Suddenly his arms reached out and his hands fastened around her throat. His hands were strong, very strong. They had got that way from the crutches.

Her voice died away and she looked at him in sudden helpless terror. She tried to speak but she couldn't. She couldn't breathe. Her hands clutched at his, trying to break his grip on her throat.

He was shaking her. Shaking her so fiercely she thought her neck would snap. There were low growling animal-like sounds deep in his throat.

He looked over her shoulder as her head swung back and forth in front of him. In the bedroom Warren was staring at him, his face white and drawn, as if hypnotized.

He looked back at Dulcie. He saw her as if for the first time. "What am I doing with you?" he said in a voice filled with disgust and loathing. He took his hands from her throat and hit her across the face with the back of one of them.

She fell to the floor. He looked down at her. "This is my wife," he said to himself over and over. "This is my wife."

She looked up at him and there seemed to be a strange smile on her face—a mixture of triumph and fear. Her hand went to her throat. "That's what I always expected from a cripple!" she flung at him. "You never really thought you were good at anything else, did you?"

For a moment he stared at her, then he turned stiffly and walked to the door. He closed it behind him softly and quietly walked down the hall to the elevator.

The night clerk was still asleep as he walked out past him into the raining night. The rain beat down on his head, reminding him he had left his hat and coat upstairs on the floor where he had dropped them. He turned the collar to his jacket up and started walking.

He didn't know how long he had been walking, but the sky above was beginning to turn gray over his head. It was still raining and his clothes were wet through to his skin. His head hurt and there were dull throbbing pains all through his body. With every step he took, shooting pains would come up from the stump of his leg and run through his side.

Words were racing through his mind. Words she had flung at him in scorn. What was it she had said? "Go back to Doris," she had screamed. "The little bitch still has hot flashes when you're around!" That was when he had grabbed her by the throat.

Suddenly his mind was clear. Everything was clear to him now. He should have known it before. He looked around him

on the street. It was a familiar street. He had seen it somewhere before.

He began to run wildly toward the end of it. Then it came
back to him. This was the street of his dreams. The street he
ran up after that girl. He strained his eyes to the corner. There
should be a girl standing there. He thought he saw a skirt
turn the corner away from him. She was there. She had to
be there. He knew who it would be now.

He ran out into the gutter and called after her. His voice
was a shrill scream. "Doris! Doris! Wait for me!" His voice
echoed hollowly in the empty street.

He stumbled and fell. He struggled to his feet, ran a few
steps, and fell again. This time he lay in a puddle of water.
Wearily he tried to get to his feet again, but he couldn't, he
was too tired. He laid his head down in the puddle of water.
It felt good against his face. It was so nice and cool while
his face was so hot and burning.

As if in a dream he heard the screech of an automobile's
brakes and a car skidding to a stop. As if from a distance he
heard a man's voice saying: "It looks like somebody is lying
there in the road."

He heard footsteps approaching. Suddenly the man's voice
was excited. "It is a man!" he shouted.

He felt hands turning him over. He wished they would go
away and leave him alone. He was just beginning to feel
good.

"Why, it's Mr. Edge!" he heard the man's voice exclaim
incredulously.

"And what's so unusual about that?" he thought lazily to
himself. "Did he expect me to be anybody else?"

He felt the hands lift him and carry him to a car and put
him in it. He sank into the seat. He was cold again and began
to shiver.

"What should we do with him?" he heard the man's voice
ask. "He looks sick."

A woman's voice answered. "He's probably drunk," she said
coldly. "Do you know where he lives? We'll have to take
him home."

The word "home" dug deeply into Johnny's mind. He
forced his eyes open. "Not home," he said weakly, his voice
cracked and hoarse. "I ain't got no home!"

The faces in the front seat turned around and looked

startledly at him. Johnny recognized the man. It was Bob Gordon, who did the Westerns at the studio. He didn't know the woman. It was probably his wife.

"Gordon," he said wearily. They could hardly hear him. "Take me to Doris Kessler's house." He shut his eyes.

9

PETER stirred restlessly in his bed. He opened his eyes and looked toward the window. The sky outside was gray with morning and the thin sound of the falling rain echoed hollowly in the rain gutters on the side of the house. He looked at the alarm clock near the bed. It was six o'clock. He sighed with relief. Another hour and he could get out of bed. He hadn't slept all night.

He stretched his body wearily. He had been a fool to worry about Johnny, everything had probably been all right. The sound of an automobile coming up the driveway came to his ears. He sat up in the bed and listened.

There were the sounds of a man's footsteps on the gravel. He could hear them coming up the front steps and then stop. Suddenly the doorbell rang. It sounded like an alarm through the house.

He sprang from his bed and, snatching up his bathrobe, ran down the stairs. He was tying the bathrobe around him when he got to the front door and opened it.

Bob Gordon was standing there. He looked at Peter's suddenly frightened face. "Mr. Kessler," he said excitedly, "I got Mr. Edge in my car outside."

Peter looked at him dumbly.

"I found him lying in a puddle of water on your street just two blocks from the house," Gordon hastened to explain. "He looks sick."

Peter found his voice. "Bring him in, bring him in," he almost stammered. "What are you waiting for?"

He followed Gordon down the steps to his car, neglectful of the rain that was falling on him. There was a woman in the car. He paid no attention to her.

Gordon opened the door to the back seat. Johnny was lying there, huddled in a small ball, his lips blue and cold. Gordon got in the car and began to lift him out. Johnny didn't move. Gordon looked at Peter.

Peter took Johnny's legs and Gordon slipped his arms under Johnny's shoulders and they carried him into the house.

Esther was standing in the door when they got there. "What happened?" she asked, her frightened eyes on Johnny's limp form.

"I don't know," Peter answered in Yiddish. They put Johnny on the couch in the foyer. His wet clothes dripped water down over the couch onto the rugs.

Esther ran over to Johnny and knelt by his side. Her hands flew over him, loosening his collar and tie. She pressed her hand against his forehead as the butler came up. She looked at them. They were watching her with typical male uselessness in time of sickness. "He's burning up," she said, getting to her feet. She turned to them, her voice crisp and assured. "Papa," she said to Peter, "go and call the doctor right away." She turned to the other two men. "Take him upstairs and undress him and get him in bed."

The men sprang to do her bidding. "Put him in Mark's room," she said to the butler. Mark was in Europe and would not be using it. She followed them upstairs.

A few minutes later Peter came into the bedroom. "The doctor will be right over," he told them. He looked at the bed. "How is he?"

"I don't know," Esther said, "but I think he's got a terrible fever."

Peter sneezed.

Esther looked at him. "Papa," she ordered, "go and change into dry clothes. One sick one around here is enough."

Peter hesitated a moment and then went into his own bedroom. Esther turned to Gordon. "You must be soaked," she said sympathetically. "Come downstairs and I'll get you some hot coffee."

"I'm all right," Gordon protested. "My wife is in the car and I have to get down to the studio."

"You left your wife in the car?" she asked incredulously. Her tone became emphatic. "Go bring the poor girl into the house. I won't let you go until you've both warmed up. The studio can wait."

Peter came into the dining-room while Gordon was telling how he had found Johnny. Gordon saw him and repeated the story for his benefit. "I was driving down to the studio early to get some work done before the crew came on when we saw him lying in the road."

"It's a good thing you found him," Peter said when the doorbell rang. He got out of his chair and hurried to the door.

It was the doctor. They followed him upstairs and stood anxiously in the room while he examined Johnny. At last he got up and turned to them. "You've got a very sick man here," he said in a low voice. "I ought to get him to a hospital, but I'm afraid to move him in this kind of weather. He's got a bad case of double pneumonia complicated by some sort of shock that I can't understand. I'll have to put him in an oxygen tent."

Peter looked at Esther, then back at the doctor. "Whatever is necessary, doctor," he said. "Don't spare any expense. That boy's gotta be all right."

The doctor looked at him. "I can't promise anything, Mr. Kessler," he said quietly, "but I'll try. Where is the phone?"

They could hear the doctor's muted voice coming from the hall through the closed door as they stood around the bed. Esther looked at Peter. "We'll have to call Dulcie and let her know," she half whispered.

Peter nodded hesitantly, looking down at Johnny. "I guess so," he agreed.

Johnny stirred on the bed. He opened his eyes and they stared out feverishly at the others. He tried to raise his head but couldn't, it fell back weakly against the pillow. His eyes closed wearily. His voice was faint, so faint they could hardly hear him, but it was filled with a desperate determination that made it sound like an explosion in the quiet room. "Don't tell—Dulcie—" His lips were barely moving. "She's—no good!"

Unconsciously Peter's hand found Esther's and squeezed it tightly. His eyes filled with tears and he looked down at Johnny. Now he knew what had happened.

It was a late Sunday afternoon, three weeks later. The slanting rays of the sun sparkled against the water in the pool, making it soft and iridescent. Its warmth fell across their faces as they looked down at the chessboard between them.

Peter made a move. He looked up at Johnny and smiled

"Knight to rook seven, check!" he announced. "That ought to hold you."

Johnny's face was still wan and pale as he studied the board. His position was hopeless, for on Peter's next move he was checkmate. He looked up at Peter; his eyes sparkled with a faint mischievous light. "This calls for something brilliant." He grinned.

Peter's smile was triumphant. "Nu, so go ahead and be brilliant," he chortled. "It won't do no good."

Johnny looked at him for a moment, then his grin broadened into a smile. "I will be brilliant," he said, laughing, "I resign!"

Peter began to reset the chessmen on their board. "Another game?" he asked, looking at Johnny.

Johnny shook his head. "No, thanks," he answered, "two lickings in one day is enough for me."

Peter leaned back in his chair and let the sun play on his face. They were silent for a while. Johnny took out a cigarette and lit it. The smoke drifted idly from his nostrils.

Peter watched him. Johnny's face was somber and thoughtful. "You made up your mind?" Peter asked. "You're going down there tomorrow?"

Johnny nodded his head. "I want to get it over with as quickly as possible," he answered tersely.

"I know," Peter said, "but do you feel well enough to go yet?"

"Reno is as good a place as any to recuperate," Johnny replied.

They were silent again for a few minutes, then Peter spoke. "I sent out their contracts Friday. Canceled. Morals clause."

Johnny didn't answer for a moment. When he spoke, his voice was harsh and strained. "You didn't have to do that," he said quietly. "After all, I know they mean boxoffice."

Peter looked at him. "Do you think I would have them around my studio after that?" His voice was indignant. "I couldn't stand seeing their faces any more!"

Johnny looked across the pool. "If I had only known before, if I only could have guessed! What a fool I was! I should have known better. All those things in the paper and I laughed at them, didn't believe them. And all the time the laugh was on me!" His voice was bitter. He covered his face with his hands. "Why didn't somebody tell me?" he asked brokenly between opened fingers.

Peter's voice was filled with pity. He dropped his hand on Johnny's shoulder. "Nobody could tell you, Johnny," he said softly. "It was something you had to find out for yourself."

The air in the musty old courtroom was dull and lifeless as the court clerk intoned in a singsong voice: "In the case of John Edge versus Dulcie W. Edge, is the plaintiff in attendance?"

"He is." Johnny's lawyer motioned to him to get to his feet.

Johnny stood up slowly and faced the white-haired judge. The judge's face looked tired and bored. This was nothing but routine for him. He looked down at Johnny. "Mr. Edge," he asked in a low monotonous voice, closing his eyes as he spoke, "is it still your desire that this divorce be granted?"

Johnny hesitated a moment. His voice sounded strange to his ears. "It is, your honor."

The judge opened his eyes and looked at him and then down at the papers before him. He picked up his pen and wearily signed his name to the bottom of them, turning each paper over to the clerk, who stood next to him with a blotter in his hand. Finished, he looked down at Johnny. "Then it is the judgment of this court that this divorce be granted."

The clerk picked up the papers and walked to the side of the bench. He looked up at the courtroom. "In the case of Edge versus Edge, the decision of the second district court of Nevada, the Honorable Justice Miguel V. Cohane presiding, the divorce is granted to the plaintiff on the grounds of incompatibility."

Johnny's lawyer turned to him and smiled. "That's it, Mr. Edge," he said. "You're a free man now."

Johnny didn't answer. He watched the lawyer step forward and take the papers from the clerk's hand and come back to him. The lawyer held out the papers toward him.

Johnny took the papers and put them inside his jacket without looking at them. He held out his hand to the lawyer. The lawyer took it. "Thank you," Johnny said.

He turned and started to leave the court. At the door he paused a moment and looked back. The walls of the room were a dirty worn gray, paneled in brown rotting wood. The benches were a light yellow and covered with knife cuts and pencil marks. It was a fitting place for his marriage to come to an end.

Suddenly his eyes were wet and he turned and hurried out into the street. What was it the lawyer had said? "You're a free man now." He shook his head. Would he ever be free? He didn't know. There was a heavy sunken feeling inside him.

He stopped at a news-stand and bought a paper. Idly he opened it and glanced at the headlines. There was a streaming red banner across the top of the front page.

STOCKS TUMBLE FOR SECOND TIME IN MONTH!

MILLIONS LOST AS WALL STREET PANICKED!

N.Y. Oct. 29 (AP)—The ticker ran more than three hours behind sales today as on the floor of the staid New York Stock Exchange excited ordinarily conservative businessmen screamed and fought their way through milling mobs. Their only concern was to sell, sell, sell! Sell, before their fortunes were gone and the stocks fell any lower in this, the greatest recorded break in stock-market history.

AFTERMATH

1938

SATURDAY

I WOKE up with a splitting headache. The pulses in my forehead were pounding like trip hammers. I sat up in bed and swayed for a moment. I tried pressing my hands against my temples to quiet the pain, but it was no good. It didn't help at all.

A sudden nausea ripped through my stomach. I fought it down as a foul taste came into my mouth. The wretched feeling passed and I knew the worst was over. I looked up. "Christopher!" I yelled.

Where the hell was he? He was never around when I wanted him. "Christopher!" I yelled again.

The door opened and he came in carrying the breakfast tray. He hurried to the bed and put the tray down in front of me. "Yes, suh, Mistuh Johnny," he said, lifting the cover off the tray.

The smell of the food almost made me sick all over again. It seemed to turn my stomach. "What's the matter with you today?" I shouted exasperatedly. "Take it away and get me a bromo!"

Chris hurriedly put the cover back on the tray and picked it up. He started for the door. I stopped him.

"You don't have to take away the papers," I said.

He came back to me and I took the papers from the tray. There was a hurt expression on his face, but I ignored it. I looked at the headline in the *Reporter*.

"Farber and Roth to Magnum Board," it read.

I put the paper down and leaned against the back of the bed. It hadn't been just a dream, then. Dreams didn't make headlines in the *Hollywood Reporter*.

I read the story slowly. It was just as I had heard it from Bob. At the board meeting last night they had elected Roth

397

vice-president in charge of production and Farber to the board with special advisory powers.

God damn them! Angrily I rolled the paper up into a small ball and flung it on the floor just as Christopher came back into the room. "They couldn't do this to me," I said aloud.

Christopher's black face was startled. "Whut dat you say, Mistuh Johnny?" he asked as he hurried to the bed with the bromo in his hand.

"Nothing," I answered shortly as I took it from him and drank it. I sat there for a minute feeling the bromo go down inside me and soothe my excited stomach. I belched. I began to feel better.

"Whut suit you want to wear today, Mistuh John?" Christopher's face looked concernedly at me.

I looked at him. Suddenly I was ashamed of myself for shouting at him. "Any suit you say, Chris," I answered. "I'll leave it up to you." I watched him walk to the closet and open the door. "I'm sorry I shouted at you, Chris," I apologized.

He turned to look at me. Suddenly his face broke into a wide smile. "Why, that's all right, Mistuh Johnny," he said gently. "I knowed you didn't mean to, you got lots o' things in your mind, that's all."

I smiled back at him and he turned happily back to the closet. I closed my eyes and leaned back. The pains in my head were subsiding slowly, leaving my mind cold and clear.

I almost spoke my thoughts aloud. It was my turn now. First it was Borden, then it was Peter. Now it was me. One after the other we had been forced out. Was there no way we could lick them? I clenched my fist on the sheet. The linen tore under my fingers. Well, they hadn't got me out yet. And they wouldn't. Not without knowing they'd been in a fight. Slowly I let my fingers relax. I could remember how it all had started.

It was early in '31 that it began. Peter was in New York on one of his semiannual visits and I was sitting in my office bulling with the boys. There was a good deal of smoke in the air besides other things, but, all in all, things weren't too bad.

We were losing money all right, but so was every other

picture company except Metro, and they couldn't lose money. They had a pipeline to the mint.

We were still writing off that nine million bucks' worth of silent film we had in inventory when the big noise came in. Our new pictures were no better and no worse than any of the other companies'. We still hadn't got wise to the technique of sound.

But the future looked good. We had one picture under our belt that looked like money in the bank. It was a war story about a group of German soldiers and just about expressed everything a human being could say about the futility of war. And there were others coming. Peter had said so. I hoped so, though I privately doubted it.

I had to keep my mouth shut about production. When we had changed over to sound pictures I had insisted that we use sound on disks instead of sound on the film itself. Peter reluctantly gave in to me after I pointedly told him that I had been right about sound pictures in the first place.

Now it was costing us another million bucks to make the change to sound on film.

Peter had been decent enough about it. He didn't rub it in even though he made it clear enough to me that he wanted me to keep my hands off production.

I had been sore about it at first, but I calmed down after a while. I figured the whole argument would blow over once things got back to normal.

I don't remember who was talking when the interoffice communicator on my desk gave forth with a loud buzzing sound that was as good an imitation of the Bronx cheer as any I ever heard. A hush fell across the room as I pressed the answer lever down. "Yes, Peter," I said into it.

"Johnny, come into my office right away," Peter's voice rasped through.

"Yes, Peter," I said.

"And, Johnny," he added chucklingly before he switched off, "tell those loafers in your office to get back to work." The box clicked off.

I got to my feet. There was a burst of laughter from them. "You heard him, boys," I said, smiling. "Back to the salt mines."

I watched them filing out of my office. They were a good bunch of men, as good as any in the business. Some of them had been with us since before the war. When the last of them had gone I walked to the door that connected Peter's office and mine. I opened it and walked through.

Peter was seated behind that big desk of his. He had a mania for big desks even though he was a small man himself. This was big enough to keep even him happy. It made him look like a midget. He looked up at me with a serious face. "Johnny," he said, "I want we should lend Bill Borden a million and a half dollars."

"A million and a half!" I choked on the words. That was all the reserve we had in case anything went wrong. And in this business it was peanuts.

Peter nodded his head slowly. "I said a million and a half. You heard me."

"But, Peter," I protested, "that's all the mad money we got. What if something should go wrong?"

There was a discreet cough behind me. I turned around. Bill Borden was sitting in a chair behind me. He had shrunk into his seat and I had not seen him as I walked by. Shocked, I noticed that his face was haggard and drawn. His hair was completely gray. I walked over to him and held out my hand. "Bill," I said embarrassedly, "I didn't see you."

He stood up and shook my hand. "Hello, Johnny," he said. I didn't recognize his voice. It had changed. There was a sound of uncertainty about it.

"I meant no offense, Bill," I said quietly.

He smiled wanly at me. "I understand, Johnny. I know how you feel. I'd feel the same way myself if I was in your shoes."

I looked at him a moment, then turned back to Peter. "Maybe I wouldn't seem like such a fool if I knew what this was all about."

"Well, it's like this," Peter began, but Borden interrupted him.

"Let me tell it, Peter," he said, holding up a hand. "After all, it's my problem."

Peter nodded and I turned back to Borden.

He seated himself slowly in the chair and looked at me for a few seconds. Then he began to speak. His voice was bitter and from it I knew that he was ashamed.

"It must seem funny to you, Johnny," he said slowly, "that Willie Borden has to come to you to borrow a few dollars.

That Willie Borden, who is the president of the biggest picture company in the world, can't go to the banks and get all the money he wants, just for the asking. But it's true. You people are my only hope."

He leaned forward in his chair earnestly and I stared at him fascinated. The man was stripping himself bare before our eyes. We could see the gradual disintegration of his spirit and his pride.

"Before the market crashed in '29 I was sitting on top of the world. When I got those theaters from you, my dreams were complete. I had more theaters than anybody in the picture business, I grossed more each year than any other company. I was smart all right. Too smart." He laughed bitterly. "I forgot when you can do the biggest business, you can also lose the most money. And that's just what happened. I lost the most money. A year after the market crashed, our theaters were worth exactly half what we had paid for them. Even the theaters we bought from you. You don't know how lucky you were to sell them just at that time."

I started to speak but he held up his hand. "I'm not blaming you, Johnny," he said quickly. "You didn't know what was going to happen any more than I did. I wanted them and I bought them. We wound up '29 with an eleven-million-dollar loss. I thought '30 would be better, but it wasn't. It was worse. We lost close to sixteen million dollars and the first six months of this year didn't show much improvement. Our loss came to seven million."

He looked at me. "Maybe you think I'm crazy to come to you and expect you to lend me a million and a half after what I just told you?" He waited for a minute and then, when I didn't answer, he continued: "I'm not asking the money for the business, Johnny, it's for myself."

I looked puzzled. He read the expression on my face correctly. "You see, Johnny," he explained, "it's not like it was in the old days, when Willie Borden was boss and could do what he wanted with his own business. Today it's different. Willie Borden doesn't own Borden Pictures any more. Sure, he's president of the company, but he doesn't really run it. A group of directors run it. Men elected by stockholders who don't know from nothing about the business give the orders and Willie Borden has to carry them out. And if he doesn't want to carry them out, he can quit."

He stopped for a few seconds and rested his head wearily against the back of the chair; then he leaned toward me again. His tone was full of subtle irony. "Even the great Borden Company cannot afford to lose thirty-four million dollars without being embarrassed in some ways. Sure, they still got twenty million in cash and seventy million in other assets, but somebody has to be the goat. Somebody has to be held up before the stockholders and crucified so that they can say: 'See, it was all his fault. He was to blame!' And who is this goat going to be? None other than little Willie Borden, who started with nothing, from a pushcart on Rivington Street, and made all this great company possible. So they got the bright idea. They would arrange to issue new stock and call in the old. Certificates of equal value would be given for each share of old stock, only there was a trick in it. A hidden trick. Now they got over two million shares outstanding. They would give two million shares for the two million shares that were out, but they had an ace up their sleeve. Instead of issuing just two million shares, they would issue four million."

He took a deep breath. "They would put an additional two million shares on the market. It made no difference to them that the market could not absorb the extra shares, because they had a plan. There was an agreement between Willie Borden and the Borden Pictures Company to the effect that Willie Borden was entitled to own outright up to twenty-five per cent of the stock outstanding and that he was to have first option on any new offerings that affect his percentage. If he did not exercise this option, then these shares would be offered on the market. Very clever." He shook his head. "Very clever. They knew that Willie Borden did not have the five million necessary to buy up to twenty-five per cent of the additional stock offered. They knew just how much he had. They figured first to reduce his holdings to about half of what they were and then to start blaming him publicly for the debacle. His reduced holdings would not give him enough votes at the stockholders' meetings to carry any weight. Especially if almost all the other votes were proxied the other way. But they forgot one important thing. Willie Borden was in the picture business before they even heard about it and he has many friends. Friends who would not want Willie Borden to get a screwing."

He looked at me. "With the help of my friends, I managed to get together three and a half million dollars. And it is to you I turn for the rest. I know your position well, I know how precarious it is, how uncertain tomorrow can be, but I have nowhere else to turn."

His voice faded out in the room and we were quiet. At last Peter shifted in his seat behind the massive desk and said uncomfortably: "Nu, Johnny, what do you say now?"

I looked from him to Borden and then back to him. I smiled slowly. "Like you always say, Peter, what good is money if you can't use it to help your friends?"

Borden sprang from his seat and came toward us. He grabbed for our hands excitedly. There was a new life, a new brightness in his face. He smiled happily. "I won't forget it, I promise," he said. "It's only a loan. I'll pay you back within a year!"

Borden left the office with our check in his pocket. After he had gone, Peter and I sat and looked at each other. At last Peter took his watch out of his pocket and looked at it and sighed. He put the watch back in his pocket and said to me: "Got a date for lunch, Johnny?"

I had a date, but I could cancel it. "No," I answered. "I'll be with you in a minute. I just have something on my desk to clean up."

I went back into my office and made a phone call that killed my previous appointment, then went back and joined him.

Peter was very quiet throughout luncheon. I could see he was thinking. I did not disturb him. He didn't open up until we had reached our coffee and he had lighted up one of those big cigars of his. Then he looked at me thoughtfully. He spoke to me, but he was really thinking aloud.

"You know," he said, pointing his cigar at me, "what this means?" I shook my head and he continued. "It means a new era is coming to the picture business. I saw it coming years ago when I warned Willie not to have anything to do with those people in Wall Street. You see, deep inside them they don't like us. Because we're new, because we made a big business without them, and because we're Jewish." He pulled his eyebrows down and squinted at me to see the effect of his words.

I kept my face blank and didn't answer. I didn't agree

with him, but at the same time I didn't want to argue with him just now. It was simply a matter of money the way I saw it. The fact that they were Jewish was only incidental.

He took my silence for acquiescence. He leaned forward in his seat and spoke in a low voice across the table. "And now, with what's happening to Borden and with what's happening to others, I know I was right. The anti-Semiten are out to steal the picture business away from us."

I looked at him. For a moment I felt sorry for him. He couldn't understand. His attitudes had been forced upon him by years of persecution, of deprivation, of living in crowded dirty ghettos. The history of the Jews was filled with oppression. It was only natural those years should instill in him their fears and effects.

But he must realize deep inside him that he was wrong. The picture business was no more a Jewish business than the banking business, or the insurance business. If our own company was any criterion, that would be the truth. Of the three of us who started it, only Peter was Jewish. Joe Turner was Irish-Catholic. I was a Methodist as far as I knew. And the three of us got exactly nowhere until an Italian loaned us the money.

Peter paid the check and got to his feet. As we walked to the door of the restaurant slowly, he whispered to me: "We'll have to watch our step very carefully now, Johnny. They'll be out to get us!"

I got back to my office very perturbed over Peter's attitude. I lit a cigarette and leaned back in my chair thinking. An attitude such as he expressed could very well becloud a man's judgment and bring him harm. At last I shook my head and decided to forget it. Probably Peter only spoke that way because he was upset over what was happening to his friend.

Borden was as good as his word. Within three months he had repaid his loan. But the struggle went on.

The pattern had become clearly established by now. It was the old struggle for control. Which would dominate the industry, financial power or production power? The eyes of the industry were on the fight that was going on in the Borden Companies. The trade papers ran daily reports on the latest developments and were very careful to be impartial. They didn't know whom they would be doing business with when the fight was over and they didn't want to prejudice their daily bread and butter.

By the end of 1931 the Borden Companies had lost an additional six million dollars and a group of stockholders instituted suit against William Borden and several of the principal stockholders and officers of the company, charging mismanagement and appropriation of company funds and acting in a manner prejudicial to the best interests of that company. They asked that a receiver be appointed to examine the company and control it until its difficulties were cleared up and the company was once more returned to a sound and profitable basis.

It was common gossip in the industry that several of the very people named as defendants in the suit were secretly aiding in its prosecution in order to remove Borden from a position of control. The case was finally brought to court early in 1932.

Bill Borden had taken the stand early in the hearings and revealed the fact that he had been serving as president for the past two years without one cent as compensation. He further disclosed that he had not drawn any reimbursement for expenses during that time, paying all expenses from his own pocket. He made public a list of recommendations he had submitted to the board throughout the past few years which would have enabled them to reduce their operating expenses and save them millions of dollars. The board had rejected those recommendations summarily as they had any other suggestions he had made.

The complainants on the other hand had an equally long list of abuses they presented to the court. One of the items mentioned was Borden's purchase of our theaters without consultation with the board. I knew it was a lot of poppycock, as he had approval from his board a year prior to the actual purchase. Borden pointed this out to them. They countered with the charge that the approval given was for that specific time, and if it came up again, the entire matter should have been resubmitted.

I remember the day the decision was handed down in the Borden case. I remember it well for many reasons. It was the day after the inauguration of President Roosevelt and I could still thrill, twenty-four hours after I had heard his voice over the radio, saying the very same words I now read in the morning papers: "The only thing we have to fear is fear itself."

It had been only that morning that I had spoken to Peter and he had assured me that Borden couldn't lose. The phone in my office rang and I picked it up.

"Peter is calling," Jane's voice told me.

"Okay," I said, "put him on." I wondered what he wanted. I looked at my watch. It was nine thirty. That made it six thirty on the coast and it was a little early even for Peter to call.

Peter's voice came on. "Hello, Johnny?"

"Yes, Peter," I said. "What gets you up so early this morning?"

"I wanted to make sure you called me as soon as you get word of the decision in the Borden case," he said.

"That's today, isn't it?" I asked.

"Yes," he replied. "And I want you to keep watch on what's happening and call me as soon as you get some word."

"I'll do that, Peter," I promised. I hesitated a moment. "How do you think it will turn out?" I asked.

"Willie will win." he said confidently.

"What makes you think so?" I asked him. I wasn't so sure.

His voice sounded surprised that I should doubt him. "Why, I just spoke to Willie Borden this morning before I talked to you and he told me that he can't miss."

After a few more words we hung up. I looked down at my desk. I hoped Bill would win, but the other side had thrown up a hell of a case. And they had better connections too.

I called Bannon in newsreel and told him to have the trial covered. I didn't want any pictures, I just wanted a man to report to me the moment a decision was handed down.

At two o'clock in the afternoon I was on the phone, talking to Peter, with the decision of the court already a matter of record.

Peter came on the phone briskly. His voice was confident and full of snap. "Well, Johnny"—I could almost see him smiling—"what was it?"

I tried to keep my voice as unemotional as possible. "He lost," I said succinctly. "Gerard Powell, of Powell & Company, was appointed temporary receiver."

I could hear Peter's breath rush out against the phone. For a moment there was silence. "Peter," I said quickly, "are you there? Did you hear me?"

Then his voice came back on. It was very low and very crushed. "I heard you," he said, and then the phone went dead in my hands.

I flashed the operator. "Was my call disconnected?" I asked.

"No, Mr. Edge," she replied in that snotty tone that comes automatically to telephone operators when their efficiency is doubted, "Mr. Kessler has hung up."

I put the phone down and stared at my desk. This morning Borden had told Peter he was sure he would win the case. I wondered how he felt now. It couldn't be too bad for him, he was still a wealthy man.

I didn't have long to wait to find out. The next morning he committed suicide.

I had just returned from lunch and was settling in my chair when the phone rang. I picked it up.

It was Irving Bannon. "Johnny," his voice was excited, "Bill Borden just committed suicide!"

For a moment I was numb, my mind was spinning like a top in my frozen body. At last I managed to speak. "Are you sure, Irving?" I asked. I still couldn't believe it.

"It just came over the Teletype," he answered.

"Where? How did it happen?"

"I don't know," he replied. "It was just a flash. They said more would follow."

"Keep me posted as soon as you hear any more," I told him, and started to hang up.

"Hold on a minute," Irving's voice said quickly. "The Teletype is going again. There may be something more on it."

I heard him put down the phone. For a second there was silence; then I could hear the clacking of the machine coming through the wire. It kept up for several minutes, then it was quiet and Irving came back on the phone. "You got something?" I asked.

"Yeah," he said, "but not much."

"Read it to me," I ordered.

His voice was very flat as he read: "The body of William Borden, prominent motion-picture magnate, was discovered dead at one fifteen p.m. today by the New York City police in a cold-water flat on Rivington Street in New York's lower East Side. He had died of a bullet wound in the temple and close to the body was a police positive .38-caliber pistol. The police believe it to be suicide. Just yesterday Mr. Borden was defeated in court in an attempt to keep his hundred-million-dollar corporation from being thrown into receivership, and the police believe this to be the motive for his taking his life. More to follow."

I sat very still. Peter would want to know about this. I didn't want to call him, but I had to. "Okay, Irving," I said, suddenly exhausted. "Thanks."

"Should I call you if any more comes in?" he asked.

"No," I answered wearily. I had heard enough. "Don't bother." I pressed down the receiver and held it for a second, then I let it up.

Jane's voice came on. "Yes, Johnny?"

"Get me Peter," I told her slowly. While I waited for the call to go through I wondered what Willie's last day had been like. Last night's paper had said that he seemed in good spirits, that he planned to carry the fight to a higher court. What had caused him to change his mind and driven him to this, the final, irrevocable act?

From the papers the following day and from what I heard and from what Peter told me, added to what I knew, I began to understand how it had come about.

Willie Borden's last day on earth started ordinarily enough. He was up early in the morning and had breakfast with his wife. She said he hadn't slept very well during the night, but in view of what had happened, it was understandable.

His breakfast was hearty, he had a good appetite. He seemed optimistic after his setback and all through breakfast he talked about his plans for the future to regain control of his company. He planned to go in to his office for a few minutes and then to his lawyer's office to make arrangements for an appeal.

The first thing that appeared which was out of the ordinary was when they called for the car to take Borden into the office. The chauffeur reported both cars to be out of order and Borden decided to go into New York by train. A taxi was summoned to take him to the station.

The taxi dropped him at the station at ten minutes after eight and he bought a *New York Times* at the news-stand. The train came in promptly—for the Long Island Railroad, that is—at eight twenty; it was due at eight fifteen. Willie Borden got on it.

With his paper folded under his arm, he walked back through the train to the last car. This was a special car known to commuters as the "Bankers Special." It was a comfortably designed car with more space and much more luxurious than the others. All seats in it were reserved for the same passengers every day. For these privileges the passengers paid five times the regular commutation rate, but to them it was worth it. They did not have to scramble with the crowds for a seat. Reservations for this car were made long in advance and it wasn't open to everyone. Willie Borden was very proud when he had been informed upon his moving to the Island that a place aboard this car was awaiting him. He felt then that he really had arrived.

He took his customary seat in the car and opened his paper. For a few minutes he scanned the headlines, read the account of his case in the paper, and then closed it. He leaned his head back against the cushion and shut his eyes. He was tired because of his restless night and he wanted to get a little rest.

After a while he opened his eyes and looked around him. The usual passengers were in their usual places. He smiled and nodded to several of them whom he knew. They did not return his glance, just looked at him coldly as if he weren't there.

Puzzled, he wondered at their strange behavior. Just yesterday these men were his friends. They spoke to him and laughed at his jokes and today they acted as if they didn't know him. Just because he had lost a case in court should make no difference to them. He was the same Willie Borden he was the day before, the same Willie Borden he always was.

He leaned forward and tapped the man in the adjoining seat on the shoulder. "It's a nice day, isn't it, Ralph?" he asked with a peculiarly ingratiating smile on his face.

The man lowered his *Tribune* and looked over the top of the paper at Willie. For a moment it seemed as if he was about to answer him, but he didn't. Instead his face set in cold reproving lines and he raised his paper again without saying a word. A few seconds later he shifted his seat to one farther away.

I often wondered whether Willie would have committed suicide if that man had exchanged a friendly word with him. Willie's face became frozen with hurt. He seemed to shrivel back into his seat, and for the rest of the forty-minute trip no one heard a word from him or saw him make a movement until the train stopped and he got out of his chair to leave. The rest of that trip must have seemed like a nightmare to Willie. I knew him. He was essentially a friendly, gregarious little man who liked to talk and laugh. He had a genuine fondness for people, combined with a native talent for getting along with them, which had contributed a great deal to his success.

At his office it was pretty much the same story. He had suddenly became a stranger in his own home. The few people who did stop to talk to him did so with such furtive glances and backward looks to see if they were being observed that even Willie himself terminated their conversations abruptly to spare them further embarrassment.

It was twenty minutes of eleven when he climbed into the taxi in front of the nineteen-story Borden Pictures Company Building and gave the driver an address on lower Pine Street. The address was that of his lawyer's office, but he never got there.

The taxi sped south on Park Avenue, through the ramp at Grand Central, and into the tunnel at Fortieth Street. It came out of the tunnel at Thirty-second Street and continued down Park Avenue to Twenty-second Street, where the driver made a left turn. The driver made a right turn on Fourth Avenue and followed that avenue down to Cooper Square, where it joined Third. He sped along under the el tracks, and just when they were crossing Delancey Street, he heard a rapping on the window behind him. He slowed down and looked back.

Willie Borden was leaning forward in his seat, looking at him. "I changed my mind, driver," he said, "I think I'll get out here."

The driver pulled the hack over to the curb and stopped. Willie got out. The meter had clocked one dollar and thirty cents. Willie gave him two dollars and told him to keep the change. He turned and walked back to Delancey Street and was lost in the crowds.

He was next seen on Rivington Street just around the corner from Houston, where he stopped at a pushcart and bought two apples. He gave the man a dime and solemnly put one apple in his pocket along with the nickel in change the old man gave him.

He bit into the apple after wiping it on his sleeve and smiled at the old man. "Nu, Schmulke," he said in Yiddish, "How is business?"

The old man peered at him out of rheumy eyes. His white beard fluttered in the wind as he tried to recognize this person who knew his name. Slowly he walked around the pushcart to see him better. Suddenly his face broke into a wide toothless smile. He threw out his arms. "If it isn't little Willie Bordanov!" he cackled in the same tongue. "How are you?" Excitedly he grabbed Willie's hand and pumped it.

Willie smiled, pleased that the old man should recognize him. "I'm all right," he said, biting again into the apple.

The old man looked at him shrewdly. "It seems funny," he said in Yiddish, "you should be buying apples from me instead of swiping them."

"I'm a little older than I was then." Willie smiled.

The old man shook his head. "Ach," he said reminiscently, "you were a wild one all right. Always up to something. I had to have a thousand eyes in my head to watch you."

"Times have changed." Willie nodded.

The old man came closer to him. Willie could smell his foul breath and see the yellow tobacco stains in his beard. He put his hands on Willie's coat. "A fine piece of goods," he said critically, rubbing the cloth between his fingers. "Like butter, so soft." He squinted at Willie. "*Mocht a leben* in the movie business?" he asked.

"I make a living," Willie answered, but the smile was gone from his face now. He turned away from the old man and started to cross the street. "So long, Schmulke," he called back over his shoulder.

The old man watched him reach the sidewalk on the other side of the street. Then he went over to the next pushcart and took the man there by the arm. "Hershel, look!" he said excitedly, pointing with his other arm. "Look over there. That's Willie Bordanov. He is a *grosse mocher* in the movies! His father and me came on the same boat together. See him? He's standing in front of that house, he used to live there!"

The other man turned curiously and looked in the direction the old man was pointing. "An ector, is he?" he asked, mildly interested.

The old man looked at him indignantly. "Vot else?"

They turned back to look at Willie Borden. He was standing in front of the building looking up at it. While they were watching, he slowly started to climb up the front steps and disappeared into the hallway.

A woman brushed past him just as he neared the inside staircase. He flattened himself against the wall to let her pass. A loose board in the floor squeaked as he put his weight on it, and a cat, frightened by the sudden noise, jumped from a garbage can behind the staircase and scurried out past him after the woman.

He stopped in front of a door two flights up. He stood there for a moment catching his breath. There had been a time he ran up those stairs three steps at once and never even felt it. He looked at the door for a second in the dim light of the small electric bulb overhead.

He reached into his pocket and took out a key case. He opened it and fished through several keys looking for a certain one. He found it and put it in the lock and turned it.

The door squeaked rustily on its hinges as it swung open and he stood there for a second before he entered the apartment. The apartment was empty. It had been that way ever since his father had died. He had wanted his father to move in with him, but the old man wouldn't. He was only happy where he was. After he had died, for some unknown reason, Willie had kept on paying the rent every month. It was only nineteen dollars.

He closed the door behind him and looked around the room. The meager furniture was rotting and covered with dust. There was a box standing in the middle of the floor. He walked over to it and looked down on it. It was the box the old man used when he sat *shiveh* for Willie's mother. He never let it be thrown out. He always kept it there to remind him of her.

Willie put his foot out and turned the box over. A little mouse ran out from under it and into a hole along the floor against the wall. The floor beneath the box was a clean shining square in the dust of the room.

Willie turned and walked through the rooms to the front of the apartment. At the room next to the front one he stopped. This had been his bedroom. His bed was still there. Slowly he rubbed his hands against the wall over the bed, just under the window that separated the two rooms. It was still there.

He struck a match and bent forward to look. In its jumping and flickering light he could read the words. They were carved awkwardly into the wall WILLIAM BORDEN. He had done it that night he lay on the bed and decided to shorten his name. Make it more American. The match flickered and went out.

He straightened up and went into the front room. There were two windows in it. They were the only windows in the apartment and the rest of the rooms got their air from them. In the summer they used to be opened wide and he would sleep on the floor right beneath them.

The panes were dirty and he tried to peer through them into the street, but he couldn't see anything. He put his hands on the window grips and tried to lift it. The window was stuck. The air in the room was dank and damp as Willie looked about him for a stick to press against the window.

He couldn't find one, so he banged his hands against the side and then tried to open it. The window opened suddenly, letting in a gust of air and the sound of the peddlers hawking their wares in the street below.

He stood there by the window looking down. The street below him was lively with color and people. How long he stood there I don't know. What he thought while he stood there I don't know, and nobody ever will.

We only know that he reached into his pocket and took out the other apple he had bought from the pushcart peddler and began to eat it. Apparently he had lost his taste for it, because after a few bites he put it down on the window sill.

Then he walked back into the center of the room and from another pocket took out a revolver. The police were never able to find out how he got it or where.

The sound of a muffled shot rang out in the empty room. There was the dull thud of a body falling. Tiny bits of plaster came down from the decaying ceiling and settled on the floor. In the street outside, there was a sudden frightened silence as the noise reached them.

Willie Borden had come home to die. The hard way.

"How about the gray one, Mistuh Johnny, the one with the chalk stripes?" It was Christopher's voice.

I looked up at him blankly. My mind had been far away.

"It'll go nice with yo' red and blue tie an' brown shoes, Mistuh Johnny," he assured me earnestly.

I took a deep breath. "Sure, Christopher," I said. "Anything you say."

I went into the bathroom and shaved while the hot water ran into the tub. Then I got into the tub and leaned back in the water. It was hot and I could feel its warmth seeping through my body, soothing my jumping nerves. Soon I was relaxed, almost drowsy.

Christopher came into the room and looked down at me. "Ready to get out now, Mistuh John?"

I nodded my head.

He reached out a hand and helped me up. I placed both hands on the parallel bars next to the tub and swung myself out. He covered me with a bath towel and rubbed me dry. My skin was pink and tingling when he got through. I grinned at him. My headache was all gone.

I got to Peter's house a little after three. It was one of those unusually warm days that spring often brings to California and I wiped my face with a handkerchief as I walked up the front steps. Doris's voice called to me from the pool. I turned around.

She was just coming out of the water, little drops were clinging iridescently to her black bathing suit, shooting sparkles of sunlight into the air around her like tiny diamonds. She took off her bathing cap and shook her hair free. "It looked so inviting," she said as I approached her, "I just couldn't resist taking a dip."

She held up her face as I kissed her. We began to walk back toward the house and she slipped a terry-cloth robe around her shoulders as we walked.

"How's Peter?" I asked.

She turned a smiling face to me. "He seems much better today," she answered happily. "He's sitting up in bed and is acting more like himself. He asked if you were coming over. He wants to see you."

"I'm glad," I said simply.

We entered the house through the finished basement and walked on up the stairs. We stopped in front of his door.

"You go on in and talk to him," she told me. "I'll slip on some clothes and join you in a little while."

"Okay," I said. I looked at her. "Is Mother around?"

"She's taking a nap," she answered over her shoulder as she walked away.

I opened the door and walked into his room. He looked up and smiled at me as I came in. The trade papers were spread all over the bed in front of him and I knew that he was aware of everything that had been going on the last few days. The nurse was sitting in a chair near the window reading. She got to her feet.

"Don't tire him too much, Mr. Edge," she admonished me and then she turned and left the room.

Peter smiled again and reached out a hand as I reached the bed. I took it. There was a warmth and strength in his grip that had been lacking the day before. "How're yuh doin'?" I asked looking down at him.

"All right," he said ruefully. "I want to get out of bed, but they won't let me."

I smiled as I sat down in a chair next to the bed. "Don't be a *shtarker*," I said. "Just do what they tell yuh and you'll be okay."

He laughed at my pronunciation of the Yiddish word meaning strong man. "They think I'm a baby," he protested.

"You were a pretty sick man," I told him, "so don't try to rush things."

He looked down at the bed for a moment, then back up at me. A serious look had come on his face. For the first time he spoke about Mark. "I was paying for my mistakes," he said. "I should never have treated the boy like that."

"Don't reproach yourself," I said slowly. "It wasn't a question of making a mistake. No one could tell you whether you did right or wrong. It wasn't even that. You did what you felt you had to."

He shook his head. "I should have known better."

"Forget it," I said sternly. "It's over and done with and you can't turn back the clock."

"No." He echoed my words hollowly: "You can't turn back the clock." His hand played with the sheet for a few seconds. I could see the blue veins on the back of them. He looked over at me. His eyes were moisture-bright. "I know he was a spoiled and selfish kid," he said. "But it was my fault he was that way. I gave in to him too much. I always let him have his own way, thinking he was young yet, there was time enough tomorrow for him to change. But tomorrow never came."

He looked down at the sheets clutched in his hand. I could see the tears rolling silently down his cheeks. I didn't speak; there was nothing I could say.

He lifted his head and wiped his cheek with the back of his hand. "I'm not crying so much for him," he said brokenly, trying to explain away his tears. "It's for myself. I was such a fool, I never gave him time to prove himself. He was my son, my own flesh and blood, and I cast him out in my wicked rage and anger. It was I who was really selfish; if I hadn't been so crazy I would have stopped to think." He took a deep breath. "He was my only son, and I loved him."

We were silent a moment, then I reached out a hand and placed it on his shoulder. "I know, Peter," I said quietly. "I know."

I could hear the clock on the night table ticking away as we sat there without talking. At last Peter stirred and turned to me again. I could see the tears were gone.

"They're after you now," he said tonelessly, his hands waving at the copy of today's *Reporter* lying in front of him.

I nodded silently.

He looked at me closely. "How do you think you'll make out?"

I shrugged my shoulders casually. I didn't want him to see how concerned I really was. "I don't know," I confessed. "I honestly don't know. They got all the money."

He nodded his head in agreement. "Yes, that's it," he said slowly. "They got all the money." He looked at me frankly. "I was wrong, you know. That's what it really was all the time. You were right when you said it wasn't anti-Semitism and this only goes to prove it."

I was curious. "What do you mean?"

A peculiar look came over his face, a strange mixture of sympathy and sorrow. "If it were anti-Semitism they wouldn't be trying to bring Farber and Roth in, over your head. They're Jewish and you're not."

I hadn't thought about that. He was right. I didn't answer, but inside me there was a strange sort of gladness that at last he could see the way things really were.

"What are you going to do?" he asked after a little pause. I rubbed my hands wearily across my forehead. I was beginning to get tired. The restless night I had spent was beginning to catch up with me. "I haven't made up my mind yet," I answered. "I don't know whether to stay until I'm forced out or quit now."

"You don't want to quit, do you?" he asked.

I looked at him and shook my head.

"No, you wouldn't," he continued thoughtfully. "I didn't think you would. We've spent too much time there, you and I. Put too much into it to ever want to leave it. It has become a secret part of us, part of our souls perhaps. You feel now as I did when I had to sell out. I've felt sort of empty ever since."

We were silent, again, each with his own thoughts, until Doris came into the room. Her face was bright and scrubbed and smiling, her dress crinkled as she walked toward us. The clean refreshing scent of pine came to my nostrils as she stood by my side and looked down at the bed. "Your bed's a mess, Papa," she exclaimed.

He smiled up at her as she picked up the papers and put them in a neat little stack on the night table. She turned back to the bed and straightened up the sheets and fluffed up the pillows behind him. Her face was flushed as she straightened up and looked at him. "There," she said. "Isn't that better?"

He nodded his head, then looked at her questioningly. "Mamma is still sleeping?" he asked.

"Yes," Doris answered, coming around the bed and sitting down next to me. "She's so tired. She hasn't had a good night's rest since you were sick."

Peter looked at her. There was a warm light in his eyes; his voice was very soft and gentle. "A wonderful woman, your mother," he said quietly. "You can't know how wonderful. I couldn't get along without her."

Doris didn't answer, but I could tell from the look on her face that she was very proud. She turned to me. "Have you had lunch yet?"

"I ate before I got here," I replied.

"You didn't hear me, maybe," Peter persisted. "I said your mother is a wonderful person."

She smiled at him. "I'm not arguing with you." She laughed, "I think you're both wonderful people."

Peter turned to me. "I been thinking," he said. "If it's a question of money, maybe Santos could help you."

For a moment I was puzzled. "But Al has retired," I protested. "Besides, what could he do anyway? They get all their money from the Boston banks."

"The loan must be due now," he said. "It's almost two years old. What if they can't get an extension? They got enough money to retire it?"

I looked at him respectfully. There was always some way in which he would surprise me. Generally when I thought him far away from something and out of touch with it, he would pop up with some remark or question that made me realize he had been watching the situation very closely. This was one of those times. "No, we haven't the money to repay it," I answered slowly. "But it doesn't make much difference. We started negotiations for an extension last month and Konstantinov assured us we would get it without trouble." Konstantinov was president of the Greater Boston Investment Corporation, from whom Ronsen had borrowed the money to buy Peter out. The loan was subsequently transferred to the picture company.

"It wouldn't hurt to talk to Al anyway," Peter insisted peculiarly. "Four million dollars is a lot of money and anything can happen when there's that much involved. Why don't you run over and see him just in case?"

"Do you know something?" I asked him. It seemed to me that he had a reason for his peculiar insistence.

He shook his head. "No, I just think you should not overlook anything. It doesn't hurt to be prepared."

I looked at my watch. It was past four o'clock. I don't know why, but suddenly I could feel a surge of hope and confidence sweep through me. Al had retired to a ranch out in the valley about three hundred and fifty miles from Los Angeles. It would take about six hours to get out there and that would be too late. Al went to bed at eight o'clock. I looked up at Peter. "Maybe you're right," I said suddenly, "but it's too late for today."

"Why don't you spend the night here?" Doris volunteered, "and I'll drive you out tomorrow. That way we can get off to an early start."

I looked at her and smiled. Peter answered for me. "A good idea," he said quickly.

I laughed aloud for the first time since last night. "Well, it seems to be settled," I said.

Peter looked at me. "Of course it's settled." He turned back to Doris with a funny smile on his face. *"Liebe kind,"* he said, "would you do your old papa a favor and bring up the chessboard from the game room?"

He was feeling better all right. I lost two games before the nurse came back and chased Doris and me out of the room and we went down to supper.

THIRTY YEARS

1936

1

JOHNNY picked up the letter from his desk and looked at it. There was a grimace of distaste on his face as he read it. This part of his job he didn't like, writing letters like this one.

Another pay cut. Ten per cent this time for the whole company. The third since '32. Angrily he pressed the buzzer for Jane to come into his office.

She stood in front of him silently, her face grave.

"Send it out on Friday," he said, giving it to her.

She took it from him without a word and left the office. He turned his chair to the window and stared out of it unseeingly. The futility of the letter ran through him.

Pay cuts weren't the answer, they never were. Friday, when a copy of the letter would be placed on each employee's desk, faces would grow longer, more worried. They would talk quietly to one another or not speak at all. Each would be trying to figure out how he could exist with this new burden. But few would dare to complain, jobs were too scarce. They would pass him silently in the hall and their eyes would stare at him resentfully and accusingly. They would blame him and Peter for it. Maybe they were right.

They couldn't know that Peter and he had not taken any salary from the company for almost three and a half years now. They couldn't know that Peter had put back almost three million dollars into the company to keep it going. That it was all the money that Peter had.

Yet, in spite of it, maybe they were right. Certainly Peter and he had not acted from altruistic motives entirely. They were trying to save their own necks. Several of the other picture companies had already filed petitions in bankruptcy, and Peter had sworn that he would never do that.

"Whom were they to blame if not Peter and himself?" he

asked himself accusingly. Certainly the average employee had not made the mistakes that were responsible for the company's predicament. The mistakes were their own, he told himself, going over them in his mind, Peter's and his. He had made his share of them too.

So what if Peter had guessed wrong about sound pictures? He himself had guessed wrong about what type of sound-recording methods they should use. He remembered his insistence on using sound on disks instead of on the film itself. Look at the phonograph, he had said, it was the only proved method of reproducing sound, you couldn't go wrong with it. But they had.

The disks were cumbersome to transport; they broke easily, were too difficult to synchronize with the film. It cost almost a million dollars to replace the equipment they had bought when they had to switch to sound on film.

Since that time he had kept his hands off production. Peter had been angry, but he had to admit that Peter had enough reason. A million dollars' worth of reason. He would have felt the same way if he had been in Peter's place. Peter had been in charge of production, not he, and Peter had paid for the mistake.

There were other mistakes too, but what was the use of rehashing them? They proved nothing except that Peter and he were human and couldn't bat a thousand. But most of all it was the pictures.

If the pictures had been good, they would have been all right no matter what had happened. The pictures were bad. It was almost as simple as that. Peter never caught on to the technique and use of sound in pictures.

He had made one good sound picture. That was back in '31. The war picture. It was the only one and it was good because Peter had put tremendous effort into it. He had salved his conscience toward his homeland with it, compensated for the picture he had to make about German atrocities during the war, but after that he seemed to lose his touch.

Johnny thought that Peter had gone wrong about the time he had become obsessed with the idea that the industry was in the throes of a religious war, that the Jewish people in it were under attack. Johnny couldn't be sure about it, but it was a possibility. Making pictures was a highly specialized and creative art and no artist could do his best while torn by seething tensions.

He lit a cigarette and walked to the window. That was part of it. You could go farther back than that—back to when the business was starting and no one had ever dreamed how big it would become. The picture business was a relatively simple thing then. You made pictures and you sold them. It was different now. Very different.

Today a picture man had to be a financier, an economist, a politician, and an artist all rolled up into one. He had to read balance sheets as well as scripts, market analyses as well as stories. He had to be able to forecast public tastes and preferences six months to a year in advance because that was how long it would take for the picture he was working on to reach the public.

Johnny turned around and picked up the small bust of Peter that stood on his desk and looked at it. Maybe that was what was wrong with Peter. Peter was trying to be too many things. He had never learned really to delegate duties and responsibilities. He tried to do everything himself, not trusting anyone else to do it for him, and his methods were the same as they had been when he first started in the business years ago.

That was it, Johnny thought. A man had to be flexible in order to survive in the complex world of motion pictures today. Peter wasn't flexible, he was too used to running the whole show, and the habits of years were difficult to break.

Johnny put the little statue back on the desk. Many things had happened that convinced him he was right. Like Peter's refusal to do business with the Borden Company after Borden had committed suicide. He wouldn't trade with those anti-Semiten, he had insisted. They had murdered his friend.

That had hurt too. Not only did they lose the Borden theaters as showplaces for their pictures, but they also lost the advantages of trading with the Borden studio for stars, directors, and other talent which they had enjoyed up to that time.

Business had grown steadily worse, but if Peter regretted his hasty actions in connection with the Borden Company he never allowed it to show. And this last thing he had just done, leaving Mark in charge of the studio while he went to Europe to dig up some business, was as bad as any of them as far as Johnny was concerned.

Mark had come back to the studio from Europe in '32. He was supposed to take a load of details off Peter's shoulders. The only detail he lifted from Peter's already overburdened shoulders was, in Johnny's estimation, the duty to keep the night clubs in Hollywood prosperous.

Mark was the columnists' darling. He was always good for an item; all they had to do was stop at his table and listen to him talk. He would gladly tell them what was wrong with the picture business in Hollywood. That always made good copy. Johnny didn't object to that if only Mark would back it up with some work, but work was something that Mark successfully avoided, until Peter had decided to stump the country for business and then go to Europe.

Until then everybody, Johnny included, had thought that if Peter left the studio for any length of time, Bob Gordon would remain in charge. He was the logical man for the job. He knew the business, had come up the hard way, and Johnny privately thought that the company would be better off if Peter had left all production in his charge.

Peter's announcement had fallen like a bombshell upon him. He had called Peter demanding to know why Gordon had not been given the job. Angrily Peter told him that he didn't trust Gordon. Bob was entirely too friendly with those anti-Semiten at Borden. Mark was his son. He could depend on him where he couldn't on anyone else. Besides, Mark was a smart boy. Didn't all the papers say so? Didn't they always quote him on what was wrong with the business? All he needed was the chance to prove himself. He was going to see that Mark had that chance.

Johnny was tired. His leg ached and he massaged it reflectively. Where was it all going to lead to? He didn't know. He was worried. The business had changed a great deal since they had entered it. It was changing more every day. They had to be ready to change with it. What was needed was a rare combination of experience and adaptability. He knew of no one in the company that had it. Peter had experience, but lacked flexibility. Mark was flexible, entirely too flexible, but lacked experience. That left only himself.

And there was nothing he could do. Peter was running the show. But even if he had the chance, he wondered if he could do the job that had to be done. It would be a dirty job. When it was over, a man wouldn't have many friends left. The whole company had to be put through the wringer, from the top down.

Unconsciously he shrugged his shoulders. Why was he thinking about it? It was Peter's headache, not his. Peter had told him the exact extent of his responsibilities. Peter had made it plain that he would stand for no interference. It had been almost four years, ever since they had got into trouble, since Peter had asked him for his opinion.

A sigh escaped his lips. Yet he knew that Peter liked him, still thought highly of him. Then what had gone wrong between them? Was it that Peter had suddenly grown conscious of his power and decided to show it? Or was it that Peter had decided he was growing old and was afraid that Johnny would cheat Mark of his inheritance?

Johnny didn't know, but his heart hung heavy in him. The old days when they had struggled toward a common goal were warm in his memory. Things were better then; all they had to worry about was the business. They weren't afraid to trust each other.

Johnny shook his head and picked up the phone. Jane answered it. "You better send that letter out tomorrow, Janey," he said into it, and hung up the phone.

Peter had said to get the pay-cut announcement out right away. Friday was still three days off. Peter wouldn't like his holding it up until then.

2

MARK emptied the champagne bottle into their glasses. The softly lit room had already taken on a rose-colored hue for him. He looked over at her wonderingly. God, she was even more beautiful than he had remembered, than any woman he had ever known. No wonder Johnny couldn't hold on to her, he wasn't man enough for a woman like this. It was funny the way he had met her again.

He had been at his table at the Trocambo with a few friends. He had just started to get out of his seat to go and talk to a friend he had seen at the bar. As he stood up and turned around, his shoulder had bumped into a woman who was passing behind him. He had grabbed her arm to steady her. "So sorry. Such little room between these damn tables," he had apologized when he recognized her.

She had looked up at him, an amused smile on her face. "That's all right," she had said. "No harm done."

He smiled down at her. Her blond hair shimmered in the blue lights of the night club. She didn't know how wrong she was when she said that. The harm had been done, but not to her. " 'Straordinary way to meet again, Miss Warren," he said.

"Hollywood is really a small town, Mark," she had replied still smiling.

A pleased look came onto his face that she knew his name. He forgot about the friend at the bar he had wanted to see. Instead he persuaded her to join his table for a drink.

That had been about six weeks ago, just after his father had gone to New York to see if he could stimulate the sales department into greater efforts.

With a smile he remembered how Johnny had argued with his father over his appointment as production boss. Johnny thought he did not have the necessary experience and that Gordon should have the job, but the old man had put his foot down. He did not trust Gordon, he had told Johnny flatly, Gordon had quit in a huff when he heard the news, and Johnny was left without an argument.

Last week his father had left for Europe, having done all he could in New York. With his domestic market in the condition it was, he thought he might be able to get more results over there. Magnum's foreign offices were always among the best in the industry.

Since he had first met her in the night club, Mark had called Dulcie several times and had gone out with her once. And each time he saw her, he became more enchanted with her.

In Paris many years ago he had learned that there were only two basic types of women: those who appealed to the flesh and those who appealed to the spirit. He had long ago made up his mind that those who appealed to the spirit were not for him. He preferred the tangible to the intangible. Dulcie Warren was a very tangible woman.

This was the first time he had ever been to her home. He

had been very happily surprised when he had called her that afternoon and she had said she was much too tired to go out that evening and suggested that he drop in for a few drinks afterward.

The few drinks had added up to two bottles of champagne up to the present moment. She had greeted him at the door in a black velvet hostess gown tied with a red silk sash. Her blond hair framed her tanned golden heart-shaped face, and her white teeth shone at him as she smiled.

He thought the smile was for him, but he was wrong. It was a smile of amusement that he should be here. She took a peculiar delight in the fact that he was Peter's son—the son of the man who had so righteously fired her, using the morals clause as an excuse. She didn't dare fight the contract at the time because it would have meant bringing the whole business out into the open, but she had promised herself that one day she would even the score.

She looked at Mark. His eyes were slightly glazed, he was a little bit drunk, she thought. Maybe she would get even through him, she didn't know. She had listened to him talk about the company. It hadn't been easy for them the past few years. And now Peter had gone off on a begging trip to try to raise some money and had left Mark in charge of the studio.

Mark had tried to persuade his father to let him make some of the ideas he had into pictures, but Peter had firmly refused. They were too impractical at the moment, he had said, they would cost too much. Peter had told him to proceed with the pictures that had been already scheduled. Those were his orders, and Mark grumblingly obeyed them.

As the liquor took hold, he began to tell her about his plans and how his father had refused him permission to make the pictures. He knew that his ideas were new and would be far superior to what they were making, but there wasn't anything he could do about it. He told her of one of the pictures he had in mind.

She listened to the story. Something inside her made her refrain from laughing at the idea. It was not only too expensive and impractical; it was downright stupid. She knew almost immediately that Mark had no more conception of what made a picture than he had of flying to the moon. She looked at him speculatively. Maybe this was the opportunity she had been waiting for.

She smiled slowly at him. Her eyes widened slightly. "Why, Mark," she said in an impressed tone of voice, "what a wonderful idea! How foolish of your father not to see it!" She shrugged her shoulders prettily and tilted her head to one side. "But then, it's not unusual out here," she added. "They haven't the appreciation for subtlety and finesse that you have. What is it they say about a prophet being without honor in his own country?"

Mark had difficulty in framing his words. "That's juth it," he answered, lisping lightly. "They resent ideas. They're alwayth afraid of something new." He stared down at his glass dejectedly.

She leaned toward him, her gown parting a little. She turned his face toward her. "Maybe there's some way you could manage to make the picture anyhow," she said encouragingly.

His eyes were on the cleft of her bosom, revealed by the parting garment. "How?" he asked. "There's only enough money to make the pictures he wants."

Her hand stroked his cheek lightly. "There are some ways you might be able to manage it. I heard of a case over at another studio where the production manager wanted to make a certain picture and they didn't want to let him do it, so he made it anyway and hid it on the production reports of a picture they wanted him to make. When it was all over, the picture was a tremendous hit and everybody thought he was a genius."

"Do you think I could do it?" he looked questioningly at her.

"I don't know," she said carefully. "I'm only mentioning it as an idea. After all, you're in charge of the studio while your father is away."

He straightened up, a thoughtful look on his face. His hand reached out for another bottle of champagne and he unsteadily filled his glass again and drank it. He looked at her. "Maybe I can do it," he said unsteadily.

"Of course you can, Mark," she said softly, leaning back against the couch. "You're smart enough to find a way."

He bent toward her. She let him kiss her, let his hands roam over her. Suddenly she caught them, held them.

"How are you going to do it, Mark?" she asked.

He looked at her stupidly. "Do what?" he asked her.

She tossed her blond head impatiently. "Make the picture without them knowing about it," she said sharply, restraining an impulse to ridicule him.

He shook his head slowly. "I didn't say I was going to do it," he said, a look of cunning coming into his face, "I only said I would think about doing it."

She watched him take another drink. "I thought you were going to do it," she pouted. "I didn't think you were afraid."

He got to his feet dizzily. The fumes of the alcohol were running around in his brain. He drew himself up proudly. "Who's afraid?" he asked drunkenly. "I'm not afraid of nobody."

She looked up at him and smiled. "Then you are going to show them?"

He looked down at her. He weaved gently in front of her. Doubt came back into his face. "I thure would like to," he lisped. "But the work reportsth we thend to New York would show it up."

"You could always say it's a title change. They'd never know the difference until it was all finished," she suggested sagaciously.

He stood there a moment thoughtfully, then his face broke into a wide smile. "Thay, Dulthie!" he exclaimed. "That'th a good idea!"

She got up and stood very close to him. "Of course it's a good idea, Mark." She pressed against him and kissed him.

He put his arms around her and buried his face against her throat. She let him kiss her until she could feel the tenseness of his body against her, his lips more demanding; then she broke loose from his grip. "Mark, don't!" she said sharply.

He looked at her bewildered. "Why, Dulcie?" he asked in an anguished voice. "I thought you liked me."

She smiled dazzlingly at him. "I do like you, darling," she said softly, coming close to him and kissing him lightly on the lips. "But I have to work tomorrow and you know what those cameras can see."

He tried to hold her, but she grabbed his hands and gently steered him toward the door. He went docilely with her. At the door he turned and kissed her again.

His cry of pain was like a strange music to her ears.

"Dulcie, I want you so much I hurt!" His eyes were wild and glazed with a drunken passion.

She opened the door and pushed him through it gently. "I know, darling," she said softly. Her eyes were filled with many promises. "Later, maybe."

She closed the door behind him and leaned against it smiling. Absently she rearranged the front of her parted gown, then she slowly crossed the room and lit a cigarette. She stared at the closed door, still smiling softly. There were many ways. . . .

3

PETER sat quietly in the chair, appraising the man who sat opposite him. He shifted his position slightly. These British had no idea of what comfort meant. If a man's behind was comfortable, he could work better, think better. He looked quickly around the office. It was dark and dull and looked exactly like what it was, the British sales manager's office.

He turned his face back to the man, Philippe X. Danvere. A month ago he had never even heard of him but, concurrently with his arrival in London, the trade papers were filled with that name.

Philippe X. Danvere, one of the richest men in Europe, had gone into the picture business. How the man had got the idea no one seemed to know. Born in Switzerland, he had been sent to England to complete his education before the World War. The war had come along while he was still at Oxford and he had enlisted in the British army. His father, head of the world-famous Danvere Textile Company, had objected to this with typical hard-headed Swiss neutrality, to no avail. His father died when the war ended, and Philippe, then a captain, returned to his native land to take over as titular head of his father's company. He had remained quietly in that position until a month ago.

The announcement that he had purchased controlling interest in several theater circuits on the Continent and finally that he had acquired the Martin Theaters Circuit, the largest in the British Isles, had startled the film world. Speculation was rife about his motives but Mr. Danvere kept his own counsel. He was a tall man with dark, wide eyes, a prominent nose, and a firm mouth and chin. His speech and mannerisms were more English than those of many a home-grown Briton.

Peter had immediately dispatched Charley Rosenberg, his London office manager, to see Mr. Danvere and try to secure the Martin circuit account for Magnum. It would be a great thing for Magnum to have four hundred guaranteed outlets for their product in the British Isles inasmuch as Great Britain represented one half of the foreign market for American pictures.

Mr. Danvere had been most polite to Rosenberg. He had also been most cautious. He explained to Mr. Rosenberg that as far as the picture business was concerned he was still a beginner and would not consider entering into any agreement with an American company for their product until he had assured himself of their complete reliability.

Mr. Rosenberg had pointed out to him that Magnum had been in the picture business since 1910 and was from the standpoint of age one of the oldest names in the business.

Mr. Danvere had indicated he was well aware of Magnum's position, since his accountants had already made a study of the more prominent companies. He also indicated he would be most interested in coming to some kind of agreement with Magnum under the proper terms and auspices.

Mr. Rosenberg had inquired what he meant and had been told that as a textile merchant, mind you, not speaking as a member of the motion-picture industry, Mr. Danvere had found the most profitable sort of arrangement where the retailer had some close connection with the manufacturer.

Mr. Rosenberg then mentioned the fact that Mr. Kessler, the president of Magnum Pictures, happened to be in London at the moment and would welcome an opportunity to meet him, and a meeting was arranged to take place in Magnum's London offices the following week.

The meeting had been delayed two weeks by the unexpected illness of Mr. Danvere, who had inconveniently taken cold, and Peter stayed in London until Mr. Danvere had recovered. Now they sat opposite each other, with Mr. Rosenberg hovering solicitously over them.

Mr. Danvere was speaking. "I must confess to a certain interest in your company, Mr. Kessler, ever since the war. I was an officer in His Majesty's armed services then, and I can remember the motion pictures you supplied the armed services without charge with a great deal of personal gratification."

Peter smiled slowly. Free motion pictures to the armies of the Allies had been one of his most treasured projects. He had realized that supplying entertainment for the soldiers would create a great deal of good will for motion pictures. "That's something I felt very grateful for being able to do, Mr. Danvere."

Mr. Danvere smiled, revealing his rather large teeth. "That's why I suggested to Mr. Rosenberg when he came to see me that a meeting might be in order between us. I should like to be able to speak to you frankly and confidentially if I may."

Peter looked at Charley Rosenberg, who immediately excused himself and left the room. Then he turned to Mr. Danvere inquiringly.

Mr. Danvere settled comfortably in his chair. "As I understand it, Mr. Kessler, and please correct me if I am wrong in my assumption, you are the sole owner of your company."

"For the most part you are correct, Mr. Danvere," Peter explained. "That is, I own all but ten per cent of the stock. That ten per cent is owned by a Mr. Edge, who helped me found the company and is at present executive vice-president."

"I see," said Mr. Danvere, nodding his head. He paused for a moment, then continued. "I believe Mr. Rosenberg made my viewpoint clear to you in connection with the showing of your pictures in the Martin theaters?"

"Not exactly," Peter replied cagily. "I would appreciate it if you would go over the idea with me."

Mr. Danvere leaned forward in his chair. His manner was still elaborately casual. "You see, Mr. Kessler," he said ingenuously, "basically I am nothing but a simple textile merchant. As such I have developed certain primary rules, which I endeavor to follow since they served me most successfully in the past. One of these rules applies to the sale of merchandise. I have found out by experience that an article is more successfully retailed when the retailer has an interest in the manufacture of the product itself. I believe that this same rule can be applied to the sale of motion pictures. For example, the Martin theaters would be more interested in securing the greatest grosses possible for Magnum pictures if they had an interest in the pictures themselves and could see the rewards for that additional effort being gainful in two ways. From the production as well as the exhibition of the pictures."

Peter looked at him steadily. What Danvere meant in plain talk was "You cut me in and I'll see that you do all right." Back in the states they called it protection. "I take it then, Mr. Danvere," he said gently, "you are interested in acquiring an interest in the Magnum company."

Danvere smiled slowly. "Something of the sort, Mr. Kessler," he admitted.

Peter rubbed the side of his face reflectively. "About how much of an interest are you considering, Mr. Danvere?"

Mr. Danvere cleared his throat. "Harumph," he coughed. He looked at Peter appraisingly. "About twenty five per cent, I should say."

"And for how much?" Peter asked.

Mr. Danvere looked around the office. He hesitated for a moment before he answered. "Five hundred thousand pounds," he replied.

Peter converted the money into dollars mentally. It came to almost two and a half million dollars. That would solve a lot of problems. He was curious as to how Danvere had arrived at that figure. "Why that particular amount, Mr. Danvere?"

Danvere's eyes met his levelly across the desk. "I make it a point never to go into any business venture half blind, Mr. Kessler. Before I purchased the Martin theaters my accountants had thoroughly investigated the entire company. When I decided to purchase them I realized that an association with an American motion-picture company would prove most beneficial to both parties. The record of your company was the most interesting one to me personally. You have a record of independence that commands my respect. You see, sir, my family fortunes, too, were founded on a principle of continually fighting the vested interests in its field. It was only natural that I should think of you in that light."

In spite of himself Peter was impressed. The fact that his struggle against odds had been recognized by this man and acknowledged was a very flattering one. Slowly he relaxed in his seat, a broad smile coming to his face. "Very kind of you to tell me this, Mr. Danvere," he said modestly.

Mr. Danvere held up a protesting hand. "It's nothing of the

sort, Mr. Kessler. You have my respect sir, no matter what decision you make in this matter."

Peter nodded in a pleased manner. "I will give serious thought to your kind offer, Mr. Danvere, but there is one important fact I would like to know beforehand."

"What is that, Mr. Kessler?"

"You may not know of this, but I would like you to know that the last several years have been difficult ones for Magnum. Its losses since '29 have been in excess of ten million dollars."

Danvere nodded thoughtfully. "I was aware of that, Mr. Kessler, but I appreciate your honesty in calling it to my attention. However, I believe some of those losses were inevitable, due to your rather difficult position in relation to the rest of the industry—those vested interests we have mentioned. I believe, however, that I have a plan which would materially aid Magnum in its struggle for finances."

Peter raised an eyebrow. He had already developed a high regard for this man's opinions. The entire conversation had convinced him that Danvere was a very solid, conservative businessman. "What is that?" he asked.

Mr. Danvere crossed his legs comfortably. "My idea is basically a very simple one. I will purchase twenty five per cent of the present company's stock from you. We will then dissolve the present company and reorganize a new one with the stock issued to the present holders on a pari passu basis; that is, sixty-five per cent to you, twenty-five per cent to me, and ten per cent to Mr. Edge. In order to gain public and industry-wide acceptance and confidence in the new company I would then suggest that you place twenty per cent of the stock on the public market. This would leave you with a forty-five-per-cent interest, which would still ensure you a satisfactory controlling interest in the company." He paused for a moment to observe the reaction on Peter's face. It was calm and interested. Mr. Danvere continued: "The public sale of those shares should bring you approximately four hundred thousand pounds. That plus what you receive from me would come to a total of nine hundred thousand pounds, or about four and a half million dollars in your currency. Then the Martin Theaters Circuit would advance to Magnum on account of advance film rentals four hundred thousand pounds, and you concurrently would lend Magnum the same amount.

This would provide Magnum with approximately four million dollars of working capital, which would be sufficient to guarantee its production program. It is also possible that, with the announcement of the new association with the Martin Theaters, Magnum's credit position will be improved materially and additional financing could be acquired if so needed."

Peter sat there quietly. If the same type of offer had come from a Wall Street financier he would have rejected it peremptorily. But this man was not a Wall Street financier. He was merely a simple textile merchant by his own admission. His family had made their fortune in much the same manner that he had, by fighting the bigger companies and their financial connections. Besides, he was in London, a long way from Wall Street, and the proposition he had just heard was a very attractive one. It would restore his personal fortune as well as place the business on an even keel.

He got out of his seat, walked around the desk, and stood in front of the chair in which Mr. Danvere was seated. He looked down at him seriously. "Of course I will have to discuss the matter with my associate, Mr. Edge, before I could give you an answer, but I will admit I am most impressed with your proposition, Mr. Danvere."

Danvere looked up at him. He got out of his chair. "Of course, Mr. Kessler." He held out his hand and Peter took it. His grip was firm and strong. "It's been a great pleasure talking to you, Mr. Kessler," he said, towering over Peter.

"My pleasure," Peter insisted.

Mr. Danvere looked down at him and smiled. "Oh, I say, Mr. Kessler, I have a small place in Scotland, and if you have no other plans for the week-end, I should very much like to have you up there for a bit of shooting."

Peter looked up at him. "I'd like it very much," he said, smiling. "I have no other plans."

"Good thing," Mr. Danvere said warmly. "I'll have my chauffeur pick you up Friday afternoon. Let my office know a convenient time for you."

"Thanks a lot, Mr. Danvere," Peter said.

"Make it Philippe," Mr. Danvere said genially, holding out his hand again. "There's no need for formalities between us. We understand each other."

"Right you are, Philippe," Peter said, smiling broadly and shaking his hand.

"Good-by, Peter," Philippe X. Danvere said from the door.

Peter walked back to his desk and sat down. Rosenberg came back into his office. He stood there looking down at Peter with an excited expression on his face. "Well, Peter," he asked, "how'd we make out?"

Peter looked up at him with a puzzled expression on his face. "What is this week-end shooting business?" he asked. "I don't know one end of a gun from the other."

4

JOHNNY looked down at the studio work reports on his desk with a puzzled look on his face. What the hell was this new picture, *United We Stand*, doing on there? He scratched his head trying to remember if Peter had told him about it before he had gone to London. He couldn't remember having heard about it before.

He pressed the buzzer on his desk and Jane came into the office. "Yes, Johnny?" she asked.

He looked up at her. "Did you ever hear Peter mention a picture by the name of *United We Stand* while he was here?"

"You mean that picture on last week's work sheet?"

"Yeanh," he said.

"No," she answered. "I don't remember it. I was going to ask you what it was all about."

He looked at her in apparent confusion. "Search me," he said at last. "Damned if I know anything about it." He looked down at the work sheet again. "Funny too," he said thoughtfully. "It pops up on the report with a hundred grand sunk into it already and only six days' shooting on it. No final budget either." He looked up at her again. "Call Mark at the studio for me, will ya, Janey?"

She nodded and left the office. A few seconds later his phone buzzed and he picked it up. "Yes, Jane?"

"There's a call coming in from Peter in London for you," her voice said. "Do you still want me to call Mark?"

He thought for a moment. "No," he decided. "Hold it. I'll ask Peter about the picture."

He put the phone down and stared at it thoughtfully. He wondered what Peter wanted. It must be damned important if Peter would spend the dough to call him from London in these difficult times. The phone buzzed again. He picked it up.

"Peter is on the phone, Johnny."

"Okay," he said. "Put him through."

Peter's voice sounded thin and far away. "Hello, Johnny," his voice was shouting.

"Peter, how are yuh?" Johnny answered. "What's on your mind?"

Peter's voice sounded excited. "I think we got our troubles licked," he said.

"What do you mean?" Johnny asked. The excitement in Peter's voice was contagious, he began to feel it sweep through him.

"You know this guy Danvere the trade papers been full about?" Peter asked.

"You mean the Swiss textile king?" Johnny asked.

"Yes, that's the guy," Peter answered quickly. "I just finished a talk to him and he made me a very interesting proposition."

"About what?" Johnny asked cautiously.

"I sent Charley Rosenberg after him to get the Martin Theaters account and he come back to me with a proposition. He'll give me preferred time in the theaters in return for a twenty-five-per-cent piece of the company."

"Wait a minute," Johnny interrupted him. "I thought you didn't want to sell any part of the company."

"That's what I thought," Peter said, "but this guy sounds all right to me. He offered me two and a half million bucks for the percentage and he'll advance the company two million bucks against film rentals."

"I don't get it," Johnny said. "What's the guy got in mind?"

"Nothing, absolutely nothing," Peter shouted back. "He's got a business principle which says a retailer will work harder if he has a connection with the manufacturer, that's all. It makes sense to me." He cleared his throat. "What do you think about it, Johnny?"

Johnny thought for a moment. "I don't know what to think," he answered cautiously. "I don't know enough about it, but the dough sounds awful good to me."

"Not only that," Peter added enthusiastically. "He's got an idea that will bring in another two million bucks and improve our credit. I'm telling you, Johnny, he's a smart feller, that one. I think he knows what he's talking about."

"Well, you're there, Peter," Johnny said slowly. "You know what's best for us."

"You got no objections if I decide to sell him a piece?" Peter asked.

Johnny hesitated. He didn't like the idea, but couldn't see how he could object to it. After all, Peter owned the company, he had a right to sell part of it if he so desired. Peter must be almost clean now and this was a chance for him to recoup some of his personal fortune.

"I haven't any objections," he replied slowly. "But, Peter—be careful."

"Sure," Peter said, his voice still excited, "I'll be careful."

Johnny remembered the picture on the work sheet. "Do you know anything about a picture called *United We Stand?*" he asked.

"No, I never heard of it. Why?"

"It just showed up on last week's studio work sheet," Johnny said.

Peter laughed. "Then what are you worrying about? It must be a new title Mark put on one of the pictures."

"But—" Johnny started to protest.

Peter's voice cut in on him. "I left Mark with complete instructions on the program. He just changed a title, that's all. After all, we got to let him have a little freedom, don't we?"

Resentment rose in Johnny's throat. With difficulty he managed to keep it from spilling over into his voice. Every time he said something about production since that fiasco with sound on disks Peter had shut him up. "The title is a phony," he said flatly. "We haven't anything on the schedule it would fit."

"How would you know?" Peter asked belligerently. "Mark is running the studio, not you. He would know better." He was still sensitive over the argument Johnny had given him when he left Mark in charge of the studio.

Johnny recognized the tone in his voice. It meant that Peter had closed his mind to argument and nothing he could say would change it. He decided not to push it any further at the moment, he did not want to upset Peter while he was in the midst of negotiations with this guy Danvere. Johnny had a hunch that Danvere was a pretty smooth article and that

Peter would need all his wits about him. "All right," he said reluctantly. "When are you coming back?" he asked. Time enough to settle it then, he thought.

"I don't know," Peter replied. "If I set this deal with Danvere, I was thinking of taking a two-month trip through the Continental offices and see how they're doing. It's been more than two years since I looked them over."

"Good idea," Johnny said. "Maybe you can hump 'em up a little."

"I'll try," Peter said.

"You want me to forward any messages to the family?" Johnny asked.

"No, thanks," Peter replied. "I've got a call in for Esther now and I'll be talking to her as soon as I get through with you."

"Okay, I won't keep you then," Johnny said. "So long."

"Good-by, Johnny," Peter answered.

Johnny put the phone down and looked at it thoughtfully. He hoped Peter knew what he was doing. He looked at his watch. It was eleven o'clock in the morning. That made it five o'clock in the afternoon in London and eight o'clock in the morning in California. Peter's call should catch the family at breakfast.

Doris was seated at the table reading the paper and drinking her orange juice when Mark came into the room. She looked up at him.

His eyes were puffed and rimmed with lack of sleep. He grinned at her. "Morning, sis," he said, his voice still husky with sleep.

"Good morning, Mark," she said, still looking at him. "What time did you get to bed last night?" she asked curiously.

He glanced at her quickly. "Why?"

She shrugged her shoulders. "I was just curious. I was up until after three o'clock and I didn't hear you come in."

He felt a peculiar irritation at her statement. "I'm not a baby any more," he growled surlily at her. "You don't have to wait up for me."

"I wasn't waiting up for you. I was working," she said, putting down her paper and looking at him. "What's eating you lately?" she asked. "You've been grouchy as a bear the last month."

He managed a conciliatory smile. "I've been working too hard, I guess," he said placatingly.

She picked up her paper again. "You might try getting to bed a little earlier," she said quietly. "It won't hurt."

He didn't answer her. He picked up the glass of juice in front of him and drank it. He heard her laugh and looked at her. "What's funny?" he asked.

"This item here in Marian Andrews's column," she said. She read it aloud. "'A prominent son of a prominent father in this town is in for a rude awakening when Papa comes home from a business trip. Said son has been running around with an actress his father fired from the lot on a morals-clause threat.'" She laughed again. "I wonder whom she means?"

He looked down at the table in front of him. He could feel a flush running up into his face and hoped she wouldn't notice it. God damn that columnist! He didn't know where she got her dope. They had been very careful not to be seen together after that first time. He was glad when the phone rang, distracting her.

"Sit there," she said to him, "I'll get it." She got out of her chair and picked up the phone. "Hello," she said into it.

A look of excitement came into her face. "Get Mamma quick," she said, covering the mouthpiece with her hand. "It's Papa calling from London!"

He looked at her stupidly for a minute. What the hell! Had the old boy heard about the picture already? No, he couldn't have; he didn't get any of the work sheets. He ran into the kitchen.

As usual Esther was at the stove frying the eggs and the cook stood by, watching her. "Mamma," he said, "come quick. Papa's on the phone!"

Esther dropped the frying-pan on the stove and, wiping her hands on her apron, hurried after him into the dining-room.

Doris saw her coming. "All right operator," she said into the phone. "Put him on. Here she is now." She handed her mother the phone and stood by, watching her with excited eyes.

"Hello, Papa?" Esther shouted into the phone. Her hand was shaking so that she could hardly hold it. "How are you feeling? Are you all right?"

They could hear their father's voice buzzing and crackling in the receiver.

Esther was silent a moment, then she spoke again. "I'm all

right Papa," she shouted into the phone again. "Doris and Mark are all right too." She turned and looked at them with proud shining eyes. "Yes, Papa," she said, "Mark is working very hard. He gets home from the studio late almost every night. Last night he didn't come in until almost four o'clock. . . ."

5

SHE saw him as he stepped down from the train. She stood on tiptoes and waved to him. "Johnny!" she called. "Over here!"

His eyes turned toward her and a broad smile crossed his face. The porter followed him with his valise as he walked toward her. She ran to him. "Oh, Johnny," she cried, "I'm so glad you could come!"

He looked down at her still smiling, the corners of his eyes crinkling good-humoredly. "I'm glad I did come, sweetheart," he said. "But why all the mystery?"

She looked up at him, her eyes clouding suddenly. "It's Mark," she said quickly. She looked up at him, a sudden fear in her eyes. "Johnny, there's something the matter with him! I don't know what it is."

His face grew serious as he took her by the arm and walked toward the car. He waited until they were settled in the car before he spoke again. "What seems to be the trouble?"

She started the motor and rolled out into traffic. "Johnny, there's something wrong out at the studio. That picture he's working on, it's not what it seems."

"I don't understand what you mean, Doris." His voice was puzzled.

"Mamma got a letter from Papa last week and her glasses weren't handy, so she asked me to read it to her. In it Papa said that he expected things to be a lot easier once Mark delivered the six pictures he was working on." She stopped for a traffic light and looked at him.

"That's right," he nodded. "But there's nothing wrong with that. We all expect things to pick up with those six pictures."

"But there is something wrong," she said swiftly. "I went

down to the studio the next day to pick up something for Mother from Papa's office, and his secretary, Miss Hartman, said something to me about everybody being so excited over *United We Stand* that almost all the other work at the studio was at a standstill."

"Did you ask her what she meant?" Johnny questioned.

"I did," came her answer, "and she said that this picture was the biggest thing Magnum ever did. She said something about it costing over two million dollars."

"Two million dollars!" Johnny ejaculated. "She must be nuts! All six of the pictures on the work report don't come to that much."

"That's what I thought, even though I didn't know all the figures," Doris said. "I knew about the money Papa got from Danvere, but I couldn't believe that Papa would throw it all into one picture."

"Did you ask Mark about it?" Johnny could feel a sudden anxiety run through him.

"I did at dinner that night and he became angry and told me to mind my own business. He said that Papa left him in charge of the studio, not me, and it was about time somebody showed them how to do things properly." She looked at him out of the corner of her eyes. He was sitting very still. "I asked him if Miss Hartman was right when she told me that the picture would cost more than two million dollars."

"What did he say?"

"He didn't answer me at first, just looked at me angrily. Then he said very nastily: 'What if it does? What are you going to do about it? Run and tell Johnny?' I told him that I wasn't prying, but was only curious because of Papa's letter. 'Papa must have been thinking of something else,' he said, trying to make a joke of it. Then he smiled at me very sweetly, and you know how sweet he can be when he wants to, and said: 'Don't worry your little head over it, sis. Your brother knows what he's doing. Besides, Papa okayed everything.' I let it drop then, but later in the evening, when I thought things over, I thought I ought to call you and see if you'd come out. Naturally I didn't want to talk about it over the phone. But I thought you should come anyway. Mark wouldn't dare fool around with you." She looked at him.

His face had settled into grim lines. If what she said was true, they were in a hell of a mess right now. Under the terms of their agreement with Danvere they had to deliver six pictures to the Martin theaters in the next month and a half. In addition to that, at the first meeting of the newly appointed board of directors, which had been held in New York just two weeks ago, he had glowingly told them of the six pictures now in progress and what it meant to the company to have them ready on time.

They wouldn't like that. Had Mark forgotten that, according to the law now, he had to have approval by the board for anything he did? The board had already approved the program of six pictures and that guy Ronsen, who was on it as Danvere's representative, was no fool either. He already had an extensive experience with the Borden Company. And there was something peculiar about the way he acted, too. Johnny couldn't put his finger on it, but the man seemed to be waiting for something to go wrong. He reminded Johnny of a hawk circling around and around in the sky waiting for prey.

He was silent for so long that at last she looked at him anxiously and asked: "What are you thinking about, Johnny?"

There was a hint of anger in his blue eyes as he turned and looked at her. "I think we ought to pay the kid a visit at the studio and see for ourselves what's going on," he said grimly.

Something in his voice frightened her. Her grip tightened on the steering wheel. "Johnny, if he did that, would we be in trouble?"

His answering laugh was flat and completely devoid of humor. "Honey, if he did that, we'd be in real trouble, the likes of which we never been in before!"

Mark looked at his watch. It was a little after two o'clock. "I got to be getting back to the studio, Dulcie," he said, looking up. "It's getting late."

She smiled back at him. "And I have the whole afternoon to kill by my lonesome," she pouted.

"Got that picture to make, baby," he said. "You wouldn't want me to be late for that."

A mischievous look came into her eyes. "No, I wouldn't want that to happen," she said quickly, "but—"

"But what?" he asked.

She eyed him daringly. "I heard so much about it, I would like to see for myself how it's going."

His voice was surprised. "You know you can't do that," he said.

She raised an eyebrow. Her voice was challenging. "Why not?" she asked. "Are you afraid to take me there?"

He laughed unconvincingly. "I'm not afraid. I was just thinking that it might be unpleasant for you, that's all."

"I don't think I'd mind," she replied. "And I do so want to see how you're doing," she added appealingly.

"No," he decided. "You'd better not. It would cause too much talk and there's enough of that already."

"You are afraid!" Her voice was accusing.

"I'm not," he insisted, standing up. He glanced at his watch again. "I'd better be going." He turned and started for the door.

She let him go as far as the door before she called him. A sudden obstinacy swept over her. "Mark!" she called.

He stopped and looked back at her questioningly.

"If you don't take me back with you, you don't have to call me any more," she told him quietly.

She restrained an impulse to smile at his haste to get back to her. He tried to take her in his arms. "Dulcie, you know I can't."

She disengaged herself from his grasp. "I don't know anything," she replied coolly, "except that you don't want to take me with you."

His hands still reached out for her. "But Dulcie—" His voice was miserable and pleading.

She turned away from him. Her voice was still cold. "That's all right, Mark. I understand. You just don't want to be seen with me."

"Dulcie, that's wrong," he pleaded. "Didn't I ask you to marry me?"

She didn't answer. She picked up a cigarette from the tray in front of her and lit it slowly.

He stood there watching her. Her face was calm and impassive. He gave in suddenly. "Oh, all right Dulcie," he said at last. "Come on."

The face she turned toward him was radiant with triumph.

He could see the surprised look on all faces when he helped her from the car and they walked on the set. He could hear the sudden excited buzz of the voices as they walked past. "Let them talk," he thought angrily, but all the same he was glad when he could get her off the set and back to his office.

He shut the door and looked at her. "Now are you satisfied?" he asked, as near to anger with her as he'd ever come.

There was a satisfied look on her face. Peter had said she would never set foot in his studio again, and look who had brought her in! She walked to him and kissed him lightly on the cheek. "Yes, darling," she answered contentedly, "I'm satisfied."

He looked at her. A strange admiration came into his eyes. One thing you could say for her, she had guts all right. Not many people had the nerve to go where they were not wanted and ignore what went on around them. He smiled slowly. He put his arms around her and kissed her. "There's something mad about you, baby, but I like it. You're my kind of woman!"

He watched her walk toward the door slowly. She walked like a panther, slowly and easily, her magnificent body saying more than words.

"Call me tonight?" her husky voice came back to him over her shoulder.

He was about to answer her when the door opened suddenly. Doris and Johnny were standing there. They came partly into the room and stopped, looking at them.

Dulcie looked at Doris and Johnny and then back at Mark. A slow smile came to her lips. She walked past them slowly. Her hand went out and patted Johnny's cheek gently. "Don't let me interrupt anything, darling," she said in a low, husky voice. "I was just leaving anyway."

6

THE crickets were chirping in the grass on the side of the hill. The night was dark and the moonlight sparkled iridescently in the rippling waters of the pool beside which they were sitting. They had been quiet for a long time, the silence between them heavy and somber with thought.

Her eyes were questioning in the darkness. "Johnny, what are you going to do?"

He shook his head slowly. He didn't know what he was going to do, he didn't know what he could do. It had turned out to be much worse than he had thought it could be. Over a million and a half of the two million ticketed for the production of six pictures had gone into *United We Stand*.

"You're not going to tell Papa," she said. "It would—" She left the unfinished sentence hanging expressively in the air.

He looked at her. Her face was tense and worried. His voice was low, hesitant. "I don't want to tell him," he said slowly, "but I'm afraid not to. We're pretty low on cash and there's not enough left to make those pictures with."

"But, Johnny," she cried out impulsively, "it would break his heart. He had such faith in Mark."

He smiled bitterly. That was the trouble. If Peter hadn't gone off half-cocked and let Gordon quit they wouldn't be in the pickle they were in now. He was suddenly tired of running interference for his mistakes. He leaned back against the chair and closed his eyes wearily. He might be tired of it, but a sense of duty kept tugging at a corner of his mind. He couldn't let Peter down. Peter had gone all the way down the line for him every time, personally as well as in business. No, he couldn't stop now. There were too many years behind them.

His face turned away from her. "I know," he said quietly. "Why do you think I'm sitting here trying to find a way out?"

She moved closer to him, her arm slipped through his. "You know I like you," she whispered.

He turned his head and looked down at her. Her face was calm and her eyes warm and trusting. He put an arm around her shoulders. "I can't imagine why," he said, a faint note of amusement coming into his voice.

She looked into his eyes seriously. "There's a strength inside you, Johnny, that people can feel and trust." Her voice was low and thoughtful. "They feel they can trust you and rely on you and draw some of that strength into themselves. Like Papa has."

He turned his face away again and looked down the hill. He didn't want her to see the sudden doubt that had sprung into his eyes. He wanted to believe she was right, but he couldn't. He was afraid of too many things himself.

As when he had first seen Dulcie in Mark's office that afternoon. He had trembled suddenly. He was afraid to talk to her because he did not know what he might say. And when she had touched his cheek. It had been a hot flame running through his flesh to his brain. A strange recollection of long nights and passionate whispers. Even now he could still feel the touch of her hand on his cheek. Would he ever stop remembering?

"I wish you were right," he said bitterly.

Her hand turned his face back to her. Her eyes were deep pools of understanding. "I know I'm right, Johnny."

They were silent again and she was thinking. It was Dulcie that had made him feel as he did. The thought of her sent a sharp pain through Doris's breast. The pain was for his suffering, his tortuous memories, not for herself. Could she ever make him forget all that had gone before? Maybe she could, maybe she couldn't. She didn't know. She only knew that she loved him. She had always loved him. Her hand crept into his palm, it was warm and soft in there. She would try to mend the pain in him. It was like mending a Chinese vase smashed to bits on the floor. It might be difficult at first, but with patience—and time—it could be done.

"Maybe I could raise some money, enough to complete the other pictures, and throw it back in there without your father knowing about it." His voice was speculative. He was thinking aloud.

"Where would you get that much money, Johnny?" she asked, her eyes suddenly lighting up. "Oh, Johnny, if you only could!"

He looked down at her. "I could sell my stock," he said.

"Johnny, you wouldn't do that?" Her voice was shocked. "Why, you've worked all your life for it."

He tried to smile. "So what?" he asked. "I can buy it back when things get straightened out. It's the only way I can see that might work."

"But what if you can't get it back?" she asked him. "Then you've lost everything."

Something inside him knew he would never get it back. Once it was gone, it was finished, that was all there was to it. A slow smile came to his lips. His heart began to hammer inside him and the words came from his lips before he knew he was saying them. "You wouldn't mind marrying a poor man, would you, sweetheart?"

She looked up at him in surprise. For a moment she sat very still, then tears began to rush into her eyes. She threw her arms around his neck and kissed him. "Oh, Johnny!" She was half laughing, half crying. "I'd marry you no matter what! I love you, darling!"

He held her very close and closed his eyes. This was what a man really lived for, to hear things like these.

Mark sat in his room nervously looking at the telephone. He glanced at his watch. Two thirty a.m. A warm breeze came in through the open window, rustling the drapes. He went over to it and shut it quietly. Through the window he could see the dim figures of Johnny and Doris seated near the pool. "Damn them!" he thought angrily.

He went back into the room and turned off the light. He didn't want them to know he was still awake. He sat down near the phone and lit another cigarette. Why didn't that damn call go through? It must be eleven in the morning in Paris. Peter should be in the office there at that time.

The phone began to ring. He snatched it up quickly, his heart pounding. It had sounded like a fire alarm in the quiet night. He was silent for a moment before he answered it. He hoped that its ring hadn't been overheard. At last he spoke into it in a quiet voice. "Hello."

The operator's voice was slightly nasal. "Mr. Mark Kessler?"

"Speaking," he answered.

"I have your Paris call for you," she said tonelessly. "Go ahead, please."

"Hello, Papa?" he asked nervously.

His father's voice was excited. "Mark, what's the matter? Is Mamma all right?"

"Mamma's all right, there's nothing the matter with the family," he said quickly.

He heard his father's sudden sigh of relief. "You scared me."

He put his cigarette in the tray near the phone, where it smoldered slowly. He hesitated a moment before he spoke. When he did, his voice was calm again. "I didn't mean to, Pa," he said slowly. "I just wanted to talk to you on business."

Peter's voice was alert. "So go ahead and talk," he said. "But at almost twenty dollars a minute, be quick about it."

His eyes glowed in the dark. There was a trace of cunning in his voice that his father didn't recognize. "I called about Johnny, Pa," he said.

"Johnny?" Peter asked in a puzzled voice. "What's wrong?"

"He came out to the studio today and raised hell here. I think there's something on his mind."

"What did he say?" Peter asked.

"It was nothing in particular, but he complained about everything in general. He didn't like the way the pictures were coming through. He's insisting that we finish *United We Stand* before anything else," Mark told him.

Peter laughed. "Don't get upset, Mark. You'll have to get used to it. New York is always telling us what to do. You just ignore them, that's all."

"But Johnny is insisting on it," Mark repeated.

"Did you ask him why?" Peter asked.

"I did, but he wouldn't give me a straight answer. I can't figure it out. He's been acting very strange lately."

Peter was silent for a moment, then his voice came through the phone again. "Maybe he's got a good reason. Johnny's a very smart boy."

"Then why won't he tell me?"

"Johnny's like that sometimes. He gets stubborn. Don't worry about it, though. You make the pictures and stop worrying. I'll talk to him when I get back." Peter's voice was reassuring.

"I don't know," Mark persisted doubtfully. "He's acting awfully funny. I overheard him talking on the phone today to Bob Gordon over at Borden's. He was laughing at something that Bob must have said. Then he said: 'You can't tell what will happen, Bob, maybe we'll be working together again, sooner than you think.'"

Peter's voice was puzzled again. "I don't understand that."

"I don't either," Mark said quickly, "but that plus the way he's been acting made me think I ought to call you." He hesitated a moment. Might as well go the whole hog, he thought. "Don't forget what we're up against, Pa," he added meaningly. "And when you scratch 'em deep enough, there isn't a one of them that really likes us. They're all the same."

Peter's voice was doubtful. "Johnny isn't like that," he said.

Mark smiled to himself as he heard the doubt in his father's voice. "I'm not saying he is, Pa, but it doesn't hurt to be careful."

Peter's voice was still unsure. "That's right, Mark," he said slowly. "We got to be careful."

"That's why I called you," Mark said. "I wanted your opinion on it."

Peter's voice was hesitant. "You go ahead with your work," he said. "We'll talk about it again when I get back."

"All right, Pa." Mark's voice was very deferential. "How are you feeling?" he asked, suddenly changing the subject.

"Fine," Peter answered, his voice belying his words. Mark could tell that he was still thinking about what he had just heard.

"That's good, Pa," he said. "Take care of yourself."

"I will," his father answered absently.

"Good-by, Pa," Mark said. He heard his father's reply and then hung up the phone. He lit another cigarette and sat there motionlessly for a minute. Then he got out of his seat and walked to the window and looked out.

In the dark he could see Johnny and Doris walking up the path to the house hand in hand. He smiled again to himself. He'd take care of Johnny. The smile faded from his lips. And Doris too.

7

VITTORIO GUIDO slowly lumbered to his feet. He was a big man and moved heavily. He held his hand out, unsmiling. "Hello, Johnny," he said with an attempt at geniality that merely served to emphasize the lack of warmth in his voice.

Johnny took his hand and shook it. "Vic, how are you?" he asked.

Vittorio nodded his head. "Good," he said slowly.

"And Al?" Johnny asked.

Vittorio looked at him. He wondered why Johnny had come to his office. He knew it wasn't a social call, they didn't like each other that much. "Al's all right considering his age," he said portentously. "The doc wants him to take it easy and stay on the ranch." He picked up a box of cigars on the desk and offered it to Johnny. Johnny shook his head. He took one from the box. "Sit down, Johnny," he said, lighting up. He watched Johnny.

Johnny remained standing. Vic didn't like him. He knew it. If only Al were here, things would be different. There would be a warmth in the air that was lacking now. Slowly he sat down opposite Vic.

The cigar was exuding small clouds of smoke. A smile crossed Vic's face. "What's on your mind, Johnny?" he asked. Almost as quickly as the words passed his lips, he wished he hadn't asked them. He had wanted to make Johnny come to him, but his curiosity had got the better of him.

"I need money, Vic," Johnny said reluctantly. He didn't want to talk to Vic about it either, but he had no choice.

Vic leaned back in his chair and half-closed his eyes. He studied Johnny. There was a faint veiled contempt behind the half-closed eyelids. These picture people were all alike. They couldn't manage their own money. It wasn't that they didn't make enough either. No matter how much they made, sooner or later they would come to him. "How much?" he asked.

Johnny looked at him. The sum came reluctantly to his lips. He could see what Vic was thinking. "A million dollars," he said.

Vic didn't answer. He sat there quietly thinking. He blew some smoke through pursed lips and regarded it satisfactorily. He was right. Johnny was no better than the rest, no matter what Al said about him. At last he looked at Johnny. "What do you need the money for?" he asked.

Johnny shifted uncomfortably in his chair. Vic didn't make it easy to talk to him. "I want to buy a half interest in a picture we're making out there, *United We Stand.*"

Vic's eyes were still half-closed. He had heard about that picture. Mark Kessler's folly, they were calling it in Hollywood. It had been rumored that the picture would cost in excess of two million dollars. Suddenly he wondered why Johnny wanted to buy half of it. From what he had heard, it was a stiff. Besides, his accountant's mind told him, Magnum couldn't even hope to break even on a two-million-dollar picture. Their grosses weren't big enough. His voice was expressionless. "You know our policy on pictures like those, Johnny," he said quietly. "Magnum owes us two million dollars and we can't make cross-loans against their pictures."

"Crap!" Johnny thought angrily. Vic could do whatever he wanted. He just didn't want to lend him the money. "Is there any other way I could get the money, then?" he asked, his voice revealing none of his inner thoughts.

Vic looked at him with new interest. Something really important must be going on out at Magnum if Johnny persisted in his attempt to get money. "Have you anything else to offer as collateral?" he asked cautiously.

Johnny hesitated. He didn't want to do it, but he saw no other way out. "How about my ten-per-cent stock interest in the company?" he suggested.

Vic's pulses suddenly began to race strangely. Ownership was the one thing these people did not hock. They would trade stars, directors, contracts. Some of them he knew would even hock their wives if they had to, but never their proprietary rights. Johnny must be in a desperate situation to come to this. Johnny's interest in Magnum was worth a million dollars at current market values. It was good security for a loan of seventy-five per cent of its value. "I couldn't make you a long-term loan on that, Johnny," he said carefully. "The market is too erratic. But I could give you three quarters of its value for a three-month note."

Johnny looked at him. Seven hundred and fifty thousand was better than nothing. Besides, if things went right he would have a chance of getting the money back by that time. The air rushed out of his lungs suddenly. He had unconsciously been holding his breath while he thought. "All right, Vic," he agreed. "How soon can I get the money?"

Vic smiled at him. "As soon as you deliver the stock to us here," he answered.

Johnny got out of his chair and stood looking down at him. "You'll have the stock here tomorrow," he said.

Vic rose to his feet. "Good," he nodded. "Then it's settled." He held out his hand.

Johnny shook it. "Thanks, Vic," he said expressionlessly.

Vic smiled at him. "Glad to be of help, Johnny."

Johnny's eyes glanced at him quickly. Vic's face was imperturbable. "So long, Vic," he said, turning and walking to the door.

"So long, Johnny," Vic called after him. A smile of satisfaction crossed his face as he watched Johnny go out the door. He looked down at his desk for a moment, frowning in thought. He would have to find out what was happening over at Magnum.

He walked over to the window that overlooked the main floor of the bank. Johnny was making his way through the crowds to the entrance. He disappeared through it and Vic went over to the other window, which looked out on the street.

Johnny was getting into an automobile that had been parked outside the door. It was a convertible coupe and the top was down. There was a girl sitting inside it. She had dark hair. Vic caught a glimpse of her face as she turned toward Johnny when he got into the car. It was Doris Kessler. He watched the car turn into the traffic and out of sight around the corner.

He went back to his desk and sat down heavily. The smile of satisfaction came back to his lips. Maybe Santos wouldn't think so much of Johnny when he told him of what had happened.

Mark sat behind his desk. A resentment was burning inside him. Resentment toward Johnny, toward Doris, toward what they were saying. They were only trying to help him, they had said. Baloney! They just wanted to get him under their thumb. But an inner voice kept telling him they were right. He had gone too far out on the limb with that one picture.

Maybe he had, but when the picture was finished he would make them all look sick. They would see then who had been right. He looked up at Johnny. "Yes, Johnny," he said, inwardly ashamed of himself for caviling at him. "I understand."

Johnny looked down at him, his face set in hard frozen lines. His eyes were cold as ice: "Make sure that you do," he said in clipped, emphatic tones. "I'm not doing this for your sake alone. Your father's heart would break if he ever found out what had happened. Now, here's what we tell him when he gets back. We have to agree on the story."

Mark didn't answer. He continued to look sullenly at Johnny.

"We'll tell him that I liked the picture so much I put up half the dough for it. It ran a little over budget and I agreed to split the difference with you and gave you first claim on it for that much. After that I collect even-Steven with you until the cost comes back." He looked questioningly at Doris. "Does that sound all right to you?" he asked.

She nodded. "It sounds all right."

Mark looked up at him. He could barely repress a smile. The damn fool was playing right into his hands. With that story he would have no trouble in convincing his father that Johnny had caused all the trouble.

8

THE snow falling outside the window had covered the city with a white blanket that already was beginning to show signs of stain as the traffic in the streets churned it into a sloppy black. Johnny turned back from the window as Peter spoke.

"I can't understand why we haven't received any reply to our cable to Danvere yet," he said worriedly.

Johnny looked at his watch. "There's not much time left before the board meeting," he said.

Peter nodded. "I wanted the answer before the meeting started," he told Johnny. He shook his head. "I can't understand why he didn't advance us the money like he promised."

Johnny looked at him. The deal with Danvere had looked like a good thing at the time Peter made it. Peter had been optimistic. The air had been filled with promises. But since that time there had been nothing but trouble. Mark had loused up their production schedule. Only two pictures of the six that had been promised were ready and they were nothing to talk about. *United We Stand* was still a headache after eating up over two million dollars and it looked as though it would take a few hundred thousand more to complete it.

Business had been slow in addition to all that, and their bank balance had dwindled. The money that Peter had loaned the company under his agreement with Danvere had almost completely disappeared even with the additional money that Johnny had advanced. Now Peter had cabled Danvere asking him for the money that he had promised to advance them. More than four months had gone by and the money had not been forthcoming.

Johnny looked at his watch again and then back at Peter. "I guess the reply won't come before the meeting," he said. "We might as well get started now."

"Tell Janey to call me if the cable comes in while we're at the meeting," Peter said, taking his hat and coat from the rack.

November 12, 1936

Magnum Pictures Company, Inc.
New York City

Minutes of Regular Meeting of Board of Directors on November 12, 1936

Place of meeting: Waldorf Astoria Hotel, New York City
Time: 2.30 p.m.

Directors present: Mr. Peter Kessler
Mr. John Edge
Mr. Laurence G. Ronsen
Mr. Oscar Floyd
Mr. Xavier Randolph
Directors absent: Mr. Mark Kessler
Mrs. Peter Kessler
Mr. Philippe X. Danvere

The meeting was called to order at 2.35 p.m. by the president. The minutes thereof were kept by Mr. Edge, who acted as secretary.

The following recommendations were placed before the board for approval:

Renewal of lease on Albany Exchange building at same terms as previously held.

Approved.

Agreement with Local W-70, I.A.T.S.E., covering employment of studio technicians at salary scale agreed to by joint negotiating committee of all companies.

Approved.

Terms contract to be entered into with Marian St. Clair, artist, for her services for a period of seven years, with options in usual manner. First year's salary to be paid at the rate of $75 per week for forty weeks' guarantee. Right to terminate contract at end of each year of employment retained by company.

Approved.

Legal fees of $12,500 submitted to company by Dale, Cohen & Swift in connection with their preparation of corporation papers.

PAYMENT APPROVED.

A general business discussion then ensued.

The president rose and gave his opinion as to the business prospects for the coming year. He reported that he was very optimistic about the immediate outlook for the company in the domestic market because they have increased their total sales contracts by six hundred in the past year and intend to garner at least one thousand contracts more in the coming year. He reported on his recent visit to Europe and said that at the present he finds the European market very unsettled because of the constant political disturbances on the Continent. He was very optimistic, however, about business in British Isles because of an agreement that had been made with Mr. Danvere regarding the distribution of Magnum pictures in that territory. He pointed out that a close working arrangement with Mr. Danvere had resulted in securing additional playing time in the largest circuits in England. He also indicated he was awaiting word almost momentarily from Mr. Danvere in connection with an advance against future film rentals to be earned in that territory amounting to $2 million, which would help their cash position immediately.

Mr. Ronsen then asked the president why the six pictures that were to be completed by this time were only one third ready for release.

The president replied that unforeseen production difficulties had arisen, but that they were in the process of being worked out and that he expected the balance of the program to be completed in short order.

Mr. Ronsen then presented to the board a cable he had just received from Mr. Danvere. A transcript of the cable follows at the request of Mr. Ronsen that it be read into the minutes.

Dear Mr. Ronsen, I am greatly disturbed at the product outlook for the Magnum company. In my last conversation with Mr. Kessler he assured me that six pictures would be available for showing in the theaters by Sept. 15th last, and to this time only two pictures have been made available, both late in October. I have just received a cable from Mr. Kessler requesting an advance of two million dollars as agreed upon. I should like you to notify Mr. Kessler that according to our existing agreement that said advance is still subject to approval by the board of directors of Martin Theaters, Ltd. Despite personal desire to accommodate Mr. Kessler, board of Martin refuses to grant such advance until it has secured the six pictures promised. Signed Philippe X. Danvere.

The president then rose and said he was greatly disturbed by the news that the board of directors of Martin had rejected his request for an advance. He said that he had been informed by Mr. Danvere that said approval was merely a formality and had been assured that nothing would go wrong. He also said that he regretted that Mr. Danvere had not replied directly to his cable and that he felt if he were in the same position he too would be ashamed to communicate directly with him.

Mr. Ronsen then placed the following proposal before the meeting:

That a committee be appointed to make a survey of the studio with a view toward finding out what was wrong with our present method of operation and why pictures could not be delivered according to schedule.

The president said the motion was improper and could not be put before the meeting unless there were sufficient grounds for such an action. He maintained there were not sufficient grounds.

Mr. Ronsen then asked the board to decide if the motion was in order. A vote was then taken and the motion was placed before the meeting.

The foregoing motion was then carried by a vote of three to two.

Mr. Ronsen then requested that the vote be recorded in the minutes.

For the motion: Mr. Ronsen
Mr. Floyd
Mr. Randolph

Against the motion: Mr. Kessler
Mr. Edge

Mr. Ronsen was then appointed a committee of one to go out to the studio and prepare a report to be delivered to the board at its next monthly meeting.

There being no further discussion to come before the board, the meeting was then adjourned. The time was 5.10 p.m.

Peter was walking up and down his office excitedly. It was dark outside his window. The clock on his desk read ten minutes past seven. For almost two hours since the meeting had adjourned he had been raving mad.

Now he turned to Johnny and looked at him. A thought had come to him suddenly. He glared at Johnny angrily. "Those God-damn besteds!" he shouted. "Why did you have to give them a chance, Johnny?"

Johnny's mouth fell open. "Me?" he asked, not believing his ears. "What kind of a chance did I give them? You made the agreement with Danvere!"

"Agreement, shmagreement!" Peter shouted at him. "If you stuck your nose out of the studio this wouldn't have happened. We would have had the six pictures ready on time!" He turned and walked angrily to the window and looked out. "But no," he said bitterly over his shoulder. "You had to be a genius! A *mocher,* a know-it-all! Mark told me how you came out to the studio and kept pushing him for that picture and made him forget about everything else." He turned to Johnny. There was a look of misery in his eyes. "Why did you do it, Johnny?" he asked reproachfully. "Was it because of the money you put into it? Was that a good enough reason to take chances like that with our business?"

Johnny didn't answer. His face had lost its color and he gripped the desk in front of him. He stared back at Peter, his eyes boring into him.

Peter turned back to the window, his shoulders slumping suddenly. "Why did you do it, Johnny?" he asked again, almost brokenly. "That ain't the only reason I feel bad either."

He walked over to Johnny and looked up into his face. Sudden tears seemed to come into his eyes. "It's just as bad thinking when I needed the money all that time, you had it for this and not for me. If I had the money and you asked me for it, Johnny, I would have given it to you."

9

THE coolness that had developed between Peter and Johnny was immediately apparent to everyone except the two principals themselves. They prided themselves on being able to keep it from general knowledge. But Jane knew about it and she was worried. She was not afraid for herself, but she felt bad that her two friends should act as they did toward each other.

A small example of it was the time the phone on her desk rang. She answered it.

"Jane," Peter's voice came through the receiver, "tell Johnny I want to see him in my office."

She hung up the phone feeling oddly disturbed. Ordinarily Peter would call Johnny direct on the interoffice communicator or walk into his office and call him. It was easy enough to do, since their offices were adjoining and had a connecting door. She pressed Johnny's signal.

He came on the phone immediately. "Yes, Jane."

"Peter wants to see you, Johnny," she said.

There was a moment's silence. Then he sighed into the phone wearily. "All right, I'll go in to see him."

Her voice kept him from hanging up the phone.

"Johnny," she said.

"Yes, Jane?"

"What's going on between Peter and you? You have a fight or something?" she asked.

His laugh rang into her ear, but his voice was cool. Something in it was telling her to mind her own business. "Don't be silly," he said, and hung up the phone.

Slowly she put the phone down. No matter what Johnny said, she still didn't like it.

He came back into his office wearily. He wished Peter would stop harping on the subject. He was getting damn sick and tired of listening to how he had got them into all this trouble. But he couldn't say anything in reply. He had promised Doris that he wouldn't.

The phone on his desk rang. He walked over to it and picked it up. "Yes, Jane?"

"Mr. Ronsen is out here and would like to see you," her voice came through.

He wondered why Ronsen had come to his office. "Send him in," he said, and hung up the phone.

The door opened and Ronsen came into the office. A thin smile came to his face as he saw Johnny. He crossed the room to him. "I wanted to see you before I left for the coast, Mr. Edge," he said, holding out his hand to Johnny.

They shook hands and Johnny was surprised at the strength he found in the pudgy fingers. "I'm glad you did, Mr. Ronsen," he said, waving toward a chair. "Sit down, won't you?"

Ronsen seated himself in a chair opposite Johnny's desk and looked at him. "I suppose you're wondering why I came to see you, Mr. Edge?" he asked.

Johnny nodded his head. "A little," he admitted.

Ronsen leaned forward in his chair eagerly. Lights were dancing in his eyes behind the thick tortoise-rimmed spectacles. "I was wondering if you had anything you wanted to tell me."

Johnny looked at him. "About what?" he asked cautiously.

Ronsen smiled slightly. "About the studio. You know I'm going tomorrow."

Johnny smiled back at him. Two could play at that game. His face was blank. "I'm afraid there's nothing I have to tell you, Mr. Ronsen," he said in a carefully polite voice. "Except to reassure you that the studio is in capable hands. As to its operation, that is Mark Kessler's responsibility, not mine, and I feel that he knows what he is doing."

The smile was still on Ronsen's face, but he sat there quietly for a moment. Then he seemed to stir himself as a thought came to him. "Perhaps in that case the fault does not lie with the studio. Maybe it properly belongs elsewhere."

The pretense stripped from Johnny's voice. "Just what are you implying, Mr. Ronsen?" he asked.

"Larry," Ronsen suggested, with the smile on his lips.

"Larry," Johnny agreed. "But that's still not an answer to my question."

Ronsen looked at him. Edge knew more about this company than any other man alive with the exception of Kessler himself. He could be damn useful if he could be persuaded to come over to his side. "Perhaps the responsibility rests with Mr. Kessler." He studied Johnny's face intently.

Johnny's face was calm, controlled. It revealed no expression. "What makes you think that, Larry?" he asked.

Ronsen sank back comfortably into his seat. "The man is getting old, you know. I believe he's over sixty. He may be subject to some slight degree of senility. Who can tell?"

Johnny laughed aloud. "That's ridiculous, Larry. You don't know the man the way I do. All right, I admit he's no youngster, but he has a greater capacity for work and a better comprehension of the business than many a younger man could possibly have."

"Than you, for example?" Ronsen prompted cagily.

Johnny smiled slowly. "He's the president, isn't he? He owns the company."

Ronsen thought of correcting the latter statement, but he decided to let it pass. "Don't you think you could do just as well if you were president, Johnny?"

"I doubt it," Johnny said flatly. His voice was cold.

Ronsen laughed. "Come now, Johnny," he said, still chuckling, "don't be so modest."

Johnny looked at him. What in hell did this guy want? Surely he hadn't come here to compliment him. "It's not modesty that compels my answer, Larry," he said slowly. "I've been associated with Peter Kessler almost thirty years now and I don't know of a more capable executive in the industry."

Ronsen clapped his hands together silently. "Bravo!" he applauded in a low voice. "Such loyalty is indeed commendable."

"Not to me, Larry," Johnny answered quickly, "but to the

man who inspires it. Loyalty is the most precious thing in life. It's one thing money can't buy."

Ronsen disagreed with the latter statement too, but again he did not pursue the point. He sat there in the chair regarding Johnny silently.

Johnny looked back at him. If Ronsen wanted to play charades, he could play the game as well. He didn't speak.

Ronsen leaned forward in his chair again. An acquisitive note crept into his voice. "I would like to speak to you, in confidence if I may, Johnny."

Johnny's voice betrayed no curiosity. "If you like," he said calmly.

Ronsen hesitated a moment. "A group of people have indicated to me that they would be interested in purchasing Mr. Kessler's interest in the company."

Johnny raised an eyebrow. So that was it. He should have guessed. "Who were they?" he asked.

Ronsen looked into his eyes. "I'm not at liberty to disclose their names, but they have indicated to me that you would make a most acceptable president to them if such an arrangement could be worked out."

Johnny looked at him and smiled. The man really wasn't foolish enough to think he could be bribed as easily as that, was he? "I'm very much flattered at their generosity, but the decision to sell the company rests with Mr. Kessler, doesn't it?"

"You could be of great help in securing Mr. Kessler's approval," Ronsen said.

Johnny leaned back in his chair. It was a good thing that they didn't know just how matters stood between Peter and himself. "I wouldn't presume even to try to influence Mr. Kessler as to the propriety of such a matter. Mr. Kessler has his own ideas on that subject."

Ronsen laughed again. "And they are ridiculous in this modern day and age, aren't they?"

"Again it's Mr. Kessler's personal opinion and he has his own reasons for the attitude. I make no attempt to judge matters with which I have no concern."

Ronsen looked at him inquisitively. "What do you suggest, then, Johnny?"

Johnny looked at him for a moment. The man was either an idiot or a complete fool if he thought he would commit him self one way or the other. "I suggest you speak to Mr. Kessler about it directly, Larry," he answered. "He would be the only person to give you an answer to that question."

"These people would be willing to give Mr. Kessler a good price for his interest, considering the present condition of the business," Ronsen said.

Johnny stood up to indicate the interview was over. "That's up to Mr. Kessler, Larry."

Ronsen got to his feet slowly. He resented being dismissed summarily in this manner, but none of the resentment showed in his voice. "Maybe I'll speak to him when I get back from the coast, Johnny. He might be willing to listen to reason then."

Johnny looked at him. There was a note of confidence in Ronsen's voice that he recognized. It was the voice of a man who was used to power and knew that he had it. "Who else besides you and Danvere are behind this business, Larry?" he asked suddenly.

Ronsen's head came up sharply. He smiled at Johnny. "I'm not allowed to say at the moment, Johnny. I believe I mentioned it before."

Johnny eyed him speculatively. "It isn't Floyd or Randolph," he probed in a gentle voice. "They're just figureheads, they don't count." He looked at Ronsen's face. It told him nothing. "It could be Berard Powell over at Borden's," Johnny guessed. "It sounds like the sort of thing he would be mixed up in."

The look on Ronsen's face told him that his guess had gone home. He smiled inwardly and walked around the desk to Ronsen and held out his hand. "I won't plague you with any more guesses, Larry," he said as they shook hands. "I'm glad you dropped in, however. I did want to know you better."

Ronsen smiled. "I felt the same way about you, Johnny."

Johnny walked out of the office and down the hall with him. "Have a nice trip, Larry," he said, smiling as they parted.

He didn't notice Peter standing in the door of his office wide-eyed and staring at them. Peter closed the door silently and walked back to his desk. What was Johnny doing with that guy? And acting so friendly too. As if they were the best of friends.

He put his hands behind him and clasped them together. He rocked gently back and forth on his toes, thinking. He didn't want to believe it, but maybe Mark was right. Johnny had been acting strangely lately.

10

DULCIE listened to Mark's voice absently. She was beginning to be bored with him. It was time for her to cut him loose. There was nothing more she could get from him.

It had been like that ever since Warren had left her. She had been restless and moved frenetically from one man to another, always seeking one who would hold her attention as he had. But she hadn't found him. Sooner or later they would give in to her and come crawling for her favors and then she would be tired of them.

It hadn't been that way with Warren. He was too much like her to ever give in. There had always been a challenge about him that had continually intrigued her. He had a faculty for making her seem alive. She was aware of every nerve in her body when he was near, her mind would race with excitement.

But he had gone back to his wife, Cynthia. She sneered to herself. That pale imitation of a woman. What was there about her that could hold a man like Warren? But she had held him. And now there were two children. She supposed it had all started that night that Johnny had come home and found her with Warren.

After Johnny had gone, she had turned and walked back into the bedroom. He was dressing hurriedly. She put an arm on him. "What are you doing?" she had asked.

He had looked at her. "Going after him," he had answered nervously. "That man is sick. He shouldn't be out in weather like this."

"Don't be a fool," she had said. "Let him go. He'll only kill you if you come near him. You saw what he tried to do to me."

He was buttoning his shirt. He looked at her strangely.

"What did you expect him to do? Applaud our performance?" He snapped the last button into place viciously. "That was a hell of a thing for him to come home and find," he added bitterly.

She pressed herself against him and put her arms behind him. She looked up into his face. "Don't look now," she said with a peculiarly irritating look on her face, "but your morals are showing."

He looked down at her. "The man is sick," he said. "Anyone with half an eye could see it."

She still was looking up into his face. "So what?" she asked in that same unemotional voice. "He has somewhere to go."

He looked into her eyes. They were wide and the pupils were black and dilated and he could see his own face in their shadowed depths. His hand suddenly grasped her hair, pulling her head back. A look of pain came into her face, but there was no fear in her eyes. She looked at him confidently as her body clung to his.

For a moment they had stood there like that and then the words seemed to be torn from his lips. "Dulcie, you're a bitch!" he said savagely.

A strange look of passion had come into her face. Her lips parted a little and he could see the white teeth behind them. "So I'm a bitch," she half whispered quietly as her arms pressed him closer to her. "But come back to bed. We have some unfinished business to attend to!"

Things hadn't been the same afterward. Then one day she had come into the apartment to find his things gone and a note on the table. It had been brief and to the point:

Dulcie—I have gone back to Cynthia. Warren.

She had even cried a little and sworn vengeance on him. But it was over and that was all there was to it. And ever since she had been alone. No matter what man she would go with, there was not one who could capture her, mind and body, as had Warren Craig.

She looked at Mark quietly. What a bore he was with his constant whining and slobbering over her! At first it had been fun to tease him. She could see how excited he would get and used to laugh to herself at him. Then when he was a little drunk he would lisp like a child. Sometimes she wondered herself how he could stand her teasing, why he hadn't seized her before this. She supposed he didn't have the nerve. She smiled again to herself. And he thought he was a man of the world. He had lived in Europe, in Paris, in Vienna, where men were supposed to know how to handle women like her. Suddenly she thought of going to Europe herself. She could imagine being the center of attraction wherever she went. Her pictures were very popular there.

She looked up at him suddenly, her attention focusing. What was that he was saying? She listened to him. He was talking about some man the board of directors had sent out to investigate the studio and how Mark was pulling the wool over his eyes and he couldn't get anywhere. It was really funny to see him prying around, not knowing where to look first.

"What did you say this man's name was?" she asked curiously.

He looked down at her. "Ronsen," he said proudly. "He's supposed to be a pretty sharp article, too, but I handle him like taking candy from a baby."

She was interested. "What's behind it?" she asked.

He shrugged his shoulders. "Some guys are trying to upset the applecart for the old man, I guess. But they don't have a chance."

She looked at him and smiled slowly. "Tell me more," she said. She wanted to know all about it. Maybe there was something she could do about evening the odds.

Ronsen sat on the edge of his seat uncomfortably. His eyes kept turning to the cleft of her bosom as it showed beneath the décolletage of her dress and then guiltily away.

She leaned forward and picked up the Silex. "Some more coffee, Mr. Ronsen?" she asked sweetly. She had already classified him in her mind. A money man. Very dull. Probably a wife and four children in a very proper home back East.

His face looked away from her. "No, thank you, Miss Warren," he said politely. He cleared his throat. "About that business we spoke over the phone—uh."

She put the Silex down and interrupted him. "Yes, Mr. Ronsen," she said, leaning back against her chair. "About that business. If I understand correctly you came out here to investigate the situation at the Magnum studios?"

He nodded his head uncomfortably. This was a peculiar way to get information. But this was Hollywood, not Wall Street. They did things a little differently out here. And this woman—she made him nervous, she was so—so—his mind groped for the correct word. He suddenly found it. So flagrantly sexual. Or was the word "fragrantly"? A flush began to creep up into his face.

"Perhaps I could help you," she suggested.

"I would be most grateful, Miss Warren," he said stiffly.

Slowly and in detail she told him about what Mark Kessler had done. As her soft voice spoke on he could feel an excitement growing in him and he could barely keep from interrupting her. At several points he did in spite of himself.

"You mean to say that the work reports were issued showing improper allocation of funds between pictures and this was done deliberately?" he asked at one time.

She had nodded. "Yes. This had gone on until Johnny Edge came out to the studio and found out about it. He put a stop to it."

"But how did he succeed in replacing the money that had been already spent on the picture improperly?" Ronsen asked.

She looked at him. "It was really very simple." Mark had told her just what Johnny had done. "He borrowed money from the Bank of Independence on his stock in Magnum. Then he bought a half interest in the picture from Magnum and the money was replaced."

"For how long a term was the loan?" he asked excitedly. The breaks were beginning to come his way at last. Maybe things would be easier than he thought.

Her brows wrinkled together in concentration. "For three months, if I remember rightly. It was while Kessler was still in Europe."

"The note should be due about now," he said reflectively.

"About this time," she agreed.

"I wonder if he has the money to cover it?" he speculated aloud.

She smiled at him. "I don't think he has," she said quietly. "He was depending on the money from the picture to cover the note, and the picture is only just about finished now."

A broad smile came to his face. He leaned back in his chair and took off his glasses and wiped them with a handkerchief quickly. Then he put them back on and looked at her. "Extraordinary," he said for a lack of other words to describe his emotions.

"I think it's a most interesting little story, Mr. Ronsen," she asked, looking directly into his eyes, "don't you?"

He blinked his eyes rapidly several times. "Most interesting," he said. He leaned back in his chair and smiled at her.

She was smiling back at him. They understood each other.

11

THE phone on Johnny's desk began to ring urgently. He picked it up. Jane's voice came crackling through it. "Vittorio Guido is on the phone, Johnny," she said.

Johnny hesitated a moment. What did Vic want? The note wasn't due for another week. He shrugged his shoulders. Might as well ask for an extension now as then. He wouldn't have the money anyway until the picture came out and that didn't look like a possibility for another month and a half. "Okay, put him on," he said.

He heard the phone clicking, then Vic's heavy voice. For a change Vic's voice was hearty, almost human. "Hello, Johnny?"

"Hello, Vic," he replied. "How are you?"

"Never better," Vic replied. "And you?"

"Okay," Johnny answered. He waited for Vic to come to the point. Suddenly he started. A thought had just come to him. Al. Had something happened to Al? He began to speak again, but Vic's voice cut him off.

"I just called to remind you about your note, Johnny," he said. "It's due next week, you know."

Johnny sank back into his seat. He didn't know whether to be happy or sorry. He felt a wave of relief sweep over him that there hadn't been anything the matter with Al. "I know, Vic," he answered quietly. "I was going to call you on it."

There was a strange change in Vic's voice. A note of anxiety seemed to creep into it. "You have the money to meet it?" he asked.

"No, Vic," Johnny answered. "That's what I wanted to talk to you about. I'd like an extension."

The anxiety seemed to leave Vic's voice and again it was genial and hearty. "I'm sorry, Johnny, but I can't," he said carefully. "We ran into a rough situation out here lately and the board won't approve my extensions without additional collateral being offered."

"Holy Christ!" Johnny exploded. "How much collateral do they want anyhow? Isn't one hundred and thirty-three per cent good enough for them?"

"I don't make the rules, Johnny," Vic protested mildly. "You know that."

"But, Vic, I can't afford to lose that stock," Johnny protested. "It's more important than ever now!"

"Maybe you can raise the money somewhere else to cover it," Vic suggested.

"That's impossible," Johnny said. "I haven't any place to turn for dough like that."

"Well, try anyway," Vic told him. "I'd hate like hell to sell that stock out from under you. Though of course you won't lose anything by it. If we get anything over the excess of the loan, we just deduct the interest and credit the rest to your account."

"That's not the idea," Johnny said. "I don't care about the money, that's not the important thing. I need the stock."

Vic's voice was hesitant but strong. There was a sound in it that seemed to give it a double meaning. "I'll see what I can do for you, Johnny," Vic said. "Keep in touch with me if anything breaks."

"Yeanh, Vic," Johnny said dryly.

"So long, Johnny," Vic said. His voice was cheerful.

"So long, Vic." Johnny stared at the dead phone in his hand. Vic would see what he could do for him all right. He knew just where he stood with that guy. For a moment he thought of calling Al at the ranch. Then something inside him rebelled at the thought. He couldn't be running to Al all his life every time he was in trouble. He was old enough to stand on his own feet. He put the phone down. Maybe everything would turn out all right anyway. Mark had said that Ronsen hadn't picked up anything out at the studio. He hoped Mark was right for once. But deep inside him he knew he was wishing with one hand and reaching for the moon with the other.

Vic put down the phone and smiled across his desk at his visitor. "It looks as if you will get that stock, Mr. Ronsen," he said slowly.

Ronsen smiled. "I'm glad, Mr. Guido." He looked right across the desk at Vic. "I must admit that it will be a great relief to me personally when Magnum is once again operating in the manner it should. I can't stand seeing a business being operated in such a slipshod way."

Vic looked at him. "I agree with you perfectly, Mr. Ronsen," he said. "I feel very much the same way about it. If it hadn't been for Mr. Santos they wouldn't have one cent in loans from us."

"You can rest assured, Mr. Guido," Ronsen said, getting to his feet, "that under proper auspices Magnum will again be in a position to discharge its obligations to you. I will see to that myself."

Vic lumbered from his chair. "I will be in touch with you next week, then," he said.

Ronsen nodded. "That's right. Next week."

Vic walked to the door with him. Maybe now Al would believe him when he said that Johnny wasn't such pumpkins.

Johnny stared up into the night. He couldn't sleep. His talk with Vic had disturbed him more than he had realized. He sat up in bed and switched on the light. He looked at the phone.

The call went through quickly. In a few seconds Doris's voice was answering. "Johnny!" she exclaimed. "I'm so glad you called!"

He smiled at the happy note in her voice. "I had to cry on somebody's shoulder, sweetheart, and I figured it might as well be yours," he said wryly.

A note of concern leaped into her voice. "Why, darling, what's wrong?"

He told of his conversation with Vic.

"Does that mean he will sell the stock away from you?" she asked.

"That's just what it means, sweetheart," he replied.

"Why, that's wicked!" she cried. "If he'll only wait, he'll get his filthy money back!"

"I think Vic knows that as well as we do," Johnny said, his voice bitter. "But he just wants to make things as tough for me as he possibly can."

"The beast!" she exclaimed. "I have a good mind to call him up and tell him off!"

He almost laughed at the fierce note that seemed to leap into her voice. Unaccountably he began to feel better. There was no real reason for him to do so, nothing had changed. She seemed to be very close to him suddenly, almost as if she were in the room with him. "You'd better not, sweetheart," he said to her. "It wouldn't help anyway. All we can do is wait and see what happens."

"Johnny, I'm sorry." Her voice sounded perilously close to tears.

Now he was reassuring her. "Don't worry about it, sugar," he said consolingly. "It's not your fault."

"But, Johnny," she wailed unhappily, "everything's going wrong. Papa's mad at you. Vic won't give you back the stock. The business is in trouble." She sniffed into the phone.

"Don't cry, sweetheart," he said consolingly. "Everything will turn out all right."

She was silent for a moment. "Do you really think so, Johnny?" she asked in a small, doubtful voice.

"Sure I do," he lied magnificently. His voice rang with assurance he did not feel.

Her voice perked up. "Then as soon as Papa gets over being mad at you," she said, "we can get married!"

He smiled into the phone. "Sooner if you like, sweetheart," he replied.

The telegram lay on his desk when he got back from lunch. He picked it up and tore it open. He sank into a chair as he read it. A chill seemed to be running through him. It was over. Vic had sold him out. He clenched his fist suddenly. The bastard! He didn't believe he would do it. But he did, damn him!

He read the telegram again:

DEAR JOHNNY, REGRET NECESSITY FOR DOING SO BUT HAVE
SOLD COLLATERAL TODAY FOR ONE MILLION DOLLARS PLUS
ACCRUED INTEREST ON YOUR NOTE. BALANCE OF TWO
HUNDRED AND FIFTY THOUSAND PLACED TO YOUR AC-
COUNT. AWAIT YOUR ORDERS AS TO DISPOSITION OF SAME.
REGARDS, VIC.

He crumpled the telegram angrily in his fist and threw
it into the basket under his desk. Await his orders as to
disposition. He knew what he would tell him to do with
it if he could. He could take the God-damn dough and
shove it. One dollar at a time.

Mark came into the room just as Doris folded the letter.
He looked down at her, smiling. "From the boy friend?"
he asked pleasantly.

She looked up as if she was seeing him for the first time.
"Yes," she answered in a dull voice.

"What's he got to say?" he asked curiously.

She looked away from him. "Vic Guido sold him out
yesterday," she said in the same toneless voice.

"He did?" Mark's voice was filled with surprise.

She nodded her head.

"That's too bad," he said aloud. Inside him there was an
elation.

Suddenly Doris was staring at him. Her voice was almost
a whisper. "It's your fault!" she said accusingly.

Mark looked back at her. "I didn't ask him to do it," he
protested defensively.

She moved quickly, impulsively. Her open palm made a
cracking sound as it came in contact with his face.

His hand flew to his cheek instinctively. Her slap hadn't
hurt, but he could feel his face tingling with shame. He
looked at her.

She stared back at him. The tears were rushing to her
eyes. "That's for Johnny," she said fiercely. Her voice began
to falter. "He's lost everything he ever had because of you!
You—you louse!" She turned from him and fled from the
room, a handkerchief pressed close to her eyes.

12

PETER's face was drawn and tired as he stood by the window looking down into the Plaza. The big Christmas tree was up and glittering with a thousand lights. The ice in the rink had turned a creamy ivory color in the light from the tree, and the few skaters that were on it moved lazily and gracefully. It was almost six o'clock and crowds of people were hurrying homeward.

Another million dollars had gone into the company from Peter's pocket when Danvere had refused to advance him the money. He had to do it. Cash had run perilously low.

Wearily he walked back to his desk and looked down at the teletype message that lay on it. The final version of *United We Stand* was at last ready for screening. They were going to sneak preview it at a small theater in the suburbs of Los Angeles tomorrow.

He sat down in his chair and closed his eyes. He wished he were home. It was almost six months since he had been home, but business had kept him in New York. There was so much to do. Thank God at least that he didn't have to worry about the studio. Mark was a good boy. You could depend on your own flesh and blood where you couldn't on anyone else.

He straightened up in his chair and looked out the window. If it only hadn't been such a rotten winter he would have had Esther join him in New York. It wouldn't seem so bad then. But he couldn't ask her to do it. Her arthritis would have made her miserable.

The door opened and a man stood there smiling. "Mr. Kessler?" he asked, a curious look on his face.

Peter looked at him. He didn't know him. How did he get there without going through his secretary's office? That was his private door. Usually no one entered by it except himself. "Yes," he answered in a tired voice.

The man came into the office and walked toward him. He took a piece of paper from his inside coat pocket and laid it on the desk in front of Peter. A smile flashed across his face and was gone in a moment. "Merry Christmas," he said and, turning, hurried back out the door and closed it behind him.

Peter leaned forward slowly and picked up the paper. He looked after the man. What was the matter with him? He acted as if he were crazy. Peter looked down at the paper in his hand. There was a word printed across the back of it in big black letters: SUMMONS.

The meaning of the word did not penetrate his tired mind at once. He opened it dully and began to read. Suddenly he came to life. His face grew flushed and excited and he sprang from his chair and ran to the door and opened it. He looked out, but the man was nowhere in sight. The hall was empty.

He closed the door and crossed his office into Johnny's. Johnny was dictating a letter to Jane and they looked up at him startled as the door opened. Peter hadn't come in that way in a long time.

Peter's face was almost purple as he angrily stamped his way to Johnny's desk and flung the paper down on it. "Read that," he said in a strangled choking voice, "and see what your friends have done!"

The city outside the window behind Peter was ablaze with electric light. The lawyer sat opposite him and slowly tapped the folded paper with his fingers. He looked at Peter solemnly.

"As I see it, Peter," he said slowly, "the gist of their whole case is this one picture, *United We Stand*. There are other charges—incompetence, peculation, mismanagement—but they are vague and difficult to substantiate. If this picture turns out to be good they have no real case, because then it becomes a matter of judgment, yours against theirs. If the picture is not, then it's another matter, a more difficult case. Then you have to fight it in the stockholders' meetings. There are many things you can do there to delay and protract matters almost indefinitely. That is, as long as you control enough votes to give you a majority."

Peter nodded his head. "I got enough votes to do that," he

said confidently. Between him and Johnny they had fifty-five per cent of the stock.

"Then the only thing we have to worry about is the picture," the lawyer replied. He looked at Peter. "Is it any good?" he asked.

"I don't know," Peter admitted honestly. "I ain't seen it yet."

"It would be a help if we did know," the lawyer said reflectively. "Then we would know just where we stand."

Peter looked at him. "We should know the day after tomorrow. We're sneaking it out in Los Angeles." He paused, struck by a sudden thought. "I'll fly out there and see it myself. We'll know for sure that way."

"That might be a good idea," the lawyer agreed. He looked at his watch. "You'll be on the plane all night."

"So I'll be on the plane all night," Peter said quickly. "But at least this way I'll be ready for the besteds at the next board meeting."

"When is that?" the lawyer asked.

"Next week," Peter replied. "Wednesday." There wouldn't be time to let Esther know he was on his way home, but it didn't make much difference anyway. He would be there late in the afternoon.

Dulcie's voice was merry on the phone. "Of course I'm coming to the preview, Mark." She laughed. "I wouldn't miss it for anything!"

He smiled into the phone. "I'll pick you up at six thirty?" he asked.

"Yes," she answered. "We'll have dinner at my place and then go right to the show."

"That's fine," he said, still smiling, "just fine." He hung up the phone and wheeled around in his chair, whistling. Maybe now that the picture was finished she would listen to reason.

13

PETER burst into the house just as they were sitting down to dinner. He stood there in the entrance to the dining-room, his face flushed with the exertion of running up the steps to the house. He had landed in Los Angeles less than an hour ago.

Esther rose from the table quickly with a welcoming cry. In a moment she was in his arms. She kissed him. "Peter, you're home! I can't believe it!"

A suspicious moisture came to his eyes as he looked down at her. Her head was against his breast; her hair was still rich and darkly lustrous despite the gray in it. "Nu, Mama," he said gruffly, "you see I'm home."

Doris was on the other side of him. She kissed his cheek. "Hello, Papa," she whispered against his ear. "I had a hunch you'd be home for the holidays."

With his arm still around Esther he walked to the table. It was good to be home. Sometimes he wondered whether the business was worth all it took out of you. Your time was never your own. And he had been away more than six months. He looked around the room. "Where's Mark?" he asked in a puzzled voice.

"He's having dinner out," Doris answered.

He looked at her as if he had not understood her. "Out?" he repeated questioningly.

Esther looked up at him and nodded her head. "He said he had some important business to attend to."

He looked down at her questioningly. Whenever they planned to sneak a picture the whole family would have dinner and then go to the preview together. "Ain't you going to the preview?" he asked.

Esther looked up at him, her face uncomprehending. "What preview?" she asked.

"The preview," he said impatiently. He drew away from her. "The preview of *United We Stand*."

"We didn't know anything about it," Doris interposed. "When are they holding it?"

He turned to her. "Tonight. At eight thirty. At the Rivoli."

"It's news to us," Doris told him.

He looked at Esther. "Sometimes I can't understand that boy," he said in an exasperated voice. "Why didn't he tell you about it? He knows the family goes to previews together."

Esther looked at him. "Maybe he was busy and he forgot." She offered the excuse gently.

"He shouldn't forget," Peter said impatiently.

She took his hand and smiled. "So why get excited over it?" she asked quietly. "You're home and we'll go together and nothing is lost. After all, Papa, the boy has been working very hard. Sometimes he can forget too." She drew him toward the table gently. "So sit down now quietly and eat your dinner. You must be tired from your trip."

Mark was already at the lisping stage. His face was flushed and there were small beads of sweat across his upper lip. His hands waved excitedly in the air. "And after the picture, we'll go out and thelebrate. We'll do the whole town. Then everybody will know who I am."

Dulcie looked at him with an amused smile. Hollywood already knew what he was. They had an instinct that told them who was going to be successful out there and who was not. Success acted as a magnet that drew people. You could always tell how successful a person would be by the people with whom he was close. If you were a real success, the biggest people in Hollywood were your friends. If you weren't, you drew a crowd of spongers and opportunists who were only trying to promote themselves at your expense. All Mark's friends were of the latter class. She didn't know of anyone who had any real respect for him. Behind his back they continually snickered and tore him apart.

It wasn't that she really wanted to see the picture. She knew it would be bad. The word had already seeped through town. But she did want to see how bad it was. She couldn't let this last moment of triumph escape her. Then when she came home she would get rid of him. This time for good.

She looked at her watch. "It's getting late, Mark," she said. "We'd better be leaving."

He looked at her owlishly. "There'th lots of time," he replied.

She smiled at him. "Come now," she murmured. "You wouldn't want to be late to a preview of your own picture, would you?"

He looked at her seriously. "That's right," he nodded sagely. "It wouldn't look good, would it?"

Hollywood sneak previews were conducted with all the privacy of a circus. The original idea was to slip the picture, unannounced, into some small local theater in order to get the reaction of a typical audience to it. Postcards were then distributed to the audience on the back of which they were invited to write their opinion of the picture they had just seen. These cards were addressed to the studio that made the picture, and in that manner the producer was supposed to learn whether his picture was good or not.

In time, however, the element of surprising the audience with the picture had been lost. Almost mysteriously when a sneak was planned the word would get around that such and such a picture was going to be shown at the Blank Theater that night and a crowd would form a line outside it. The attraction was twofold. One was to be able to say snidely to your neighbor: "Oh, that picture? We saw it at a preview before it came out. It's not so much." The other attraction was that very often the preview would be attended by the important members of the cast, and the crowd would gather to look at the celebrities.

The lobby of the theater was crowded when Peter got there with Esther and Doris. The studio publicity man standing at the door near the ticket-taker recognized him. "Hello, Mr. Kessler," he said deferentially. "The picture's just going on now. I'll find you some seats."

They followed him into the theater and down the aisle. The theater was dark and their eyes could make out the shapes of people sitting expectantly in their seats only vaguely. In the center of the theater several aisles had been roped off for the studio representatives. Quietly they moved into the last row of the section.

Peter sat down and looked around him. His eyes were

rapidly getting used to the dark and he recognized several people there. An atmosphere of tension hung over this section that was evident nowhere else in the theater. These were the people who would rise or fall by the picture on the screen. He felt the sweat break out on his forehead. It wasn't that the theater was warm, he always felt like that at a preview.

His hand reached out for Esther. When he found her hand, his own was already moist. She smiled to him in the dark. "Nervous?" she whispered.

He nodded to her. "More than for my own pictures," he whispered back.

She shook her head understandingly. She knew how he felt, how important it was to him. Besides, it was their son who had made it. In some ways they were more anxious for him than they were for themselves.

Peter looked around for Mark. He heard his voice directly in front of him. Mark was talking to a girl in the seat next to him. There was a vaguely familiar look about her profile as she turned to answer Mark, but in the dark Peter couldn't recognize her. He was just leaning forward to tap Mark on the shoulder and let him know he was there when the sound of the Magnum theme music hit his ears. He leaned back in his seat and smiled to himself. He would surprise Mark after the picture was over. He looked up at the screen expectantly.

There was a dark blue light on the screen. In the lower right-hand corner there was a glowing green bottle with a small gold label on it. Swiftly the bottle moved toward the center of the screen, looming larger and larger, until the red-lettered words on the label could be read: "A MAGNUM PICTURE."

Suddenly there was a sharp popping sound and the cork flew from the bottle. The golden sparkling liquid came gushing from its neck. A man's hand reached from out of nowhere and picked the bottle up. A woman's hand holding a crystal-clear goblet moved toward it. Slowly the bottle tilted and the liquid poured into the goblet, overflowing the rim. The bottle and the glass began to recede to the back of the screen, and words began to appear, superimposed over the scene in majestic gothic lettering.

Mark G. Kessler, Vice-president in Charge of Production
Presents

UNITED WE STAND

Peter turned to Esther excitedly. "What's this Mark G. business?" he whispered. "What does this 'G.' mean?"

She looked at him bewildered for a moment. Then a light of comprehension came into her eyes. "It must be for Greenberg," she guessed, "my maiden name."

A hand tapped him on the shoulder. He turned around. A voice from the seat behind him whispered fiercely: "Just because you people got in for free, you don't have to make so much noise!"

"Pardon me," he apologized, and turned his face back to the screen. The man was right. He had no business antagonizing the paying customers.

Something inside Peter turned sick as the picture wore on. Within a few minutes he knew it was a stinker. He didn't have to look at the screen to know that. He could tell from the comments in the audience behind him, from the sounds of restless shifting and the coughs that rang out desultorily, from the laughter in the wrong places. A misery seemed to sweep over him and he shrank back into his seat, growing smaller and smaller.

For the first time it all became clear to him. The whole thing. You had to see someone else make the same mistakes you so confidently made all along, thinking you were right, before you could tell how wrong you had been. That was the way it was with Peter. When he saw Mark's picture on the screen he first began to see his own mistakes. It was then perhaps that a sense of failure came over him. It was then that he realized that the business had outgrown him, that he never had really understood the use of sound in his pictures.

He looked up at the screen. Johnny was right all along about Gordon. He should have listened to him. He looked at Esther; her eyes were miserable. He looked back at the screen. He felt an anger sweep through him. Even if he had been right about Gordon, Johnny should never have insisted on pushing this picture through.

In front of him Mark's head bent toward the girl. He

could see him whispering something to her. He could hear her quiet laugh. There was such a familiar ring about it. Suddenly he wanted to hear what Mark was saying. He leaned forward in his seat, hunching himself behind them.

He could hear Mark's voice whispering to the girl. Suddenly he seemed to freeze to his seat. What was it that Mark was saying? He was joking about how he had put it over on everybody. The old man was even blaming Johnny for it. Was he smart, baby, or was he smart? The girl laughed with him and slipped her arm through his; she seemed to be pleased at what he was saying.

Peter shrank back into his seat. He was trembling. He couldn't tell what the rest of the picture was about. He didn't see it. His eyes had filled with burning, blinding tears. Time lost all its meaning for him. His own son. His own flesh and blood. If they could do this to him, who in the world was there that a man could trust?

The picture was over. He sat there in his seat, his eyes closed tightly together, as the house lights came on. Slowly he opened them.

Mark was getting out of his seat. He was helping the girl on with her wrap. Dully Peter watched him move toward the aisle, where he was surrounded immediately by people. He saw the girl's face turn to him and his eyes widened in shocked surprise.

Dulcie Warren! What was Mark doing with her? He knew what his father thought of her. While he was watching them he saw her kiss Mark's cheek lightly; then the people were all around them and he couldn't see what they were doing.

"It's too good a picture for the masses, they won't appreciate it, Mark," someone was saying consolingly as Peter angrily pushed his way through the crowd around them. Dulcie was leaning on Mark's arm, looking up at him with an amused smile on her face.

"I had been afraid of that," Mark admitted. "The average movie-goer isn't too bright, you know," he added snidely. Then his gaze suddenly fell upon his father.

Peter was standing in front of him, his face almost choleric with rage.

"Peter!" Mark tried to smile. He didn't quite succeed. His face looked almost sickly. "What are you doing here?"

He could feel Dulcie's arm slip quietly from his. "I didn't know you were here!"

For a moment Peter couldn't talk, he was almost speechless. Then his voice burst from him in a shrill scream. "You didn't know I would be here!" he mimicked. His voice grew even louder. "Well, I was. I sat behind you through the whole rotten picture and heard everything you said to that—to that—" He looked at Dulcie, standing next to Mark. His mind searched frantically for a word to describe her. "To that cheap *courveh!* Every word you said I heard!"

Mark looked around him anxiously. There was a look of eager expectancy on the faces about him. Already other people were being attracted by the commotion. They were beginning to look at them with a morbid relish. "Papa!" he said through white lips, his hands indicating the people.

But Peter was too angry to pay any attention to his imploring glances. "What's the metter, Marcus?" he asked, slipping unconsciously into his accent. "You ashamed the pipple should know what you done? You made a picture too good for the masses?" He drew himself up as high as he could and shook an excited finger under his son's nose. "Vel, let me tell you somet'ing! The only time a picture is too good for the masses is ven it's a stinker like the vun you just made!"

A titter of appreciative laughter went up from the people around them. Mark could feel his face turn a brick-red. He wished the floor would open up and swallow him. He turned to look helplessly at Dulcie, but she was already gone. She was walking swiftly up the aisle away from him. He turned back to his father miserably. "But, Papa—" he said, his voice perilously close to tears.

"Vot are you looking for, Marcus?" his father asked him, still shouting. "Your hooer? Maybe you vant to go vit her?"

Mark looked down at the floor. He didn't answer.

"Vel, vot are you vaiting for?" Peter roared. "Go after her! Go!" His arm pointed after her dramatically. "You already done all the damage you could do here! The business already you cost me! In the same gutter vit her you belong!" His voice broke suddenly as Esther came up to him through the crowd.

Mark looked up at his parents. His mother's eyes were filled with tears, she was turning Peter away from him. He took a step toward her. She shook her head gently over Peter's shoulders and nodded toward the exit. Mark started up the aisle.

His father turned and shouted after him: "And don't come back neither, you—you bloodsucker, you!"

Mark stumbled blindly toward the exit. He heard someone laugh and say maliciously: "That was a better show than the picture. It was worth the price of admission alone. I'm telling you all the picture people are like that. They're no good, none of them!"

An anger began to rise in him. His throat was dry and parched. Tomorrow all Hollywood would be talking about him and laughing at him. He yanked open the door of his car viciously. He climbed into it and put his head on his arms across the steering wheel. He began to cry.

Peter and Esther sat in the back of the car, Doris sat in the front seat driving. Her father's head lay wearily against the back of the seat and he was talking in a low voice. She couldn't hear what he was saying.

His face turned slowly to Esther. His voice was close against her ear. It was dull and empty of feeling. All his strength seemed to have left him. "The only chance we got now," he was saying weakly, "is the stock. If Johnny votes with me, maybe things will be all right."

Esther shushed him. "Rest," she said gently, pulling his head down to her shoulder. "Don't worry. On Johnny you can depend." But all the time her heart kept crying out to her son: "Mark, Mark, you were such a sweet little baby. How could you do this to your father?"

14

"Aren't you going to take me home?" Dulcie's voice came calmly from the back seat. When she had left the theater he couldn't find a cab, so she had climbed into Mark's car to get out of the sight of the gaping crowds.

He raised his head from his arms slowly. He turned around and looked at her. Her cigarette glowed brightly in the darkness as she drew on it. Its light revealed her eyes; they were dark and imperturbable.

They drove home in silence. Occasionally he looked at her out of the corner of his eyes. There was no expression on her face at all. To look at her you would think nothing had happened to upset her. Yet he knew she was upset. He could tell from the way in which she lit one cigarette from another.

She put her key in the lock and turned it. The door opened a little and she turned back to him and looked up at him. "Good night, Mark," she said calmly.

He looked down into her eyes. Anger came over his face. "Is that all you have to say after what happened tonight? 'Good night, Mark'?" His voice was hoarse.

She shrugged her shoulders quietly. "What else is there to say?" she asked in that same calm, infuriating manner. She stepped inside the door. "It's over and done with." She began to close the door.

His foot stopped it. He glared at her angrily.

She looked up at him, still calm, still sure of herself. "I'm tired, Mark. Let me go to sleep."

He didn't answer. For a moment he stood there quietly, then he put an arm on her shoulder and pushed her into the room ahead of him and closed the door.

Her eyes were wide and unafraid. "What are you doing, Mark?" she asked quickly. "Why don't you go home? It's been a pretty rough day for all of us."

He went to a cabinet and took a bottle of whisky from it. He opened it and drank right from the bottle. He could feel the hot liquor burning its way down his throat. He turned back to her. "You heard what my father said?" he asked hoarsely.

"He'll get over it by morning," she answered quietly. She came toward him. "Now will you go home?"

His hands reached out and seized her roughly. He pulled her to him and kissed her, his mouth bruising hers.

She twisted in his grasp, trying to get loose. "Mark"— her voice was beginning to show signs of fright—"you don't know what you're doing!"

"Don't I?" he asked mockingly, his arms holding her tight. "I should have done this a long time ago!"

She was really frightened now. There was a look of madness on his face that she had never seen before. Her hands flew up and scratched at him, she tried to push him away from her. Suddenly she broke free of him. "Get out!" she screamed at him.

He smiled at her slowly. "You look real pretty when you're angry, Dulcie," he said walking toward her. "But you know that, don't you? Many men must have told you that!" His hand reached out and grabbed her shoulder.

She wrenched herself free of his grip, but he held on to her dress. The flimsy material tore in his hands. He caught her again. Her hands tore at his face, scratched at his eyes. "Let me go! Let me go, you maniac!" she screamed at him.

Suddenly his hand swept across her face. Her head reeled with the shock. He struck her again and she fell to the floor, leaving the rest of her dress in his hands. He bent over her and again his hand struck her.

Her hands flew up to cover her face. "Not my face," she screamed in abject terror. "Not my face!"

His face was very close to hers. He grinned slowly. "What's the matter, Dulcie? Afraid for your looks?"

She felt his hands tearing the rest of her clothing from her. Suddenly she didn't feel them on her any more. She took her hands from her face slowly and looked up at him. There was a trickle of blood running from the corner of her mouth. She could taste its salty flavor against her tongue.

He was taking off his jacket. Dully, almost stupidly, she saw the rest of his clothes come off. Suddenly she was cold. A chill ran through her body. She looked down at herself. There were dark-blue bruises on her white flesh. She began to tremble in her fright.

He knelt over her, grinning crazily. She looked up at him, shivering convulsively, her eyes dilated with fear. He stared into her eyes. His hand went out and hit her face again. Her mind was reeling. She could hardly hear what he was saying.

"Too bad there isn't a gutter handy," he said in a conversational tone of voice. "But the floor will have to do!"

And then he fell on her.

15

THE meeting-room in the Waldorf was already filled with smoke as Johnny looked around the room. Ronsen sat opposite him. There were small beads of sweat standing out on his forehead as he spoke in whispers to Floyd and Randolph.

Johnny looked at his watch. Peter should be here any minute now. His plane had been due at the airport almost an hour ago. He looked across the room at the men.

Ronsen shifted uncomfortably under his gaze. They had not spoken to each other since a brief greeting when Johnny had entered the room a half hour ago. They were waiting for Peter to arrive. Suddenly the room was silent and a subtle tension seemed to creep into the air.

There was the sound of voices outside the door. It opened and their eyes turned to it automatically as Peter came into the room. Esther and Doris were with him.

Johnny looked up in surprise. He had not known that Doris was coming with her father.

Awkwardly the men rose to their feet. They looked at the two women.

Peter's face was tired as he introduced them. Each man murmured an uncomfortable greeting as his name was spoken.

Johnny took advantage of their turned backs to wink at Doris. She smiled back at him.

Peter threw his hat and coat into an empty chair and took his place at the table. Esther sat down beside him, while Doris seated herself in a chair against the wall.

Peter looked around the table. "Are we ready to get down to business?" he asked. He didn't wait for their reply. "As

presiding officer at this meeting, I hereby call it to order."
He picked up a gavel from the table in front of him and
rapped the table with it sharply. The loud noise echoed
through the room.

Johnny picked up his pen, looked at his watch, and wrote
the time in his notebook. When he looked up, Ronsen was
already on his feet. Johnny smiled grimly to himself. They
weren't wasting any time.

"Mr. Chairman," Ronsen spoke to Peter.

Peter nodded his head. "Mr. Ronsen."

Ronsen's eyes were on Peter. He spoke in impersonal terms,
but his words were addressed directly to him. "In view of
the existing conditions at the studio and, in general, throughout the company—matters of great concern to this board
naturally—I was wondering whether the chair would entertain an offer to purchase his stock in the company."

Peter looked at him steadily. His voice was flat and
cold. "No."

Johnny watched him. From the way Peter sounded, he
was angry. Ronsen was in for a hell of a fight. Suddenly he
was very proud of Peter. He remembered a long time ago
when Peter had faced Segale across a desk at the old combine and had told him off. Peter had guts then. Time had
not taken that away from him. His pen scratched busily on
the paper.

Ronsen was still on his feet, looking down at Peter. His
mouth, too, had set into grim, determined lines. "I would
like to point out to the chair that a suit has been filed
against him on behalf of certain stockholders, which, if
brought into court, would prove most embarrassing."

Peter shook his head gently. "In this business we learned
a long time ago not to be embarrassed, Mr. Ronsen. We
have gotten used to the public eye and we are not afraid
of it." He got to his feet slowly and faced Ronsen across
the table. "As long as I represent the controlling interest
in this company, I will not consider selling my stock in it.
I ain't going to be intimidated by nobody. Especially people
who enter into agreements with the sole purpose of breaking them agreements. Those people are no better than
crooks to me."

A strange glitter came into Ronsen's eyes. They loomed
intensely behind his glasses. "In view of the chairman's state-

ment, would he care to let the stockholders pass upon that decision?"

Peter nodded. His eyes were on Ronsen. "The chair is willing."

Ronsen looked around him. There was a faint note of triumph in his voice. "I believe all the stockholders are represented at this meeting. Would the chair be satisfied with an oral vote? A written vote can be taken later if desired."

Peter turned to Johnny as Ronsen sat down. "The motion is whether I should sell my stock or not. Will the secretary call the roll?" He sat down and looked at Johnny expectantly.

Johnny stared at him. His heart began to pound excitedly in his breast. Didn't Peter know he had lost his stock? Hadn't Doris told him? He looked at her. Her hand was clenched before her mouth and she was staring back at him, her eyes wide in her white, frightened face.

He got to his feet. "I don't believe such a decision can be brought before the board at this meeting," he said desperately, trying to stave off the inevitable. His voice was ragged with strain.

Peter looked up at him. "Don't be a *schlemiel*, Johnny. Go ahead and take the vote!"

Johnny still hesitated.

Peter stood up angrily. "All right, then, I'll take it myself."

Johnny's legs were trembling as he sat down. He picked up his pen again, but his hand was shaking so much that he could hardly write.

Peter's voice was firm. "I'll make it snappy, gentlemen," he said. "The chair votes against the motion. That's forty-five per cent of the stock." A note of satisfaction came into his voice. "Now, Johnny," he said, turning toward him.

Johnny looked up at him without answering. He opened his mouth, but no sounds came out. He tried again to speak. He didn't recognize the croaking sounds that came from his lips as his voice. "I—I can't vote, Peter."

Peter stared at him incredulously. "What do you mean you can't vote? Don't be a fool, Johnny! Come on and get this business over with!"

The words seemed torn from Johnny's lips in an agonizing cry. "I haven't got the stock any more!"

Peter's voice was unbelieving. "If you haven't got it, then who has?"

Ronsen was on his feet again. There was a look of cold triumph on his face. "I have it, Mr. Chairman," he said quietly, his voice filled with power.

Johnny's face snapped toward him. He should have guessed it! Ronsen was out there at the time Vic sold the stock. The son of a bitch!

Peter's face turned white. He slumped against the table for a moment, then sank slowly into his seat. His eyes were bitter and accusing on Johnny's face. "You sold me out, Johnny," he said dully. "You sold me out!"

16

HE PRESSED the buzzer. He could hear the chimes ringing behind the door, then the sounds of footsteps approaching it. The door opened and Doris stood there.

He stepped into the foyer and kissed her. Her eyes were wide and looked up at him. "Did you have a chance to talk to Peter yet?" he asked.

She took his hat and led him into the living-room. She shook her head hopelessly. "No." She turned and looked up at him. "He won't let anyone talk to him about you. He won't listen. I told Mamma, but it didn't help. He won't let her talk either. He says he doesn't want to hear any more about either you or Mark."

He sank into a chair and lit a cigarette. "The stubborn old fool! This is a hell of a time for him to get his Dutch up." He looked up at her. "What about us?" he asked.

She looked down at him. "What about us, Johnny?"

"Are we getting married or aren't we?" His voice was savage.

She put a hand on his cheek. "We'll have to wait, Johnny," she said softly. "It would only make him feel worse."

He caught her hand and held it. "I'm getting tired of waiting."

She looked down at him without answering. Her eyes pleaded for his patience.

"What are you doing here?" Peter's voice came roaring at him from the doorway.

Johnny looked at him startled. Peter's eyes were wild in his face. "I came to see if I could knock some sense into your thick Dutch head!"

Peter came toward him. His voice was shrill and shaking. "Get out of my house, you Judas, you!"

Johnny got to his feet. He held his hands placatingly in front of him. "Peter, why don't you listen to reason? You ought to know I would—"

Peter interrupted him. "Don't give me no lying explanations! I know what you done!" He turned to Doris. "Did you ask him to come here?" he asked accusingly.

"She didn't," Johnny answered before she could speak. "It was my idea. We had some things to settle."

Peter turned back to him. "Some things to settle," he sneered. "You trying to turn her against me too? Ain't it enough what you done? Ain't you satisfied?"

"We want to get married," Johnny insisted stubbornly.

Peter looked up at him. "Marry you?" His voice was sharp with amazement. "Doris marry you? You anti-Semite? Sooner I would be she was dead! Gedt oudt before I throw you oudt!"

"Papa"—Doris put her arm on Peter's—"you got to listen to Johnny! He didn't sell you out. He pledged the stock for—"

"Shut up!" Peter shouted at her. "If you go with him, I'm through with you. If you go with him, you turn against your own people, your own flesh and blood! Don't you think I knew that all these years he was jealous of me? Scheming behind my back to steal the company away from me? When I look back and think what a fool I was to trust him, I could cry. He was no better than the others! They hate the Jews! All of them! And he's no better than the rest! Now he's trying to turn you against me too!"

She stared at her father helplessly. Her eyes filled with tears. She turned to Johnny.

His face was a blank stony mask. Slowly, woodenly, he turned from her to her father. "You won't listen," he said bitterly. "And if you did, you wouldn't believe. You're an old man, bitter inside and eaten with your own poisons. But you're not too old to learn some day that you could be wrong!" He picked up his hat and walked slowly to the door. He turned and looked back at Doris.

Esther brushed past him into the room. He didn't even notice her. There were tears in his eyes, burning at his eyelids. His voice shook as he spoke. "Doris, are you coming with me?" There was a note of pleading in it that had never been there before.

She shook her head and moved closer to her father and mother. Her mother reached up and took her hand.

He stood there for a long while, looking at her. At last Peter's voice came savagely to his ears.

"Go!" it was saying savagely. "Go! what are you waiting for? You can see she's not coming. Go back to your friends, your sneaking, underhanded partners! You think you can trust them? Depend on them? You'll find out otherwise. Some day they will get you and throw you out too. When they don't need you any more. Like you did when you decided you didn't need me!"

The tears filled Johnny's eyes, blinding him, but the voice still tore savagely at his ears.

"You were laughing, hah? This simple little hardware man from Rochester you would turn into a picture man? You would make him over and do what you want with him, and when you didn't need him any more, you would get rid of him? I should have known better. I trusted you, but all the time you were laughing at me. Because all the time you made me think it was my business when it was really yours! So you had your fun with the little Jew from Rochester and now it's over. You can be very proud of yourself. You had me fooled all the time. But now it's over and you can go. There's nothing more you can get from me!" Peter's voice broke and he began to cry.

Johnny took several steps toward him. Peter's face looked at him, his voice was suddenly old and broken.

"Why did you do it, Johnny?" he asked quietly. "Why? Why did you wait and do it like this when all the time all you had to do was come to me and say: 'Peter, I don't need you any more. The business has outgrown you.' Don't you think I didn't know it?" He closed his eyes wearily. "If you had come to me yourself, I would have turned the whole business over to you. I didn't need the money or the struggle any more. I had enough of it in my life!"

His voice seemed to grow stronger. It was cold and bitter. "But no! You had to do it your way! With a knife in my back!"

For a long moment they looked into each other's eyes. It seemed almost that they were alone in the room. Johnny searched Peter's eyes for a glimmer of warmth. They were hard and implacable.

He looked at Doris, then at Esther. Their faces were filled with pity for him. "Give him time," they seemed to be saying, "give him time!"

At last he turned and silently walked out the door. He closed it behind him. His heart seemed to turn to lead within him as he walked down the hall to the elevator. He looked back at their door and he could feel the tears flaming behind his eyelids.

The sound of the elevator coming up reached his ears. Grimly his face settled into thin masklike lines. His lips tightened as he put his hat on his head.

The elevator door opened and he stepped into it. Thirty years. Thirty long years. Half a lifetime to reach something like this.

AFTERMATH

1938

idiot or a complete fool if he thought he would cheat him

SUNDAY AND MONDAY

WE LEFT at six thirty in the morning and had breakfast and lunch on the road. It was two o'clock and the bright shining sun was hanging in the sky over our heads as we turned up the narrow dirt road that led to the ranch house. Some men in the fields straightened up to look at us, their faces brown and curious under the broad-brimmed straw hats they wore to keep the sun from their heads. A few minutes later we pulled to a stop in front of the house.

A man came out on the porch to look at us and see who we were. He was a big man with a round face and dark hair. I knew him. Vic Guido.

I got out of the car and walked to the porch. "Hello, Vic," I called to him.

He took a heavy-rimmed pair of glasses from his shirt pocket and put them on and peered at me. "Johnny Edge!" he exclaimed without enthusiasm. "What are you doing out here?"

I walked back to the car and held the door open for Doris to get out as I answered him. "I thought I'd take a run out here and see your boss," I said casually. "Where is he?"

He looked down at us for a moment before he answered. "He's out in the back near the old carnival wagon watching a bocca game," he replied. "Do you want me to show you the way?" he added surlily.

"No, thanks." I smiled up at him. "I know where to find it."

He didn't answer, just turned around and went back into the house silently.

"That man always gives me the creeps." Doris shuddered.

I looked down at her and smiled. "Vic's all right," I said, taking her hand as we started to walk around the house.

"He always acts like that when I'm around. I think it's because he's a little jealous of his boss's liking for me."

We were at the back of the house now and I could hear the sound of excited voices in the air. I looked toward them.

The wagon was about two hundred yards behind the house and stood there incongruously on the flat ranchland. It was painted a bright red, and the yellow words on its side spelled out: SANTOS' CARNIVAL AND SHOWS. There were about twenty men standing in front of it along the sides of the bocca alley.

Bocca was an old Italian game played with hard wooden bowling balls about the size of those used for duckpins. One man would roll a slightly smaller ball toward the other end of the alley and the other men would then try to roll the larger bowling balls as close to it as possible. I couldn't see what there was about the game that made them so excited, but then I never could understand the game anyway.

Al was sitting on the wagon steps, an unlit familiar-looking black stogie sticking out of the corner of his mouth, watching the game as we approached him. His brown wrinkled face broke into a smile as he saw us. He stood up and took the cigar out of his mouth and held his arms out to me. "Johnny," he said. His voice sounded pleased.

Embarrassed by this openly expressed pleasure of his welcome and feeling guilty over my reasons for coming out here I could only stand there and smile at him, holding out my hand. "Hello, Al," I said.

He brushed my hand aside and put his arms around me and hugged me. Then he drew back and looked up into my face. "I'm glad you came out," he said simply. "I was just a sitting here thinking about you."

I could feel my face flush as I answered. I looked quickly around me to see if any of the men were watching us, but they weren't. They were too engrossed in the game. "It was a nice day for a ride," I said lamely.

He turned to Doris and smiled at her. "It's good to see you too, my dear," he said, warmly taking her hand.

She kissed his cheek. "You're looking very well, Uncle Al," she said, returning his smile.

"How is your father?" he asked.

Her smile seemed to grow brighter. "Much better, thanks

she replied. "I think the worst of it is over. All that he needs now is time and rest."

He nodded his head. "That's right. In a littla while he'll be his old self again." He turned back to me. "And you?" he asked, "you're all right?"

I took out a handkerchief and mopped my face. It was hot out here in the field. "I feel good," I assured him.

He looked up at me anxiously. "We'd better go into the wagon," he said solicitously. "This sun is pretty strong to take. Especially if you're not used to it."

He turned and led the way up the steps and opened the door. The sun shone on the faded blue denim of his work shirt and the seat of his dark-blue overalls was shining and gleaming on his narrow shanks. The inside of the wagon was cool and dark and he took a match from his pocket and struck it. He picked up an old oil lamp and held the flame to the wick. It sputtered and caught the flame and then began to glow with a shiny golden color, lighting up the wagon.

I looked around me curiously. It was pretty much as I remembered it. The big roll-top desk was still against the wall. The bunks at the back were all made up. Even the old chair that Al used to sit in reading the paper was there. I smiled at him.

He smiled back at me proudly. "I'm glad I bought it," he said. "Sometimes a man has to have something of his youth around him to remind him of what he really is."

I looked at him curiously. It was a funny thing that he had said, but it was true. He never thought of himself as a banker, only as a carny operator, despite his tremendous success. I looked around me, and the room brought back many memories, but I couldn't feel the way he did. I was not a carny guy; maybe I had never been one. I was of the picture business. His next words surprised me.

He walked past us and closed the door carefully. Then he turned back to me, his face serious and questioning. "What's wrong, Johnny?" he asked suddenly. "Are you in trouble?"

I looked at him, then at Doris. Her eyes were wide and dark, but her lips were smiling gently. "You might as well tell him, Johnny," she said softly. "Anyone who loves you can read you like a book."

I took a deep breath, turned back to Al, and began my

story. His eyes were alert, his face attentive, his lips silent as he listened. As we sat there opposite each other in the little wagon I was taken back many years to the times when we used to sit like this and talk to each other after the show had closed down for the night. And I marveled to myself as I kept on talking. He hadn't changed very much in the years that had passed; I couldn't believe that he must be at least seventy-seven years old.

When I had finished, he struck a match on the heel of his shoe and held it to the cigar that still dangled from his lips. The flame of the match rose and fell with his breath as he drew on the cigar. At last it was going satisfactorily and he carefully shook the match until the flame went out and then threw it on the floor of the wagon. He didn't speak. Just sat there and looked at me with bright searching eyes.

We sat there so long that the atmosphere seemed to charge with tension. I felt a movement against my hand. I looked down. Doris's hand had found a way to mine. I looked up at her and smiled slowly.

Al saw it too; his sharp, bright eyes missed nothing that went on in front of them. At last he spoke, his voice very quiet. "What do you want me to do?" he asked.

I thought a moment before I spoke. "I don't know," I said doubtfully. "Nothing you can do, I guess. You were my last hope and I had to talk to you."

He looked at me closely. "You want that company, don't you?" his voice was very soft.

I looked at him. I remembered what Peter had said yesterday. He had been right. "Yes," I answered simply. "I put thirty years of my life into that company and it's not just a business any more. It's a part of me that I don't want to lose." I hesitated a second, then laughed, a little bitterly, I guess. "It's like the leg I lost in France. I can probably live without it. Maybe in time I will find something just as good, but it will always seem like this." I tapped my artificial leg. "You get along with it. It serves the purpose and gets you around. But you always know, deep inside you, that you're never the same. And you aren't."

His voice was still soft. "You could be wrong, Johnny. When I was your age I left the only business I ever liked. And I became a very rich man as a result. Maybe it's time for you to quit."

I took a deep breath and looked slowly around the wagon and then back at him. The words seemed to come out of me by themselves, my gaze was pointed. "If I did that," I said slowly, "I couldn't buy a studio and put it in my back yard."

He sat very still, only the glow on the tip of his cigar kept him from looking like a graven image. After a while he took his cigar from his lips and looked at it carefully; then he let out a long, deep breath. He stood up and opened the door of the wagon. He looked back at us. "Come into the house with me," he said.

The sun outside was still hot and bright. The men were still intent upon their game as we walked past them following Al to the ranch house. We went in through a back door into the kitchen.

A fat dark woman was rolling dough on a large wooden table. She looked at us as we came into the room. She spoke a few words in Italian to Al. He answered her in the same tongue and led us through the kitchen into the front of the house.

We stopped in the large old-fashioned parlor. Al told us to sit down and walked on into the hall and out of view. Doris and I looked at each other. We both were wondering what he was going to do.

"Vittorio!" I heard his voice calling in the hall. "Vittorio!" A muffled answer came from somewhere upstairs, followed by a short remark in Italian from Al, and then he came back into the room. He looked down at us. "Vittorio will be here in a minute," he said, and sat down in a chair opposite us and looked at us.

I wondered what good Vittorio could do. Al's voice cut into my thoughts.

"When are you two getting married?" he asked suddenly. "I'm tired of waiting for you to make up your minds."

We blushed like a pair of kids and looked at each other, smiling. Doris answered for me. "We've been so upset since Papa got sick," she explained, "we haven't had time to talk about it."

"Talk? What's there to talk about?" Al exploded, his cigar

throwing off heavy gray fumes of smoke. "Don't you know your own minds yet?"

I started to answer, when I saw the grin on his face and realized he had been teasing us. I shut my mouth, stopping the reply just as Vic came into the room.

He ignored us. "What do you want, Al?" he asked him.

Al looked up at him. "Get Constantin Konstantinov on the phone in Boston."

Vic looked quickly at me, then turned back to his boss. A flood of protesting words in Italian poured out of him.

Al held up his hand and Vic shut up like a clam, for all his size. "I said get him on the phone," he told Vic. "I want to talk to him. And after this remember your manners. When there are people around who don't understand our language, speak in English. Don't be rude." His voice was very soft, but there was a thread of steel that ran through it. "I brought Johnny up when he was a kid. And I know I can trust him not to reveal anything he might learn here."

Vic's face looked balefully at me, but he went to the phone and sat down.

I looked at Al. I didn't know he knew Konstantinov. I wondered what he was going to do. What could he do? This was Sunday and Konstantinov was in Boston. Besides, Konstantinov was supposed to be a very important guy who listened to no one in connection with his business affairs. He was rumored to be one of the richest men in the country even though nobody had heard much about him before the Greater Boston Investment Corporation began to lend money to the picture business back in '27.

"What good will it do to talk to him, Al?" I asked. "He won't listen to you."

Al smiled back at me confidently. "He'll listen to me," he said quietly. There was something in the tone of his voice that suddenly made me feel he knew what he was talking about.

Vic turned from the phone. "Constantin is on, Al," he said.

Al got out of his seat and took the phone from Vic's hand. He smiled a moment as before he began to speak into it. "Hello, Constantin," he said. "How are you?"

I could hear the crackle of a voice in the receiver he held loosely against his ear.

"I'm pretty good for an old man," Al said easily in reply

to a question. Again the crackle of the voice in the receiver. When it stopped, Al began to speak again.

"I wanted to talk to you on that situation over at Magnum," he said quietly. "I'm a little disturbed over what's going on there." He waited a moment while the voice buzzed again. "I think we ought to clarify our position in connection with that affair. My own feeling is that Farber will only bring confusion and be a highly annoying element in the company."

The voice in the phone crackled excitedly into Al's ear. He listened patiently. At last he spoke again. His voice was quiet, with authority. "I don't care what Ronsen told you," he said flatly. "Farber will only create a conflict within the company and perhaps even stop its progress back to a sound position. I want you to inform Ronsen that the loan will not be renegotiated if Farber is allowed to come into Magnum."

The voice spoke again in the phone, only this time it sounded quiet and subdued. "That's right," Al said when the voice had stopped. "Tell him that under no circumstances will we agree to allow the operating management of the company to be interfered with."

The voice spoke quietly again. "Right, Constantin," Al said into the mouthpiece. "I'll talk to you again, later in the week maybe." He looked over at me and smiled, then turned back to the phone. "Good-by, Constantin."

He put down the phone and walked back to me and looked down at us. He stood there quietly for a second before he spoke. "That's settled now, Johnny," he said slowly. "I guess you won't have any further trouble from them."

I looked up at him, my mouth almost open. "How could you tell him what to do?" I almost gasped.

Al smiled at me. I could see he was laughing at my amazement. "Very simple." He shrugged his shoulders. "You see, I own the Greater Boston Investment Corporation."

Then he told me something else that surprised me even more.

I was very quiet in the car going back. The little brown-faced, wrinkled old man in the faded blue denim shirt and the shiny blue overalls that I had left back there on a ranch was actually the most powerful man in the picture business. He controlled its money, no matter where it came from, East or West.

Now that I knew, I could see how simple it really was. Again I marveled at the brilliance of the little man who always thought of himself as a carny guy. He was smart enough to see there would come a time when the industry would outgrow its picture-by-picture method of financing, so back in '25, when the companies started making calf eyes at Wall Street, he opened a little office in the East. On the plate-glass door were painted the words: "Greater Boston Investment Corp."

Inside this office were two rooms: a reception room and a private office. The lettering on the door of this inner office read simply: "Constantin Konstantinov, Executive Vice-President—Loan and Collateral Department." Until that time Konstantinov had been a clerk in Vic's office.

In two short and hectic years as picture company after picture company turned Eastward for their financing, the office grew, and in 1927 it occupied a whole floor in a staid office building in the heart of Boston's conservative business section.

I smiled to myself as I thought about it. Loans, wholesale or retail. Finance one picture at a time? See the Bank of Independence in Los Angeles. Finance a whole picture company for forty pictures at a time? See the Greater Boston Investment Corporation. I smiled again as I thought of many of the men in the other companies that I knew who had prided themselves on getting out of Santos's clutches and never knew or would know that they were only doing business with him under another name.

I began to wonder how much Al was really worth. Fifty million? More? Suddenly it didn't matter. I was satisfied. It couldn't have happened to a nicer guy.

It was near ten o'clock when we got back to the house. We went into the library and Doris got some cubes from the kitchen and we made a couple of highballs. We were just toasting each other when the nurse came into the room.

"Mr. Kessler would like to see you right away," she said.

I looked at her in surprise. "Is he still up?" I asked.

She nodded. "He wouldn't go to sleep until he saw you," she said disapprovingly. "So be as brief as you can. He's had a pretty uncomfortable day and he must get some rest."

We put down our drinks untouched and hurried up the

stairs to his room. Esther was sitting by the bed holding his hand as we came in. "Hello, *kinder*," she said to us.

Doris went over to her and kissed her, then she kissed her father. "How are you feeling?" she asked them.

Maybe it was the light in the room—there was only one small lamp turned on—but I thought he looked rather wan and drawn. "All right," he said to her; then he raised his head and looked at me. "Nu?" he asked.

I smiled at him. "You were right, boss," I said. "He did help us. Everything is going to be all right now."

His head sank back against the pillow weakly and he closed his eyes. For a moment he lay there quietly, then he opened them. Again I thought it might be the light in the room, but his eyes seemed dull and shadowed to me. He seemed to have difficulty in focusing them. But his voice was strong enough and there was a note of satisfaction in it. "Now you'll be getting married soon?"

I started. It was the second time that day I had heard that. Again it was Doris who answered. She leaned over her father and kissed him lightly. I could see her mother squeeze her hand. "As soon as you're well enough to give the bride away, Papa," she said.

He smiled up at her. I thought I saw the tears come to his eyes, but he shut them quickly. "Don't wait too long, *kinder*," he said slowly. "I want to see yet grandchildren on my knee."

Doris looked at me and smiled. I came close to the edge of the bed and looked down at him. "Don't worry about that, Peter," I said, taking Doris's hand. "You will."

He smiled again, but didn't answer, just turned his head wearily on the pillow.

The nurse shooed us from the room then. "Good night, Peter," I said.

His voice was light and faint. "Good night, Johnny."

Doris kissed him again and turned to her mother. "Coming, Mamma?" she asked.

Esther shook her head. "I'll stay here until he falls asleep."

I remember looking back as we left the room. Esther was still sitting in the chair next to the bed. Peter's hand lay outstretched along the cover and, while I was looking, Esther covered it with hers. She smiled after us as I closed the door behind me.

Silently we went downstairs, back into the library. Once inside the room, Doris turned to me. Her eyes were wide and suddenly frightened. She shivered as if a sudden chill had come over her. "Johnny," she said in a small voice, "Johnny, I'm afraid."

I took her in my arms. "Afraid of what, sweetheart?" I asked gently.

She shook her head. "I don't know," she said vaguely, "I don't know, but I've a feeling something is wrong. Something terrible is going to happen." Her eyes began to fill with helpless, frightened tears.

I put a hand under her chin and raised her face toward me. "Don't worry, sweetheart," I reassured her confidently, "it's only your reaction to everything that has happened in the past week. And don't forget you've had a tough day today, too. You've been driving almost twelve hours. Everything will be all right."

She looked up at me, her face luminous, her eyes wide and trusting. "Do you really think so, Johnny?" she asked hopefully.

I smiled down at her. "I know so," I said positively.

But I was wrong. This had been the last time I saw Peter alive.

I got down to the office early. I wanted to be there when the boys got the sad news. It was a bright, cheerful day. The sun was shining, the birds were singing, and I was whistling as I walked past the studio gates.

The gateman came out of his little cubbyhole and stood there looking at me. "Beautiful day, isn't it, Mr. Edge?" He smiled.

I stopped and smiled back at him. "Swell day, fella," I said. It was too.

He grinned again at me and I walked on. My heels echoed on the concrete walk. Crowds of people were coming through the gate. They were going to work. All kinds of people, actors, actresses, extras; directors and their assistants, producers and their assistants, cameramen and their assistants; prop men, grips men, electricians; bookkeepers, secretaries, typists, and clerks; messenger boys and the cute little girls just out of high school who worked in the steno pool. The were going to work. All kinds of people. My kind of people. Picture people.

I walked into my office briskly. Gordon was there already. He looked up at me questioningly. "What you so chipper about, Papa?" he asked.

I smiled as I threw my hat on the couch and went to my chair. I waved my hand expansively. "It's a beautiful day outside," I said to him, "so what have I got to feel blue about?" I looked at him. "Good morning, Robert." I grinned. "You're mighty dapper this a.m. in that sky-blue pink tie."

He looked at me as if I were crazy. Maybe I was a little tetched that morning, but I didn't care. If this was being nuts, I never wanted to be sane again. It felt too good.

I sat there looking at him owlishly until he began to smile. He got out of his chair and came over to me sheepishly. "You're plastered!" he said accusingly.

I raised my right hand. "S' help me," I swore, "I didn't touch a drop!"

He looked at me skeptically for a moment. Then he grinned again. "Well then," he said, "let me in on the secret. Where did you bury the son of a bitch?"

I laughed aloud. "Why, Bob, how can you talk like that about our eminent chairman of the board?" I asked reproachfully.

He put his hands in his pockets and stared down at me. When I spoke to you Friday night, you sounded as if you had been hit over the head with a sledge hammer. Yet when see you this morning, you're as bright and cheerful as a up. That leaves me with only one conclusion. If you're not drunk, then you've murdered him." He smiled down at me gently. "Now come on, Johnny, let me in on it. Maybe we can bury the body together."

I looked up at him. "I told you I had a plan," I said.

"That you did." He nodded.

"Well, it's really very simple," I said. I made snake-dance motions with my hands and gave him a fast sample of fancy double talk. "You franisan the sanifran an' the first thing you know the old boy gets a call from his bankers in New York d phfft! Farber flies out the window with his bright little phew along with him!"

"Honest, Johnny?" he asked, smiling suddenly.

I stood up at my desk and looked him right in the eye.

"Do you doubt the word of Honest John Edge, the fairest dealer this side of Las Vegas?" I asked in a mock-heavy voice.

"I can't believe it," he said wonderingly. "How did you pull it off, Johnny?"

"Trade secret, son," I said to him, still in that heavy voice. "Some day when you're old enough, Papa John will tell you about the birds and bees. But right now—" I paused impressively and pointed to his door. "To work! Your duty calls you, Robert, and I will not have you shirk it!"

He walked smiling to his door and opened it. He bowed low in the doorway to me, his hands extended before him. "Your slave, O master," he said.

I laughed and he closed the door behind him. I wheeled around in the chair and looked out the window. What a day! It was the kind of day you saw on those vacation posters. A pretty girl in make-up walked in front of my window. I fitted right into the picture. There was always a pretty girl somewhere on those posters that read: "Come to California." I got out of my chair and went to the window sill and sat down on it. I whistled after the girl.

She turned and looked back at me. She saw who I was and smiled prettily and waved her hand to me. I waved back at her. I could hear her voice floating back to me on the morning breeze. "Hello, Johnny." I watched her practice walk until she was out of sight. She was cute. One of the kids who had beat her way up from the extra class. She had guts. She was one of my kind of people. Picture people.

I went back to my chair and sat down. I lit a cigarette. I never felt so good in my life.

It was almost ten o'clock when the intercom on my desk buzzed. I pressed the lever down and spoke into it. The indicator told me who it was. "Yes, Larry," I said.

His voice was puzzled and worried. "Will you be in your office the next few minutes?" he asked, almost abjectly for him. "I want to come down there and see you."

I smiled at the sound of his voice. "Come on down, Larry," I said genially. "I'm always in to you!"

His face was a picture of bewilderment when he came into my office. It was worried too. All I had to do was look at him to know what had happened. He had heard from Konstantinov.

"Johnny, there's been a terrible mistake!" were the first words out of his mouth. He couldn't even wait to reach my desk before he spoke.

I played dumb. I raised an eyebrow and looked at him inquiringly. "Mistake?" I repeated in a voice smooth as silk. "About what?"

He stopped short and looked at me in surprise. "You saw the papers over the week-end?" he asked.

I nodded my head without answering. I could see the sweat standing out on his forehead, all three million dollars of it.

"The board got their wires crossed," he said quickly. "They weren't supposed to approve Farber and Roth until they had your okay."

I didn't answer right away. I enjoyed watching him flounder around. I liked seeing him crawl. On him it looked good. It did something for my ego. Then I piled it on. "That's too bad," I said slowly.

The worried look on his face deepened. "What do you mean?"

"Remember what I said yesterday? 'If they come in, I go out.'" I hesitated just a second to make it look good. "Well, I'm out!"

For a moment I was willing to swear he was going to faint. His face turned a white ashen hue, his mouth opened as if gasping for air. I almost laughed in his face.

"But, Johnny"—his voice was weak—"I told you it was all a mistake. The wires got crossed!"

"Double-crossed!" I muttered under my breath. Only it had boomeranged back at him instead of me. I was sick and tired of all this flimflam. Why didn't he talk straight and say he had tried to shiv me and let it go at that? That he was very sorry only because he missed. Then we could talk plainly to each other. We were no babies. We knew we were married by a shotgun.

But of course you can't talk like that. That's being honest, and there's an unwritten law in the picture business that being honest doesn't pay. It simply isn't done.

I looked at him. My voice was patient. I sounded almost bored. "Which way is it then?" I asked.

He stared back at me for a long moment. The color began

to return to his face. "I've already sent a note to the papers denying the story," he said, a faint note of hope coming back into his voice. He leaned toward me. "I'm sorry this happened, Johnny." His voice was earnest.

I believed him, too. I knew how sorry he really was. A guy like him doesn't like to be caught off base. I stood up. "Okay, Larry," I said easily, "mistakes will happen. Let's forget it." I could afford to be magnanimous. I smiled at him.

At first his answering smile was tentative, then it broadened as relief swept across his face. I could see the three-million-dollar worry disappear from his eyes. When he left the office, he was almost back to normal and I was hungry. It was time for lunch.

I was tired and lazy when I got back from lunch. I had had a few drinks to celebrate, and the excitement of the morning had worn off. But I still felt good. It was still a beautiful day.

There was a note on my desk. I picked it up and read it. "Call Miss Kessler at home," it read. I picked up the phone and told the operator to get her.

I hummed to myself as I waited for her to answer the phone. I heard the receiver come off the hook. Her voice sounded oddly tired to me. "Hello," she said.

"Hello, sweetheart," I said into the phone. "What's on your mind?"

"Johnny," she said slowly, her voice seeming to echo in the phone. "Papa is dead."

I could feel the cold running through me. I felt as though I was in an icebox for a second. Then I found my voice. "Baby, I'm sorry," I said. "When did it happen?"

"An hour ago," she said dully.

"I'll be out there in a little while," I told her. An afterthought struck me. "How is Mamma taking it?"

"She's upstairs with him now," she answered. She began to cry into the phone.

"Get a hold of yourself, sweetheart," I said to her. "Peter wouldn't like that at all."

I could hear her sniff. "No, he wouldn't," she said slowly. "He could never bear seeing me cry. All I had to do to get anything when I was a kid was to cry in front of him."

"That a girl," I said encouragingly. "I'll be out there as soon as I can."

I put the receiver back on the hook and stared at it. I turned the chair around and looked out the window. It was a beautiful day, but something had gone out of it for me. I could feel my eyes fill with sudden tears. I remember thinking: "Come now, Johnny old boy, you're not going to act like a baby. Nobody can live forever, and he had a rich, full life." But he had a lot of heartbreak in it too. So I turned around and put my head on the desk and made like a baby. But what the hell, I had as much a right to cry for him as anybody.

I picked my head up from the desk when I heard the door open and someone come into my office. It was Bob. He stood there looking at me.

"You heard about the old man," he said. He could tell by looking at my eyes.

I got out of my chair wearily and walked around the desk. I picked my hat from the couch and stood there looking at him silently.

His eyes were filled with sympathy. "I know how you feel, Johnny," he said quietly. "He was a pretty good old guy at that."

"He was a greater man than most of us really knew," I said. "At least he didn't walk around with a knife in his hand."

He nodded his head.

Suddenly I noticed the silence. It seemed to be all around us like a big blanket that had come down and shut off all the sound. I looked at him. "It's awfully quiet," I said.

He looked at me. "The news is all over the lot. Nobody feels much like working."

I nodded my head. That was the way it should be.

I walked past him and out the door. People gathered in the corridor in small groups looked at me as I passed. Their glances were filled with compassion. One or two even came over to me and gripped my hand silently.

I went out into the sunlight. It was the same way out here. Everywhere people were standing and talking in hushed voices. I could feel their sympathy flowing toward me in a comforting wave. I walked past recording stage three. It was silent there too. It was the same way with stage four and two. In front of each building there were people whose kindness followed me down the walk.

A blare of music struck my ears. I looked up, startled. I had grown used to the silence. Sound stage one was blaring away. A pain seemed to swell up inside me and almost burst against my ribs. What right did they have to do business as usual? All the others knew enough to shut down.

I walked to the door slowly and went in. The music was as loud as thunder now. It beat against my ears as I made my way toward it. Then slowly it faded to a soft murmur and I could hear a rich young voice lifted in song. There was a young girl standing in the center of the stage singing into a microphone. Her voice poured forth from her throat as if it came from a golden flute. I turned and started back for the door.

An arm grabbed mine excitedly. I turned. It was Dave; his eyes were shining brightly. "Listen to that canary sing, Johnny," he said. "Just listen."

I looked past him to the stage. The kid could sing all right, but I was in no mood to listen to anything right now. I could see Larry and Stanley Farber walking toward us. Vaguely I wondered if Larry had told him yet. But I really didn't care about that either. All I wanted to do was to get out of there.

Dave's arm held mine again until they came up to us. Then his excited voice was in my ear again. "I'm telling you that kid is money in the bank! I can hear the old cash registers tinkle with every note in her voice!" He turned to the others for corroboration. "That's right, isn't it?"

They nodded, smiling in agreement.

I looked at them. "Did you hear that Peter Kessler is dead?" I asked.

Larry nodded his head. "Yes," he answered. "I heard. Too bad, but it wasn't unexpected. He was an old man."

I stared at them for a moment. Larry was right. It was too bad. Only he didn't know just how bad it really was I pulled my arm loose from Dave's grasp roughly and walked away from them.

I could hear Dave's voice behind me. "Say, what's eatin' that guy, anyway?" he was asking them.

I didn't hear their answer because the door had closed behind me.

The office was empty as I sat down at my desk and placed a sheet of paper on it. My pen made scratching sounds on the paper. I stopped and looked down at the words I had just written:

"To The Board of Directors of Magnum Pictures Company, Inc."

I looked up for a moment and through the open door into the corridor, then back at the sheet of paper in front of me. Everything suddenly made sense to me now. I remembered what Al had told me after he said he owned the Greater Boston Investment Corporation.

He had looked down at me with that quiet smile on his face. "Peter said that someday you would come out to see me," he said.

I had looked up at him in surprise. "He did?" I asked. "How could he know? It was only yesterday we decided!"

He shook his head. "You're wrong, Johnny," he replied quietly, "it was almost two years ago. When he sold his share in Magnum."

I was more bewildered than ever. I looked at Doris, then back at him. "How could he have known, then?" I asked incredulously.

Al looked at Vic. Vic stared at me for a moment, then angrily turned and walked out of the room. Al sat down opposite me.

"You remember that day you had a fight with him and he ordered you out of the house?" he asked.

I nodded my head. From the corner of my eyes I could see Doris watching me.

Al put a fresh stogie in his mouth. "Right after you left, he called me." He looked at Doris. "That's right, isn't it?" he asked her.

Her eyes were wide. "I remember that," she answered. "It was just before I left the room. I didn't hear him talk to you."

Al turned back to me. "His first words were: 'Johnny sold me out!' Then he asked me to lend him the money to buy control of the company.

"I had just learned from Vic what he had done. I was mad

as hell at him, but it was done and there was nothing that we could do about it. I told him I would be glad to lend him the money, but was that what he really wanted?

"'What do you mean?' he ask.

"'They're offering you four and a half million for your share,' I told him. 'Why put yourself in hock when you can get that kinda money and retire and live like a gentleman with no troubles instead of having to worry about paying off money you owe?'

"Over the phone he wasa quiet for a minute. I know he'sa thinking. Then I tell him about what Vittorio do to you. He thinks some more. Then his voice sounds bad.

"'I wasa wrong about Johnny?' he ask.

"'You wasa wrong,' I say.

"'In thata case,' he say, 'I gotta have the money!'

"'Why?' I ask.

"'Because Johnny lose everything,' he tells me. 'I gotta help him. Without me in the company, he lose his job.'

"'Johnny won't lose his job,' I tell him. 'They need him. He's the only man who knows the company.'

"Peter still doubts me. I tell him I'm right, not to worry.

"'But someday Johnny's in trouble,' Peter says. 'They do to him what they do to me. What Johnny do then? He's got nobody else to turn to but you or me.'

"'If he gets into trouble,' I say, 'I'll help him. But meanwhile I want you take it easy. You work hard building up this business. It's time you take it easy. Enjoy yourself. Your wife. Your family. With four and a half million dollars you got no worries.'

"Then he makes me promise if you ever get into trouble I help you. I promise right away because that's what I intend to do anyway. Then he says all right, he will sell."

A silence fell across the room as he lit his cigar. I looked at him. My heart was so full I couldn't speak. These two guys had always been my guardian angels. I owed them so much I could never repay them. I was never as smart as I thought I had been.

We in the picture business were so busy wrapping dreams in beautiful celluloid that we never saw that we were the only people who really believed in them. We were caught in a dream world of our own making, and every time the harsh reality of day crept into it, we screamed in sudden panic and frantically scurried around trying to patch the chinks in our celluloid armor.

I was no better than the others. I lived in a beautiful dream world that I had made up to suit myself. Like the others, I had built myself a house of celluloid.

But celluloid has a habit of melting when exposed to the heat of the sun. Like the others, I had forgotten that. I thought my house was strong enough to protect me against the world. It wasn't.

It was only as strong as the people around me helped to make it. Now I knew that most of its strength was Peter. He was its foundation and its walls. Without him, there was no house.

Without him, there was no dream world left for me to live in.

I knew that now. I should have realized it a long time ago.

My pen began to scratch across the paper again as I concentrated on the words that seemed to flow from it:

"I herewith submit my resignation as President and as a member of the Board of Directors of your company."

"You can't do that, Johnny!" Her voice was intense and close to my ear.

I looked up, startled. Doris stood there, her face white, her eyes wide and angry. For a second I couldn't find my voice; then it came back to me. "Why aren't you home with your mother?" I asked harshly.

She ignored my question. "You can't do that, Johnny!" she repeated, her eyes on mine. "You just can't quit like that!"

I stood up. My hands were trembling. I walked over to the window and opened it. A blare of music came in from the sound stage across the way. I turned and faced her. "I can't, can't I?" I asked, my voice still gruff and hoarse. "Listen to that. I don't want them to do business as usual in my house after I die. I want them to stop. Even if it's only for a day, for a minute. But I want them to stop. I want them to remember!"

She walked toward me slowly. Her eyes were suddenly fixed on the distance and far away from me. Her head tilted to one side in that habit she had when she was listening intently. She was listening, she was remembering. For a long moment she was silent. When, at last, she spoke, her voice was charged with a lyrical quality I had never heard before. "What greater monument can any man ask to leave behind him," she said softly, "than the gift of bringing pleasure and escape from the cares of everyday living to so many people?"

I didn't answer.

Her eyes came back to mine. I could see the sudden flood of tears behind them. Her voice was still soft, still singing. "That's why you can't quit, Johnny. You and Papa made a bargain, even if neither of you knew about it. You can't let him down now. He wouldn't want you to quit because of him. That's why he sent you to Santos even when he knew he couldn't ever hope to come back.

"There are other reasons you can't quit, Johnny." Her hand made a gesture toward the window. "The people out there. They're depending on you. To save their jobs, their homes, their families. And they're your kind of people, Johnny. Picture people. Yourself, Johnny—you would never be happy if you quit. Remember what you told Santos: you can't put a studio in your back yard. You said so yourself. But, most of all, you can't quit because thirty years ago in a little town you made a bargain with the little man who lived upstairs over his hardware store. A bargain that took you both a long way from that little town, three thousand miles across the country, to where you stand today."

She took my hand and looked up into my face. "Now only you are left to keep the bargain and fulfill that promise you made to each other. You see, Johnny"—her voice was almost a whisper—"that's why you can't quit."

Suddenly my breath filled my lungs and then rushed out. She was right. I had known that with the first word she had spoken. What kind of a man was I anyway to run from life at the first sign of pain?

It was her father who had died. And she was comforting me instead of me comforting her. I turned the palm of her hand toward me and kissed it. I could feel her fingers against my cheek. Lightly, ever so lightly.

I picked up the sheet of paper from the desk and together we walked out of the office. I felt better when we got out into the sunlight again. The music didn't hurt my ears. She was right. It was a monument any man could be proud of leaving behind him. Together we walked down to the gate and through it.

I could hear the splashing of the water from the big bottle over my head and I turned around and looked up at it. The water was sparkling in the sunlight. It made a light tinkling sound as it fell into the big crystal goblet beneath it.

I could feel my eyes blurring with a sudden moisture. I closed them and I could hear Esther's voice in my ear. It was such a long time ago. "Let's call it Magnum," she had said. Magnum, after a big bottle of champagne that Peter had bought for a party when we first went into business.

I opened my eyes again. A lot of living had gone by since then. A lot of people were gone too. We walked to her car. It was parked just outside the gate. I held the door open for her and she got into it and slid behind the steering wheel.

I stood there with my foot on the running board, looking down at her, when I became aware of the paper I still clutched in my hand. I looked down at it in half surprise, then I tore it into tiny bits and scattered them in the road.

We watched them flutter in the breeze, their shining whiteness like little snowflakes settling to the ground. Her face turned back to me. Her hand went out and took mine. Her eyes were shining brightly.

My heart leaped in gladness at her touch. I looked down at her. "You didn't answer my question back in there. Why aren't you home with your mother?" I asked her.

Her eyes looked up into mine. They grew soft and wise with an understanding I would never know. "She told me to come down and get you," she replied. "She said you would need me more than anyone else right now."

I looked down at her for a moment more and then got into the car beside her. "All right, Doris," I said slowly. "Let's go home."